THE RAT-PIT

PATRICK MacGILL

Introduction by Brian D. Osborne

Birlinn

This edition first published in 1999 by
Birlinn Limited
Unit 8 Canongate Venture
5 New Street
Edinburgh EH8 8BH

Reprinted 2001

ISBN 1 84158 004 X

Originally published in 1915 by Herbert Jenkins

Subsequently published in 1985 by Caliban Books
17 South Hill Park Gardens
London, NW3

The publisher acknowledges subsidy from

THE SCOTTISH ARTS COUNCIL

towards publication of this volume

Typeset by Trinity Typesetting, Edinburgh
Printed and bound by Omnia Books Limited, Glasgow

CONTENTS

INTRODUCTION

In the early summer of 1914, twenty-four year old Patrick MacGill, navvy poet and author of *Children of the Dead End*, returned to Glasgow from his post as librarian and secretary at Windsor to research the central chapters of his new novel *The Rat-Pit*. An interview with the Scottish socialist weekly *Forward* told the journal's readers that:

> His next book which is to deal largely with farmed outhouses in Glasgow and the exploitation of the poor is sure to strike deep. To gather material for the book, MacGill has been visiting old Glasgow haunts, and he promises us a bitter exposure of the rack-renting indulged in by the owners of farmed-out houses. The heroine of this book-to-be is named 'Norah Ryan', an Irish girl who has been forced to adopt the profession of prostitute through poverty and to save her child.

The subscribers to *Forward* who had read *Children of the Dead End*, published earlier in 1914, would certainly recognise the name and story of Norah, the tragic childhood sweetheart of the hero of the earlier novel, Dermod Flynn. *The Rat-Pit* is, however, not so much a sequel to *Children of the Dead End* as a skilfully interwoven companion piece to it. *Children of the Dead End* was an openly autobiographical novel and Dermod Flynn's experiences are, in broad terms, those of MacGill in his years in Ireland and Scotland working on the land and as a tramp, navvy and railway labourer. Both novels share much the same time frame, many of the same characters and even the same scenes, albeit presented from different viewpoints. *Children of the Dead End* is Dermod's story while *The Rat-Pit* is Norah Ryan's. The second novel may suffer at times from the loss of MacGill's personal experience, but, to compensate for this, it is even more strongly suffused with the author's concern for the plight of the poor and his condemnation of the hypocrisy and unconcern of the moneyed classes.

The Rat-Pit starts in an impoverished rural setting in MacGill's native Donegal with a twelve year-old Norah setting out to get yarn for stocking knitting from the Greenanore warehouse of Farley McKeown, the oppressive moneylender who dominates the life of the Donegal peasantry. Production of hand-knitted stockings is the mainstay of the Ryan household economy, even at the miserable rate of a penny farthing a pair. The Ryans, in common with their neighbours, are equally oppressed by McKeown, the landlord and the priest, all of whom make demands on them and who form an unholy combination which turns life into a perpetual struggle, where want is an everyday experience and poverty lies just around every corner.

A brief spell of easier times comes when her brother Fergus sends money home from England. This allows Norah to resume her education at Glenmornan National School where she sits beside Dermod Flynn. Norah, a bright and devout girl, is intended by her pious parents to become a nun. Indeed Norah's goodness is painted with a rather heavy hand – in the bad times she neglects herself. Her sickly mother complained:

'That is always the way with you, Norah. You never take your meals, but always leave them for somebody else.'

When she goes with other village women to Greenanore for yarn and they have to wade a sea loch her modesty is such that rather than hitch up her dress she allows it to become soaked by trailing through the waist-deep water.

Norah's fisherman father is drowned and to support her mother she leaves home to join a party of potato diggers, the same squad that Dermod joins in *Children of the Dead End*. Dermod and Norah meet for the first time in two years at Derry harbour and a gentle and tentative romance soon blossoms between the two young people.

However, when the potato squad come to work on a Renfrewshire farm Norah attracts the attention of the farmer's son – Alec Morrison. Morrison was, as MacGill puts it:

> ... a thinker, a moralist, earnest and profound in his own estimation.

Alec is a bank clerk in Paisley, in love with a member of his progressive club but finds himself drawn to Norah. MacGill was himself a Socialist, who had been a member of the Greenock branch of the Marxist Social Democratic Party while working as a railwayman there, but displays his contempt for the dilettante middle-class progressivism of Morrison and his little group of fellow intellectuals. The end of the season comes with Norah still evading Morrison's sexual advances. Dermod, having lost all his money gambling, goes off on the tramp while Norah returns to Donegal.

The next season Norah is back in Scotland, without the stabilising presence of Dermod, and finally succumbs to Morrison's advances. When she returns in the third year she is pregnant and seeks out Alec but he has become engaged to his progressive thinker and, revealing his essentially shallow nature, attempts to put matters right with Norah by giving her money – an offer she rejects.

The shame of her condition prevents her returning to Donegal and her mother. Norah's only recourse is to sink into the world of the Glasgow slums where her only support is another Donegal woman, Sheila Carrol, the *beansho* – literally 'that woman' – another 'fallen woman' despised and rejected by her own people.

Three of the most powerful chapters of *The Rat-Pit* describe the horrific conditions of the submerged part of the Glasgow population, the residents in the lodging houses, the made down dwellings, the ticketed houses. The rat-pit, from which the novel takes its name, is a lodging house for women where a bed, in a room of forty beds, can be had for three pence a night.

Sheila Carrol's last known address proves to be a condemned dwelling from which the city corporation had turned out the inhabitants but Norah finds her nearby, living in a squalid furnished room. Like many of the city's one room dwellings, or single-ends, this had a ticket affixed to it by the sanitary authorities authorising it as fit for the habitation of two adults. Ticketing was part of the city's attempt to keep some control on overcrowding and some check on the public health implications of overcrowding. Sheila rents her room from a 'house-farmer' who has sparsely furnished the room and, a fine touch this, who provided bedding stamped 'Stolen from James Moffat', lest any of his tenants feel tempted to make off with the coarse blankets. It is little wonder that Sheila describes Scotland as 'the black country with the cold heart'.

Although by 1914 MacGill had moved on from navvying, through a brief spell as a London journalist, to work under the aegis of Canon Dalton of St George's Chapel, Windsor, as secretary and librarian, his own earlier experience of the model lodging houses and slum dwellings of Glasgow enabled him to provide memorable images unlikely to come from even the most sympathetic middle-class novelist. Norah looks out of Sheila's room on to the yard behind the tenement and sees:

A four-square block of buildings with outhouses, slaty grey and ugly, scabbed on to the walls, enclosed a paved courtyard, at one corner of which stood a pump, at another a stable with a heap of manure piled high outside the door. Two grey long-bodied rats could be seen running across from the pump to the stable, a ragged tramp who had slept all night on the warm dunghill shuffled up to his feet, rubbed the sleep and dirt from his eyes, then slunk away from the place as if conscious of having done something very wrong.

Equally evocative of the life of the slum dweller is the description of the midnight inspection by the sanitary officers seeking to ensure that the ticketing restrictions were being obeyed.

Just as the women in Donegal had been wage-slaves to Farley McKeown, knitting socks for meagre reward, so Sheila and Norah scrape a living as out-workers for a textile sweatshop. Sheila explains the job of a shirt-finisher:

'For every shirt there's two rows of feather-stitchin', eight buttonholes and seven buttons sewed on, four seams and eight fasteners. It takes me over an hour to do each shirt and the pay is a penny farthing. I can make about fifteen pence a day, but out of that I have to buy my own thread.'

With four shillings a week, almost seven pence a day, going on rent, Sheila's grasp on even this lowly rung of the economic ladder is an insecure one.

Norah's tragedy continues, and she eventually is forced into prostitution to support herself and her baby. The baby dies, Norah contracts tuberculosis, but before she dies she is reunited with Dermod through the intervention of a kindly priest.

The Rat-Pit is a love story, a tragedy and a description of the underside of life. It is also an overtly political novel.

On Norah's first morning in Sheila's squalid little room their neighbour, Meg, points over the roofs of the slums and points out another, very different, building:

> 'That's the Municipal Buildin's; that's where the rich folk meet and talk about the best thing to be done with houses like these. It's easy to talk over yonder; that house cost five hunner and fifty thousand pounds to build.'

Glasgow City Chambers, opened by Queen Victoria in 1888, was a massively self-confident statement of Glasgow's role as the Second City of the Empire. The Cowcaddens tenement where Meg, Sheila and Norah scratched an existence might only have lain a few hundred yards north of the City Chambers but was light years away from the marble and satinwood extravaganza that was Glasgow's pride and joy.

When Norah becomes a prostitute the caretaker of the slum property demands half the money she receives from every man that calls on her. Meg, who has heard the conversation between Norah and the caretaker exclaims:

> 'A dirty hag she is! ... Full of money she is and so is the woman that owns the buildin'. Mrs Crawford they cry her, and she lives oot in Hillhead, the rich people's place, and goes to church ev'ry Sunday with prayer books under her arm. Strike me dead! if she isn't a swine, a swine unhung, a swine and a half. Has a motor car too, and is always writin' to the papers about sanitary arrangements.'

Mrs Crawford may have professed a public concern about sanitary arrangements but in Meg's view her support for ticketing and other measures to prevent overcrowding was not inspired by a concern for the plight of the poor but by an economic interest in ensuring that the demand for housing remained high:

'If few people stay in ev'ry room she can let more of
them; God put her in the pit, the swine!'

The housing conditions in Glasgow had given cause for
concern for years – slum clearance programmes had been
started by the City Improvement Trust in the 1870s but,
as in all other major urban centres, replacement housing
was designed for the better-off section of the working class.
The prevailing theory and hope was that they would move
out of less desirable accommodation, freeing it for the
displaced slum dwellers. This neat plan fell down in the
face of increasing urbanisation and, in Glasgow's case, in
the greater rapidity of slum clearance as opposed to house-
building. Model lodging-houses were provided by the City
Council but these had to be supplemented by common
lodging-houses, such as the Rat-Pit, run as commercial
ventures.

MacGill's clear message in *The Rat-Pit* is that the only
friends the poor have are their fellow sufferers. Even the
owner of the rag-store where Norah finds unhealthy and
distasteful work as a rag-picker proves to be a lecherous
exploiter of his more attractive employees:

'I could raise yer screw, say to ten bob a week,' said
the man, slipping his arms round her waist and trying
to kiss her on the lips.

The farmers who ill-housed their potato-pickers, Alec
Morrison who indulged himself with 'advanced ideas' and
wondered why the pickers were housed worse than
animals, the slum landlords and their factors, the sweatshop
owners and the rag-store master: all exploit and degrade
the poor.

Norah finds support, comfort and a sharing of her
misery from the poor, from the *beansho*, Sheila Carrol and
from the drunken neighbour Meg, who, when in drink,
found a few coins for Norah's baby:

'Just for the little thing to play wi',' she would explain
in an apologetic voice, as if ashamed of being found
guilty of a good action.

At the end, Norah meets up again with Gourock Ellen, a Scot
from the potato picking team, who 'bore all the indelible marks
of dissolute and careless living' but brings comfort to Norah
both by aiding her in her physical distress and by reading to
her the words of Jesus about the woman taken in adultery:

'He that is without sin among you, let him cast a stone
at her'

In a 1911 poem MacGill wrote:

> I sing of them,
>   The underworld, the great oppressed,
>   Befooled of parson, priest, and king,
> Who mutely plod earth's pregnant breast,
>   Who weary of their sorrowing
>   – The Great Unwashed – of them I sing.

MacGill's identification with 'the great oppressed', so
evident in *Children of the Dead End*, is, if anything even
more clearly expressed in *The Rat-Pit*. There is, perhaps, a
redeeming rough vitality in the navvy's huts and the
tramping life but the grey, grinding misery of the Rat-Pit
and the slum and the whole rat-infested city seems designed
to provide evidence to support Sheila Carrol's remark that:

'... people can stand a lot one way and another, a
terrible lot entirely.'

Norah, the saintly Donegal girl forced into poverty,
prostitution and degradation, has indeed to 'stand a lot
one way and another'. As Gourock Ellen says:

'Ah! it's sic a pity the way things work out in this life.
There seems to be a bad management of things
somewhere.'

By the time *The Rat-Pit* was published war had broken out and MacGill had enlisted as a private soldier. Wounded and invalided home in 1915 he married in November of that year. His bride was an Irish writer working in London, Margaret Gibbons, the grandniece of Cardinal James Gibbons of Baltimore. A report in the *Glasgow Herald* noted:

> The wedding of Rifleman Patrick MacGill of the London Irish Rifles, who is well known as the 'Navvy Poet' ... The bridegroom prior to enlistment was a librarian at Windsor Castle and amongst the numerous presents was a Georgian silver service from Canon Dalton ...

After the honeymoon MacGill rejoined his regiment and also continued his writing career. Six novels inspired by the war were published between 1915 and 1919. Later MacGill moved to the United States, continuing to write for his friend and London publisher Herbert Jenkins until 1937, when his last work, *Helen Spenser,* appeared. MacGill wrote the screenplay for an almost forgotten 1930 Hollywood war film, *Suspense,* and acted in the 1932 film of Noel Coward's *Cavalcade.* Margaret MacGill also continued her career as a romantic novelist, contributing to D. C. Thomson's Red Letter Novels series and to Herbert Jenkins's list. Her last novel, *Hollywood Madness,* appeared in 1936. Patrick MacGill died in Florida in 1963.

BRIAN D. OSBORNE
May 1999

FOREWORD

In the city of Glasgow there is a lodging-house for women known as 'The Rat-pit'. Here the vagrant can get a nightly bunk for a few pence, and no female is refused admittance: the unfortunate, the sick, the work-weary congregate under the same roof, breathe the same fetid air and forget the troubles of a miserable existence in strong drink, the solace of the sorrowful, or in heavy stupor, the slumber of the toilworn. The underworld, of which I have seen and known such a lot, has always appeared to me as a Greater Rat-pit, where human beings, pinched and poverty-stricken and ground down with a weight of oppression, are hemmed up like the plague-stricken in a pest-house.

It is in this larger sense that I have chosen the name for the title of Norah Ryan's story. By committing the 'great sin' and subsequently by allowing the dictates of motherhood to triumph over decrees of society, she became a pariah eternally doomed to the Greater Rat-pit. Whilst my former book, *Children of the Dead End*, was on the whole accepted as giving a picture of the life of the navvy, there were some who refused to believe that scenes such as I strove to depict could exist in a country like ours. To them I venture the assurance that *The Rat-Pit* is a transcript from life and that most of the characters are real people, and the scenes only too poignantly true. Some may think that such things should not be written about; but public opinion, like the light of day, is a great purifier, and to hide a sore from the surgeon's eye out of miscalled delicacy is surely a supreme folly.

A word about *Children of the Dead End*. I am highly gratified by the success attained by that book in Britain and abroad. Only in Ireland, my native country, has the book given offence. Reviewers there spoke angrily about it, and one went so far as to say that I would end my days by blowing out my brains with a revolver. The reference to a tyrannical village priest gave great offence to a number of clergy, but on the other hand several wrote to me speaking very highly of the book, and I have been told that a Roman Catholic Bishop sat up all night to read it. In my own place I am looked upon with suspicion, all because I 'wrote a book, a bad one makin' fun of the priest', as an old countryman remarked to me last summer when I was at home. 'You don't like it, then?' I said. 'Like it! I wouldn't read it for a hundred pounds, money down,' was the answer.

PATRICK MACGILL
London Irish,
St Albans,
5th Feb. 1915.

CHAPTER 1

THE TURN OF THE TIDE

I

'Have you your brogues, Norah?'

'They're tied round my shoulders with a string, mother.'

'And your brown penny for tea and bread in the town, Norah?'

'It's in the corner of my weasel-skin purse, mother.'

'The tide is long on the turn, so you'd better be off, Norah.'

'I'm off and away, mother.'

Two voices were speaking inside a cabin on the coast of Donegal. The season was midwinter; the time an hour before the dawn of a cheerless morning. Within the hovel there was neither light nor warmth; the rushlight had gone out and the turf piled on the hearth refused to burn. Outside a gale was blowing, the door, flimsy and fractured, creaked complainingly on its leathern hinges, the panes of the foot-square and only window were broken, the rags that had taken their places had been blown in during the night, and the sleet carried by the north-west wind struck heavily on the earthen floor. In the corner of the hut a woman coughed violently, expending all the breath in her body, then followed a struggle for air, for renewed life, and a battle against sickness or death went on in the darkness. There was silence for a moment, then a voice, speaking in Gaelic, could be heard again.

'Are you away, Norah?'

'I am just going, mother. I am stopping the window to keep the cold away from you.'

'God bless you, child,' came the answer. 'The men are not coming in yet, are they?'

'I don't hear their step. Now the window is all right. Are you warm?'

'Middling, Alannah. Did you take the milk for your breakfast?'

'I left some for you in the jug,' came the reply. 'Will you take it now?'

'That is always the way with you, Norah,' said the woman in a querulous voice. 'You never take your meals, but always leave them for somebody else. And you are getting thinner on it every day. I don't want anything, for I am not hungry these days; and maybe it is God Himself that put the sickness on me so that I would not take away the food of them that needs it more than I do. Drink the milk, Norah, it will do you good.'

There was no answer. A pale-faced little girl lifted the latch of the door and looked timorously out into the cold and the blackness. The gale caught her and for a moment she almost choked for breath. It was still intensely dark, no colour of the day was yet in the sky. The wind whistled shrilly round the corners of the cabin and a storm-swept bird dropped to the ground in front of the child. She looked back into the gloomy interior of the cabin and for a moment thought of returning. She was very hungry, but remembered her father and brother who would presently come in from the fishing, probably, as they had come in for days, with empty boats and empty stomachs. Another fit of coughing seized the mother, and the girl went out, shutting the door carefully behind her to stay the wrath of the wind which swept violently across the floor of the house.

The sea was near. The tide, sweeping sullenly away from the shore, moaned plaintively near the land and swelled into loud discordant wrath, far out at the bar. All round the house a tremulous grey haze enveloped everything, and the child stole into its mysterious bosom and towards the sea. The sleet shot sharply across her body and at times she turned round to save her face from its stinging lash. She was so small, so frail, so tender that she might be swept away at any moment as she moved like a shadow through the greyness, keeping a keen look-out for the ghosts that peopled the mists and the lonely places. Of these phantoms she was assured. To her they were as true as her own mother, as her own self. They were around and above her. They hid in the mists, walked on the sea, roved in the fields, and she was afraid of them.

Suddenly she called to mind the story of the Lone Woman of the Mist, the ghost whom all the old people of the locality had met at some time or another in their lives. Even as she thought, an apparition took form, a lone woman stood in front of the little girl, barely ten paces away. The child crossed herself seven times and walked straight ahead, keeping her eyes fixed on the figure that barred the path. This was the only thing to be done. Under the steady look of the eyes a ghost is powerless. So her mother had told her, and the girl, knowing this, never lowered her gaze; but her bare feet got suddenly warm, her heart leapt as if wanting to leave her body, and the effort to restrain the tremor of her eyelids caused her pain. The ghost spoke.

'Who is the girsha[1] that is out so early?' came the question.

'It's me, Norah Ryan,' answered the child in a glad voice. 'I thought that ye were the Lone Woman of the Mist or maybe a beanshee.'[2]

'I'm not the beanshee, I'm the beansho,'[3] the woman replied in a sharp voice. 'D'ye know what that means?'

'It means that ye are the woman I'm not to have the civil word with because ye've committed a great sin.'

'Who said that? Was it yer mother?'

'Then it was,' said the child, 'I often heard her say them words.'

'D'ye know me sin then?' enquired the woman, and without waiting for an answer she went on: 'Ye don't, of course. This is me sin, girsha; this is me sin. Look at it!'

The woman loosened the shawl which was drawn tightly around her body and disclosed a little bullet-headed child lying fast asleep in her arms. The wind caught the sleeper; one tiny hand quivered in mute protest, then the infant awoke and roared loudly. The mother kissed the wee thing hastily, fastened the shawl again and strode forward, taking long steps like a man, towards the sea. She was barefooted; her feet made a rustling sound on the snow and two little furrows lay behind her. Norah Ryan followed and presently the older woman turned round.

'That's me sin, girsha, that's me sin,' she said. 'That's a sin that can never be undone. Mind that and mind it always.... . Ye'll be goin' into the town, I suppose?'

'That I am,' said the child. 'Is the tide full on the run now?'

---

[1]Girsha, girl.
[2]Beanshee, a fairy woman. (Bean, a woman; shee, a fairy.)
[3]Beansho, 'That woman'. (A term of reproach.)

'It's nearly out. See! the sky is clearin' a bit; and look it! there's some stars.'

'I don't like the stars, good woman, for they're always so cold lookin'.'

'Yes, they're middlin' like to goodly people,' said the woman. 'There, we're near the sea and the greyness is risin' off it.'

The woman lifted her hand and pointed to the rocky shore that skirted the bay. At first sight it appeared to be completely deserted; nothing could be seen but the leaden grey sea and the sharp and jagged rocks protruding through the snow that covered the shore. The tide was nearly out; the east was clearing, but the wind still lashed furiously against the legs and faces of the woman and the girl.

'I suppose there'll be a lot waitin' for the tide,' said Norah Ryan. 'And a cold wait it'll be for them too, on this mornin' of all mornin's.'

'It's God's will,' said the woman with the child, 'God's will, the priest's will, and the will of the yarn seller.' She spoke sharply and resentfully and again with long strides hurried forward to the shore.

II

How lifeless the scene looked; the hollows white with snow, the gale-swept edges of the rocks darkly bare! Norah Ryan stepping timidly, suddenly shrieked as her foot slipped into a wreath of snow. Under her tread something moved, the snow rose into the air as if to shake itself, then fell again with a crackling noise. The girl had stepped upon a sleeping woman, who, now rudely wakened, was afoot and angry.

'Mercy be on you, child!' roared the female in Gaelic, as she shook the frozen flakes from the old woollen handkerchief that covered her head. 'Can you not take heed of your feet and where you're putting them?'

'It's the child that didn't see ye,' said the beansho, then added by way of salutation: 'It's cold to be sleepin' out this mornin'.'

'It's Norah Ryan, is it?' asked the woman, still shaking the snow from her head-dress. 'And has she been along with you, of all persons in the world?'

'Is the tide out yet?' asked a voice from the snow.

A face like that of a sheeted corpse peered up into the greyness, and Norah Ryan looked at it, her face full of a fright that was not unmixed with childish curiosity. There in the white snow, some asleep and some staring vacantly into the darkness, lay a score of women, some young, some old, and all curled up like sleeping dogs. Nothing could be seen but the faces, coloured ghastly silver in the dim light of the slow dawn, faces without bodies staring like dead things from the welter of snow. An old woman asleep, the bones of her face showing plainly through the sallow wrinkles of the skin, her only tooth protruding like a fang and her jaw lowered as if hung by a string, suddenly coughed. Her cough was wheezy, weak with age, and she awoke. In the midst of the heap of bodies she stood upright and disturbed the other sleepers. In an instant the hollow was alive, voluble, noisy. Some of the women knelt down and said their prayers, others shook the snow from their shawls, one was humming a love song and making the sign of the cross at the end of every verse.

'I've been travelling all night long,' said an old crone who had just joined the party, 'and I thought that I would not be in time to catch the tide. It is a long way that I have to come for a bundle of yarn - sixteen miles, and maybe it is that I won't get it at the end of my journey.'

The kneeling women rose from their knees and hurried towards the channel in the bay, now a thin string of water barely three yards in width. The wind, piercingly cold, no longer carried its burden of sleet, and the east, icily clear, waited, almost in suspense, for the first tint of the sun. The soil, black on the foreshore, cracked underfoot and pained the women as they walked. None wore their shoes, although three or four carried brogues tied round their necks. Most had mairteens (double thick stockings) on their feet, and these, though they retained a certain amount of body heat, kept out no wet. In front the old woman, all skin and bones and more bones than skin, whom Norah had wakened, led the way, her breath steaming out into the air and her feet sinking almost to the knees at every step. From her dull, lifeless look and the weary eyes that accepted everything with fatalistic calm it was plain that she had passed the greater part of her years in suffering.

All the women had difficulty with the wet and shifty sand, which, when they placed their feet heavily on one particular spot, rose in an instant to their knees. They floundered across, pulling out one foot and then another, and grunting whenever they did so. Norah Ryan, the child, had little difficulty; she glided lightly across, her feet barely sinking to the ankles.

'Who'd have thought that one's spags could be so troublesome!' said the beansho. 'It almost seems like as if I had no end of feet.'

'Do you hear that woman speaking?' asked the aged female who led the way. 'It's ill luck that will keep us company when she's with us: her with her back-of-the-byre wean!'

The sun was nearing the horizon, and the women, now on the verge of the channel (dhan, they called it), stood in silence looking at the water. It was not at its lowest yet; probably they would have to wait for five minutes, maybe more. And as they waited they came closer and closer to one another for warmth.

The beansho stood a little apart from the throng. Although tall and angular, she showed traces of good looks which if they had been tended might have made her beautiful. But now her lips were drawn in a thin, hard line and a set, determined expression showed on her face. She was barefooted and did not even wear mairteens, and carried no brogues. Her sole articles of dress were a shawl, which sufficed also for her child, a thick petticoat made of sackcloth, a chemise and a blouse. The wind constantly lifted her petticoat and exposed her bare legs above the knees. Some of the women sniggered on seeing this, but finally the beansho tightened her petticoat between her legs and thus held it firmly.

'That's the way, woman,' said the old crone who led the party. 'Hold your dress tight, tighter. Keep away from the beansho, Norah Ryan.'

The child looked up at the old woman and smiled as a child sometimes will when it fails to understand the purport of words that are spoken. Then her teeth chattered and she looked down at her feet, which were bleeding, and the blood could be seen welling out through the mairteens. She shivered constantly from the cold and her face was a little drawn, a little wistful, and her grey eyes, large and soft, were full of a tender pity. Perhaps the pity was for her mother who was ill at home, maybe for the beansho whom everyone disliked, or maybe for herself, the little girl of twelve, who was by far the youngest member of the party.

III

'It's time that we were tryin' to face the water in the name of God,' said one of the women, who supported herself against a neighbour's shoulder whilst she took off her mairteens. 'There is low tide now.'

All mairteens were taken off, and raising their petticoats well up and tying them tightly around their waists they entered the water. The old woman leading the party walked into the icy sea placidly; the others faltered a moment, then stepped in recklessly and in a second the water was well up to their thighs. They hurried across shouting carelessly, gesticulating violently and laughing loudly. Yet every one of them, with the possible exception of the woman in front, was on the borderland of tears. If they had spoken not they would have wept.

Norah Ryan, who was the last to enter the water, tucked up her dress and cast a frightened glance at those in front. No one observed her. She lifted the dress higher and entered the icy cold stream which chilled her to the bone. At each successive step the rising water pained her as a knife driven into the flesh might pain her. She raised her eyes and noticed a woman looking back; instantly Norah dropped her clothes and the hem of her petticoat became saturated with water.

'What are ye doin', Norah Ryan?' the woman shouted. 'Ye'll be wettin' the dress that's takin' ye to the town.'

The child paid no heed. With her clothes trailing in the stream she walked across breast deep to the other side. Her garments were soaked when she landed. The old woman, placid fatalist, was pulling on her mairteens with skinny, warty hands; another was lacing her brogues; a third tied a rag round her foot, which had been cut by a shell at the bottom of the channel.

'Why did ye let yer clothes drop into the dhan?' croaked the old woman. She asked out of mere curiosity; much suffering had driven all feeling from her soul.

'Why d'ye ask that, Maire a Crick (Mary of the Hill)?' enquired the beansho. 'It's the modest girl that she is, and that's why she let her clothes down. Poor child! she'll be wet all day now!'

'Her petticoat is full of water,' said Maire a Crick, tying the second mairteen. 'If many's a one would be always as modest as Norah Ryan they'd have no burden in their shawls this day.'

'Ye're a barefaced old heifer, Maire a Crick,' said the beansho angrily. 'Can ye never hold yer cuttin' tongue quiet? It's good that ye have me to be saying the evil word against. If I wasn't here ye'd be on to some other body.'

'I'm hearin' that Norah Ryan is a fine knitter entirely,' someone interrupted. 'She can make a great penny with her needles. Farley McKeown says that he never gave yarn to a soncier girl.'

'True for ye, Biddy Wor,' said Maire a Crick grudgingly. 'It's funny that a slip of a girsha like her can do so much. I work meself from dawn to dusk, and long before and after, and I cannot make near as much as Norah Ryan.'

'Neither can any of us,' said several women in one breath.

'She only works about fourteen hours every day, too,' said Biddy Wor.

'How much can ye make a day, Norah Ryan?' asked the beansho.

'Three ha'pence a day and nothing less,' said the girl, and a glow of pride suffused her face.

'Three ha'pence a day!' the beansho ejaculated, stooping down and pulling out the gritty sand which had collected between her toes. 'Just think of that, and her only a wee slip of a girl!'

'That's one pound nineteen shillin's a year,' said Maire a Crick reflectively. 'She's as good as old Maire a Glan (Mary of the Glen) of Greenanore, who didn't miss a stitch in a stockin' and her givin' birth to twins.'

The party set off, some singing plaintively, one or two talking and the rest buried in moody silence. It was now day, the sun shot up suddenly and lighted the other side of the bay where the land spread out, bleak, black, dreary and dismal. In front of the party rose a range of hills that threw a dark shadow on the sand, and in this shadow the women walked. Above them on the rising ground could be seen many cabins and blue wreaths of smoke rising from the chimneys into the air. A cock crowed loudly and several others joined in chorus. A dog barked at the heels of a stubborn cow which a ragged, bare-legged boy was driving into a wet pasture field ... the snow which lay light on the knolls was rapidly thawing ... the sea, now dark blue in colour, rose in a long heaving swell, and the wind, blowing in from the horizon, was bitterly cold.

'When will the tide be out again?' asked Judy Farrel, a thin, undersized, consumptive woman who coughed loudly as she walked.

'When the sun's on Dooey Head,' came the answer.

An old, wrinkled stump of a woman now joined the party. She carried a bundle of stockings, wrapped in a shawl hung across her shoulders. As she walked she kept telling her beads.

'We were just talkin' of ye, Maire a Glan,' said Biddy Wor. 'How many stockin's have ye in that bundle?'

'- Mother of God, pray for us sinners now and at the hour of our death, Amen,' said the woman, speaking in Gaelic and drawing her prayer to a close; then to Biddy Wor: 'A dozen long stockings that I have been working on for a whole fortnight. The thread was bad, bitter bad, as the old man said, and I could hardly get the mastery of it. And think of it, good woman, just think of it! Farley McKeown only gives me thirteen pence for the dozen, and he gives other knitters one and three. He gave my good man a job building the big warehouse in Greenanore, and then he took two pence off me in the dozen of stockings.'

'You don't say so!'

'True as death,' said Maire a Glan. 'And Farley is building a big place, as the old man said. He has well nigh over forty men on the job.'

'And what would he be paying them?'

'Seven shillings a week, without bit or sup. It is a hard job too, for my man, himself, leaves here at six of the clock in the morning and he is not back at our own fire till eight of the clock at night.'

'Get away!'

'But that isn't all, nor the half of it, as the man said,' Maire a Glan went on. 'Himself has to do all the work at home before dawn and after dusk, so that he has only four hours to sleep in the turn of the sun.'

'Just think of that,' said Maire a Crick.

'That's not all, nor half of it, as the old man said,' the woman with the bundle continued. 'My man gets one bag of yellow meal from Farley every fortnight, for we have eight children and not a pratee, thanks be to God! Farley charges people like yourselves only sixteen shillings a bag, but he charges us every penny of a gold sovereign on the bags that we get. If we do not pay at the end of a month he puts on another sixpence, and at the end of six months he has three extra shillings on the bag of yellow meal.'

'God be praised, but he's a sharp one!' said the beansho.

'Is this you?' asked the woman with the bundle, looking at the speaker. 'Have you some stockings in your shaw too?'

'Sorrow the one,' answered the beansho.

'But what have ye there?' asked Maire a Glan; then, as if recollecting, she exclaimed: 'Oh, I know! It is the wean, as the man said.... And is this yourself, Norah Ryan?'

'It's myself,' replied the child, and her teeth chattered as she answered.

'The blush is going from your cheek,' said Maire a Glan. 'And your mother; is she better in health? They're hard times that are in it now,' she went on, without waiting for an answer to her question. 'There are only ten creels of potatoes in our townland and these have to be used for seed. God's mercy be on us, as the old man said, but it was a bad year for the crops!'

'It couldn't have been worse,' said Judy Farrel, clapping her thin hands to keep them warm. 'On our side of the water, old Oiney Dinchy (that's the man who has the dog that bit Dermod Flynn) had to dig in the pratee field for six hours, and at the end of that time he had only twenty-seven pratees in the basket.'

'If the crows lifted a potato in Glenmornan this minute, all the people of the Glen would follow the crow for a whole week until they got the potato back,' said old Maire a Crick. 'It's as bad now as it was in the year of the famine.'

'Do you mind the famine year?' asked Norah Ryan. The water was streaming from the girl's clothes into the roadway, and though she broke into a run at times in her endeavour to keep pace with the elder women, the shivering fits did not leave her for an instant. The wind became more violent and the sleet which had ceased for a while was again falling from the clouds in white wavy lines.

'I mind the bad times as well as I mind yesterday,' said Maire a Crick. 'My own father, mother, and sister died in one turn of the sun with the wasting sickness and the hunger. I waked them all alone by myself, for most of the neighbours had their own sick and their own dead to look after. But they helped me to carry my people to the grave in the coffin that had the door with hinges on the bottom. When we came to the grave the door was opened and the dead were dropped out; then the coffin was taken back for some other soul.'

'At that time there lived a family named Gorlachs at the foot of Slieve a Dorras,' said Maire a Glan, taking up the tale; 'and they lifted their child out of the grave on the night after it was buried and ate it in their own house. Wasn't that the awful thing, as the old man said?'

'I wouldn't put it past them, for they were a bad set, the same Gorlachs,' said Maire a Crick. 'But for all that, maybe it is that there wasn't a word of truth in the whole story.'

IV

Norah Ryan, who was now lagging in the rear, got suddenly caught by a heavy gust of wind that blew up from the sea. Her clothes were lifted over her head; she tried to push them down, and the weasel-skin purse which she held in her hand dropped on the roadway. The penny jingled out, the coin which was to procure her bread in Greenanore, and she clutched at it hurriedly. A sudden dizziness overcame her, her brain reeled and she fell prostrate to the wet earth. In an instant the beansho was at her side.

'Norah Ryan, what's coming over ye?' she cried and knelt down by the girl. The child's face was deathly pale, the sleet cut her viciously, and her hands, lying palm upwards on the mire, were blue and cold. The beansho tried to raise her but the effort was too much; the child which the woman carried impeded her movements. Maire a Crick now hurried up and the rest of the women approached, though in more leisurely fashion.

'Mother of God! What's wrong? What's wrong?' asked the old woman anxiously. 'What has come over the child atall, atall? She's starving,' the old body went on, kneeling on the roadway and pressing her warty hands on the breast of the young girl. 'She's starving, that's it. In her own home she hardly eats one bite at all so that her people may have the more. So I have heard tell…. Norah Ryan, for God's sake wake up!'

The girl gave no heed, made no sign. The sleet sang through the air and the women gathered closer, shielding the little one with their bodies.

'What's to be done?' asked the beansho. Biddy Wor told how people were cured of fargortha (hunger) at the time of the famine, but little heed was paid to her talk. The beansho unloosened her shawl, wrapped her offspring tightly in it and handed the bundle to one of the women, who crossed herself as she caught it.

'Now up on my back with the girsha,' said the beansho authoritatively, stooping on her knees in the roadway and bending her shoulders. 'Martin Eveleen has a house across the rise of the brae and I'll carry her there.'

Three of the party lifted Norah and placed her across the beansho's shoulders.

'How weighty the girsha is!' one exclaimed; then recollecting said: 'It's the water in her clothes that's doing it. Poor girsha! and it'll be the hunger that's causing her the weakness.'

The beansho with her burden on her shoulders hurried forward, her feet pressing deeply into the mire and the water squirting out between her toes. The rest of the party following discussed the matter and, being most of them old cronies, related stories of the hunger that was in it at the time of the great famine. Again it faired, the sun came out, but the air was still bitterly cold.

A cabin stood on the crest of the hill and towards this the beansho hurried. Strong and lank though she was, the burden began to bear heavily and she panted at every step. At the door of the house she paused for a moment to collect her strength, then lifted the latch and pushed the door inwards. A man, shaggy and barefooted, hurried to meet the woman and stared at her suspiciously.

'What do you want?' he asked in Gaelic.

'It's Norah Ryan that's hungry, and she fainted on the road,' explained the beansho.

'In with her then,' said the man, standing aside. 'Maybe the heat of the fire will take her to. Indeed there's little else that she can get here.'

Inside it was warm and a bright fire blazed on the cabin hearth. In a corner near the door some cows could be heard munching hay, and a dog came sniffing round the beansho's legs. A feeling of homeliness pervaded the place and the smell of the peat was soothing to the nostrils.

'Leave her down here,' said the woman of the house, a pale, sickly little creature, as she pointed to the dingy bed in the corner of the room near the fire. Several children dressed in rags who were seated warming their hands at the blaze rose hurriedly on the entrance of the strangers and hid behind the cattle near the door.

'Is it the hunger and hardships?' asked the man of the house as he helped the beansho to place the inert body of the little girl on the bed.

'The hunger and hardships, that's it,' said Maire a Crick, who now entered, followed by the rest of the women.

'Then we'll try her with this,' said the man, and from behind the rafters of the roof he drew out a black bottle which he uncorked with his fingers. 'It's potheen,' he explained, and emptied some of the contents into a wooden bowl. This he held to the lips of the child who now, partly from the effects of the heat and partly from the effects of the shaking she had received on the beansho's back, awakened and was staring vacantly around her. The smell of the intoxicant brought her sharply to her senses.

'What are ye doin'?' she cried. 'That's not right, and me havin' the holy pledge against drink!'

The man crossed himself and withdrew the bowl, whereupon the woman of the house brought some milk from the basin that stood on the dresser, and this being handed to Norah Ryan, the child drank greedily. The beansho gave her a piece of bread when the milk was consumed.

'Where is me purse?' asked Norah suddenly. 'It's lyin' on the road and the brown penny is in the clabber. Where are we atall?'

'In Martin Eveleen's house, the house of a decent man,' said the beansho. 'Eat yer bit of bread, child, for ye're dyin' of hunger.'

For a moment the child looked earnestly at the bread, then, as if stifling the impulse to return it, she began to eat almost savagely. Maire a Crick placed the purse and penny which she had lifted from the road by the bedside and withdrew to the door, already sorry perhaps for having wasted so much time on the journey. The beansho found her baby, kissed a crumb into its mouth, tied it up again in her shawl and, when Norah had eaten the bread, both went to the door together.

'God be with ye, decent people,' said the child. 'Some day I hope to be able to do a good turn for you.'

'We're only glad to be of help to a nice girsha,' said the man, taking down a bottle of holy water from the roof-beam. He made the sign of the cross, dipped his fingers in the bottle, and shook the holy water over the visitors.

'God be with yer journey,' he said.

'And God keep guard over your home and everything in it,' Norah and the beansho made answer in one voice.

CHAPTER 2

AN UNSUCCESSFUL JOURNEY

I

The hour was half-past ten in the forenoon. In the village ('town' the peasantry called it) of Greenanore two rows of houses ran parallel along a miry street which measured east to west some two hundred yards. At one end of the street were the police barracks and at the other end the workhouse. Behind the latter rose the Catholic chapel, and further back the brown moors stretched to the hills which looked down upon the bay where the women crossed in the early morning.

The houses in the village were dull, dirty and dilapidated. There were eight public-houses, a few grocers' shops, a smithy where the blacksmith, who mended scythes or shod donkeys, got paid in kind for his services. The policemen, one to every fifty souls in the village, paraded idly up and down the street, their heavy batons clanking against their trousers, and their boots, spotlessly clean, rasping eternally on the pavement. Their sole occupation seemed to be the kicking of unoffending dogs that spent their days and nights in a vain search for some eatable garbage in the gutter. The dogs were skeletons; and when kicked they would slink quietly out of the way, lacking courage either to snap or snarl. Even a kick brought no yelp from them, they were almost insensible to every feeling but that of the heavy hunger which dulled their natural activity. At night they were silent ghosts prowling about looking for a morsel to eat. Now and again they howled mournfully, sitting on their haunches in a circle; and when the people heard the lonely sound they would say: 'There, the dogs are crying because they have got no souls.'

A little pot-bellied man stepped briskly along the street of the village, one gloved hand grasping a stout stick, the other, also gloved, sunk in the capacious pocket of a heavy overcoat. He walked as if he lacked knee-joints, throwing the legs out from his hips, but, save for this, there was nothing remarkable about the man except perhaps his stoutness. The people of Greenanore, battling daily against the terrible spectre of hunger, had no time to grow fat, yet this man measured forty inches round the waist. In the midst of extreme poverty he, strange to say, had grown corpulent and rich. His name was Farley McKeown, now possessor of £200,000, part of it invested in South American Railways and part of it in the Donegal Knitting Industry, and nearly all of it earned in the latter.

Farley McKeown was now seventy years of age and unmarried. At one time, years before, he had his desires as most young men have, and the sight of a comely girl going barefooted to Greenanore imparted a fiery and not unpleasant vigour to his body and caused strange but not unnatural thoughts to enter into his mind. He was then a young man of twenty, thoughtful and ambitious. Although his father was poor, the boy, educated by some hedge schoolmaster, showed promise and evinced a desire to become a priest. 'It is an easy job,' he said to himself, 'and a priest can make plenty of money.' Farley McKeown desired to make money anyway and anyhow.

When the black potato blight, with the fever and famine that followed it, spread over Donegal, Farley McKeown saw his chance. By dint of plausible arguments he persuaded a firm of Londonderry grain merchants to ship a cargo of Indian meal to Greenanore and promised to pay for the consignment within two years from the date of its arrival. When the cargo was landed on Dooey Head the people hailed it as a gift from God and the priest blessed Farley McKeown from the altar steps. The peasants built a large warehouse for McKeown, and in return for the work they were allowed a whole year in which to pay for their meal. Meanwhile the younger generation went off to America, and money flowed in to Donegal and Farley McKeown's pocket. At the end of two years he had paid the grain merchants, but the peasants found to their astonishment that *they* had only paid interest on the cost of their food. They were in the man's clutches, always paying for goods received and in some strange way never clear of debt. This went on for years, and Farley McKeown, a pillar of the Church and the friend of the holy priest, waxed wealthy on the proceeds of his business.

Then he started a knitting industry and again was hailed by the priest as the saviour of the people. From far and near, from the most southerly to the most northerly point of Donegal the peasant women came to Greenanore for yarn, crossing arms of the sea, mountains and moors on their journey, and carrying back bundles of yarn to their homes. The journey was in many cases thirty miles each way, and these miles were tramped by women between a sleep and a sleep, often with only one meal in their stomachs.

The daughters of Donegal are splendid knitters. But how difficult to make are those wonderful stockings when there is nothing but the peat fire or the rushlight to show the women the dreary and countless stitches that go to make the whole marvellous work. How quick those irons flash in the firelight, how they tinkle, tinkle one against another as the nimble fingers wind the threads around them, but alas! how wearying the toil! And the time usually taken to make a pair of socks was sixteen hours, and the wages paid for sixteen hours' work was a penny farthing.

II

Farley McKeown strutted along the street, inflating his stomach with dignity as he walked and casting careless looks around him. All those whom he met saluted him, the men raised their hands to their caps, the women bowed gravely, and the children, when they saw him coming, ran away. An old sow, black and dirty from her wallow in some near midden, rushed violently into the street and grunted as she mouthed at the grime in the gutter. A peasant boy, dressed in trousers and shirt, got hold of one of the young pigs and the animal squealed loudly. This startled the mother and she peered round, her little stupid eyes blinking angrily. On seeing that one of her young was possibly in danger she charged full at the youth, who, hurriedly dropping the sucker, sought the safety of a near doorway. A few hens rushed off with long, remarkable strides that made one wonder how the spider-shanked, ungainly birds saved themselves from toppling over. A rooster – a defiant Sultan – who did not share in the trepidacious exit of his wives, crowed loudly and looked valiantly at the sow, as much as to say: 'I, for one, am not the least afraid of you.' The boy finding himself safe ventured out again into the street, but coming face to face with Farley McKeown hurried off even more rapidly than when pursued by the sow. The man noticed the doubtful mark of respect which the youth showed him, purred approvingly and smiled, the smile giving him the appearance of an over-fed, serious frog.

McKeown walked along the street towards a spacious three-storied building containing many large windows and heavy, painted doors. This was the warehouse in which he stored his yarn. One door was open, and in front of this a crowd of barefooted women and children were standing, most of them holding large bundles of stockings which they frequently changed from one hand to another. They did not dare to rest their bundles on the street, which was wet with the slabbery sleet of mid-November.

Farley McKeown came to the door and from there surveyed the women with a fixed stare. They shuffled uneasily, a few crossed themselves, and one, a young girl, ventured to say: 'It's a cold morning this, Farley McKeown, thanks be to God!'

The merchant made no answer. To see those creatures, shrinking before his gaze, filled him with a comfortable sense of importance. They were afraid of him, just as he was afraid of God, and he thought that he must be like God in their eyes. He fixed another withering glance on the crowd, then turned and hurried upstairs to the top floor, there to enter a room where two young men were seated over a desk struggling with long rows of figures in dirty ledgers. A peat fire blazed brightly in one corner of the room, and the cheerful flame was a red rag to the eyes of the proprietor. He looked sternly at the fire, then at the clerks, then at the fire, then back to the clerks again.

'Warm here, isn't it?' he exclaimed. 'Yes, it's warm, very warm; very comfortable indeed, isn't it? It's nice to have a fire on a cold morning, very nice indeed. If you were working in your fathers' fields you'd have a fire out by your sides, you'd carry a fire about in your pockets all day, you would indeed. Is it not enough for you to have a roof over you?' he cried in an angry tone, his voice rising shrilly; 'a roof over your head and four good walls to keep the winds of heaven away from your bodies? No, it isn't, it isn't, it isn't atall, atall! I gave you orders not to put a fire on till I came into the office myself, and what do I see here now? One would think that it's not me that owns this business. Who does own it, I'd like to know! Is it me or is it you?'

Gasping for breath, he flopped down suddenly into a chair, and drawing off his gloves he stuffed them into the pocket of his coat. Then taking an account book he stroked out several figures with his pen, while between every pen stroke he turned round and shouted: 'Is it me that owns this business or is it you? Eh?'

After a while he ceased to speak, probably forgetting his rage in the midst of the work, and for two hours there was almost total silence save for the low scratchings of pen on paper and the occasional grunt which emanated from the throat of Farley McKeown. Suddenly, however, he stopped in the middle of his work and looked at the skylight above, through which snow was falling, and some of it skiting off the window-ledge dropped on the top of his head, which being bald was extremely sensitive to climatic changes. Then he gave an order slowly and emphatically:

'Dony McNelis, close the window.'

One of the clerks, a tall lank youth, rose like a rubber ball, bounded on top of his seat and closed the window with a bang. On stepping down to resume his work, he noticed the crowd of women, now greatly increased by the party which had crossed the bay in the morning, standing huddled together in the street. The sleet was falling thickly – it was now more snow than sleet – and the clothes of the women were covered with a fleecy whiteness. The clerk paused in his descent and looked at the women, then he spoke to the yarn-seller.

'Would it not be better to attend to these women now?' he asked. 'Some of them have been out on the cold street since the dawn.'

Farley McKeown turned round sharply. 'Is this my business or is it yours?' he cried, rising from the chair and stamping his feet on the floor. 'Mine or yours, eh? Have I to run like a dog and attend to these people, have I? I've kept them from death and the workhouse for the last forty years, have I not? And now you want me to run out and attend on them, do you? I've taken you, Dony McNelis, into my office out of pure charity, and how much money is it that your mother owes me? Couldn't I turn her out of house and home at a moment's notice? And in face of that you come here and tell me how to run my own business. Isn't that what you're trying to do? Eh?'

The boy sat down without a word, and catching a piece of waste paper off the table, he crumpled it angrily in his hand; then rising again he confronted his master.

'There are women out there from Tweedore and Frosses,' he said. 'They have travelled upwards of thirty miles, hungry, all of them, I'll go bail, and maybe not a penny in their pockets. If they don't catch the tide when it's out they'll have to sleep on the rocks of Dooey all night, and if they do there'll be more curses on your head in the morning than all the masses ever said and all the prayers ever prayed will be fit to wash away. It's nearly one of the clock now, and they'll have to race and catch the tide afore it's on the turn, so it would be the best thing to do to attend to them this minute.'

The youth stood for a moment after he had delivered this speech, the longest ever made by him in his life, and seemed on the point of saying something more vehement. All at once, however, he sat down again and went on with his work as if nothing unusual had happened.

Farley McKeown was a superstitious man. He feared the curse of an angry woman as much as he feared the curse of a priest of the Catholic Church. And those women would curse him if they slept all night on Dooey Head. For a moment he glared angrily at Dony McNelis, then went to the window facing the street, opened it and looked out on the shivering creatures assembled in the falling snow.

'Are there many Tweedore and Frosses people here?' he shouted.

'There's a good lot of us here, and we're afraid that we'll be a wee bit late for the tide if we don't get away this very minute,' said a voice from the crowd. Maire a Crick, the fatalist, was speaking.

'Have ye any stockings with ye?'

'Sorrow the one has one that's not on her feet, save Maire a Glan, and she doesn't come from our side of the water,' Maire a Crick answered. 'When we were here the last day we couldn't get a taste of yarn and we had to sleep all night on the rocks of Dooey. All night, mind, Farley McKeown, and the sky glowering like a hangman and the sea rushing like horses of war up on the strand. God be with us! but it will be a cold place on a night like this. For the love of

Mary, give us some yarn, Farley McKeown,' said the old woman in a piteous voice. 'Twenty-four hours have passed since I saw bread or that what buys it.'

McKeown turned round to his clerks. 'Is there much yarn down below?' he asked.

'Plenty,' said Dony McNelis, wiping his pen on his coat-sleeve.

'If they had my yarn with them and miss the tide, they'd ruin the stuff,' thought Farley McKeown; then turning to the women he shouted in a loud voice: 'There's no yarn for the Tweedore and Frosses women this day. Maybe if they come tomorrow or the day after they'll get some.'

Having said these words he shut the window.

CHAPTER 3

ON DOOEY HEAD

I

Outside, the women who had taken up their stand at dawn were still changing their bundles of stockings from one hand to another and sheltering them under their shawls whenever they changed them. All the time they kept hitting their feet sharply against the gritty street, trying to drive the cold and the numbness away. On the other side of the pavement a policeman stood for a moment and eyed them disdainfully, then marched on, his baton striking soberly against his leg. One of the party, a handsome girl, stepped out from the crowd and lifting her dress well over her ankles wrung the water from her petticoats. A young fellow passing on a donkey-cart looked slyly at the girl and shouted: 'Lift them a bit higher, girsha; just a little bit!' Whereupon the maiden blushed, dropped her dress as if it was red-hot and returned hurriedly to her companions.

The Tweedore and Frosses women had gone away, speaking loudly and lamenting over their ill-luck. Many of them were eating white bread (a new importation into Greenanore), but without butter to give it relish or liquid to wash it down. The bread cost a penny a chunk and one penny represented a whole day's wages to most of the women. Norah Ryan walked with them, but in her lagging gait could be detected great weariness, and in her eyes there were traces of tears. The poor child of twelve, who felt her suffering very keenly, offered to share her dry crust with Maire a Crick, who had no money, and the old woman looked greedily at the bread for a moment but refused to accept it.

The party hurried clear of the town, their bare feet pattering loudly on the road. Suddenly they encountered the parish priest, Father Devaney, an old, grey-haired, sleek-looking fellow, with shiny false teeth and a pot-belly like McKeown. He pulled his rosary from his pocket and began to pray when he observed his parishioners.

'Tweedore and Frosses people,' he cried genially, turning his eyes from the rosary cross to the women, 'have ye got no yarn this good day? No. That's a pity, but believe me when I say that Mr McKeown is doing his very best for the whole lot of ye. He's a good man, a sturdy man, a reliable man, and there's not his equal, barrin' the priests themselves, in all Ireland. Are you the daughter of James Ryan of Meenalicknalore?' he asked, turning to Norah Ryan.

'That I am, father,' answered the child.

'Does he forget about the money that I'm wanting for the building of my new house?' asked the old man in a severe tone of voice. 'I want five pounds from every family in the parish, and I'm not givin' them one year or two years, but a whole five years in which to pay it. They're most of them payin' up now like real good Christians and Catholics, for they want to see their own soggarth's house a good house, a strong house and a substantial house. But there is some of my own flock, and James Ryan is one of them, that won't give a penny piece to the soggarth who is goin' to save their souls for them. Listen, girsha! Tell James Ryan when you get home that the first pound should be paid at Michaelmas and it's now long past Hallowe'en. Tell him that I pray every night for them that's not behind in comin' forward to help the priest at the buildin' of his house, the soggarth's house and the house of all his people. Tell James Ryan that there's no prayer for him as yet, but if he hurries up with just one pound–'

The priest suddenly spied the beansho staring at him, and he noticed that there was a look of unfeigned contempt in her eyes. He observed the bundle in her shawl, and suddenly recollected that it was the woman's child – the talk of the parish barely six months before. The priest looked at the woman fixedly for a moment, then knowing that all the party was watching him intently, he raised his hand and made the sign of the cross on his forehead. This was as much as to say, 'God save me from this woman, for there is nothing good in her.' Old Maire a Crick crossed herself in imitation of the soggarth and cast a look of withering contempt at the beansho. Norah Ryan also raised her hand, but suddenly it was borne to her that the action of Maire a Crick was very unseemly, and she refrained from making the sign of the cross. Of course the priest was right in what he had done, she knew; the people were forbidden to see anything wrong in the ways of the soggarth.

Suddenly the old man turned away. He walked off a short distance, his head sunk on his breast and his hands clasped behind his back, the rosary dangling from his fingers. Perhaps he was deep in thought, or maybe he was saying a prayer for the beansho; the poor woman, buried beneath her weight of sin and sorrow, had no doubt filled him with compassion. What would he, the father of the flock, not do to make lighter the woman's burden? All at once he paused, turned round and faced the women who were staring after him.

'Norah Ryan!' he called, and his voice was pregnant with priestly gravity. 'If yer father doesn't send me the pound before the end of the next month he'll have no luck in this world and no happiness in the next. Tell him that I, meself, the parish priest, said these very words.'

Having thus spoken, the good man went on his way, telling his beads; perhaps counting by their aid the number of sovereigns required for the construction of his mansion.

'That will make some people sit up if they don't sink into their brogues,' said Maire a Crick, glancing in turn at Norah Ryan and the beansho. 'Mother of Jesus, to have the priest talking to one like that! Who ever heard the likes of it?'

'Do you know how much the priest is goin' to spend on a lav-ha-thury for his new house?' asked the beansho drily.

'Lav-ha-thury?' said Judy Farrel. 'What's that?'

'Old Oiney Dinchy of Glenmornan said that it is a place for keeping holy water,' said Maire a Crick.

'Holy water, my eye!' said the beansho. 'It's the place where the priest washes himself.'

'I've heard of them washin' themselves away in foreign parts all over and every day,' said a woman. 'But they must be far from clean in them places. They just go into big things full of water just as pigs, God be good to us! go into a midden. Father McKee, I wish him rest! used to wash his hands in an old tub, and that's all the washin' ever he did, and wouldn't ye think that a tub was good enough for this man? But what am I talking about!' exclaimed the woman, making the sign of the cross. 'Isn't it the priest that knows what is best to do?'

'He's goin' to spend two hundred and fifty pounds on his lav-ha-thury, anyway,' said the beansho. 'Two hundred and fifty pounds on one single room of his house! Ye'll not fill yer own bellies and ye'll give him a bathroom to wash his!'

'Mercy be on us!' exclaimed Biddy Wor, staring aghast at the beansho. 'Ye're turnin' out to be a Prodisan, Sheila Carrol. Talkin' of the priest in that way! No wonder, indeed, that he puts the cross on his forehead when he meets you.'

'No wonder, indeed!' chimed a chorus of voices.

'The sun, God forgive me for callin' it a sun! will be near Dooey Head this minute,' Maire a Crick reminded the party, who had forgotten about the tide in the heat of the discussion. Now they hurried off, breaking into a run from time to time, Judy Farrel leading, her little pinched figure doubling up almost into a knot when she coughed. Last in the race were Norah Ryan and Maire a Crick.

II

The darkness was falling as the women raced down the crooked road that ran to Dooey foreshore. A few birch bushes, with trembling branches tossing hither and thither like tangled tresses, bounded the road at intervals. The sky was overcast with low-hanging, slatey clouds, and in the intervening distance between foreshore and horizon no separate object could be distinguished: everything there had blended together in grey, formless mistiness. There was hardly a word spoken; the pattering of bare feet, Judy Farrel's cough and the hard, laboured breathing of the elder women were all that could be heard.

One of the party, well in advance, barefooted and carrying her shoes hung round her neck with a piece of string, struck her toe sharply against a rock.

'The curse of the devil!' she exclaimed; then in a quieter voice: 'It's God's blessin' that I haven't my brogues on my feet, for they would be ruined entirely.'

A belated bird cried sharply and its call was carried in from the sea ... somewhere in the distance a cow lowed – the sound was prolonged in a hundred ravines ... the bar moaned fretfully as if in a troubled sleep ... the snow ceased to fall and some stars glittered bright as diamonds in the cold heavens.

'Mother of God! It's on the turn,' Maire a Crick shouted, and hurried as rapidly as her legs would permit down the hill. At intervals some of the party following her would stumble, fall, turn head over heels and rise rapidly again. They came to the strand, raced across it, making little noise with their feet as they ran and with their bodies as they fell. Norah Ryan's head shook fitfully from side to side as she tried to keep pace with her companions.

They were not aware of the proximity of the dhan until they were in the water and splashing it all around them. When half-way across Maire a Crick found the water at her breast; another step and it reached her chin. Those behind could only see a black head bobbing in the waves.

'Come back, Maire a Crick!' Biddy Wor shouted. 'Ye'll be drownded if ye go one step at all further.'

The old woman turned, came back slowly and solemnly, without speaking a word.

On reaching the strand she went down on her knees and raised her eyes to heaven, looking up through the snowy flakes that were now falling out of the darkness. Then she spoke, and her voice, rising shrill and terrible, carried far across the dhan:

'May seven curses from the lips of Jesus Christ fall seven times seven on the head of Farley McKeown!'

The waves rolled up to her feet, stretching out like black, sinuous snakes; a long, wailing wind, that put droumy thoughts into the hearts of those who listened to it, swept in from the sea. Behind on the shore, large rocks, frightful and shapeless, stood out amidst stunted bushes that sobbed in dismal unison. The women went back to the rocks, passing through bent-grass that shook in the breeze like eels. All round the brambles writhed like long arms clutching at their prey with horrible claws. A tuft of withered fern flew by in the air as if escaping from something which followed it, and again the cry of the solitary sea-bird pierced the darkness.

Between the clefts of a large rock, which in some past age had been split by lightning, the women, worn out with their day's journey, sat down in a circle, their shawls drawn over their heads and their feet tucked well up under their petticoats. The darkness almost overpowered Norah Ryan; she shuddered and the shudder chilled her to the heart. It was not terror that possessed her but something more unendurable than terror; it was the agony of a soul dwarfed by the immensity of the infinite. She was lonely, desperately lonely. In the midst of the women she was far from them. They began to speak and their voices were the voices of dreams.

Maire a Crick, speaking in Gaelic, was telling a story, while wringing the water from her clothes, the story of a barrow that came across the hills of Glenmornan in the year of the famine, and on the barrow, which rolled along of its own accord, there was a large coffin with a door at the bottom of it. Then another of the party told of her grandfather's wake and the naked man who came to the house in the middle of the night and took up a seat by the chimney corner. He never spoke a word but smoked the pipe of tobacco that was handed to him. When the cock crew with the dawn he got up from his seat and went out and away. Nobody knew the man and no one ever saw him again.

'We might get shelter in one of the houses up there,' said Norah Ryan, rousing herself and pointing to the hill above, where the short-lived rushlights flickered and shone at intervals in the scattered cabins.

'We might,' said Maire a Crick, 'we might indeed, but it's not in me to go askin' a night's shelter under the roof of a Ballybonar man. There was once, years ago, a black word between the Ballybonar people and the people of our side of the water. Since then we haven't darkened one another's doorsteps, and we're not going to do it now.'

'Maybe someone on our side will send a boat across,' said the beansho.

'Maybe they'll do that if they're not at the fishin',' Judy Farrel answered. 'And when are they not at the fishin'? They're always out on the diddy of the sea and never catching a fish atall, atall!'

'We'll walk about; it will keep our feet warm.'

'And maybe fall down between the rocks and break our bits of legs.'

The rushlights on the hill above went out one by one and the darkness became intense. The Ballybonar people had gone to bed. One of the women on the rock began to snore loudly, and those who remained awake envied her because she slept so soundly.

'I suppose Farley McKeown will have a feather bed under him now,' said Maire a Crick with a broken laugh. It seemed as if she was weeping. The beansho, who was giving suck to her babe, turned to Norah Ryan who sat beside her.

'What are you thinking of, Norah?' she asked in Gaelic.

'I'm just wondering if my mother is better,' answered the child.

'I hope she is,' said the beansho. 'Are you sleepy? Would you like to sleep like the earth, like the ground under you?'

'In the grave you mean?'

'No, no, child. But like the world at night; like the ground under you? It's asleep now; one can almost hear it breathing, and one would like to sleep with it. If ever you think that the earth is asleep, Norah, be careful. Maybe when you grow up some man will say to you: "I like you better than anyone else in the world." That will be very nice to listen to, Norah. Maybe you'll walk with the man on a lonely moor or on the strand beside the sea. It will be night, and there will be many stars in the sky, and you'll not say they're cold then as you said this morning, Norah. All at once you'll stop and listen. You'll not know why you listen for everything will be so quiet. But for a minute it will come to you that the earth is asleep and that everything is in slumber. That will be a dangerous hour, child, for then you may commit the mortal sin of love.'

'Was that your sin, Sheila Carrol?' asked Norah Ryan, calling the woman by her correct name for the first time.

'That was my sin, Norah.'

'But you said this morning –'

'Never mind what I said this morning,' answered the woman in a tone of mild reproof. 'I'm only saying that the ground under us and around us is now sleeping.'

'The ground sleeping!' exclaimed Maire a Crick, who overheard the last words of the conversation. 'I never heard such silly talk coming out of a mouth in all my life before.'

'Neither have I,' said Norah Ryan, but she spoke so low that no one, not even the beansho, heard her.

Maire a Crick sang a song. It told of a youth who lived in Ireland 'when cows were kine, and pigs were swine and eagles of the air built their nests in the beards of giants'. When the youth was born his father planted a tree in honour of the event. The boy grew up, very proud of this tree, and daily he watered and tended it, and one day the boy was hung (why the song never stated) from the branches of his own tree.

'There never was a man hung either in Frosses or Tweedore,' said the woman who had just been snoring. 'Never a mother's son!'

'So I have heard,' Maire a Crick remarked, pulling her feet well up under her petticoats. 'In Frosses and Tweedore there never was a tree strong enough to bear the weight of a man, and never a man with a body weighty enough to break his own neck.'

Having said this the old woman, who came from the south of Donegal, chuckled deep down in her throat, and showed the one remaining tooth which she possessed in a hideous grin.

III

About the hour of midnight the heavens cleared and the moon, hardly full, lighted up the coast of Western Donegal. On the bosom of the sea a few dark specks moved to and fro, and at intervals the splash of oars could be heard. When the oars were lifted out of the sea the water, falling from them, looked like molten silver.

'Norah will be warm in bed by now,' said a voice.

'If she caught the tide when it was standing,' a voice clearer and younger replied.

'If she caught the tide,' repeated the first speaker in a thoughtful tone; then after a short silence, 'Does not the land look black, back from the sea?'

The youth studied the shore-line attentively, allowing his oar to trail through the water. 'Mother of God! but it looks ugly,' he replied. 'I hate it! I hate it more than I hate anything!'

On shore most of the women were now asleep amongst the rocks, their shawls drawn tightly over their heads and their feet tucked up under their petticoats. Maire a Crick, still awake, hummed a tune deep down in her throat, and Judy Farrel coughed incessantly. One white, youthful face was turned to the heavens, and the moon, glancing for a moment on the pale cheeks of the sleeper, caused a tear falling from the closed eyelids to sparkle like a pearl.

CHAPTER 4

RESTLESS YOUTH

I

James Ryan's cabin lay within half a mile of the sea, and his croft, a long strip of rock-bespattered, sapless land, ran down to the very shore. But this strip of land was so narrow that the house, small though it was, could not be built across, and instead of the cabin-front, an end gable faced the water. In Frosses most of the land is divided into thin strips, for it is the unwritten law that they who have no land touching the sea may not lift any seaweed to manure their potato patches. In Frosses some of the crofts, measuring two miles in length, are seldom more than eight paces in width at any point.

All over the district gigantic boulders are strewn, huge rocks that might have been flung about in play by monstrous giants who forgot, when their humour was at an end, to gather them up again. Between these rocks the people till for crops, plots of land which seldom measure more than four yards square, and every rock conceals either a potato patch or cornfield. It was said years ago that Frosses had twenty-one blades of grass to the square foot, but this was contradicted by a sarcastic peasant, who said that if grass grew so plentifully with them they would all be wealthy.

Fishing was indulged in, but very little fish was ever landed: Scottish and English trawlers netted the fish off-shore, and few were picked up by the peasantry, whose boats and nets were of the most primitive pattern. The nets were bad, the boats, mere curraghs, were untrustworthy, and a great deal of the fishermen's time was usually spent in baling out water. At best fishing was for them an almost profitless trade. They had no markets and no carts to send their fish to town. For the most part the fishers used the fish themselves or traded them in kind with their neighbours.

On the morning following the women's visit to Greenanore two men came up from the sea towards the door of James Ryan's cabin. One was an old man, bearded and wrinkled, whose brows were continually contracting as is the habit with those who live by the sea and look on the wrath of many winds. He was dressed in a white wrapper, a woollen shirt, open at the neck, trousers folded up to the knees, and mairteens. The other was a youth of nineteen, dark-haired, supple of limb and barefooted. In the two men a family likeness might be detected; they were father and son, James Ryan and his only boy, Fergus. There were now only four in the family; death had taken away most of the children before they were a year old.

Fergus opened the door of the cabin, to be met with the warm and penetrating breath of the cattle inside. The cows, always curious to see a newcomer, turned round in their beds of fresh heather and fixed their big, soft eyes on the youth. Beside the cow nearest the door, a young calf, spotted black and white, turned round on long, lank, awkward legs and sniffed suspiciously; then, finding that no danger was going to befall him, snuggled up against his mother, who commenced to lick her offspring with a big rough tongue. Suddenly a pig ran in from the outside, rushed between the youth's legs and disappeared under the bed. Its back was bleeding as if a dog had bitten it.

'Is not the pig's flesh like a human's?' said Fergus, turning to his father. 'White; almost without hair and it bleeds just like a man's. I hate pigs; I wish we could live without keeping them… . Oh! here is Norah at the fire. Have you just got up?'

The child, shivering from cold, was sitting on the hassock her hands spread out to the peat blaze.

'She has only just come in from the other side of the water,' said the mother, who was sitting up in bed, knitting stockings. 'She lay out all night, poor creature! Twenty-seven women in all were lying out on the snow. And she got no yarn! Thanks be to God! but it's a bad time.'

'A bad time, a hard time, a very hard time!' said the old man, sitting down on an upturned creel and taking off his mairteens. 'No yarn! and there was not a fish in all the seas last night.'

'None but the ones we didn't catch,' said Fergus. 'It is that dirty potato-basket of a boat that is to blame… . Are you cold, Norah?'

'I am only shivering; but the fire will do me good.'

'She didn't ate one bit of her breakfast yesterday,' said the mother. 'Left it all for you when you came in from the sea, she did!'

Norah blushed as if she had been caught doing something wrong; then drank from the bowl of milk which was placed on the floor beside her. The father looked greedily at the bowl; the mother spoke.

'It is nice and warm, that milk,' said the old woman. 'I wish we had more of it, but at this time of the year the milk runs thin in the cow's elldurs. But even if we had got enough bread, never mind milk, it would not be so bad…. And there is not one bit for you this morning…. Do you know what the soggarth says, Shemus?'

II

The husband looked at his wife, and an expression of dread appeared on his face. 'What does he say, Mary?'

'He is offering up no prayers for your soul.'

'Mother of God, be good to me!'

'You must pay him that pound at once, he says.'

'But barring what we are saving up for the landlord's rent, bad scran to him! we have not one white shilling in the house.'

'That does not matter to the priest, the damned old pig!' exclaimed Fergus, who had been looking gloomily at the roof since he had spoken to Norah.

'Fergus!' the three occupants of the house exclaimed in one breath.

'What's coming over the boy at all?' the mother went on. 'It must be the books that Micky's Jim takes over from Scotland that are bringing ruin to the gasair.'

'It is common sense that I am talking,' Fergus hotly replied. 'What with the landlord, Farley McKeown, and the priest, you are all in a nice pickle!'

'The priest, Fergus!'

'Robbing you because he is a servant of the Lord; that is the priest's trick,' the youth exclaimed. 'We are feeding here with the cows and the pigs and we are not one bit better than the animals ourselves. I hate the place; I hate it and everything about it.'

'Sure you don't hate your own people?' asked Norah, rising from her seat and going timidly up to her brother. 'Sure you don't hate me, Fergus?'

'Hate you?' laughed the young man stroking her hair with an awkward hand. 'No one could hate you, because you are a little angel... . Now run away and sit down at the fire and warm yourself... . They are going to make you a nun, they say.'

There was a note of scorn in his voice, and he looked defiantly at his mother as he spoke.

'What better than a nun could she be?' asked the mother.

'I would rather see her a beggar on the rainy roads.'

'What is coming over you atall, Fergus?' asked the old man. 'Last night, too, you were strange in your talk on the top of the sea.'

'How much money have you in the house?' Fergus asked, taking no heed of his father's remark. 'Ten shillings will be enough to take me out of the country altogether.'

'Fergus, what are you saying?' asked his mother.

'I am going away from here and I am going to push my fortune.' He looked out of the window and his eyes followed the twist of the road that ran like a ribbon away past the door of the house.

'But, Fergus dear –!'

'It does not matter, maghair (mother), what you say,' remarked the youth, interrupting his mother. 'I am going away this very day. I have had it in my head for a long while. I'll make you rich in the years to come. I'll earn plenty of money.'

'That's what they all say, child,' the mother interposed, and tears came into her eyes. 'It's more often a grave than a fortune they find in the black foreign country.'

'Could any place under the roof-tree of heaven be as black as this,' asked the youth excitedly. 'There is nothing here but rags, poverty, and dirt; pigs under the bed, cows in the house, the rain coming through the thatch instead of seeping from the eaves, and the winds of night raving and roaring through wall and window. Then if by chance you make one gold guinea, half of it goes to Farley McKeown and the priest, and the other half of it goes to the landlord.'

'But Farley McKeown doesn't get any money from us at all,' said the mother in a tone of reproof. 'It is him that gives us money for the knitting.'

'Knitting!' exclaimed Fergus, rising to his feet and striding up and down the cabin. 'God look sideways on the knitting! How much are you paid for your work? One shilling and threepence for a dozen pairs of stockings that takes the two of you more than a whole week to make. You might as well be slaves; you are slaves, slaves to the very middle of your bones! How much does Farley McKeown get for the stockings in the big towns away out of here? Four shillings a pair, I am after hearing. You get a penny farthing a pair; a penny farthing! If you read some of the books that comes home with the harvestmen you would not suffer Farley McKeown for long.'

'That is it,' said the mother, winding the thread round her knitting-irons. 'That is it! It is the books that the harvestmen take home that puts the boy astray. It is no wonder that the priest condemns the books.'

'The priest!' said the youth in a tone of contempt. 'But what is the good of talking to the likes of you? How much money have you in the house?'

'Sure you are not going to leave us?' Norah exclaimed, gazing with large troubled eyes at her brother.

'I am,' snapped Fergus. 'I am going away this evening. I'll tramp the road to Derry and take the big boat from there to Scotland or some other place beyond the water. What are you crying for? Don't be a baby, Norah! I'll come back again and make you a lady. I'll earn big piles of money and send it home at the end of every month.'

James Ryan looked at his wife, and a similar thought struck both of them at the same instant. The son had some book learning, and he might get on well abroad and amass considerable wealth, which he would share with his own people. The old man drew nearer to the fire and held out his bare feet, which were blue with cold, to the flames.

'If Fergus sends home money I'll get a good strong and warm pair of boots,' he said to himself; then asked: 'How much money is there in the teapot, Mary?'

'Twelve white shillings and sevenpence,' answered the wife. 'No, it is only twelve shillings and sixpence. Norah took a penny with her to the town yesterday.'

'I have a ha'penny back with me,' said the child, drawing a coin from her weasel-skin purse. 'I only spent half of the money on bread yesterday because I was not very hungry.'

'God be merciful to us! but the child is starving herself,' said the old woman, clutching eagerly at the coin which her daughter held towards her. 'You can have half a gold guinea, Fergus, if you are going out to push your fortune.'

III

In the evening when the moon peeped over the western hills, Fergus Ryan tied his boots round his neck, placed three bannocks in a woollen handkerchief and went out from his father's door. The mother wept not when he was leaving; she had seen so many of her children go out on a much longer journey. Norah accompanied Fergus for a short distance and stopped where the road streaked with very faint lines of light merged into the darkness. The moon rose clear off the hills ... lights could be seen glowing in the distance ... a leafless birch waved its arms in the breeze ... somewhere a cow was lowing and far away, across the water, a Ballybonar dog howled at the stars.

'I never thought that I could like the place as much as I do now,' Fergus said in English.

'It's the way with everyone when they're going away,' answered his sister. 'And I'm sick at heart that ye are goin', Fergus. Is Derry far away?'

'A longish way –'

'Out beyont the moon, is it?' asked the child, pointing at the hills and the moon above them.

'Maybe,' said the youth; then in a low voice: 'D'ye know what they do in other countries when they are saying "Goodbye"?'

'Then I don't,' answered Norah.

'They do this,' said the young man, and he pressed his lips against his sister's cheek.

'But they never do that here,' said the girl, and both blushed as if they had been discovered doing something very wrong. 'I'll say a long prayer for you every night, when you are away, Fergus.'

The boy looked at her, rubbed one bare foot on the ground and seemed on the point of saying something further; then without a word he turned and walked off along the wet road. Norah kept looking after him till he was out of sight, then, with her eyes full of tears, she went back to her home.

CHAPTER 5

GOOD NEWS FROM A FAR COUNTRY

I

Towards the end of the following year a great event took place in Frosses. It was reported that a registered letter addressed to 'James Ryan, Esquire, Meenalicknalore' was lying in Frosses post office. Norah heard the news and spoke of it to her father.

'No one but your own self can get the letter,' she said. 'That is what the people at the post office say. You have to write your name down on white paper too, before the letter crosses the counter.'

'And is it me, a man who was never at school, that has to put down my name?' asked James Ryan in a puzzled voice.

'It will be a letter from the boy himself,' said the old woman, who was sitting up in bed and knitting. Now and again she placed her bright irons down and coughed with such violence as to shake her whole body. 'And maybe there is money in the same letter. It is not often that we have a letter coming to us.'

'We had none since the last process for the rent and that was two years aback,' said the husband. 'Maybe I will be going into Frosses and getting that letter myself now.'

'Maybe you would,' stammered his wife, still battling with her cough.

James Ryan put on his mairteens and left the house. Norah watched him depart, and her eyes followed him until he turned the corner of the road; then she went to the bedside and sitting on a low stool commenced to turn the heel of a long stocking.

'How many days to a day now is it since Fergus took the road to Derry?' asked the old woman. 'I am sure it is near come nine months this very minute.'

'It is ten months all but sixteen days.'

'Under God the day and the night, and is it that?'

'That it is and every hour of it.'

'He will be across the whole flat world since he left,' said the mother, looking fixedly at an awkward, ungainly calf which had just blundered into the house, but seeing far beyond. 'He will maybe send five pounds in gold in the letter.'

'Maybe. But you are not thinking of that, mother?' said Norah.

'And what would *you* be thinking of, then?' asked the old woman.

'I am wondering if he is in good health and happy.'

'The young are always happy, Norah. Are you not?'

'Sometimes. I am happy when out in the open, listening to the birds singing, and the wind running on the heather.'

'Who ever heard of a person listening to things like those? Are you not happy in God's house on a Sunday?'

'Oh, I am happy there as well,' answered Norah, but there was a hint of hesitation in the answer.

'Everyone that is good of heart is happy in God's house,' said the mother. 'Have you turned the heel of the stocking yet?'

'I am nigh finished with the foot, mother.'

'My own two eyes are getting dim, and I cannot hurry like you these days,' said the woman in the bed. 'Run those hens from the house, and the young sturk too…. I wonder what he is coming in here for now, the rascal?'

'Maybe he likes to be near the fire,' said the child, looking at the spotted calf that was nosing at a dish on the dresser. 'When Micky's Jim built a new byre it was not easy to keep the cattle in it, for they always wanted to get back into the warm house again.'

With these words she rose and chased the young animal out of doors, while a few stray hens fluttered wildly about in making their exit. 'The cows like the blaze,' Norah went on as she came back and took up her seat by the fire. 'Every evening they turn round and look at it, and you can see their big soft eyes shining through the darkness.'

'It is the strange things that you be noticing, alannah, but what you say is very true,' said the mother. 'It will be a letter from Fergus, I suppose, with five gold guineas in it,' she went on. 'Maybe he will be at the back of America by now…. If he sends five gold guineas we will make a holy nun of you, Norah, and then you can pray day and night with no one at all to ask you to do anything but that alone.'

'I might get tired of it, mother.'

'Son of Mary, listen to her! Tired of saying your prayers, you mean? There is that sturk at the door again. Isn't he the rascal of the world?'

II

Darkness had fallen before James Ryan returned from Frosses post office, which was over four miles away. He entered the cabin, breathing heavily, the sweat streaming from his brow and coursing down his blood-threaded cheeks. He had run most of the way back, and in his hand he carried the letter, the first which he had received for two whole years.

'Mercy be on us, but you are out of breath!' said his wife, laying down her knitting irons, a fault of which she was seldom guilty, save when eating or sleeping. 'Put one of the rushlights in the fire, Norah, and read the letter from foreign parts. Is it from the boy himself?'

'Maybe it is,' answered the man, seating himself as usual on an upturned creel in the centre of the cabin. 'The man at the post office, Micky McNelis, first cousin he is to Dony McNelis that works with Farley McKeown, says that it is from a far part, anyway. "You must put down your own name," said Micky to me, in English. "I cannot write, for I never had a pen in my hand," said I. "You have to make your mark then," said he. "I don't know how to do that either," said I. "I'll write your name and you have to put a line down this way and a line down that way after what I write," said he, and, just by way of showing me, he made a crooked cross with his pen on a piece of paper. Then I made my mark and a good mark it was too, for Micky himself said as much, and I got the letter there and then into my own two hands. If it is from the boy there is not one penny piece in it.'

'Why would you be saying that now?'

'I could not feel anything inside of it,' said the man. 'If there were gold pieces in it I could easily find them through that piece of paper.'

The rushlight was now ready; the father took it in his hand and stood beside Norah, to whom he gave the letter. The woman leant forward in the bed; her husband held up the light with a shaky hand; dim shadows danced on the roof; the young sturk again entered the house and took up his stand in the corner. Norah having opened the letter proceeded to read:

Dear Father and Mother and Norah,

I am writing to say that I am well, hoping to find you all at home in the same state of health. I am far away in the middle of England now, in a place called Liverpool where I have a job as a dock labourer –

'Micky's Jim had that kind of job the year before last in Glasgow,' said the mother.

The work is hard enough, heaven knows, but the pay is good. I came here from Derry and I have been working for the most part of the time ever since. I intended to write home sooner but between one thing and another, time passed by, but now I am sending you home twelve pounds, and you can get gold in Frosses post office for the slip of paper which I enclose –

'Under God the day and the night!' exclaimed the woman in the bed.

A pound of this money is for Norah, and she can buy a new dress for it. See and don't let her go to Greenanore for yarn any more, or it will be the death of her, sleeping out at night on the rocks of Dooey.

I hope my mother is well and that her cold is getting better. I spend all my spare time reading books. It is a great, great world once you are away from Donegal, and here, where I am, as many books as one would want to carry can be had for a mere song –

'Getting things for a song!' said the man. 'That is like the ballad singers –'

It would be nice to hear from you, but as I am going away to America on the day after tomorrow, I have no fixed address, and it would be next to useless for you to write to me. I'll send a letter soon again, and more money when I can earn it.

Your loving son, Fergus

III

'This is the paper which he talks about,' said Norah, handing a money order to her mother.

'A thing like that worth twelve pounds!' exclaimed the old woman, a look of perplexity intensifying the wrinkles of her face. 'I would hardly give a white sixpence, no, nor a brown penny for the little thing. Glory be to God! but maybe it is worth twelve golden sovereigns, for there are many strange things that come out of foreign parts.'

'Alive and well he is,' said Norah, reading the letter over again. 'Thank God for that, for I was afraid that he might be dead, seeing that it took him so long to write home. Wouldn't I like to see him again!'

'It will be worth twelve pounds without a doubt,' said the husband, referring to the money order, as he threw the rushlight which was burning his fingers into the fire. 'I once heard tell that a man can get hundreds and hundreds of guineas for a piece of paper no bigger than that!'

'Mother of God!' exclaimed the old woman, making the sign of the cross and kissing the money order rapturously.

'Poor Fergus!' said Norah, laying down the letter on the window-sill and taking up her needles. 'It is a pity of him so far away from his own home!'

'Twelve gold sovereigns!' said the mother. 'A big pile that without a doubt. Hardly a house in Frosses has twelve pounds inside the threshold of its door. Put out that animal to the fields,' she called to her husband. 'We'll have to build a new byre and not have the cattle in the house any longer. A funny thing indeed to have them tied up in a house along with people who can get twelve pounds in bulk from foreign parts! No decent body would dream of such a thing as having them tied up here now! Norah, leave down that stocking. Let me never see you knitting under this roof again.'

'Why, mother?'

'You are going to be a nun, a holy nun, Norah, and nuns never knit; they just pray all day long and all night too. You have to set about and go to school again. You are not to be like other people's children any more, knitting stockings in the ashes. You are going to be a nun – and there never was a nun in Frosses yet!'

'I would like to go to school again,' said the child, clinking her irons nervously and following with her eyes the blue flames that rose from the peat fire and disappeared in the chimney. 'There is a map of the world in the school, hanging on the wall, and one can see Liverpool on it and America as well. I could look at them and think that I am seeing Fergus away in foreign parts, so far from his own home.'

'And there is a pound due to the priest this minute,' said the old man, who had just chased the calf out into the darkness. 'It would be well to give the soggarth the money in the morning.'

'And you'll go to school again tomorrow,' repeated the mother, who was following up some train of thought, and who, curiously enough, made no mention of her son since the letter had been read. 'You'll go again tomorrow and learn well. The master said that you were getting on fine the last time you were there and that it was a sin to take you away from the books.'

Having said this, the old woman lay back in her bed with a sigh of relief, the man closed the door of the house, and drawing near to the fire he held out his feet to the blaze. Norah, glad to be released from the labour of the knitting irons, looked into the flames, and many strange pictures came and went before her eyes. From time to time the woman in the bed could be heard speaking.

'Twelve pounds for a piece of paper!' she would exclaim. 'Mother of God! But there is strange things in foreign lands!'

Suddenly Norah arose and approached the bed. 'Am I a good girl, mother?' she asked, with a slight catch in her voice.

'What silliness is entering your head?' enquired the old woman. 'Who said that you were not good?'

'You said that good people were happy in God's house, but I am not always happy there.'

'Did I say that?' asked the mother, who had forgotten all about the remark. 'Maybe I did say it, maybe indeed. But run away now and don't bother me, for I am going to sleep.'

'A little bit of paper to be worth twelve pounds!' she mumbled to herself, after a short interval of silence. 'Mother of God! but there are many strange things in foreign parts of the world!'

CHAPTER 6

SCHOOL LIFE

I

On the Monday of the week following Norah Ryan went to school again. She had been there for two years already but left off going when she became an adept at the needles. Master Diver had control of the school; he was a fat little man, always panting and perspiring, who frightened the children and feared the priest. On the way to school he cut hazel rods by the roadside, and when in a bad mood he used them on the youngsters. After he had caned three or four children he became good tempered, when he caned half a dozen he got tired of his task and allowed the remainder (if any remained) to go scot free. Some of the boys who worked in their spare time at peat saving and fishing had hands hard as horses' hooves. When these did something wrong their trousers were taken down and awkward chastisement was inflicted with severe simplicity in full view of a breathless school.

The school consisted of a single apartment, at one end of which, on a slightly elevated platform near the fire, the master's desk and chair were placed. Several maps, two blackboards, a modulator, which no one, not even the master himself, understood, and a thermometer, long deprived of its quicksilver, hung on the walls. In one corner were the pegs on which the boys' caps were hung; on a large roof-beam which spanned the width of the room the girls' shawls were piled in a large heap. The room boasted of two wide open fireplaces, but only one of these was ever lighted; the other was used for storing the turf carried to school daily by the scholars. The room was swept twice weekly; then a grey dust rose off the floor and the master and children were seized with prolonged fits of sneezing. Outside and above the door was a large plate with the inscription;

GLENMORNAN NATIONAL SCHOOL 1872

Over the plate and under the eaves of the building a sparrow built its nest yearly, and it was even reported that a bat took up its daily residence in the same quarter.

From his seat beside the fire in the schoolroom the master watched his pupils through half-closed eyes, save when now and again he dropped into a sound sleep and snored loudly. Asleep he perspired more freely than when awake. He was very bald, and sometimes a tame robin that had been in the schoolhouse for many years fluttered down and rested on the skinny head which shone brilliantly in the firelight. There the robin preened its feathers. Now and then a mouse nibbled under the boards of the floor, and the children stopped their noisy chatter for a moment to listen to the movements of the little animal.

Prayers were said morning and evening. The children went down on their knees, the master prayed standing like a priest at the altar. The prayers of the morning were repeated in English, those of the evening in Gaelic.

Norah Ryan took her place in the third standard. In the class the boys stood at top, the girls at bottom, and those of each sex were ranged in order of merit. Norah, an apt pupil, easily took her place at the head of the girls, and the most ignorant of the boys, a youth named Dermod Flynn, was placed beside her. Although this lad got caned on an average three times a day, he never cried when he was beaten; still, Norah Ryan felt mutely compassionate for him when she heard the sharp hazel rod strike like a whiplash against his hand. His usual punishment consisted of four slaps of the rod, but always he held out his hand for a fifth; this, no doubt, was done to show the master that he did not fear him. Dermod could not fix his mind on any one subject; there was usually a far-away look in his eyes, which were continually turning towards the window and the country outside. On the calf of his left leg a large red scar showed where he had been bitten by a dog, and it was known that he would become mad one day. When a man is bitten by an angry dog he is sure to become mad at some time or another. So they say in Frosses.

The third class was usually ranged for lessons in a semi-circle facing the map of the world, which, with the exception of the map of Ireland, was the largest in the school. On the corners of the map were pictures of various men and animals with titles underneath; which, going the round of the two hemispheres, could be read as follows: Dromedary; A Russian Moujik; Wild Boar; A Chinaman; Leopard; An Indian; Lion; A Fiji Islander; etc., etc.

II

One day the master asked Dermod Flynn if he knew what race of people lived in Liverpool. As usual Dermod did not know.

'Dockers and Irishmen,' Norah Ryan, whose mind reverted to the letter which had been received from Fergus, whispered under her breath.

'Rockets and Irishmen,' Dermod blurted out.

No one laughed: a rocket had never been seen in Glenmornan, and it would have surprised none of the children if Dermod were correct; it would have surprised none of them if he were wrong. The master reached for the hazel rod.

'Hold out your hand, Dermod Flynn,' he commanded and delivered four blows on the boy's palm. Flynn held out his hand for a fifth slap: the master took no notice.

'Now, Norah Ryan, hold out your hand,' said the master. 'Promptin' is worse than tellin' lies.'

Norah received two slaps, much lighter than those delivered to the boy. The master knew that she was going to be a nun one day, and he respected her accordingly, but not to such an extent that he could refrain from using the rod of correction.

Dermod Flynn turned and stared at Norah. A red blush mantled her cheeks, and she looked at him shyly for a moment; then her lashes dropped quickly, for she felt that he was looking into her very soul. He appeared self-possessed, impervious to the pain of the master's chastisement. After a while Norah looked at him again, but he was gazing vacantly out of the window at a brook tumbling from the rocky hills that fringed the further side of the playground.

When school was dismissed and the scholars were on their way home, Dermod spoke to Norah.

'Why did you help me in the class today?' he asked.

She did not answer but turned away and stared at the stream falling from the dark rocks.

'It's like white smoke against a black cloud,' he said following her gaze.

'What is?'

'The stream falling from the rocks.'

On the day following Dermod got into trouble again. His class was asked to write an essay on fire, and Dermod sat biting his pen until the allotted time was nearly finished. Then he scribbled down a few lines.

'A house without fire is like a man without a stomach; a chimney without smoke is like a man without breath, for –'

That was all. Dermod pondered over the word 'stomach' for a while and felt that it made the whole sentence an unseemly one. He was stroking out the word when the master, awakening from his sleep, grabbed the essay and read it. He read it a second time, then took down a hazel rod from the nail on which it hung. The ignorance of the boy who wrote such a sentence was most profound. The master caned Dermod.

Norah Ryan made rapid progress at her work, and when she went home in the evening she sat down on the hassock and learned her lessons by the light of the peat fire. She considered old Master Diver to be a very learned man, but somehow she could not get herself to like him. 'Why does he beat Dermod Flynn so often?' she asked herself time and again, and whenever she thought of school she thought of Dermod Flynn.

Her mother, who had improved in health, now that there was food to eat, brought a looking-glass from Greenanore one day. She paid fourpence halfpenny for it in 'McKeown's Great Emporium', the new business which had just been started by the yarn merchant. Norah dressed her hair in front of this glass, and one day when engaged in the task, she said: 'I wish I could see Dermod Flynn now!' Perhaps she really meant to say: 'I wish Dermod Flynn could see me now!' In any case she got so red in the face that her mother asked her what was wrong.

Shortly afterwards Dermod Flynn's school troubles came to an end. His class was standing as usual, facing the map of the world, and Master Diver asked Dermod to point out Corsica. The boy did not know where Corsica was; he stared at the map, holding the idle pointer in his hand.

'Point out Corsica!' the master repeated, and seized the youth by the ear, which he pulled vigorously. The blood mounted to the boy's cheeks, and raising the pointer suddenly he hit the master sharply across the face.

'You've killed him, Dermod Flynn!' Norah Ryan gasped involuntarily. The old fellow put his hands over his face and sank down limply on the form. Blood trickled through his fingers ... a fly settled on his bald head ... the scholars stared aghast at their fallen master. Dermod gazed at the old man for a moment, then seizing his cap he rushed out of the schoolroom. Most of the boys followed the example, and when the master, who only suffered from a slight flesh wound, regained his feet and looked round, the school was almost deserted.

Dermod Flynn did not return again, and after his departure Norah found that she did not like the school so much as formerly.

CHAPTER 7

PLUCKING BOG-BINE

I

The May of 1903 came round, and on every twelfth day of May the young boys and girls of Donegal start for the hiring fair of Strabane. The rumour went that Dermod Flynn was going now, but no one knew for certain; the Flynns being a close-mouthed people gave no secrets away. On the evening preceding the twelfth, Norah heard of Dermod's intended departure and that night she was long in falling asleep. Her bed was made on the floor beside the fire; a grey woollen blanket served a double debt to pay, and was used as a blanket and sheet. But the sleeping place was not cold; the heat of the fire and the breath of the kine kept it warm.

The first bird was twittering on the thatch and the first tint of dawn was tinging the sky when Norah awoke, sat up in bed and threw part of the blanket aside. At the further end of the house where it was still dark cattle were stamping, and bright eyes could be seen glowing like coals. The child rose, went to the window, pulled up the blind and looked out on the sea. She stood there for a moment rapt in reverie, her pure white bosom showing above her low-cut cotton chemise and her long tresses hanging down loosely over her shoulders. She was now fourteen.

Her short reverie came to an end; she crossed herself many times and proceeded to dress, taking unusual care with her hair, weaving it into two long plaits, and polishing her boots carefully. These, the second pair of her life, were studded with nails which she liked to hear rasping on the ground as she walked. At night she noticed that the nails were bright and shiny; in the mornings they were always brown with rust. She recollected, not without a certain amount of satisfaction, that she was the only girl wearing shoes at Frosses school. But she could well afford it; Fergus had sent twenty pounds to his parents and three pounds to herself since he left home.

Her father and mother were asleep in the bed; the former snoring loudly, the latter coughing drowsily from time to time. The cat, which had been in the house since Norah could remember, was curled atop of the blanket and fast asleep.

A movement occurred in the bed as Norah finished her toilet; the cat stirred itself, stretched its front legs, spreading out its claws, yawned and fell asleep again.

'Son of Mary! but you are up early, Norah!' exclaimed her mother, sitting up in bed; then seeing the cat she gave the blankets a vigorous shake and cried: 'Get out, you little devil! You lie in bed as if you were a person and no less!'

'I am going to pull bog-bine on the hills of Glenmornan for your sickness, mother.'

'But would it not be time enough for you to go there come noon?'

'It is as well to go now, mother.'

'Then it is, alannah, if you have the liking for it,' said the old woman. 'See and turn the cattle into the holm below the Holy Rocks before you go away.'

'I will do that, mother.'

'And put the blind up on the window again, for the light is getting into my eyes.'

Norah untied the cattle from their stakes and opened the door. The old brindled cow went out first, lazily lashing her legs with her long tail, and smelt the door-post as she passed soberly into the open. The second cow, a fawn-grey beast, was followed by a restless, awkward calf that mischievously nudged the hindquarters of the animal in front with its nose. The Ryans possessed three cattle only, and the byre which the old woman had wanted erected was now in process of construction.

When the young calf got into the field he jumped exultantly into the air and rushed madly off for the distance of a hundred yards; then, planting his forefeet squarely in the earth, as suddenly stopped and turned round to look at the two cows. Surprised that they had not followed him, he scampered back to where they were cropping noisily at the short grass, and with his head dunted the brindled cow on the belly. The old animal turned round, her mouth full of grass, and gave a reproving nudge with her warm, damp nose which sent the calf scampering off again.

The houses of Meenalicknalore were arranged in a row on the top of a brae that swept down to the sea, shoving its toes into the water. A curl of smoke rose from some of the houses; others gave no hint of human activity. 'A chimney without smoke is like a man without breath,' quoted Norah. 'I wonder how Dermod Flynn thinks of things like that; and today he is goin' away all alone by himself across the mountains.'

She came to the Three Rocks; three large masses of limestone, one long and perpendicular, the other two squat and globular, which the peasantry supposed to represent the Holy Trinity. Here Norah said her prayers, one 'Our Father' and three 'Hail Marys' in front of each of the two smaller stones, and the Apostles' Creed in front of the large rock in the centre. When her prayers were finished she drove the cattle into a holm, put a bush in the gap and resumed her journey.

The sun had just risen ... a wind cool and moist blew in from the bosom of the sea ... little tufts of thistledown trembled through the air, dropped to the ground, rose again and vanished in the distance ... wrens chirped in the juniper ... frogs chuckled in the meadows ... a rabbit with eyes alert, ears aback and tail acock ran along the roadway and disappeared under a clump of furze ... clouds floating across the sky like large, lazy, wingless birds slowly assumed a delicate rosy tint until they looked like mother-of-pearl inside a giant shell.

Norah, very excited and very happy, stood for a moment to look into a clear well by the roadside. On her face was the expectant look of a sweet kitten that waits for the ball to be thrown to it; her two plaits of hair hung over her shoulders, one delicate strand that had fallen away fluttering in the breeze. She looked approvingly into the calm water at the laughing face that smiled up at her.

'How good to be out here, to be alive, to be young,' she seemed to say to herself. 'Everything is so fair, so beautiful, so wonderful!'

II

About six o'clock Norah entered Glenmornan. Here she met three boys and two girls bound for the rabble market of Strabane. One of the boys was whistling a tune, the other two chattered noisily; the girls, who were silent, carried each a pair of hob-nailed boots hung over their shoulders.

'Good luck to your journey,' said Norah Ryan, by way of salutation.

'And to yours,' they answered.

'Are there lots of ones a-goin' this mornin'?' she asked in English.

'Lots,' answered one of the girls, making the sign of the cross on her brow. 'Two gasairs of Oiney Dinchy's, one of Cormac of the Hill's ones, seven or more from the townland of Dooran, and more besides.'

'Many goin' from Glenmornan?'

'Lots,' said the boy who had been whistling.

Norah waited for him to proceed, but finding that he remained silent, she enquired as to who was going.

'Condy Dan, Hudy Neddy, Columb Kennedy, Unah Roarty and' – the boy paused for a moment to scratch his head – 'and Dermod Flynn, the gasair that struck Master Diver with the pointer.'

'Well, good luck to yer journey,' said Norah, shaking the hand of each of them in turn. 'May God be with ye all till ye come back!'

'And with yerself for ever.'

The crooked road twisted round copse and knoll, now bordering the river, now rising well up on the shoulder of the hill, and along this road Norah hurried, her hands hanging idly by her side and her plaits when caught by an errant breeze fluttering over her shoulders. Half-way along the Glenmornan road she met Dermod Flynn.

'Where are ye for this mornin', Dermod?' she asked. She knew where he was going, and after speaking felt that she should not have asked him that question.

'Beyond the mountains,' answered the youth with a smile which showed his white teeth. In one hand he carried a bundle, in the other an ash-plant with a heavy knob at the end. The young fellows of Glenmornan had got into a habit of carrying sticks in imitation of the cattle drovers who came once every month to the fair of Greenanore.

'Ye'll not come back for a long while, will ye?' Norah asked.

'I'm never goin' to come back again,' Dermod answered. At this Norah laughed, but, strangely enough, she felt ready to cry. All that she intended to say to him was forgotten; she held out her hand, stammered a confused goodbye and hurried away.

'His eyes are on me now,' she said several times to herself as she walked away, and every time she spoke a blush mounted to her cheeks. She wanted to look back, but did not do so until she came to the first bend of the road. There she turned round, but Dermod Flynn had gone from sight and a great loneliness entered the girl's heart. A steer with wide, curious eyes watched her from a field beside the road, the water sang a song, all its own, as it dropped from the hills, and the Glen River, viewed from the point where Norah stood, looked like a streak of silver on a cloth of green. But the girl saw and heard none of these things, her eyes were fixed on the crooked road which ran on through holt and hollow as far as the village of Greenanore, and miles and miles beyond.

She stood there for a long time lost in reverie. Dermod Flynn was gone now, and he would never come back again. So he had told her. Suddenly she recollected why she had come out on the journey. 'To pluck bog-bine it was,' she murmured. 'I am after forgetting that!'

She went across the river by the ford and climbed the hill. From the top of the knoll she could see the train steam out from the station of Greenanore. In it were the children bound for the rabble market of Strabane. Norah stared and stared at the train, which crawled like a black caterpillar across the brown moor, leaving a trail of white smoke behind it.

'I'm after forgettin' that I came out to pluck bog-bine,' she repeated when the train had disappeared from sight, and taking off her boots, she picked her way across the soft and spongy moor.

CHAPTER 8

THE TRAGEDY

I

Often a youth leaves Donegal and goes out into the world, does well for a time, writes frequently home to his own people, sends them a sum of money in every letter (which shows that he is not a spendthrift), asking them for a little gift in return, a scapular blessed by the priest, or a bottle of water from the holy well (which shows that he has not forgotten the faith in which he was born); but in the end he ceases to write, drops out of the ken of his people and disappears. The father mourns the son for a while, regrets that the usual money-order is not forthcoming, weeps little, for too much sentiment is foreign to the hardened sensibilities of the poor; the mother tells her beads and does not fail to say one extra decade for the boy or to give a hard-earned guinea to the priest for masses for the gasair's soul. Time rapidly dries their tears of regret, their sorrow disappears and the more pressing problems of their lives take up their whole interests again. In later years they may learn that their boy died of fever in a hospital, or was killed by a broken derrick-jib, or done to death by a railway train. 'Them foreign parts were always bad,' they may say. 'Black luck be with the big boat, for it's few it takes back of the many it takes away!'

A year had passed by since James Ryan last heard from Fergus his son. No word came of the youth, and none of the Frosses people, great travellers though the young of Frosses were, had ever come across him in any corner of the world.

'We are missing the blue pieces of paper,' Mary Ryan said to her husband one evening in the late autumn, fully three years after Fergus's departure. She now spent her days sitting at the fire, and though her health was not the best it had greatly improved within recent years. 'They were the papers!' she exclaimed. 'They could buy meal in the town of Greenanore and pay the landlord his rent. Maybe the gasair is dead!'

'Maybe he is,' the husband answered. He was a man of few words and fewer ideas. Life to him, as to the animals of the fields, was naturally simple. He married, became the father of many children, all unnecessary to an overcrowded district, and most of them were flicked out by death before they were a year old. Once every eighteen months James Ryan's wife became suddenly irritable and querulous and asked her husband to leave the house for a while. The cattle were allowed to remain inside, the husband went out and walked about in the vicinity of his home for two or three hours. From time to time he would go up to the door and call out: 'Are you all right, Mary?' through the keyhole. 'I am all right, Shemus,' she would answer, and the man would resume his walk. When the wife allowed him to come in he always found that his family had increased in number.

One day a child was born to him, and its third breath killed it. It was the seventh, and the year was a bad one. Potatoes lay rotting in the fields, and the peat being wet refused to burn. Somehow James Ryan felt a great relief when the child was buried. Twelve children in all were born to him, and ten of these died before they reached the age of three. 'The hunger took them, I suppose,' he said, and never wept over any of his offspring, and even in time forgot the names of most of those who were dead. The third who came to him was the boy Fergus; Norah was the youngest of all.

'Maybe, indeed, he is dead,' he repeated to his wife. 'I suppose there is nothing for it but to put out the curragh to the fishing again.'

'And never catch anything,' said his wife, as if blaming him for the ill-luck. 'It is always the way.... If Fergus would send a few gold guineas now it would be a great help.'

'It would be a great help.'

'We could keep Norah at school for another year.'

'We could.'

'And then send her to the convent like a lady.'

'Just.'

'When are you going to put the curragh out again?'

'Maybe this very night,' answered the husband. 'It is now Michaelmas a week past. There were blue lights seen out beyond the bar last night, and a sea-gull dropped from the sky and fell dead on the rocks of Dooey. The same happened ten years ago, and at that time there was a big catch out by Arranmore.'

'Then you had better go out tonight, for there is not much money in the teapot this minute.'

'The byre cost a big penny,' said James Ryan, and he spoke as if regretting something.

'It did that, and the house does not look half as well with the cattle gone from it.' So saying the woman turned over some live turf on the pile of potatoes that was toasting beside the fire, and rising emptied part of the contents of a jug of milk into a bowl. 'It is a wonder that Norah is not in,' she remarked. 'She should be back from school over an hour ago.'

II

At that moment Norah entered, placed her cotton satchel and books on the window sill, and sat down to her meal. She was a winsome girl, neat, delicate and good-looking. She had grown taller; her tresses were glossier, her clear grey eyes, out of which the radiance of her pure soul seemed to shine, were dreamy and thoughtful. She was remarkable for a pure and exquisite beauty, not alone of body, but of mind. She was dressed in peasant garb, but her clothes, though patched and shabby, showed the lines of her well-formed figure to advantage. Her feet were small, an unusual thing amongst country children who run about barefooted, and her dainty little hands matched her feet to perfection. Her accomplishments were the knowledge of a few Irish songs and country dances, and her intellectual gifts could be summed up in the words, simple innocence.

'Are you getting on well with your lessons, Norah?' asked the father.

Every day for the last two years, on her return from school, he asked a similar question and took no heed of the answer, which was always the same.

'I am getting on very well, father.'

'He's going out to the fishing tonight,' said the mother, handing a bowl of milk to Norah and pointing her finger at her husband.

'Any letter from Fergus?' asked the girl.

'Never a word,' said the mother. 'Maybe one will be here tomorrow.'

'Tomorrow never comes,' said James Ryan. He had heard somebody use this phrase years ago and he repeated it almost hourly ever since. 'It is off on the curragh that I am going now.'

He rose and went out. The dusk had fallen and a heaven of brilliant stars glittered overhead. A light gust of wind surged up angrily for a moment and swept along the ground, crooning amidst rock and boulder. Outside James Ryan stood for a moment and looked up at the sky, his thoughts running on the conversation which had just taken place inside. 'Tomorrow never comes,' he repeated and hurried towards the sea.

Mary Ryan lit the paraffin lamp which hung from the great beam that stretched across the middle of the house. The rushlight was now used no longer; the oil lamp had taken its place in most of the houses in Frosses. Norah finished her meal and turned to her books. For a long while there was silence in the cabin, but outside the wind was rising, whirling round the corners and sweeping in under the door.

'Tell me a story, mother,' Norah said, putting her books aside and curling up like a pretty ball on the earthen floor in front of the fire.

'All right, I will tell you a story, silly baby that you are!' said the old woman, sitting down on the hassock by the hearth. 'Will it be about the wee red-headed man with the flock of goats before him, and the flock of goats behind him, and the salmon tied to the laces of his brogues for supper?'

'Not that one, a maghair, I know it myself.'

'Will it be about Kitty the Ashy pet who said "Let you be combing there, mother, and I'll be combing here," and who went up the Bay of Baltic, carrying the Rock of Cattegat on her shoulders?'

'I know that one, mother.'

'And the Bonnie Bull of Norway you know as well. Then it will be about the cat that would not dress its whiskers if it wasn't in front of the biggest looking-glass in all the world. The biggest looking-glass in all the wide world is the broad ocean in a calm.'

'Not that one, mother.'

'You are hard to please this very night. I will tell you the story of the little green-coated boy who wandered on the rainy roads… . There's the wind rising. Mercy of God be on your father if the sea is out of order!'

Mary Ryan began the story which she knew by heart, having heard it so often from the lips of her own mother. Here, it may be remarked, most of the folk stories of Donegal are of Norwegian or Danish origin and have in many cases been so well preserved that the Scandinavian names of people and places are retained in the stories until the present day.

'Once upon a time when cows were kine and when eagles of the air built their nests in the beards of giants, a little green-coated boy with a stick in his hand and a bundle of bannocks over his shoulder went out on the rainy roads to push his fortune –'

III

'I'm going to marry a prince when I get very old, mother,' said Norah, interrupting the story-teller. 'Prince Charming, for that's what the girl did in the fairy stories when she grew up and got old at twenty or twenty-one. She was very poor at first and did nothing grand, but stopped at home, sweeping the floor and washing dishes. Then one night an old woman came down the chimney and told the girl to go to a dance, and the girl didn't leave the dance in time and she lost one of her slippers and – Oh! it was a great story, mother. I read it in a book that Fergus had.'

'You were reading those books, too!'

'Just only that one, mother, and Fergus didn't like it at all. He said it was very silly!'

'So it was, alannah, when it put thoughts like that into your head. Marry Prince Charming, and you going to be a holy nun! Nuns never marry like that.'

'Don't they? Well, I'll not marry a Prince Charming. I'll marry one of the White Horsemen who are under the mountain of Aileach.'

'But nuns never marry anybody.'

'They don't?' exclaimed Norah in a puzzled voice. Then with childish irrelevance: 'But tell me the story about the White Horsemen of Aileach, mother. That's the best story of all.'

'Long, long ago, when the red-haired strangers came to Ireland, they put nearly everybody to the sword; the old and young, the fit and feeble, and mind you, Ireland was in worse than a bad way,' the mother began, drifting easily into her narrative. 'Ireland was a great place in those days with castles and kings. Kings, Norah! There were five of them; now there isn't even one in the four corners of the country. But the red-haired strangers came like a storm from the sea and there was no standing before them. Red were their swords, red as their hair, but not with rust but with the blood of men, women, and children. And the chieftains of Ireland and the men of Ireland could make no stand against the enemy atall. "What am I to do?" cried the Ardrigh, the top king of the whole country, speaking from the door of his own castle. "There will soon be no Ireland belonging to me, it will all go to the red-haired strangers." Then up spoke an old withered stick of a man, that nobody knew, and who had been listening to the words of the King.

"Have you asked the Chieftain of the White Horsemen for help?"

"I never met him, decent stranger," answered the King. "I know him not."

"Go to the sea when it strikes in storm on the coast of Tir Conail," said the old man to the king, "and call out to Maanan MacLir for aid and he'll send to your help his ten score and ten white horsemen. You'll see the white horses far out, rearing on the top of the waves, every steed pawing the ocean and all mad for the fight before them."

Well, to cut a long story short, the King did as he was told and called to the White Horsemen to come and help him, and they came, ten score of them and ten, with their shields shining like polished silver and lances bright as frosty stars. Down from the North they rode, driving the foe on in front of them, and never was seen such a rout, neither in the days that went before nor the days that came after. The White Horsemen cut their way right through mountains in their haste to get to the other side; for nothing could stand against their lances. Nobody could go as quickly as them, not even the red-haired strangers who were in such a hurry to get out of their way.

And when victory was theirs, the White Horsemen came back here to Tir Conail again and stood on the verge of the ocean while Maanan MacLir headed his horse out on the waves. But lo, and behold! the steed could no longer gallop across the water. The poor animal sank into the sea and the chieftain was nearly drowned. At that moment a voice, nobody knew where it came from, called to Maanan MacLir:

"Long enough has the sea called for the rest and quiet that was not given to it by the white horses of MacLir.

Never more will the sea bend under them; now it will break apart and let them through!"

When they heard these words the White Horsemen turned away from the sea and went galloping to the foot of the Mountain of Aileach. When they arrived there the mountain raised itself upon one side just like the lid of a kettle and Maanan MacLir and his White Horsemen disappeared under it. Since that day they have never been seen again.'

'But the mountain didn't close on top of them, did it?' asked Norah.

'Of course it did. Isn't it closed to this very day?'

'And will it be a true story?'

'True, child!' exclaimed the mother. 'Sure the mountain is there to this very hour. And besides, Saint Columbkille talks about it in his prophecies.'

'Then the White Horsemen will come out again?'

'They'll come out when the great war comes,' said the mother. 'And that will be when there are roads round every mountain like the frills round the cap of an old woman. It will start, the great war, when the nights lengthen and the year grows brown, between the seasons of scythe and sickle; murder and slaughter, madder than cattle in the heat of summer, will run through the land, and the young men will be killed and the middle-aged men and the old. The very crutches of the cripples will be taken out to arm the fighters, and the bed-ridden will be turned three times three in their beds to see if they are fit to go into the field of battle. Death will take them all, for that is how it is to be; that way and no other. And when they're all gone it will be the turn of the White Horsemen, who have been waiting for the great war ever since they chased the red-haired strangers from the country. They'll come out from under Aileach when the day arrives, ten score and ten of them with silver shields and spears, bright as stars on a frosty night. They'll fight the foe and win and victory will come to Ireland. These are the words of the great saint, Columbkille.'

'Are the White Horsemen very tall, mother?' asked Norah, her eyes alight with enthusiastic interest.

'Tall is not the word!'

'High as a hill?'

'Higher!'

'As Sliab a Tuagh?'

'It's as nothing compared to one of the men of Maanan MacLir.'

'Then I'll marry one of the White Horsemen,' said Norah, decision in her clear voice. 'I'll live in a castle, polish his lance and shield, and – Who will that be at the door?'

IV

Norah paused. Someone was moving outside as if fumbling for the latch; then a tall, heavily-bearded man pushed the door of the cabin inwards and entered, bringing with him a terrific gust of wind that almost shook the house to its foundations. On his face was a scared look, and his clothes were dripping wet, although it was not raining.

'Was it himself?' cried the old woman, alluding to her husband and speaking to the man who entered. It was evident from the tone in which she spoke that she anticipated something terrible.

'It was himself,' said the man in a low, hoarse voice. 'He's coming on the flat of two oars. God bless us! But it is a black heart that the sea has.'

With these words the visitor went out again, and the excited voices of men could be heard floating on the wind.

'It's your father, Norah,' said the old woman. 'He went down with the curragh, I'm thinking; down through the black water. Mother of God! but it's the sea that has the black heart! There they are coming with him. Open the door wider, Norah!'

The girl, who had risen from her seat, pulled the door inwards and placed a stone against the sill to keep it open. She felt as if a thousand pins were pricking her legs; her head was heavy, her fingers felt enormous and when they pressed against the door it seemed to Norah as if they did not belong to her at all. Outside it was very dark, the heavens held no stars and it looked as if the howling gale had whirled them away. In the darkness a torch swayed in the wind, and behind the torch black forms of men and white, pallid faces could be discerned. Norah's mind turned to the stories which her mother had been telling her. She knew it was wrong to think of them at that moment but she felt an inordinate desire to laugh at something; what she wanted to laugh at she did not know; why she wanted to laugh she could not fathom.

'Are they coming, Norah?' asked the old woman, rising from her seat and hobbling with difficulty towards the door. 'Mother of Christ! but the hand of God is heavy on me this night of nights! Children of my own and man of my own, all, all going away from me! I'll see the last of them go down into the grave before me, for with my hard cough and the long sickness I'll outlive them all: that is the will of God. Ten sons and daughters of my body; every one of them gone, and one away in black foreign parts.... Are they coming, Norah?'

The woman reached the door and leant against the jamb for support. The torch was flaring outside and very near.

'Watch that you don't set the thatch on fire!' a voice cried.

Two men entered the house, the water streaming from their clothes and each holding a burdened oar in his hands. Across the oars a sail was bound tightly, and cold in death on the sail lay James Ryan, his grey beard sticking out stiffly, his eyes open, his head shaking from side to side, his bare feet blue with the cold. The oars, which brushed sharply against the old woman in passing, were laid on the floor and the dead man was placed on the bed.

'I'm sweatin' like a pig!' said one of the bearers, and he rubbed his wrinkled brow violently with the back of his hand.

'Watch the thatch!' someone outside shouted. The torch was extinguished and a crowd of men entered the cabin. An old red-haired fisherman lifted the oars; the sail was rolled into a bundle and carried out again. Pools of water formed on the floor and tracks of wet feet showed all over it. The old woman hobbled back to her bed and gazed long and earnestly at her husband; some of the men took off their hats; one was smoking, another dressed a bleeding foot and told how he hit it against a sharp rock when carrying the dead man up from the sea; several of the neighbouring women were already in the house. Maire a Crick was on her knees by the bedside.

'I am used to it now,' said the old woman, as she sorted the blankets on the bed with her withered hands. 'Ten sons and daughters, and another away and maybe never hearing from him again.… Himself said when he was going out that the morrow never comes.'

She sat down on the edge of the bed, ran her fingers over the wet clothes of her husband, opened his vest, put her hand on his heart, shook her head sadly and buttoned the coat again.

'Just when he was putting out the wind caught him, and he dropped like a stone over the side of the curragh,' the red-haired fisherman was saying. 'But the boat was no good anyway. It is one of the Congested Districts Board's boats that he should have.'

'Where would he get the money to buy one?' asked Maire a Crick, turning round from the prayer which she was saying for the dead man.

'The money can be paid in instalments,' answered the red fisherman. He spoke the Gaelic, as nearly everybody in Frosses did, but the words 'instalments' and 'Congested Districts Board' were said in English. 'Ten pounds the new boats cost, and there is five years allowed for paying the money.'

'The Congested Districts Board is going to be a great help,' someone remarked.

'Is the curragh safe?' asked Mary Ryan, turning round. She was still sitting beside the bed, turning over the clothes with lean, shaky fingers.

'It is at the bottom,' said a neighbour, Eamon Doherty by name. 'It was rotten anyhow, and it hadn't been in wet water for close on two years…. Now, I wonder what made Shemus go out on it?'

'Nothing atall, atall left,' said the old woman in a feeble voice. 'If I only had the curragh even…. And himself dead after all the times that the sea has bent under him! Never to see him again, never! Isn't it hard to think that a thing like that could be?'

Whereupon, saying this she began to cry, at first quietly, but afterwards, as if getting warmed to the task, more loudly, until her sobs could be heard a hundred yards away from the house.

'If I only had the curragh left!' she repeated time and again.

Norah approached the bed timidly. She had been weeping silently by the door ever since the corpse had been carried in. Death was here in the house; it had already taken possession of her father. And it was with her also. Not tonight nor tomorrow, but at the end of forty years or of fifty, and was it not all the same? And what was this death? She did not know; she only thought it cruel and strange. Her own helplessness in face of such a crisis almost overpowered her. For death there was no help, from it there was no escape. It was all powerful and terrible. Tomorrow and tomorrow might come and go, but her father would lie still and unheeding. He would not return, he could not return. This fact hammered at her mind, and the cruelty of her own thoughts tortured her. She tried to think of something apart from the tragedy, but ever her mind reverted to the one and same dreadful subject. Of a great fact she was certain; one that would never be contradicted. Her father was dead; thousands of years might pass and one truth would still remain unquestioned. Her father was dead. 'To think of it!' she said in a low voice. 'Dead for ever!'

She went down on her knees by the bedside but could not pray. God was cruel; He had no mercy. She sobbed no longer, but with wide, tearless eyes she gazed at the face of her father. It had now become yellow, the lips blue, the nose was pinched and the eyes sunken. The water from his clothes was dripping underneath the bed, and she could hear the drip-drip of it falling on the floor.

Everything in the house had suddenly taken on a different aspect. The bed appeared strange to her; so did the fire, the low droning voices of the neighbours, and the play of light and shadow on the walls. The old cat sitting on top of the dresser, gazing down at her, had a curious look in its wide-open eyes; the animal seemed to have changed in some queer way. Outside the wind was beating against the house and wailing over the chimney. Never in her life before had she heard such a melancholy sob in the wind.

CHAPTER 9

THE WAKE

I

Several more neighbours, men, women, and children, were now coming in. With eyes fixed straight ahead they approached the corpse, went down on their knees on the wet floor by the bedside and said their prayers, crossing themselves many times. Those who carried the dead body up from the sea drew near to the fire and dried their sodden garments in the midst of a cloud of vapour that almost hid them from view. Eamon Doherty remarked that Ireland would have Home Rule presently, and a loud discussion mingled with many jokes was soon in progress.

'The Irish will never agree,' said old Oiney Dinchy, a one-eyed ancient who had just risen from his knees by the bedside. 'That is the worst of the Irish; they never agree. Look at them now in the House of Commons; one member is always fighting against another member, and it was ever the same, for contrairiness is in their blood to the very last drop of it.'

'There is always bound to be two parties,' said Master Diver with dogmatic assurance. 'In England and America there are always two parties, sometimes more.'

'They'll never get on, then,' said Eamon Doherty. 'There are no two parties in the holy Church, and that's why it gets on so well.'

The door opened and Sheila Carrol, the beansho, entered, her child, now a chubby little boy of three, toddling at her heels. Without looking round she went down on her knees by the bedside, and a couple of women who were praying crossed themselves and rose hurriedly. A few of the younger men winked knowingly and turned their thumbs towards the newcomer. Old Mary Ryan muttered something under her breath and turned a look of severe disapproval on the kneeling woman, then on the little boy who had run forward to the fire, where he was holding out his hands to the blaze.

'Who'll be the ones that will go to Greenanore and get tea, bread, snuff, and tobacco for the wake?' asked Mary Ryan.

'I'll go if Eamon Doherty comes along with me,' said old Oiney Dinchy, getting to his feet and putting a live peat to the bowl of his pipe.

'The two of you always get drunk if you go to Greenanore together,' said the old woman. 'I'd as soon send the –' she pointed with her thumb over her shoulder at the beansho but did not mention her name, 'to Greenanore, as send you two.'

'It is not everyone that would be treated that way if they offered to help a person,' Eamon Doherty remarked in a loud voice to Oiney Dinchy.

'I'll go if Willie the Duck comes with me,' said a long, lank, shaggy youth, rising from one corner of the room and stretching his arms.

'You're the man for the job, Micky's Jim,' answered Mary Ryan, coming from the bedside and tottering through the press of neighbours to the dresser where the Delft tea-pot stood. She raised the lid, dipped her hand into the tea-pot and drew out a fistful of money.

'Four shillings for tea,' she began to calculate; 'eightpence for sugar; five shillings for loaves of bread; four shillings and sixpence for tobacco, and sixpence for snuff, and – How much potheen did you get for your father's wake, Eamon Doherty?'

'Four gallons and no less,' Eamon answered in a surly tone of voice.

'Two gallons of potheen, Micky's Jim, and get it as cheap as you can,' said the old woman, turning to the long-limbed youth. 'From what I hear Martin Eveleen sells good potheen. Get it from him, for it was Martin, I wish him luck! that helped Norah when she took the fargortha on the road to Greenanore three winters agone.'

The money was handed to Micky's Jim, and he left the house followed by Willie the Duck, a small man, dark and swarthy, with a hump on his left shoulder, and a voice, when he spoke, that reminded one of the quacking of ducks.

'Thirty-four shillings in all,' mumbled Mary Ryan as she took her way back to the fireside. 'It costs a lot to bury a body, and there will never be left one at all to bury me, never a one at all. If only the curragh was left me it would be something.'

Meanwhile Norah had slipped out, and went from house to house borrowing candlesticks (Meenalicknalore townland consisted of thirty families and there were only two candlesticks amongst them), baskets of peat, holy water, a lamp, extra chairs, stools, and many other things required for the wake.

II

At midnight the cabin was cleared of everybody but the washers of the dead, Eamon Doherty and Master Diver. Oiney Dinchy was very angry because Mary Ryan did not ask him to give a hand at the washing of her husband.

'It wasn't as if Shemus and me weren't good friends,' said Oiney. 'And besides, I have washed more dead men in a year of my life than all washed by Eamon and Master Diver put together.... And to think that I wasn't allowed to help at the washin' tonight!'

The men and women who had left the cabin went down on their knees at the doorstep and recited the rosary. The night being very dark the young men drew near the girls and tickled them on the bare feet while they prayed. When admittance was again possible the dead man lay in the bed, his body covered with a white sheet and a large black crucifix resting on his breast. His clothes were already burned in the fire, it being a common custom in Frosses to consign the clothes of the dead to the flames on the first night of the wake.

About two o'clock in the morning provisions came from Greenanore. The house was now crowded, and several games such as 'The Priest of the Parish', 'Catch the Ten', and 'Put your fingers in the Crow's Nest' were in progress. An old man who sat in the corner was telling a story of the famine, and a few mischievous boys were amusing themselves by throwing pieces of peat at his hat.

While tea was being made, the rosary was again started. Micky's Jim, a trifle the worse for liquor, went down on his knees on a chair and gave out the prayers. The mischievous boys turned their attentions from the old man to Jim, who was presently bombarded by a fire of turf. One went past his ears; one hit him on the back, another on the head, a third on the brow. Jim got angry.

'Pray away yourselves and be damned to you!' he roared at the kneeling house and, jumping off the chair, he sat down in a corner from which he had a view of the whole party. Prayers came to an abrupt conclusion; the chair was taken by the beansho, who placed her child between its legs, and the little boy, who had shown a wonderful propensity for running to the bedside and pulling the corpse by the beard, was held a fast prisoner. Four or five women moved about hurriedly preparing tea; whisky was served without skimp or stint, but pipes were found to be scarce; one had to do for three persons, each pulling at it in turn.

The old man in the corner took up the famine story at a point where the prayers had interrupted the recital. It told of a corpse that rose from the bed of death, sat down at the table, lifted a bowl of tea, drank it and went back to bed again. 'And the man was dead all the time,' said the story-teller.

Willie the Duck, speaking in a quavering voice, began to ask riddles: 'What bears but never blossoms?' he enquired.

'The hangman's rope,' was the answer.

'What tree never comes to fruit?' he asked.

'The gallows-tree,' was the answer.

'This is the best guess of the night,' said Willie, taking a pinch of snuff and sneezing violently. 'No one will be able to answer it.... In the morning four legs; at noon two legs; in the evening three legs and at night four legs; and what would that be?'

'It's a man,' said Eamon Doherty, looking round with a triumphant glance. 'In his young days a man walks on his hands and knees, when he grows up he walks on two legs; when he gets older he walks on three legs, two and a stick; and if he lives long enough he'll walk on crutches, God be good to us! and that's four legs!'

'You're a man with a head, Eamon,' said Willie the Duck. 'And how did you guess it atall?'

'I heard the same guess often and I knew the answer every time,' Eamon replied, and a smile of satisfaction lit up his face.

About four o'clock in the morning most of the men and a few of the ancient females were drunk. Mary Ryan had fallen asleep by the fire, her head touching the white ashes of her husband's clothes. Norah placed a pillow under her mother's head and took up a seat near her, gazing in turn at the silent figure which lay in the bed and the blue flames chasing one another up the black chimney.

Two lamps, one at each end of the house, spluttered dismally; the wind outside battered loudly against the door and wailed over the chimney. Oiney Dinchy was asleep and snoring loudly, and two youngsters blackened his face with soot. The beansho slept, and her child, long since released from the prison of the chair, was blubbering fitfully. On the damp earth of the mid-floor a well-made young woman slumbered, the naked calves of her finely formed legs showing. Micky's Jim slapped the legs with his hand; the girl awoke, put down her dress until it covered her toes, made a face at the tormentor and went to sleep again. Beside Norah, old Master Diver, now remarkably rotund, was asleep, his bald head hanging to one side and a spittle slobbering from his lips.

Norah looked round at the sleepers, saw the stiff legs stretched on the floor, the long, awkward arms hanging loosely over the backs of the chairs, the bowls and the upturned whisky glasses on the table; heard the loud snoring, the rustle of petticoats as a woman changed her position on a stool, the crackle of falling peat on the hearth, the whimpering of the beansho's child, and the sound made by the lips of a sucking babe pulling at its mother's breast.

The strange fear, that which had taken possession of her three years before on the rocks of Dooey, seized her again. To her all things seemed to lack finish as they lacked design. A vague sense of repulsion overcame the girl as she gazed at the sleepers huddled on form and floor. She shuddered as if in a fever and approached the bed; there the awful stillness of the dead fascinated her. She was looking at the dead, but somehow Death had now lost its terror: it was the living who caused her fear. She knelt down and prayed.

CHAPTER 10

COFFIN AND COIN

I

For two days and nights the neighbours came in, prayed by the bedside, drank bowls of tea, smoked long white clay pipes and departed, only to return later and renew the same performance. A coffin and coffin-bearer, the latter shaped like a ladder, the sides of which were cushioned to ease the shoulders of the men who carried it, were procured. On the rungs of the coffin-bearer a number of notches, three hundred and fifty-two in all, told of the bodies carried on it to the grave. The bearer had been in service for many years and had been used by most of the families in Frosses. The man who made it was long dead; number seventy-seven represented his notch on the rungs.

On the morning of the third day Oiney Dinchy and Micky's Jim lifted the dead man from the bed and placed him in the coffin. Before the lid was screwed down, Mary Ryan knelt over the coffin, gripping the side near her with thin, long fingers, which showed white at the joints, and kissing her husband she burst into a loud outcry of grief. Norah, more reserved in her sorrow, knelt on the floor, said a short prayer and then kissed the face of the corpse as her mother had done.

The lid was fastened, but here an interruption occurred. The wife wanted to look at her husband for 'just one other minute'. With a gesture of impatience old Oiney Dinchy, who was discussing the best means of catching flukes and tying the coffin, lifted the lid again and stood silently by, his hat drawn down well over his eyes. Mary Ryan gave vent to another outburst of grief; the coffin was again closed and lifted on the wooden bearer. An idle child was busily engaged in counting the notches.

'Seventy-seven; that's for the man who made it,' someone was saying.

'Listen, Micky's Jim,' whispered Mary Ryan as the youth passed her, going towards the door with a basket of pipes and tobacco.

'Well, Mary, what is it?' Jim asked.

'Was this a good year beyond the water?'

Jim went yearly to the potato-digging in Scotland, taking with him a squad of men and women from his own country, and over these he was master while they were at work.

'It was not so very bad,' said Jim cautiously. He was afraid that the old woman might ask the loan of money from him.

'Next year I have a mind to send Norah.'

'And not to make a nun of her, after all?'

Norah was piling peat on the fire, lifting them from the floor and dropping them into the flames. As she bent down Jim noticed every movement of her body and paid very little attention to the words of the old woman. Norah, having finished her task, stood upright; Jim waited eagerly for a repetition of her former movement, but seeing that she was weeping he turned his attention to the task of getting the coffin through the doorway.

Norah would be a light girl for heavy work on the Scottish farms, Jim thought, as he stooped down and lifted a rung of the bearer. Could he take her with him? That was a ticklish question. She was clever with the needles, he knew, but she had not done any heavy manual work for the last two years. Learning lessons was to Jim an idle task. But the movement of her body, and especially of her legs when bending over the fire, appealed to Jim. The grace of her carriage, the poise of her head, the soft hair that fell over her shoulders, all these found favour in the eyes of the healthy young man.

'My cripes, I'll take her with me next year!' he said under his breath. He spoke in English and had learned many strange oaths abroad.

II

Outside a large crowd of people were waiting; the women dressed in red flannel petticoats and woollen shawls, the men in white wrappers and corduroy trousers. The coffin bearer was raised on high; four men placed their shoulders under it; a bottle of holy water was sprinkled over bearers and burden indiscriminately; the men and women crossed themselves many times, and the mournful procession started.

Mary Ryan stood at the door and watched it wending its way across the dreary, uneven fields, past the Three Rocks, now getting lost in some hollow, again rising to the shoulders of a hillock, the coffin swaying unevenly on the shoulders of the bearers, the red petticoats of the women in the rear shaking in the breeze. The widow, almost too weak to move, was with difficulty restrained from going to the churchyard. Norah, having arranged the hassock in the corner for her mother, had followed the procession, and now the old woman thought that she could detect her child a quarter of a mile away, following in the rear of the party. Micky's Jim, who had not gone away yet, was engaged in sorting a rope on the thatch which had been blown askew by the wind of the previous nights.

'I'll overtake the funeral, Mary,' he said when he completed the work. 'I was just making the thatch strong against the breeze and I have tied a broken rope.'

'Mother of God be good to you, Jim, but it is yourself that has the kindly heart!' said Mary in a tremulous whisper. 'Could you take Norah with you beyond the water next year?'

Jim called to mind the movements of the girl's body when she stooped to lift peat for the fire, and the remembrance filled him with pleasure. 'When next summer comes round, I'll see, Mary Ryan,' he answered. 'If there is a place to spare in the squad I'll let you know and your Norah will have the very first chance of it.'

'Mother of God bless you, Jim, for the kindness is in you!' said the old woman. 'It is me that is the lone body this very minute, with never a penny in my house and not even the old curragh left to me to make a penny by.'

'Well, I'm off, Mary,' said Jim. 'The coffin is going out of sight and they'll be needing new blood under it.'

He hurried across the fields, his long legs covering an enormous spread of earth at every stride. Over the brae he hurried, and at the turn of the road halted for a moment and looked back at Mary Ryan's cabin. The woman still stood at the door, one hand shading her eyes, looking towards the Frosses churchyard, which lay more than three miles away. 'Thinkin' that she could get anything for an old curragh!' he muttered contemptuously, as he resumed his stride. 'She's an old fool; but Norah! Ah! she's a soncy lass, and she was good to look at when making that fire!'

III

The graveyard, surrounded by a stone wall, broken down
in several places, served as a grazing plot for bullocks,
donkeys, and sheep, as well as for the burial place of the
dead. A long walk, lined with stunted hazel bushes, ran
half-way through the yard, and at the end a low stone vault,
hardly higher than a man's head, stood under the shadow
of an overhanging sycamore.

The funeral procession was delayed on the journey, and
Father Devaney, round-faced and red-cheeked, stamped
up and down while waiting its arrival. He had come all the
way from Greenanore and was in a hurry to get back again.
The morning was cold and caused him to shiver a little,
and when he shivered he clapped his hands vigorously, the
palm of one against the back of the other.

His large mansion, complete now and habitable, had
not been fully paid for yet, and most of his parishioners
were a pound or two in arrears; when this money came to
hand matters would be much better. Old Devaney had
developed a particularly fine taste in wine and cigars and
found these very expensive; and at present he called to mind
how James Ryan was two pounds in arrears with the
mansion tax. The old priest knew that this money would
never come to hand; the widow was ill, no word had been
heard of Fergus for years, and Norah Ryan was a light slip
of a girl who would probably never earn a penny. Devaney
knew all the affairs of his flock, and he stamped up and
down the graveyard, a little angry with the dead man who,
being so long in coming to his last home, had kept him
waiting for thirty minutes.

The funeral came in sight, creeping up over the brow
of the hill that rose near at hand, the bearers straining under

their burden as they hurried across the uneven ground, with the coffin rising and falling on their shoulders like a bark in a storm at sea. The gate of the graveyard was already open; the procession filed through, Father Devaney stepping out in front, his surplice streaming in the wind. The good man thought of the warm dinner waiting for him at home, and being in a hurry to get done with the burial service he walked so quickly that the bearers could hardly keep up with him. On the floor of the little vault in the centre of the graveyard the coffin was set down and the basket of snuff, pipes, and tobacco was handed round. All the men took pipes, filled them with rank plug and lit them; the older women lit pipes also, and everybody, with the exception of the priest and Norah Ryan, took snuff.

'Hurry up!' said Father Devaney. 'Ye can smoke after ye do yer duty. It would be as well if ye were puttin' yer hands in yer pockets now and gettin' yer offerin's ready.'

Immediately a stream of silver descended on the coffin. All the mourners paid rapidly, but in turn, and the priest called out their names as they paid. A sum of ten pounds seventeen shillings was collected, and this the priest carefully wrapped up in a woollen muffler and put into his pocket.

'Now hurry up, boys, and get a move on ye; and open the grave!' he shouted, making no effort to hide his impatience now that the money was safely in his keeping. He felt full of the importance of a man who knows that everybody around him trembles under his eyes. Three or four young fellows were digging the grave and joking loudly as they worked; a crowd of men stood round them, puffing white clouds of smoke up into the air. Many of the women were kneeling beside graves that held all that remained of one or another near and dear to them. Norah Ryan stood alone with the priest, her dark shawl drawn over her white forehead, and a few stray tresses, that had fallen over her face, shaking in the breeze.

'It is a black day this for you, Norah, a black day,' said the priest, speaking in Gaelic. Two tears coursed down the girl's cheeks, and she fixed a pair of sorrowful grey eyes on the man when he spoke.

'Don't cry, girsha beag (little girl),' said the priest. 'It is all for the best, all for the best, because it is the will of God.'

He looked sharply at the girl, who, feeling uncomfortable in his presence, longed to be away from the man's side. She wondered why she had not gone off to the other end of the graveyard with Sheila Carrol, whom she could now see kneeling before a black wooden cross that was fast falling into decay. But it would be wrong to go away from the side of her father's coffin, she thought.

'Any word from Fergus of late?' the priest was asking.

'No; not the smallest word.'

That Mary Ryan owed him two pounds, and that there was very little possibility of ever receiving the money, forcibly occurred to the priest at that moment. 'Ye'll not be in a good way at home now?' he said aloud.

'There's hardly a white shilling in the house,' answered the girl.

'Is that the way of it?' exclaimed the priest, then seemed on the point of giving expression to something more forcible, but with an effort he restrained himself. 'Well, it cannot be helped, I suppose, but there are two pounds owing for the building of my new house.'

IV

'The grave is ready,' said Micky's Jim, approaching the priest and saluting. The youth was perspiring profusely; his shirt open at the neck exposed his hairy chest, on which beads of sweat were glistening brightly.

'In with the coffin then,' said the priest, taking a book from his pocket and approaching the open grave. A pile of red earth, out of which several white bones protruded, lay on the brink, and long earthworms crawled across it. The coffin was lowered into the grave with a rope. Norah wept loudly; old Oiney Dinchy remarked that the bones belonged to her grandparents whom she did not remember.

'Remember man that thou art dust and unto dust thou shalt return,' the priest chanted in a loud, droning voice. Norah, kneeling on the wet ground, her head bent down over her bosom, so that her hair hung over her shoulders, saw nothing but the black coffin which was speedily disappearing under the red clay, and heard nothing but the thud of the earth as it struck the coffin.

The priest took his departure; the grave was filled up and the crowd began to disperse.

'Come away home now,' said Sheila Carrol to Norah, who was still kneeling on the wet ground. The girl rose without a word, brushed her dress with a woollen handkerchief and accompanied the beansho from the churchyard.

'Don't cry, Norah,' said Sheila, observing that tears were still falling down the cheeks of her companion. 'Everyone must die and go away just the same as if they had never been at all, for that is the will of God. How is yer mother this morning?'

'Much the same as she was always,' said Norah. 'She cannot get rid of her cough, and she has shiverin' fits of late.... Hasn't the sea the black heart?'

'Black enough, indeed, my child,' said the beansho. 'Your mother will feel it a big lot?'

'Not so much,' said the girl. 'She'll soon be with him, she's thinkin'.'

'At the wake I heard her say that she would be the last of the family to die. What put that into her head?'

'I don't know what put it into her head, but if I were to die on the wet road this very minute I wouldn't care one haet.' On Norah's face there was a look of infinite sadness, and the pathos of her words cut Sheila to the heart.

'Don't speak like that, Norah Ryan,' she exclaimed. 'Death is black and bitter, but there are things much worse than death, things far, far worse.'

They had now reached a stile, and far in front the soft caishin (path) wound on by rock and rath across the broad expanse of moor. Several people, walking one after another, were in front; the soft ooze was squirting under their feet and splashing against their ankles. In the midst of the heather a young bullock lay chewing the cud, and looked upon the passers-by with that stupid, involved look peculiar to the ox; a moor-cock, agitated and voluble, rose into the air and chattered as it swept across the brown of the moor.

'I'm goin' to leave Ireland come Candlemas,' said the beansho, pulling her feet wearily out of the mire.

'And where would ye be goin' to then, Sheila Carrol?'

'Beyont the water.'

'Mercy be on us, and are ye goin' surely?'

'True as death, I'm goin',' said Sheila Carrol with rising voice. 'I'm sick of this place – not the place itself but the people that's in it, them with their bitin' tongues and cuttin' talk, them that won't let those that do them no harm a-be. Nothin' bad enough that they wouldn't put past me, the same Frosses people. For me it's always the hard word that they have; even the priest himself when he meets me on the high road crosses himself as if he met the red-hot devil out of hell. But did he refuse my shillin' today? ... Even at the wakes the very people point their thumbs at me when I go down on my own two knees to say a prayer for the dead.... But what am I talkin' about! Why should I be tellin' my own sorrows to one that has heavy troubles of her own to bear.... I'm goin' beyont the water come next Candlemas, anyway, Norah Ryan!'

CHAPTER 11

THE TRAIN FROM GREENANORE

I

When one is leaving home every familiar object seems to take on a different aspect and becomes almost strange and foreign. The streets, houses, and landscape which you have gazed on for years become in some way very remote, like objects seen in a dream, but under this guise every familiar landmark becomes dearer than ever it has been before. So Norah Ryan felt as she was leaving home in the June of 1905 bound for the potato fields of Scotland.

'Is this the road to Greenanore, the road that our feet took when goin' to the town for the stockin' yarn?' she asked herself several times. 'It is changed somehow; it doesn't seem to be the same place, but for all that I like it better than ever. Why this is I do not know; I seem to be in a dream of some kind.'

Her thoughts were confused and her mind ran on several things at the same time; her mother's words at leave-taking, the prayer that the child might do well, the quick words of tearless farewell spoken at the doorstep; and as she thought of these things she wondered why her mother did not weep when her only child was leaving her.

The girl was now walking alone to the village of Greenanore. There she would meet all the members of the party, and every step of the journey brought a thousand bygone memories vividly to her mind. Fergus she thought of, his goodbye at the cross-roads, the dog whining in Ballybonar, the lowing cow, the soft song of the sea. Would she ever see Fergus again? Where had he been all these years? Looking into the distance she could see the mountains that hemmed Glenmornan, and light clouds, white and fleecy as Candlemas sheep, resting on the tops of them. Further down, on the foothills, the smoke of peat-fires rose into the air, telling of the turf-savers who laboured on the brown bogs at the stacks and rikkles. Norah thought of Dermod Flynn; indeed she called him to mind daily when gazing towards the hills of Glenmornan, recollecting with a certain feeling of pride the boy's demeanour at school and his utter indifference towards personal chastisement. The dreamy eyes of Dermod and his manner of looking through the school window at nothing in particular fascinated her; and the very remembrance of the youth standing beside her facing the map of the world always caused a pleasant thrill to run through her body. Now, as she looked at the hills of Glenmornan, the incidents of the morning on which she went to pull bog-bine there came back to her mind, and she wondered if Dermod Flynn thought the hills so much changed on the day when he was setting out for the rabble of Strabane.

A large iron bridge, lately built by the Congested Districts Board, spanned the bay between Frosses and Dooey. Norah crossed over this to the other side, where the black rocks, sharp and pointed, spread over the white sand. It was here that the women slept out on the mid-winter night many years ago; and now Norah had only a very dim remembrance of the event.

Up to the rise of the hill she hurried, and from the townland of Ballybonar looked back at Frosses: at the little strips of land running down to the sea, at the white lime-washed cabins dotted all over the parish, at Frosses graveyard and the lone sycamore tree that grew there, showing like a black stain against the sky. Seeing it, she thought of her father and said an 'Our Father' and 'Hail Mary' for the repose of his soul. Then her eye roved over Frosses again.

'Maybe after this I'll never set my two eyes on the place,' she said, then added, 'just like Fergus!'

The thought that she might never see the place again filled her with a certain feeling of importance which up to now had been altogether foreign to her.

II

At the station she met the other members of the potato squad, fifteen in all. Some were sitting on their boxes, others on the bundles bound in cotton handkerchiefs which contained all their clothes and toilet requisites. The latter consisted of combs and hand-mirrors possessed by the women, and razors, the property of the men. Micky's Jim was pacing up and down the platform, his hands deep in his trousers' pockets and a heavy-bowled wooden pipe in his mouth. From time to time he pulled the pipe from between his teeth, accompanying the action with a knowing shrug of his shoulders, and spat into the four-foot way.

'Is this yerself, Norah?' he exclaimed, casting a patronising glance at the girl as she entered the railway station. 'Ye are almost late for the train. Did ye walk the whole way? ... Ah! here she comes!'

The train came in sight, puffing round the curve; the women rose from their seats, clutched hastily at their bundles and formed into a row on the verge of the platform; the men, most of whom were smoking, took their pipes from their mouths, hit the bowls sharply against their palms, thus emptying them of white ash; then, with a feigned look of unconcern on their faces, they picked up their belongings with a leisure which implied that they were men well used to such happenings. They were posing a little; knowing that those who came to see them off would tell for days in Frosses how indifferently Mick or Ned took the train leading to the land beyond the water. 'Just went on the train with no more concern on their faces than if they were going to a neighbour's wake!' the Frosses people would say.

The train puffed into the station, the driver descended from his post, yawned, stretched his arms, and surveyed the crowd with a look of superior disdain. The fireman, with an oil can in his hands, raced along the footplate and disappeared behind the engine, only to come back almost immediately, puffing and wiping the sweat from his face with a piece of torn and dirty rag.

'All aboard!' Micky's Jim shouted in an excited voice, forgetting pose for a moment. 'Hurry up now or the train will be away, leavin' the biggest half of ye standin' here. A train isn't like Oiney Dinchy's cuddy cart; it hasn't to stop seven times in order to get right started. Hurry up! Go in sideways, Willie the Duck; ye cannot go through a door frontways carrying a bundle under yer oxter. Yer stupid ways would drive a sensible man to pot! Hurry up and come on now! Get a move on ye, every one of the whole lot of ye!'

Presently all, with the exception of the speaker, were in their compartments and looking for seats. Micky's Jim remained on the platform, waiting for the train to start, when he could show by boarding it as it steamed out of the station that he had learned a thing or two beyond the water in his time; a thing or two not known to all the Frosses people.

A ticket collector examined the tickets, chatting heartily as he did so. When he found that Norah had not procured hers he ran off and came back with one, smiling happily as if glad to be of assistance to the girl. A lady and gentleman, tourists no doubt, paced up and down the platform, eyeing everybody with the tourists' rude look of enquiry; a stray dog sniffed at Micky's Jim's trousers and got kicked for its curiosity; the engine driver yawned again, made the sign of the cross on his open mouth and mounted to his place; the whistle sounded, and with Micky's Jim standing on the footboard the train steamed out of the station.

Norah, who had never been on a train before, took up her seat near the window, and rubbed the pane with her shawl in order to get a better view of the country, which seemed to be flying past with remarkable speed. The telegraph wires were sinking and rising; the poles like big hands gripped them up, dropped them, but only to lift them up again as threads are lifted on the fingers of a knitter.

There were eleven people in the compartment, four women and seven men. One of the latter, Eamon Doherty, was eating a piece of dry bread made from Indian meal; the rest of the men were smoking black clay pipes, so short of shank that the bowls almost touched the noses of the smokers. But Jim's pipe was different from any of these; it was a wooden one, 'real briar root' he said, and was awfully proud of it. It had cost three shillings and sixpence in a town beyond the water, he now told the party, not indeed for the first time; but none of the listeners believed him. Two of the women said their prayers; one wept because she was leaving Ireland, and Norah Ryan spent her time looking out of the window.

III

'Who'll take a drink?' asked Micky's Jim, pulling a half-bottle of whisky from his pocket and drawing out the cork with his fingers. 'Good stuff this is, and I'm as dry as the rafters of hell.... Will ye have a wee drop, Willie the Duck?'

'No, sure,' answered Willie, who was sitting beside the weeping woman, his one leg across the other, and his hands clasped over his stomach. 'I would take it if I hadn't the pledge against drink, indeed I would. Aye, sure!'

'Aye sure, be hanged!' Jim blurted out. 'Ye've got to take it, for it's die-dog-or-eat-the-gallows this time. Are ye goin' to take it?'

'No, sure –'

'Why d'ye always say "Aye, sure" and "No, sure" when talking to a person?' asked Jim, replacing the cork in the bottle, which he now tried to balance on the point of his finger. 'Is it a habit that ye've got into, Willie the Duck?'

'Aye, sure,' answered Willie, edging away from Micky's Jim, who was balancing the bottle successfully within an inch of the roof. 'Ye'll let that bottle fall on me head.'

'Aye, sure,' answered Willie, edging away from Micky's Jim, who was balancing the bottle successfully within an inch of the roof. 'Ye'll let that bottle fall on me head.'

'Aye, sure,' shouted Micky's Jim and shook the bottle with perilous carelessness, holding out the free hand in case it should fall. 'It wouldn't crack a wooden head anyhow.'

'That's Brockagh station that we're comin' into now, as the man said,' remarked one of the women who had been praying. The woman was Maire a Glan, who had been going beyond the water to work for the last four or five years. Things were not going well at home; her husband lay ill with paralysis, the children from a monetary point of view were useless as yet – the oldest boy, thin and weakly, a cripple from birth, went about on crutches, the younger ones were eternally crying for bread. Maire a Glan placed the rosary round her neck and took a piece of oaten bread from the bundle at her feet.

'Will ye have a wee bit to eat, Norah Ryan?' she asked.

'My thanks to ye, Maire a Glan, but I'm not hungry,' answered Norah, rubbing the window where her breath had dimmed it.

'I thought that ye might be, seeing that yer eye is not wet on leavin' home,' said the woman, breaking bread and putting a bit of it in her mouth. 'There, the train is stopping!' she went on, 'and I have two sisters married within the stretch of a mile from this place.'

'Aye, sure,' said Willie the Duck with his usual quack. 'I know both, and once I had a notion of one of them, meself.'

'Lookin' for one of God's stars to light yer pipe with, as the man said,' remarked the woman contemptuously, fixing her eyes on the poor fellow's hump. 'Ye have a burden enough on yer shoulders and not to be thinkin' at all of a wife.'

'Them that carries the burden should be the first to complain of it,' said Willie the Duck, edging still further away from Micky's Jim, who was now standing up and balancing the whisky bottle on the point of his nose. The women tittered, the men drew their pipes from their mouths and gave vent to loud guffaws. The train started out from Brockagh station, a porter ran after it, shut a door, and again Norah Ryan watched the fields run past and the telegraph wires rise and fall.

'I'll bet that not one of ye knows who's comin' to join us at Derry,' said Micky's Jim, tiring of his play and putting the bottle back in his pocket, after having taken a sup of its contents.

'Who?' asked several voices.

'Dermod Flynn from Glenmornan.'

'I haven't seen that gasair for the last two years or more,' said Murtagh Gallagher, a young man of twenty-five, who came from the townland of Meenahalla in the parish of Frosses. 'If I mind right, he was sort of soft in the head.'

A faint blush rose to Norah Ryan's cheek, and though she still looked out of the window she now failed to see the objects flying past. The conversation had suddenly become very interesting for her.

'He has been working with a farmer beyont the mountains this long while,' said Micky's Jim. 'But I'm keepin' a place for him in the squad, and ye'll see him on the Glasgow boat this very night. Ye have said that he was soft in his head, Murtagh Gallagher. Well, that remark applies to me.'

Jim spat on his hands, rose to his feet, shoved his fist under Murtagh's nose and cried: 'Smell that! There's the smell of dead men off that fist! Dermod Flynn soft in the head, indeed! I'll soft ye, ye – ye flat-nosed flea-catcher ye!'

'I was only making fun,' said Murtagh.

'Make it to his face then!'

'D'ye mind how Dermod Flynn knocked Master Diver down with his fist in the very school?' asked Judy Farrel, who was also one of the party.

'Aye, sure,' said Willie the Duck. 'But it wasn't with his fist but with a stick that he struck Master Diver, and mind ye he made the blood to flow!'

'*I'll* soon make blood to flow!' said Micky's Jim, still holding his fist under Murtagh Gallagher's nose.

'I was only in fun,' Gallagher repeated. 'Ye're as hasty as a briar, Jim, for one cannot open his lips but ye want to blacken his eyes.'

'Now sit down, Micky's Jim,' said Maire a Glan. 'It's not nice to see two people, both of them from Donegal, fighting when they're away from home.'

'Fightin'!' exclaimed Jim, dropping into his seat and pulling out his pipe. 'I see no fightin' ... I wish to God that someone would fight ... Sort of soft in the head, indeed! ... I never could stand a man from Meenahalla, anyway.'

IV

The train sped on. House, field, and roadway whirled by, and Norah, almost bewildered, ceased to wonder where this road ran to, who lived in that house, what was the name of this village and whether that large building with the spire on top of it was a church (Bad luck to it!) or chapel (God bless it!).

'I'll see him again,' she thought, her mind reverting to Dermod Flynn. 'I wonder how he'll look now; if his hair is still as curly as when he was at Frosses school.... Two years away from his own home and the home of all his people! Such a long while, and now he'll know everything about the whole world.' Mixed with these lip-spoken words was the remembrance of her mother all alone in the old cabin at Frosses, and a vague feeling of regret filled her mind.

'Are you getting homesick, Norah?' Maire a Glan enquired, speaking in Gaelic, which came more easily than English to her tongue. 'It's not the dry eye that always tells of the lightest heart, I know myself.'

'Old Oiney Dinchy has a fine daughter,' Eamon Doherty was saying.

'She's as stuck-up as Dooey Head,' piped Judy Farrel in a weak, thin voice.

'Micky's Jim has a notion of her, I hear,' remarked Willie the Duck. 'But what girl hasn't Jim a notion of?'

Jim cleaned out the bowl of his pipe with a rusty nail and fell asleep while engaged on the task. The conversation went on.

'Old Farley McKeown is goin' to get married to an English lady.'

'A young soncy wench she is, they say!'

'Think of that, for old Farley! A wrinkled old stick of seventy! Ah! the shameless old thing!'

'It'll be a cold bed for the girl that is alongside of him. She'll need a lot of blankets, as the man said.'

'Aye, sure, and she will that.'

'But he's the man that has the money to pay for them.'

Norah, deep in a dreamy mood, listened idly to snatches of song, the laughter, and the voices that seemed to be speaking at a very remote distance; but after a while, sinking into the quiet isolation of her own thoughts, the outside world became non-existent to the young girl. She was thinking of Dermod; why he persisted in coming up before her mind's eye she could not explain, but the dream of meeting with him on the streets of Derry exerted a restful influence over her and she fell into a light slumber.

'It's the soncy girl she looks with the sleep on her.'

Almost imperceptibly Norah opened her eyes. The transition was so quiet that she was hardly aware that she had slept, and those who looked on were hardly aware that she had wakened. It was Maire a Glan who had been speaking. The train now stood at a station and Micky's Jim was walking up and down the platform, his pipe in his mouth and his hands deep in his trousers' pockets. Facing the window was a bookstall and a white-faced girl handing to some man a newspaper and a book with a red cover, Norah recollected that Fergus often read books with red covers just like the one that was handed over the counter of the bookstall. That it was possible to have a shop containing nothing but books and papers came as a surprise to Norah Ryan. Over the bookstall in white letters was the station's name – Strabane. Of this town Norah had often heard. It was to the hiring market of Strabane that Dermod Flynn had gone two years ago. Other two trains stood at the station, one on each side, and both full of passengers.

'Where are all those people going, Maire a Glan?' asked Norah.

'Everywhere, as the man said,' answered the old woman, who was telling her rosary and taking no notice of anything but the black beads passing through her fingers.

A boy walked up and down in front of the carriage, selling oranges at fourpence a dozen. Micky's Jim bought sixpence worth and handed them through the window, telling all inside to eat as many as they liked; he would pay. Maire a Glan left her beads aside until the feast was finished. The engine whistled; Micky's Jim boarded the moving train and again the fields were running past and the telegraph wires rising and falling.

''Twon't be long till we are on the streets of Derry now,' said Micky's Jim, drawing another half-bottle of whisky from his pocket and digging out the cork with a clasp-knife.

''Twon't be very long, no, sure,' said Willie the Duck, edging away from Micky's Jim.

CHAPTER 12

DERRY

I

They stepped on the dry and dusty Derry streets, the whole fifteen of them, with their bundles over their shoulders or dangling from their arms. Norah Ryan, homesickness heavy on her heart, had eyes for everything; and everything on which she looked was so strange and foreign: the car that came along the streets, moving so quickly and never a horse drawing it; the shops where hair was taken off for a few pence and put on again for a few shillings; shops with watches and gold rings in the windows; shops where they sold nothing but books and papers; and the high clocks, facing four ways at once and looking all over the town and the country beyond.

The long streets, without end almost, the houses without number, the large mills at the waterside, where row after row of windows rose one above another, until it made the eye dim and the head dizzy to look up at them, the noise, the babble of voices, the hurrying of men, the women, their dresses, filled Norah with a weary longing for her own fireside so far away by the shores of the sea that washed round Donegal.

A bell tolled; Micky's Jim turned round and looked at Norah, who immediately blessed herself and commenced to say the Angelus.

'That's not the bell above the chapel of Greenanore, that's the town clock,' laughed one of the women.

'There's no God in this town,' said Micky's Jim.

'No God!' Norah exclaimed, stopping in the midst of her prayer and half inclined to believe what Micky's Jim was saying.

'None at all,' said Micky's Jim. 'God's choice about the company He keeps and never comes near Derry.'

The party went to the Donegal House, a cheap little restaurant near the quay. The place was crowded. In addition to the potato squad there were several harvestmen from various districts in Donegal, and these were going over to Scotland now, intending to earn a few pounds at the turnip-thinning and haymaking before the real harvest came on. Most of the harvesters were intoxicated and raised a terrible hubbub in the restaurant while taking their food.

Micky's Jim, who was very drunk, sat on one chair in the dingy dining-room, placed his feet on another chair, and with his back pressed against the limewashed wall sank into a deep slumber. The rest of the party sat round a rude table, much hacked with knives, and had tea, bread, and rancid butter for their meal. A slatternly servant, a native of Donegal, served all customers; the mistress of the house, a tall, thin woman, with a long nose sharp as a knife and eyes cruel enough to match the nose, cooked the food. The tea was made in a large pot, continually on the boil. When a bowl of tea (there were no cups) was lifted out a similar amount of water was put in to replace it and a three fingerful of tea was added. The man of the house, a stout little fellow with a red nose, took up his position behind the bar and sold whisky with lightning rapidity. Now and again he gave a glass of whisky free of cost to some of the harvesters who weren't drinking very heavily. Those who got free drinks usually bought several glasses of liquor afterwards and became the most drunken men in the house.

After a long sleep Micky's Jim awoke and called for a bowl of tea. Followed all the way by the shrill voice of her mistress, who was always scolding somebody, the servant girl carried the tea to Jim, and the youth drank a mouthful of it while rubbing one hand vigorously across his eyes in order to drive the sleep away from them.

'This tay is as long drawn as the face of yer mistress,' grumbled Jim, and the servant giggled. 'I'm forgettin' all about Dermod Flynn too,' Jim continued, turning to Norah Ryan, who sat on the chair next to him. 'I must go out and look for him. He was to meet me at the quay, and I'm sure that he'll be on the wait for me there now.'

'Poor Dermod!' said Norah in answer to Jim. 'Maybe he'll get lost out on the lone streets, seein' that he is all be himself.'

'Him to get lost!' exclaimed Jim. 'Catch Dermod Flynn doin' anything as foolish as that! He's the cute rogue is Dermod!'

The tables and chairs in the eating-room were now cleared away and someone suggested getting up a dance. The harvestmen ceased swearing and began thumping their hobnailed boots on the floor; Willie the Duck played on a fiddle, which he had procured years before for a few shillings in a Glasgow rag-market, and in the space of a minute all the women, including old Maire a Glan, who looked sixty if a day, ranged on the floor preparatory to dancing a six-hand reel. On seeing this, the red-nosed landlord jumped over the counter and commenced to swear at the musician.

'The curse of Moses be on ye!' he roared. 'There'll be no dancin' here. Thumpin' on the floor ye gallivantin' fools! If ye want dancin' go out to the quay and dance. Dance into the Foyle or into hell if ye like, but don't dance here! Come now, stop it at once!'

'It's such a roarin' tune,' said Maire a Glan, interrupting him.

'It is that,' answered the man, 'but it needs a lighter foot than yours to do it justice, decent woman. There was a time when me meself could caper to that; aye, indeed... . But what am I talkin' about? There'll be no dancin' here.'

'Just one wee short one?' said a girl. Willie the Duck played with redoubled enthusiasm.

'No, nor half a one,' said the proprietor, tapping absently on the floor with his foot. 'God's curse on ye all! D'ye want to bring down the house over me head? ... "The Movin' Bogs of Allen" that's playin', isn't it? A good tune it, surely. But stop it! stop it!' roared the red-nosed man, cutting a caper, half a step and half a kick in front of the fiddler. 'I don't want your damned dancin', I can't stand it. God have mercy on me! Sure I'm wantin' to foot it meself!'

II

But the dancing was in full swing now, despite the vehemence of the proprietor. He looked round helplessly, and finding that his wife was already dancing with old Eamon Doherty he seized hold of the servant girl and whirled her into the midst of the party with a loud whoop that surprised himself even as much as it surprised the Donegal dancers.

Micky's Jim was dancing with Norah Ryan and pressing her tightly to his body. The youth's breath smelt of whisky and his movements were violent and irregular.

'Ye're hurtin' me, Jim,' said the girl, and he lifted her in his arms and carried her to a seat.

'Now are ye better?' he asked, not at all unkindly. 'Will I get ye a glass of cordial?'

'Don't bother about cordial,' said the girl; 'but go out and look for Dermod Flynn. Ye said that ye'd go out a good while ago.'

'Why are ye so anxious about him, girsha?' asked Jim. 'One would think that he was a brother of yours. Maybe indeed –'

He paused, looked round, then without another word he rose, went out into the street and took his way to the wharf, and there, when he could not find Dermod Flynn after a few minutes' search, he sat down on a capstan, lit his pipe and puffed huge clouds of smoke up into the air.

'Now I wonder why that Norah Ryan is so anxious about Dermod Flynn?' he muttered. 'Man! it's hard to know, for these women are all alike…. By Cripes, she's a fine built bit of a lassie. So is old Oiney Dinchy's daughter … Frosses and Glenmornan for women and fighters! … And the best fighters don't always get the best women. Now, that Norah Ryan will have nothin' at all to do with me as far as I can see; it's Dermod Flynn that she wants…. I'll have to look round for another wench, and girsha Oiney Dinchy (Oiney Dinchy's daughter) is a soncy slip of a cutty.'

When Dermod Flynn came along Jim had to look at him very closely before realising that this was the youth whom he had known in Glenmornan two summers before. Dermod stood sturdily on his legs; his shoulders were broad, his back straight, and his well-formed chest betokened great strength even now at the age of fourteen. A bundle dangled on his arm; one knee was out through his trousers, and he carried a hazel stick in his hand.

'Patrick's Dermod!' exclaimed Jim, a glance of glad recognition coming into his eyes when he had stared for a moment at Flynn. 'By Cripes! ye've grown to be a big healthy bucko since last I saw ye.'

Dermod flushed with pleasure. Jim began to ply him with questions about his work in Tyrone, his masters, whether they were good or bad, and – above all – if he had ever had a fight since he left home.

Dermod assured him that he had had many a hard, gruelling fight; knocked down a man twice his size with one blow of his fist and blackened the eyes of a youth who was head and shoulders taller than himself.

'And who have ye with ye, Jim?' he asked. 'Any of the Glenmornan people?'

'Lots,' answered Jim. 'Willie the Duck, Eamon Doherty, Judy Farrel, Maire a Glan, Norah Ryan – but she's not from Glenmornan, she's a Frosses girsha.'

He looked sharply at Dermod as he spoke.

'She was at Glenmornan school with me,' said Flynn. 'Where is she now?'

'There's a dance goin' on in the Donegal House; that's where we had our bit and sup, and she's shaking her feet on the floor there.'

'Can we go there and see the dancers?'

'There's not much time now,' said Jim. 'And there's the boat, that big one nearest us, that we're goin' on this very night. She's a rotten tub and we'll be very sick goin' round the Mulls of Cantyre.'

'Will we?'

'What I mean is that ye and all the rest of the men and women will be sick. I was never seasick in my life.'

'When is it going away?'

'In about half an hour from now.'

'How long will it take us to get across?' asked Dermod. 'Ten hours?'

'God look on yer wit!' exclaimed Jim. 'If there's a fog on the Clyde it will maybe take three days – maybe more. Ye can never know what a boat's goin' to do. Ye can no more trust it than ye can trust a woman.'

CHAPTER 13

A WILD NIGHT

I

The dance came to an end, and, worn out with their exertions, the women picked up their shawls and wrapped them round their shoulders. Then getting their bundles they went towards the wharf, Willie the Duck leading, his fiddle under his arm and his bundle tied over his shoulders with a string. Coming to the quay they passed through a gloomy grain-shed, where heating bags of wheat sent a steam out into the air. Suddenly, gazing through the rising vapour, Norah saw horses up in the sky and she could hear them neighing loudly. For a moment she paused in terror and wondered how such a thing could be, then recollected that in a town, where there was no God, anything might be possible. Once out in the open Maire a Glan pointed to the fall-and-tackle, hardly distinguishable at a distance, which was lifting the animals off the pier and lowering them down to the main deck of the boat. The horses were turning round awkwardly and snorting wildly, terrified by the sound of the sea.

Bags of grain were being lifted on long chains; dark derricks shoved out lean arms that waved to and fro as if inviting somebody to come near; cattle lowing and slipping were being hammered by the drovers' blackthorns into the hold; a tall man with face fierce and swarthy, eyes bright as fire, and mouth like a raw, red scar, was roaring out orders in a shrill voice, and suddenly in the midst of all this Norah saw Micky's Jim leaning against the funnel of the boat, his hands deep in his trousers' pockets and the eternal pipe in his mouth, apparently heedless of all that was going on around him.

Beside Jim stood one whom Norah knew, but one who had changed a great deal since she had seen him last. As she went up the gangplank, stepping timidly, cowering under the great derrick that wheeled above, she felt that a pair of eyes were fixed upon her, piercing into her very soul. She turned her gaze towards the deck and found Dermod Flynn looking straight at her as she made her way aboard. In an instant her eye had taken the whole picture of the youth, his clothes, the coat, much the worse for wear, his trousers, thin at knee and frilly at the shoe-mouth, his cap torn at rim and crown, the stray locks of hair straggling down his forehead, the bundle lying at his feet, and the hazel stick which he held in his hand, probably even yet in imitation of the cattle drovers who went along Glenmornan road on the way to the fair of Greenanore. These things Norah noticed with a girl's quick intuitive perception, but what struck her most forcibly was Dermod's look of expectation as he watched her come up the gangplank towards him.

'Dermod Flynn, I hardly knew ye at all,' she said, putting out her hand and smiling slightly. 'Ye've got very big these last two years.'

'So did you, Norah,' Dermod answered, looking curiously at the small white hand which he gripped in his own. 'You are almost as tall as I am myself.'

'Why wouldn't I be as tall as you are?' Norah replied, although Dermod had unknowingly squeezed her hand in a hard, tense grip. 'Am I not a year and a half older?'

When her hand was released her skin showed white where Dermod's fingers had gripped her, but she did not feel angry. On the contrary the girl was glad because he was so strong.

'Come over here!' cried Maire a Glan, who was sitting on her bundle beside the rail, smoking a black clay pipe and spitting on the deck.

The noise was deafening; the rowting of the cattle in the pens became louder; a man on the deck gave a sharp order; the gangway was pulled off with a resounding clash, the funnel began to rise and fall; Norah saw the pier move; a few women were weeping; some of the passengers waved handkerchiefs (none of them too clean) to the people on the quay; rails were bound together, hatches battened down; sailors hurried to and fro; a loud hoot could be heard overhead near the top of the funnel and the big vessel shuffled out to the open sea.

II

The boat was crowded with harvestmen from Frosses, potato-diggers from Glenmornan and Tweedore; cattle drovers from Coleraine and Londonderry, second-hand clothes-dealers, bricklayers' labourers, farm hands, young men and old, women and children; all sorts and conditions of people.

'There are lots of folk gathered together on this piece of floatin' wood,' said Maire a Glan, crossing herself, a habit of hers, when speaking of anything out of the ordinary. 'The big boat is a wonderful thing; beds with warm blankets and white sheets to sleep in, tables to sit down at and have tea in real cups and saucers, just the same as Father Devaney has at Greenanore, and him not out at all in the middle of the ocean on a piece of floatin' wood!'

'And will *we* get a bed to sleep in?' asked Norah Ryan.

'Why should *we* be gettin' a grand bed? We're only the poor people, and the poor people have no right to these things on a big boat like this one,' said the old woman, putting her black clay pipe into the pocket of her apron. 'There are no grand beds for people like us; they're only for the gentry.'

'Wouldn't a bed look nice on a Frosses curragh?' said Micky's Jim, sitting down on the bundle belonging to Willie the Duck and pulling the cork from a bottle of whisky which he had procured in Derry. 'Will ye have a drop, Maire a Glan?' he asked.

'I'll not be havin' any,' said the old woman, who nevertheless put out her hand, caught the bottle and raised it to her lips. 'It's a nice drop this,' she said, when she had swallowed several mouthfuls, 'but I'm not goin' to drink any of it. I'm only just tastin' it.'

'If it was my bottle I'd be content if ye only just smelt it,' said Eamon Doherty, with a dry laugh.

'Dermod Flynn had one great fight in Tyrone,' said Micky's Jim after draining some of the liquor. 'Gave his master one in the guts and knocked him as sick as a dog.'

'Get away!'

'So he was sayin'. Dermod Flynn, come here and give an account of yerself.'

The young fellow, who was watching the waves slide past the side of the vessel, came forward when Micky's Jim called him.

'Give an account of yerself, Dermod Flynn,' Jim cried. 'Did ye not knock down yer boss with one in the guts? That was the thing to do; that's what a Glenmornan man should do. I mind once when I was coal humpin' on the Greenock Docks –'

And without waiting for an answer to his question, Jim narrated the story of a fight which had once taken place between himself and a Glasgow sailor.

The sun, red as a live coal, was sinking towards the west, the murmur, powerful and gentle, of a trembling wind could be heard overhead; a white, ghostly mist stole down from the shore on either side and spread far out over the waters. The waves lapped against the side of the vessel with short, sudden splashes, and the sound of the labouring screw could be heard pulsing loudly through the air. A black trail of smoke spread out behind; a flight of following gulls, making little apparent effort, easily kept pace with the vessel.

'They will follow us to Scotland,' said Maire a Glan, pointing at the birds with a long claw-like finger.

Most of the men were drunk; a few lying stretched on the deck were already asleep, and the rest were singing and quarrelling. Micky's Jim stopped in the middle of an interesting story, a new one, but also about a fight, and joined in a song; old Maire a Glan helped him with the chorus.

III

A man, full of drink and fight, paraded along the deck, his stride uncertain and unsteady, a look born of the dark blood of mischief showing in his eyes. He had already been fighting; in his hand he carried an open clasp-knife; one eyebrow had been gashed and the strip of torn flesh hung down even as far as his high cheek-bones. He was dressed in a dirty pea-jacket and moleskin trousers; a brown leather belt with a huge, shiny buckle was tied round his waist, and the neck of a half-empty whisky bottle could be seen peeping over the rim of his coat pocket. His shoulders were broad and massive, his neck short and wrinkled and the torn shirt showed his deep chest, alive with muscles and terribly hairy, more like an animal's than a man's. His hands, which seemed to have never been washed, were knotted and gnarled like the branches of an old and stunted bush.

'This is young O'Donnel from the County Donegal, and young O'Donnel doesn't give a damn for any man on this boat!' he roared, speaking of himself in the third person, and brandishing the knife carelessly around him. 'I can fight like a two-year-old bullock, and a blow from young O'Donnel is like a kick from a young colt that's new to the grass. I'm a Rosses man and I don't care a damn for any soul on this bloody boat – not one damn! So there ye are!'

Suddenly observing Dermod Flynn staring at him, he slouched forward and struck the boy heavily across the face with a full swing of his left fist. Dermod dropped quietly to the deck; Micky's Jim, who was suggesting to Willie the Duck that the fiddle should be flung into the sea, threw down the instrument which he held and, jumping on the top of O'Donnel, with a sudden movement of his hand sent the knife flying into the sea.

'Ye long drink of water, I'll do for ye!' shouted Jim, and with feet and fists he hammered O'Donnel into insensibility.

Dermod Flynn regained his feet with a swollen cheek and a long red gash stretching along his face from ear to chin.

He was helped to a seat by one of the party; Norah Ryan procured some water and bathed his face, rubbing her fingers tenderly over the sore.

'It was a shame to hit ye, Dermod,' she said. 'One would think that a big man like that wouldn't hit a small boy like yourself!'

Dermod flushed and his eyes lit up as if he was going to say something cutting, but Norah checked the words by pressing her hand across his brow and looking at him with eyes of womanly understanding.

'I know what ye are goin' to say, Dermod,' she said. 'Ye're goin' to tell me that ye are a man: and no one can deny that. Ye were a man when ye were at school and hit the master. Sure I know meself what ye had in yer head to say.'

Dermod resented the words of consolation and felt like rising and walking away from the girl, if her fair fingers had not been pressing so softly and tenderly against his cheek. He shrugged his shoulders and resigned himself to the ministrations of Norah.

'By God, I wasn't long with him!' cried Micky's Jim, kicking idly at Willie the Duck's fiddle which still lay on the deck. 'I just gave him one in the jaw and three on the guts. Ah! that was the way to do it! It takes a Glenmornan kiddie to use his mits in this bloomin' hole. Glenmornan, and every inch of it, forever! Whoo! There's no man on this boat could take a rise out of me; not one mother's son! Fight! I could fight any damned mug aboard this bleedin' vessel. Look at my fist; smell it! There's the smell of dead men off it!'

Micky's Jim, now doubly drunk with liquor and excitement, paced up and down the deck, challenging all aboard to fight, to put up their 'fives' to him. Presently the quarrel became general.

All along the deck and down in the steerage cabin a terrible uproar broke forth; men fastened on to one another's throats, kicking, tearing, and cursing loudly. The darkness had fallen; the buoys, floating past, bobbed up and down in the water, their little bright lights twinkling merrily. The pale ghost of a moon stole into the heavens and a million stars kept it company. But those aboard the Derry boat took little heed of the moon or stars. Over coils of ropes, loose chains, boxes and bundles, sleeping women and crying babies, they staggered, fought and fell, trampling everything with which they came in contact.

A man went headlong down the steerage stair and a second followed, thrown from above. Beside the door a bleeding face, out of which gleamed a pair of lustrous eyes, glowered sinister for a moment, a fist hit sharply against the eyebrows, the eyes closed; a knife shone, glancing brightly against the woodwork, the man with the bloodstained face groaned and fell; a woman crouching at the bottom of the stairs was trampled upon, she shrieked and the shriek changed into a volley of curses, which in turn died away into a low, murmurous plaint of tearful pity. Men sought one another's faces grunting and gasping, long lean arms stretched out everywhere and fists shot through the smoke-laden atmosphere of the steerage ... splotches of blood showed darkly on the deck ... somewhere from below came the tinkle of glasses and the loud chorus of an Irish folk song.

The fighters, overcome by their mad exertion, collapsed three or four in a heap and slept where they had fallen. Outside on the open deck Micky's Jim lay prostrate, his head on the lap of Maire a Glan, who was also asleep, her two remaining upper teeth, tobacco-stained and yellow, showing in the moonlight. All over the deck men and women lay curled up like dogs. Near the rail a woman's bare arm showed for a moment over a bundle of rags, then twined snakelike round the neck of a sleeping child. On a bench astern Norah Ryan sat, her shawl drawn tightly over her head and her eyes fixed on the moon-silvered sea that stretched out behind. A great loneliness had overcome her; a loneliness which she did not understand. It seemed as if something had snapped within her, as if every fabric of her life had been torn to shreds. The stars overhead looked so cold, everything seemed so desolate. A chill wind swept against her face, and she could hear the water soughing along the vessel's side and crying wearily. Snores, groans, and sleepy voices came through the open doors and resounded in the passage at the head of the steerage stairs. Human bodies were heaped together in compact masses everywhere. The fighting had come to an end – though now and then, as a flame flickers up for a second over a dying fire, a man would totter from a drunken sleep and challenge everybody on board to fight him. But even when speaking loudest he would drop to the deck with a thud and fall asleep again.

IV

Listening to the engine pulsing heavily and the propeller hitting the water with an intermittent buzz Norah Ryan fell asleep. On opening her eyes again she could see the moon further up the sky and the stars twinkling colder than ever. Dermod Flynn, his face swollen horribly, was beside her, looking at her, and she was pleased to see him.

'Sit down beside me, Dermod,' she said. 'It will be warmer for two.'

He sat down, his eyes sparkling with pleasure; the girl nestled close to his side in the darkness, and one timid little hand stole softly into his.

'Ye nearly squeezed the hand off me when I met ye this evenin',' she said, but there was no reproof in her voice, and he understood that she was not angry with his strong handshake, even though it had given her pain.

'Did I?'

'Ye did.... Isn't it cold?'

'Cold as the breath of a stepmother,' said Dermod. 'There was great fighting!'

'Why do men always fight?' asked Norah.

'Because it's – it's their way.'

'Why is that?'

'You'll not understand; you're only a girl.'

'Will I never understand?' asked Norah.

'Never,' Dermod answered. 'And we're goin' to be sick too,' he went on with boyish irrelevance. 'That's when we're passin' round the Mull of Cantyre. So Micky's Jim said. And we're goin' to see Paddy's Milestone, that's if we aren't asleep.'

'Where's Paddy's Milestone?'

'It's a big rock out in the middle of the sea, half-way between Ireland and Scotland,' said Dermod.

'Oh, is that it? ... What kind of time had ye in Tyrone?'

'Not so bad, but Scotland will be a better place.... Is old Master Diver livin' away?'

'Dead, God rest his soul. He was only ill for three days. And poor Maire a Crick is gone as well.'

'She was as old as the Glenmornan hills. And old Oiney Dinchy?'

'He got one of his eyes knocked out with the horns of a cow. That was because the priest put the seven curses on him; but that was before ye went away.'

'Is Fergus writin' home now?'

'We haven't heard hilt nor hair of him for a long while,' said Norah sadly. 'Maybe it is that he is dead.'

'Don't say that!' Dermod exclaimed, fixing a pair of sad eyes on the girl.

'Well, it is a wonder that we're not hearin' from him,' Norah went on, 'a great wonder entirely… . Your face is very … Is it sore now?'

The conversation died away; the boy and girl pressed closer for warmth and presently both were asleep. When they awoke the pale dawn was breaking. A drunken man lay asleep at their feet, his face turned upwards, one arm stretched out at full length and the other curled over his breast. Beside him on the deck was an empty whisky bottle and the bowl of a broken clay pipe.

'Have ye seen Scotland yet?' asked the girl, rubbing her fingers over her eyelids.

'That's it, I think,' Dermod answered, pointing at the coastline which showed like a well-defined cloud against the skyline miles away.

'Have we passed Paddy's Milestone?'

'I don't know. I was sleepin'.'

'Isn't it like Ireland?' remarked Norah after she had gazed for a while in silence at the coastline. 'I would like to be goin' back again, Dermod,' she said.

'I'm goin' to make a great fortune in Scotland, Norah,' said the youth, releasing the girl's hand which he had held all night. 'And I'm goin' to make ye a lady.'

'Why would ye be goin' to do the likes of that?'

'I don't know,' Dermod confessed, and the boy and girl laughed together.

CHAPTER 14

'BEYOND THE WATER'

I

A heavy fall of rain came with the dawn, and the Clyde was a dreary smudge of grey when the boat made fast alongside Greenock Quay and discharged its passengers. Again the derricks began to creak complainingly on their pivots; a mob of excited cattle streamed up the narrow gangways, followed by swearing drovers, who prodded the dewlaps and hindquarters of the animals with their short, heavy blackthorn sticks.

A tall, thin man, somewhat over middle age, with bushy beard, small penetrating eyes and wrinkles between the eyebrows, met the squad as they disembarked. He bade good morning to Micky's Jim just as if he had seen him the night before, and in a loud, hurried voice gave him several orders as to what he had to do during the summer season at the digging. The tall, thin man was the potato merchant.

'How many have ye with ye from Ireland?' he asked Micky's Jim.

Although knowing the number of men it contained, Jim, with an air of importance, began to count the members of the squad, carefully enumerating each person by name.

'Get your squad to work as soon as you can,' said the merchant, his Adam's apple bobbing in and out with every movement of his throat. He gave Jim no time to finish the count. 'I see you're three or four short of last year – four, isn't it? There's some people waitin' for a start over there, so you'd better take a few of them with you.'

Opposite the squad a dozen or more men and women stood, looking on eagerly, all of them shivering with the cold and the water dripping from their rags. These Jim approached with a very self-conscious swagger and entered into conversation with the women, who began to speak volubly.

'What's wrong with them?' asked Dermod Flynn, and Maire a Glan, to whom he addressed the question, drew a snuff-box from her pocket and took a pinch.

'They're lookin' for a job, as the man said,' she answered and her teeth chattered as she spoke.

'When do we start our work?' asked Norah Ryan.

'Work!' laughed Judy Farrel, and her laugh ended in a fit of coughing. 'Work, indeed!' she stammered on regaining breath. 'Ye'll soon have plenty of that and no fear!'

'Come, now,' Micky's Jim shouted as he came back to his own squad followed by two men and two women who detached themselves from the crowd that was looking for work. 'We must go down to the Isle of Bute today and get some potatoes dug in a hurry. Take yer bundles in yer hands and make a start for the station.'

'It's Gourock Ellen that's in it,' said Maire a Glan, when the strange women came forward. 'Gourock Ellen and Annie, as the man said.'

Gourock Ellen was a tall, angular woman, who might at one period of her life have been very handsome, but who now, owing to the results of a hard and loose life, bore all the indelible marks of dissolute and careless living. Her face was hard, pock-marked, and stamped with a look of impudent defiance; she smiled with ill-concealed contempt at Maire a Glan and looked with mock curiosity at the warty hand which the old woman held out to her.

'There's a lot of new faces in the squad,' she said, glancing in turn at Norah Ryan and Dermod Flynn. 'Not bad lookin', the two of them, and they'll sleep in the yin bed yet, I'll go bail! And you, have you the fiddle with you?'

'Aye, sure, and I have,' said Willie the Duck, to whom she addressed this question. 'I don't go far without it.'

'You don't,' answered the woman, and her tones implied that she would have added, 'you fool!' if she thought it worth while.

Her companion, who hardly spoke a word, was somewhat older, swarthy of appearance and very ragged. Her toes peeped out through the torn uppers of her hob-nailed boots, and when she lifted her dress to wring the water from the hem it could be seen that she wore no stockings and that her dark, thin legs were threaded with varicose veins above the calves.

'D'ye see them?' Micky's Jim whispered in Dermod's ear. 'They cannot make a livin' on the streets and they have to come and work with us.'

'I don't like the look of them,' Dermod whispered, rubbing his hand over the sore on his face.

'By God! that was a great dunt that O'Donnel gave ye,' said Jim. 'They're great women, them, without a doubt,' he added. 'It's a long while since Gourock Ellen broke her pitcher.'

'How? What do you mean?'

'Ye're green, Dermod, green as a cabbage,' said Jim, chuckling. 'Them women – but I'll tell ye all about it some other time. Willie the Duck is a great friend of them same women. He knows what they are, as well as anyone, don't ye, Willie?'

'Aye, sure,' said Willie, who did not know what Jim was speaking about, but wished to be agreeable to everybody.

II

A short run on a fast train from Upper Greenock to Wemyss Bay was followed by an hour's journey on a boat crowded with passengers bound for Rothesay. It was now the last day of June, and those who had rented coast houses for the following month were flocking down from Glasgow and other Clydeside industrial centres. In the midst of the crowd of gaily dressed trippers all the members of the squad felt sensitive and shy and stood huddled awkwardly together on deck; all but Micky's Jim and the strange men and women, who paraded up and down the deck, careless of the eyes that were fixed upon them. Old Maire a Glan was praying, her rosary hidden under her shawl; Dermod Flynn was looking over the rail into the water, his main interest in turning away being to keep the naked knee that peeped through his torn trousers hidden from the sight of the elegantly dressed trippers. Norah envied the young girls who chattered noisily to and fro, envied them their fine hats and brave dresses, their elegant shoes and the wonderful sparkling things that decorated their necks and wrists. What a splendid vision for the girl's eyes! – the hot sun overhead in a sky of blue, the water glancing brightly as the boat cut through it; the fair women, the well-dressed men, the band playing on deck, the glitter, the charm and the happiness! The girl could hardly realise that such beauty existed, though once she had seen a picture of a scene something like this in one of the books which Fergus used to read at home. Poor girl! – the water was still running down her stockings, her clothes were ragged and dirty, and the boy, her youthful lover, was hiding his naked knee by turning to the rail!

Opposite the crowd in which Norah stood, a group of five persons – father, mother and their children, a son and two daughters – were sitting on camp-stools. The man, bubble-bellied and short, had taken off his hat, and in the sunlight beads of sweat glittered on his bald head like crystals in a white limestone facing. His wife, a plump, good-looking woman, who seemed full of a haughty self-esteem, gazed critically through a lorgnette on the unkempt workers and sniffed contemptuously as if something had displeased her when her examinations came to an end. The three little things regarded them wonderingly for a moment and afterwards began to ply first the father and then the mother with questions about the strange folk who were aboard the boat. But the parents, finding that the children were speaking too loudly, bade them be silent, and the little ones, getting no answer to their questions, began to puzzle over this and wonder who and what were the queer, ragged people sitting opposite.

The girls, taking into account the contemptuous stare which their mother fixed on the members of the squad, came to the conclusion that the beings who were dressed so differently from themselves were really other species of men and women altogether and were far inferior to those who wore starched collars and gold ornaments.

The boy, an undersized little fellow with sharp, twinkling eyes, looked at his father when putting his questions, but the old man pulled a paper – *The Christian Guide* – from his pocket and, burying himself in it, took no notice of the youngster's queries.

The boy solved the question for himself in the curious incomplete way which is peculiar to a child.

'I don't know who they are,' he said, 'but I'd like to play with them – that old lady who's moving something under her shawl and speakin' to herself, with the nice young lady, with the man with the hump and the fiddle; with every one of them.'

Gourock Ellen was speaking to Micky's Jim.

'Have ye ever slept under a bridge with the wind chillin' ye to the bone?' she asked.

'No. Why?'

'That's where I slept last night,' said Ellen fiercely. 'Isn't that a pretty dress that that woman has, Jim?'

'And Annie?' Jim asked, putting a match to the eternal pipe.

'She slept along wi' me,' Ellen replied. 'Blood is warm even when it runs thin.'

'If ye had the price of that lady's dress, ye'd not have to sleep out for a week of Sundays,' said Jim, pointing to the woman with the lorgnette. 'See her brats too! Look how they're glowerin' at Norah Ryan!'

'The children are very pretty,' said the woman, and a slight touch of regret softened her harsh voice. Perhaps for the moment she longed for the children which might have been hers if all had gone well. 'Norah Ryan is a very soncy wench, isn't she, Jim?' she went on. 'What is the bald man readin'?'

'*Christian Guide*,' said Jim, who spent a whole year at school and who could read a little.

'I ken him well,' said Ellen, assuming a knowing look and winking slightly. 'It was years ago, he was young – and ye ken yerself.'

'Phew!' Jim whistled, taking the pipe from his mouth and lowering the left eyelid. 'He was one of them sort? … *Christian Guide*, indeed! … A decent man, now, I suppose, and would hardly pass a word with ye!'

'I'm not as good lookin' as I was.'

'If ye told old baldhead's wife what ye told me what would she say?'

'Oh! I wadna dae that, Jim. He always paid on the nail.'

'*Christian Guide*,' sniggered Jim, hurrying to the rail and spitting into the water.

'There are some great dresses on those people,' said Maire a Glan, nipping Dermod Flynn on the thigh with her finger and thumb. 'See that woman sittin' there with the bald-headed man. Her dress is a good one. All the money that ye earned for two whole years in Tyrone would hardly put flounces on it; wouldn't flounce it, as the man said.'

'Maybe not,' said Dermod, turning round slightly, but still standing in such a way that his bare knee was concealed from everybody on board.

'It's a great dress, a grand dress and a dress for a queen,' Maire a Glan went on. 'Look at the difference between it and the dress that Gourock Ellen is wearin'!'

'Just so,' said Dermod, peeping at the exposed knee-cap. 'Could ye give me a needle and thread this night, Maire a Glan?' he asked.

'I could, indeed, Dermod,' said the old woman. 'That wife of the bald-headed man is a fine soncy-lookin' stump of a woman.'

'Is she better-lookin' than Gourock Ellen?' asked Dermod with a laugh.

'Ye are droll, Dermod,' said Maire a Glan, nipping the boy's thigh again. 'D'ye know where Gourock Ellen slept last night? Under a cold bridge with the winds of heaven whistlin' through the eye of it.'

'Could she not have gone into some house?'

'House, child? Ye are not in Ireland here!'

'When a poor man comes to our house at night, he always gets a bed till the mornin',' said Norah Ryan, who was listening to the conversation. 'And a bit and sup as well!'

'It's only God and the poor who help the poor,' said the old woman. 'And here's the rain comin' again, as the man said. It will be a bad day this to plough on our knees through the wet fields, bad luck be with them!'

III

A farmer with a bulbous nose and red whiskers met the squad on Rothesay pier. He wore a black jacket which, being too narrow round the shoulders, had split open half way down the back, a corduroy waistcoat, very tight trousers, patched at the knees and caked brown with clotted earth. This man was seated on the sideboard of a large waggon, removing the dirt from his clothes with a heavy, double-bladed clasp-knife.

'Good-day,' said Micky's Jim, coming off the boat and stepping up to the man on the waggon.

'Good-day,' answered the man without lifting his head or looking at the speaker.

'Will ye take the waggon nearer the boat, or will we carry up the bundles to here?' asked Jim, blowing a puff of white smoke into the air.

'Carry them up, of course,' said the farmer, still busy with his clasp-knife.

Jim set his squad to work, and soon the waggon was loaded with bundles of clothes, frying-pans, tea-caddies, tins, bowls, and other articles necessary for the workers during the coming months. In addition to the stores taken from Ireland by the potato-diggers, the merchant supplied them with blankets, an open stove, and a pot for boiling potatoes. It was now raining heavily; the drops splashed loudly on the streets, ran down the faces and soaked through the clothes of the workers. The rain struck heavily against the waggon; a hot steam rose from the withers of the cart-horse; the pier was almost deserted and everything looked lonesome and gloomy.

So far the farmer had taken very little notice of anybody; but now, having observed Norah Ryan, he shouted: 'Ye have a fine leg, lassie!' and afterwards, while the cart was being loaded, he kept repeating this phrase and chuckling deep down in his throat. Whenever he made the remark he looked at the girl, and Norah felt uncomfortable and blushed every time he spoke.

Dermod Flynn, who had taken a sudden dislike to the man with the bulbous nose, now felt sorry for Norah and angry with the man. At last, unable to restrain his passion any longer, he stepped up to the side of the waggon and looked straight in the face of the farmer, who was packing the blankets in one corner of the vehicle, and shouted: 'Here, Red Nose, don't try and make fun of yer betters!' The farmer straightened himself up, rested his thumb on his jaw and pulled a long black finger through his beard.

'All right,' he said at last, and did not speak another word to anybody else that day.

Dermod, who had looked for an outburst, felt frightened when the farmer became silent.

'Jim, what's wrong with that man?' he asked his ganger when the cart started on its journey home with the farmer sitting in front, waving his whip vigorously, but refraining from hitting the horse.

'He's mad,' said Jim in a whisper.

'Mad?'

'As a March hare, as an Epiphany cock, as a – He's very mad, and was in the madhouse last year when we were digging on the farm. It takes very little to set him off. Maybe he's goin' mad now; one never knows.'

'It was very good of you to stand up for me,' said Norah to Dermod about an hour later, when the party came in sight of the farmhouse. 'Ye have the kind heart, and that farmer isn't a nice man. I don't like the looks of him!'

'He's mad –'

'Mother of God!'

'– as an Epiphany cock! He was in the madhouse last year.'

'Maybe he'll do ye some harm one day!'

'Will he?' asked Dermod, squaring his shoulders and instinctively tightening his fists. Somehow he felt wonderfully elated since he had spoken to the farmer on the waggon.

CHAPTER 15

DRUDGERY

I

New potatoes were urgently needed and the potato merchant told Jim to get as many as possible dug on the first afternoon. No sooner had the squad come to the farmhouse than they were shown out to the fields where the green shaws, heavy with rain, lay in matted clusters across the drills. Every step taken relieved the green vegetable matter of an enormous amount of water, which splashed all over the workers as they stumbled along to their toil.

Work started. The men threw out the potatoes with short three-pronged graips; the women, girt bags round their waists, went down on their knees and followed the diggers, picking up the potatoes which they threw out. Two basin-shaped wicker baskets without handles were supplied to each woman; one basket for the good potatoes and the other for 'brock', pig-food.

'It's the devil's job, as the man said,' old Maire a Glan remarked as she furrowed her way through the slushy earth. 'What d'ye think of it, Judy Farrel?' But Judy, struggling with a potato stem, did not deign to answer.

Maire was a hard worker; and it was her boast that she never had had a day's illness in her life. The story had got abroad that she never missed a stitch in a stocking while giving birth to twins, and the woman never contradicted the story. She gathered after Eamon Doherty's 'graip'; old Eamon with a head rising to a point almost and a very short temper.

Biddy Wor, the mother of seven children, 'all gone now to all the seven ends of the world', as she often pathetically remarked, gathered the potatoes that Murtagh Gallagher threw out. Biddy's hair was as white as snow, except on her chin, where a dozen or more black hairs stood out as stiffly as if they were starched.

Owen Kelly, another of the diggers, was very miserly and was eternally complaining of a pain in the back. Micky's Jim assured him that a wife was the best cure in the world for a sore back. But Owen, skinflint that he was, considered a wife very costly property and preferred to live without one. He dug for Judy Farrel, the stunted little creature with the cough. She was a very quiet little woman, Judy, had very little to say and, when speaking, spoke as if her mouth was full of something. When pulling the heavy baskets, weighted with the wet clay, she moaned constantly like a child in pain.

Two sisters worked in the squad, Dora and Bridget Doherty, cheery girls, who spoke a lot, laughed easily, and who were similar in appearance and very ugly. Dora worked with Connel Dinchy, son of Oiney Dinchy, an eel-stomached youth over six foot in height and barely measuring thirty-four inches round the chest. He was a quiet, inoffensive fellow, who laughed down in his throat, and every fortnight he sent all his wages home to his parents. Bridget Doherty gathered potatoes for one of the strange men. Both girls were blood relations of Murtagh Gallagher. The other strange man worked in conjunction with Gourock Ellen; Norah Ryan gathered for Willie the Duck; and Ellen's companion, who was known as Annie – simply

Annie – crawled in the clay after Thady Scanlon, a first cousin of Micky's Jim. When the baskets were full, Dermod Flynn emptied the potatoes into large barrels supplied for the purpose.

The women worked hard, trying to keep themselves warm. Norah Ryan became weary very soon. The rain formed into a little pond in the hollow of her dress where it covered the calves of her legs. Seeing that the rest of the women were rising from time to time and shaking the water off their clothes, she followed their example, and when standing, a slight dizziness caused her to reel unsteadily and she almost overbalanced and fell. She went down on her knees hurriedly, as she did not want Micky's Jim to see her tottering. If this was noticed he might think her unfit for the job. For the rest of the afternoon she crawled steadily, fearing to rise, and wondered how Gourock Ellen, who was giving voice to a loose and humorous song, could sing on such a day. What troubled Norah most were the sharp pebbles that came in contact with her knees as she dragged herself along. They seemed to pierce through rags and flesh at each movement, and at times she could hardly refrain from crying aloud on account of the pain. Before night, and when she knew that her knees were bleeding, she had become almost indifferent to bodily discomforts.

All the time she was filled with an insatiable longing for home. The farm looked out on the Clyde – the river was a grey blur seen through the driving rain, and a boat passing by attracted her attention.

'Is it an Irish boat?' she asked Willie the Duck, who was whistling softly to himself.

'Aye, sure,' answered Willie without raising his head.

'I wish that I was goin' home in it,' she said plaintively.

'Ireland's much better than this dirty country,' said Maire a Glan, speaking loud enough for the Scotchwoman Annie to hear her.

II

When six o'clock came round Jim pulled out his watch, looked at it severely for a moment and shouted: 'Down graips and run home to yer warm supper!'

'Home!' repeated Maire a Glan, rising awkwardly to her knees. 'Mother of Jesus! It is a home! An old byre, and no less, as the man said. Shame be on ye, Micky's Jim!'

'We have no grub and no siller,' said Gourock Ellen, rising briskly and loosing the clay-coated sack from around her waist. 'I'm up to my thighs in clabber,' she added.

'We'll not let ye starve as long as there's a bit at all goin',' said Micky's Jim.

'We'd be pigs if we ate all ourselves when other people have nothin',' remarked Maire a Glan.

When the squad went back to the farm a ploughman, a flat-footed, surly fellow with a hare-lip, showed them their quarters in the steading. 'First I'll show ye where ye're to roost,' said the man, and led the way into an evil-smelling byre, the roof of which was covered with cobwebs, the floor with dung. A young fellow, with a cigarette in his mouth, was throwing the manure through a trap-door into a vault underneath. On both sides of the sink, which ran up the middle, was a row of stalls, each stall containing two iron stanchions to which chains used for tying cattle were fastened.

'No need to tie any of ye to the chains, is there?' asked the man with the hare-lip, laughing loudly. 'When ye go to bed at night, close the trap-door,' he continued. 'It will keep the smell of the midden away from you!'

'Aye, sure,' said Willie the Duck.

'Oh! Ye're here again, are ye?' asked the ploughman. 'Have ye got the music murderer with ye? This way to see where yer eatin' room is,' said the man, without waiting to hear Willie the Duck's answer to his question.

The byre was built on the shoulder of a hillock; the midden was situated in a grotto hollowed underneath. Behind the dung-hill, in the grotto, the three-legged stove was standing, and already a fire which old Eamon Doherty had kindled was sparkling merrily.

'Watch yersel'!' shouted the ploughman to Dermod Flynn, who was crossing the dung-hill on the way towards the fire. 'That young rascal above will throw down a graipful of dung on yer head if ye're not careful.'

Maire a Glan filled the pot with clean white potatoes and placed them over the blaze. The ploughman sat down on an upended box and lit his pipe; Micky's Jim took the squad back to the byre, which was now fairly clean, and proceeded to make bunks for the night. Four or five level boxes were placed on the floor of each stall, a pile of hay was scattered about on top, and over this was spread two or three bags sewn together in the form of a sheet; sacks filled with straw served as pillows, a single blanket was given to each person, and two of the party had to sleep in each stall.

'Who's goin' to sleep with me?' asked Micky's Jim.

'I will,' said Murtagh Gallagher.

'Ye snore like a pig!'

'What about me?' asked Owen Kelly.

'Ye kick like a colt.'

'Will I do?' asked Willie the Duck.

'Ye do!' cried Micky's Jim, 'ye that was chased out of the graveyard with a squad of worms. None of ye will sleep with me; Dermod Flynn is the man I want. Help me to make the bed, Dermod Flynn,' he said to the youth who was standing beside him.

'It's a fine place this,' said Gourock Ellen as she spread a pile of hay over the boxes in the stalls. 'A gey guid place!'

'D'ye know who slept in that stall last night?' asked Jim.

'A heifer like mysel' maybe,' said Ellen. 'And indeed it had a muckle better place than I had under the bridge.'

'The potatoes are nearly ready,' shouted Maire a Glan, sticking her wrinkled head round the corner of the door.

There was a hurried rush down to the midden. Boxes were upended to serve as seats, the maid-servant at the farm came out in brattie,[1] shorgun,[2] and brogues, and sold milk at a penny a pint to the diggers. All, with the exception of Annie, Ellen, and Owen Kelly, bought a pennyworth; Micky's Jim bought a pennyworth for Ellen, Maire a Glan shared her milk with Annie, and Owen Kelly bought only a halfpennyworth, half of which he kept for his breakfast on the following morning.

The potatoes were not ready yet; the water bubbled and spluttered in the pot and shot out in little short spurts on every side. Ellen complained of her legs; they had been horribly gashed during the day and were now terribly sore. She lifted up her clothes as far as her thighs and rubbed a wet cloth over the wounds. Micky's Jim tittered; Dermod Flynn blushed, turned away his head and looked at Norah Ryan. Ellen noticed this and, smiling sarcastically, began to hum:

When I was a wee thing and lived wi' my granny,
Oh! it's many a caution my granny gied me;
She said: 'Now, be wise and beware of the boys,
And don't let yer petticoats over yer knee!'

As she finished the song, Ellen winked at Micky's Jim and Jim winked back. Then she hit her thigh with her hand and shouted: 'Not a bad leg that for an old one, is it?'

---

[1]Brattie, an apron made of coarse cloth.
[2]Shorgun, short gown. The uniform of the female farm servant: the sleeves of the blouse reach the elbows, the hem of the skirt covers the knees.

The potatoes were now emptied into a wicker basket, the water running through the bottom into the midden. The men and women sat round the basket, their little tins of milk in their hands, and proceeded to eat their supper. The potato was held in the left hand, and stripped of its jacket with the nail of the right thumb. Gourock Ellen used a knife when peeling, Willie the Duck ate potato, pelt and all.

While they were sitting an old, wrinkled, and crooked man came across the top of the dung-hill, sinking into it almost up to his knees and approached the fire. His clothes were held on by strings, he wore a pair of boots differing one from the other in size, shape, and colour. Indeed they were almost without shape, and the old man's toes, pink, with black nails, showed through the uppers.

Gourock Ellen handed him three large potatoes from the basket.

'God bless ye, for it's yerself that has the kindly heart, decent woman,' said the old fellow in a feeble voice, and he began to eat his potatoes hurriedly like a dog. Dermod handed him part of a tin of milk and blushed at the profuse thanks of the stranger.

'It's a fine warm place that ye are inside of this night,' said the old fellow when he had finished his meal.

'It's a rotten place,' said Dermod Flynn.

'It's better nor lyin' under a hedge,' answered the old man.

'Or under a bridge,' Gourock Ellen remarked, lifting her dress again; then, as if some modest thought had struck her, dropping it suddenly.

'Why do ye lie under a hedge?' Dermod asked, and the old man thereupon gave a rambling account of his misfortunes, which included a sore back and inability to labour along with sound men. He had come from Mayo years ago and had worked at many a hard job since then, both in England and Scotland. Now that he was a homeless old man nobody at all wanted him.

When the party went up to the byre he stretched out his old thin limbs by the fire and fell into the easy slumber of old age. Suddenly he awoke with a start to find the fire still burning brightly and a beautiful girl with long hair flung over her shoulders looking at him. It was Norah Ryan; the old man thought for a moment that he was looking at an angel.

'God be good to me!' he cried, crossing himself; 'but who is yerself?' Then as recollection brought him a face seen at the fire, he exclaimed: 'Arrah, sure it's yerself that is the colleen I was after seein' sittin' here a minute ago. Now, isn't it a good cheery fire?'

'Have ye any home to go to?' asked Norah.

'Never a home,' said the old man, resting one elbow in the ashes. 'There is nothin' but the rainy roads and the hardships for a man like me.'

'But could ye not get inside of some house for the night?'

'God look on yer wit!' said the old fellow, laughing feebly. 'Ye're just new over, I'll warrant, and ye haven't come to learn that they have forgotten all about kindness in this country. They do not want the man with no roof-tree over his head here. They're all black and bitter Protestants.'

'So I heard say.'

'Ye'll be one of the right sort, I'll go bail.'

'I'm a Catholic.'

'Ah! that's it! The Catholics are the best, and I'm one meself just as ye are, girsha. Have ye a penny to spare for one of yer own kind?'

'Are ye goin' back to Ireland again?' asked Norah, drawing the weasel-skin purse from the pocket of her steaming dress.

'If only I had the price of a boat, I'd go in a minute,' said the man, fixing greedy eyes on the purse which Norah held in her hand. 'But I'm very poor, and mind ye I'm one of yer own sort. Maybe ye have a sixpence to spare,' he said.

Norah possessed a two-shilling piece, all the money she had in the world, and she needed it badly herself. But the desire to help the old man overmastered her, and she handed him the florin. Followed by the garrulous thanks of her penniless countryman she hurried back to the byre, feeling in some curious way ashamed of her kindness.

III

A candle fixed on the top of a stanchion threw a dim light over the byre, and long black shadows danced on roof and wall. A strong, unhealthy odour pervaded the whole building; the tap at one end was running, and as the screw had been broken the water could not be turned off. Micky's Jim sat in a cattle-trough sewing bags together with a packing needle; these were to be used as a quilt. Dermod Flynn, who was undressing, slipped beneath the blankets with his trousers still on as Norah Ryan came in, but Willie the Duck, stripped to the pelt, stood for a moment laughing stupidly, the guttering candle lighting up his narrow, hairy face and sunken chest.

Old Owen Kelly was already in bed.

'This place is a lot better than where we slept last year,' he called to Micky's Jim.

'Where did ye sleep last year?' asked Dermod Flynn.

'In the pig-sty,' said Jim. 'We were almost eaten alive by the blue lice.'

The women undressed in the shadow at the far end of the stalls, and from time to time Micky's Jim peeped round the corner. When the women looked up he would shout out: 'I see something,' and whistle lightly between the thumb and middle finger of his right hand. The Irishwomen undressed under the blankets, the two strange women, careless and indifferent to the jibes of Micky's Jim, stripped off to their chemises in full view of the occupants of the byre. Annie and Gourock Ellen had quarrelled about something; they were not going to sleep together that night.

'Ye have to sleep with me, lass,' said Gourock Ellen to Norah.

'All right,' said the young girl quietly, seeing no reason why she should not sleep with a strange woman. As she spoke she went down on her knees to say her prayers.

'Say one prayer for me, just a short one,' said Ellen in a low tone.

'All right, decent woman,' answered the girl.

'I'll put the light out now,' shouted Micky's Jim after a short interval. 'The women will not be ashamed to go on takin' off their clothes now.'

The light went out, but Jim suddenly relit the candle, and the guttering blaze again flared weakly through the gloom. There was a hurried movement of naked flesh in the women's quarters and a precipitate scampering under the blankets.

'That was a mortal sin, Micky's Jim,' Norah Ryan said in a low voice, and in her tones there was a suspicion of tears.

CHAPTER 16

LITTLE LOVES

I

To Norah Ryan the days passed by, at first remorselessly slow, burdened with longings and regrets, clogged with cares and sorrows which pressed heavily on her young heart. Each passing day was very much like that which had gone before, all had their homesickness and longings. She wanted so much to be back in her own home, picking cockles from the Frosses strand or driving the cattle into the shallow water when the heat of summer put the wild madness into their dry hooves.

All day long she trailed in the fields, her knees sore, and the sharp, flinty pebbles cutting them to the bone; and at night when she undressed she found her petticoats and stockings covered with blood. Gourock Ellen showed a great interest in the girl, bathed Norah's knees often, and when near a druggist's bought liniments and ointments which she applied to the wounds. Usually the sores, though they healed a little during the night, broke afresh when work started again in the morning, and six weeks went by before the girl hardened sufficiently to resist the rough pressure of the stones which she had to crawl over when at her work in the fields. Her hands also troubled her for a while; they became hacked and swollen and pained her intensely when she washed them at close of evening. Gradually these physical discomforts passed away, and with them went many of the girl's regrets and much of her homesickness. True, she wished to be back with her mother again, and that wish, unable to be gratified, caused her many poignant heartaches which she bravely concealed from her companions. Every Sunday afternoon she sat down and wrote a long letter home, telling her mother of the wonderful land across the water and the curious things which were to be seen there. Her mother, not being able to read or write, answered very seldom, and her letters were all penned by the new master of Glenmornan schoolhouse.

The members of the squad lived a very stirring life, changing almost weekly from one farm to another, travelling on fast trains and wonderful steamers. But in the midst of all this excitement Maire a Glan never forgot to tell her beads, Owen Kelly to save up his money, Micky's Jim to swear about nothing in particular, and Norah never forgot to speak about home when any of the Frosses people were in the mood to listen. Dermod Flynn, ever eager to hear about all that had passed in his two years' absence, was a ready talker on matters that concerned the people of Glenmornan and Frosses. But in other respects he was still the same dreamy youth who had spent the greater part of his time at school in gazing out of the window. Even now he would sometimes forget his work for a long while to gaze at a worm which he picked up from the ground and held between his finger and thumb. Whenever Micky's Jim saw this he would assert that Flynn was rapidly going mad. Norah herself often wished that Dermod would not take such an interest in things which, when all was said and done, were useless and made the boy the laughing-stock of the whole squad. But she always felt sorry for him when the rest of the party laughed at his oddities. Why should she care if everybody in the country laughed at a fool who took a great interest in common worms? she often asked herself. But never was the girl able to find a satisfactory answer to this question.

Dermod had a curious habit of going out into the fields and lying down on the green sod when the evening was a good one and when the day's work was done. Norah noticed this and often wondered what he did and thought of when by himself. The youth fascinated the girl in some strange way; this fascination she could not explain and dared not combat. She even felt afraid of him; he thronged into her mind, banished all other thoughts and reigned supreme in her imagination. Sometimes, indeed, she wished that he were gone from the squad altogether; he made her so uncomfortable. He said such strange things, too. Once he remarked that there was no God, and Norah knew instinctively that he meant what he said; not like Micky's Jim, who often said that there was no Creator, merely with the object of startling those to whom he was speaking. If Dermod did things like other people, if he played cards, passed jests, she would not fear him so much. Even now, when he spoke to her of home, there was a strange intensity in his voice that often unnerved her.

II

One evening in September Dermod Flynn stole away from the fire as was his custom and sat down in a field near the sea, where he was speedily buried in the quiet isolation of his own thoughts. Norah Ryan followed him; why, she did not know. Something seemed to compel her to go after the youth: a certain wild pleasure surged through her, she felt as if she could run and sing out to the light airs that fanned her cheeks as she moved along. Presently, looking through a row of hazel bushes that hemmed the farmhouse, she espied him, lying on the green grass, seemingly lost to everything and gazing upwards into the blue heavens where the first early star was flickering faintly through the soft loom of the evening. Below him the Clyde widened out to the sea and a few black boats were heaving slowly on the tide. As if under the spell of a power which she could not resist, Norah Ryan parted the boughs of the hazel copse and stood before Dermod Flynn.

'Is it here, Dermod, that ye are, lookin' at the sea?' she asked involuntarily.

'I was lookin' at the star above me,' he replied.

Norah wore a soft grey tweed dress that became her well. She had bought it in Greenock a week before, and when Dermod looked at the dress with a critical eye she wondered why she had put it on. But his look turned to one of admiration when his eye fell on the sweet face of the young girl, the eyes gentle and wistful, the white neck and the pure brow half hidden by the brown ruffled tresses. Something leapt into the heart of the young man, a thought which he could not put into words flashed through his mind, held him tense for a moment and then flitted away.

'Why do you keep watchin' me?' Norah enquired.

'I don't know,' Dermod answered, lowering his eyes. 'D'ye mind the night on the Derry boat?' he asked. 'All that night when you were asleep I had your hand in mine.'

'I mind it very well,' she said, and a slight blush stole into her cheeks. They clasped hands, the girl's fingers stole over

Dermod's and their eyes met. For a moment it seemed as if one or the other was going to speak, but no voice broke the stillness. The fear had now gone from Norah's heart; it seemed quite natural to her that she should be there clasping the hand of that ragged youth who always attracted and fascinated her. That she should desire to sit beside him, to press his hands so very tightly, did not appear strange to her and above all did not appear wrong. Dermod saw in her eyes a childlike admiration, a look half a child's and half a woman's. A vague longing, something which he could not comprehend and which caused him a momentary pang of fear, rose in his heart. What he had to be afraid of he did not know, as he knelt there in spirit before the most holy sanctuary in the world, the sanctuary of chaste and beautiful womanhood.

Many evenings they met together in the same way; they became more intimate, more friendly, and Norah found that her fear of Dermod was gradually passing away. When evenings were wet they sat in the byre or cart-shed, where the fire burned brightly, and talked about Glenmornan and the people at home. One day Micky's Jim said that he himself had once a notion of Norah Ryan. When Dermod heard this he flushed hotly. Norah's cheeks got very red and Jim laughed loudly.

'I have no time for them sort of capers now,' said Jim. 'Ye can have her all to yerself, Dermod, and people like yerselves will be always doin' the silly thing, indeed ye will!'

CHAPTER 17

A GAME OF CARDS

I

Micky's Jim was telling the story of a fight in which he had taken part and how he knocked down a man twice as heavy as himself with one on the jaw. Owen Kelly, Gourock Ellen, Dermod, and Norah were the listeners. The squad had just changed quarters from a farm on which they had been engaged to the one on which they were now, and it was here that they were going to end the season. The farm belonged to a surly old man named Morrison, a short-tempered fellow, always at variance with the squad, whom he did not like.

Jim was telling the story in the cart-shed. A blazing fire lit up the place, shadows danced along the roof, outside a slight rain was falling and the wind blew mournfully in from the hayricks that stood up like shrouded ghosts in the gloomy stack yard. Presently a man entered, a red-haired fellow with a limp in one leg and a heavy stick in his hand. He was a stranger to Norah and Dermod, but the rest of the squad knew him well and were pleased to see the man with the limp. Owen Kelly, however, grunted something on seeing the stranger, and a look, certainly not of pleasure, passed across his face.

'How are ye, Ginger Dubbin?' Micky's Jim shouted to the visitor. 'By this and by that ye look well on it.'

'The bad are always well fed,' said Owen Kelly in a low voice.

'Have ye the devil's prayer-book with ye, Ginger?' asked Micky's Jim.

'Here it is,' said the man, drawing a pack of cards from his pocket and running his hands along the edge of it.

'We'll have a bit of the Gospel of Chance,' said Murtagh Gallagher.

'It's no game for Christians,' remarked Owen Kelly, picking his teeth with a splinter of wood.

'D'ye know why Owen Kelly doesn't like Ginger Dubbin?' Gourock Ellen asked Dermod Flynn in a whisper. 'No? Then I'll tell ye, but never let dab about it. Four years ago Ginger, drunken old scamp that he is, came here and played cards with Owen, and Owen won at first, three shillin's in all. Then he began to lose and lost half a crown of the money that he had won. "My God!" said old Owen, and he was nearly greetin'; "My God! that I have ever lived to see this day!" He has never played since that. D'ye play, Dermod?'

'I used to play for buttons in Ireland.'

'It's a bad thing they are, the cards,' said Norah Ryan.

'Turn it up or I'll gie ye a dunt in the lug!' Micky's Jim was shouting to Willie the Duck, who was helping to turn the body of a disused cart upside down.

'Aye, sure,' said Willie the Duck, but as he spoke he fell prostrate on his face, causing all who were watching him to burst into loud peals of laughter.

When the cart was laid down a game of banker commenced and most of the squad joined in the game. Dermod Flynn watched the players for a little space; then he rose to his feet.

'Where are ye goin'?' Norah asked.

'To look at the card players.'

'Don't, Dermod!'

'Why?'

'Maybe ye'll learn to play.'

'And if I do?' There was a note of defiance in the boy's voice, and it was evident that Norah's remarks had displeased him.

'Well, do as you like,' said the girl in an injured tone. 'But mind that it's a sin to play cards.'

Dermod stretched himself, laughed and approached the table. Norah felt a sudden fear overcome her: she wanted him back, and she was angry with the cards – little squares of cardboard – that could lure Dermod away from her side.

He bent over the shoulder of Micky's Jim, who was smoking and shouting loudly. All the players, with the exception of Ginger Dubbin, were very excited: Ginger hummed tunes with equal gusto whether winning or losing. Most of the players used pence, but a few pieces of silver glittered on the table, and Micky's Jim had changed a sovereign. Dermod had never gambled, although he had often played cards before; then the stakes were merely buttons, that was not gambling; no one feels very vexed at having lost a button. Something thrilled Dermod through as he looked at the coins on the board; the two pieces of silver attracted him strongly. He had one hand deep in his trousers' pocket closing tightly over the money in his possession. How exciting it would be to put something on that card; he was certain that it would win! Dubbin turned up the card which Dermod's imagination pictured to be a good one, and showed an ace, the winning card. If only he had staked a penny on it, Dermod thought! He sat down beside Micky's Jim and gazed across the board.

'Another cut – for me,' he said, and his voice was a trifle husky. 'I'm going to play.'

He put down a penny and won.

II

The farmer's son came into the shed. He was a strongly built, handsome lad of twenty-one, and was employed as a bank clerk in Paisley. It was now Saturday. He always returned home on weekends and spent Sunday on his father's farm. Eamon Doherty was very pleased to see young Morrison, who was a great friend of his, and sometimes, when the squad went home at the end of the year, Eamon stopped with Morrison senior and worked over the winter on the farm.

The squad interested young Morrison. 'These strange, half-savage people have a certain fascination for me,' he told his friends in town – young men and women with great ideals and full of schemes and high purposes for the reformation of the human race. Morrison belonged to a club, famous for its erudite members, one of whom discovered a grammatical error in a translation of Karl Marx's *Kapital* and another who had written a volume of verses, *Songs of the Day*. Young Morrison himself was a thinker, a moralist, earnest and profound in his own estimation. Coming into contact with the potato diggers on weekends, he often wondered why these people were treated like cattle wherever they took up their temporary abode. Here, on his father's farm, kindly old men, lithe, active youths and pure and comely girls were housed like beasts of burden. The young man often felt so sorry for them that he almost wept for his own tenderness.

Before entering the shed on this evening he had looked in at them from the cover of the darkness outside. He noticed the fire shining on their faces, saw old Maire a Glan telling her beads, the card-players bent over the cart, the young women knitting, and the two harridans, Gourock Ellen and Annie, holding out their hacked hands to the blaze.

The gamblers were so interested in their game that they took very little notice of the young man when he entered the shed; even Eamon Doherty who was playing had scant leisure to greet the newcomer. Morrison sat down on an upended box beside Gourock Ellen, who was stretching out her lean, claw-like fingers to the fire.

'Good-evening, Ellen!' he cried jovially, for he knew the woman, and sitting down, stretched out one delicate hand, on the middle finger of which a ring glittered, to the stove.

'It may be a guid e'en, but it's gey cold,' said Ellen.

'There are many new faces here,' said Morrison, looking into the corner where Norah Ryan was sitting, sewing patches on her working dress. The girl was deep in thought.

'Why has Dermod gone away and left me for them cards?' she asked herself and for a while sought in vain for an answer. Then when it came she thrust it away angrily and refused to give it credence, although the answer came from the depths of her own soul. 'He cares more for the cards than he cares for me.'

She looked up and saw the glint of the fire on the ring which the visitor wore, and noticed that he was looking at her. She had not noticed the man before. Never had such a well-dressed person visited the squad.

'It's Alec Morrison, the farmer's son,' old Maire a Glan, who was sitting beside the girl, whispered. 'He just comes in here like one of ourselves, as the man said. Just think of that and him a gentleman!'

Norah bowed her head, for Morrison's eyes were fixed on her still. Why did he keep staring at her? she asked herself and felt very uncomfortable, but not displeased. And how that ring sparkled, too! It must have cost a great amount of money.

A wave of tenderness swept across Morrison as he looked at Norah. 'She's too good for this sort of life,' he said inwardly as he noticed her white brow, and the small delicate fingers in which she held the needle. 'It's criminal to condemn a girl like her to such a life. The sanitary authorities will not give my father permission to house his cattle in the stall where that girl has now to sleep. That maiden to sleep there! I, a man, who should be able to bear suffering and privation, sleep in soft clothes that are clean and comfortable, and she has to lie in rags, in straw, in a place that is not good enough for cattle. And all these people are like myself, people with souls, feelings and passions… .'

'Have you just come to this country for the first time?' he asked Norah, and when he put the question a sense of shame surged through him.

'The first time,' answered the girl.

'And you'll not think much of Scotland?' he said.

'People like yerself may like it,' said Maire a Glan; 'but as for us, it's beyont talkin' about… . In the last farm we had to sleep in a shed that was full of rats. They ate our bits of food, aye, and our very clothes. The floor was alive with wood-lice and worms… . The night before we left the shed was flooded, and there was eighteen inches of water on the floor. We had to rise from our beds in the bare pelt and stand all night up to our knees in the cold water…. . There's Norah Ryan getting red in the face as if it was her very own fault.'

'Norah! What a pretty name,' said the young man. 'And did she sleep in that shed?'

'The farmers think that we're pigs,' said Maire a Glan harshly. 'That's why they treat us like pigs.'

'It's wrong, very wrong,' said the young man, and his eyes were still fixed on Norah. The girl wondered why he stared at her in such a manner. He was handsome to look upon, clean-skinned, dark-eyed, and well-dressed. She had never spoken to such a well-dressed man in all her life before; but she felt frightened at something which she could not understand and wished that the man was gone. An idea came to her that she was doing something very wrong, and with this idea came fear, fear of the unknown.

Gourock Ellen, elbows on knees, her hands crossed over her breast and her thumbs propping her chin, began to tell a story of one of her early love affairs; how a man would not pay and how she took away his clothes and vowed to send him out naked into the streets. Morrison listened attentively and Norah, who did not understand the story fully, and who was shocked at all she understood, wondered why the farmer's son was not horrified at this episode in the life of Ellen.

About ten o'clock he rose to go and stood for a moment talking to Micky's Jim at the card table. Norah examined him attentively. He was well favoured and vigorous, and he spoke so nicely and quietly too!

'Dermod Flynn is makin' a fortune,' Jim was saying. Alec Morrison went to the door; there he stood for a moment and looked back into the shed. Norah glanced at the youth; their eyes met and both felt that this was something which they desired.

Morrison's simplicity, his interest in the squad and his kindly remarks, established a bond of sympathy between himself and Norah; but even yet she could not understand why such a well-dressed youth had visited the squalid shed in which the squad was staying. He seemed out of place; he could not feel at home in such dirty surroundings. And he had gazed so earnestly at her: in his eyes was a look of appeal, of entreaty. It seemed to Norah that it was in her power to bestow some favour on the youth, give him some precious gift that he desired very earnestly. Filled with a mixed emotion of pleasure and natural modesty, the girl wondered if all that had happened was real and if it had any significance for her.

'The way he looked at me!' she murmured in a puzzled voice. 'And him a gentleman talking to us as if we were of his own kind! He must be very learned. And why didn't Dermod Flynn stay with me here, not runnin' away to them old cards!'

She glanced at Dermod, whose face was flushed and whose fingers trembled nervously as he placed a silver coin down on the gaming-table, and instinctively it was borne to her that something black and ugly had crept into the purity of the passion which attracted her towards the Glenmornan youth.

'The blame's all on me,' she whispered, hardly realising what she was saying, and began to turn over in her mind every incident of the evening from the time when she first noticed Alec Morrison sitting by the fire up till the present moment.

'Did you see the way that the farmer's son was watchin' ye, Norah Ryan?' Maire a Glan asked. 'His two eyes were on ye all the time. He'll be havin' a notion of ye.'

'That he will,' said Gourock Ellen, and both women laughed loudly.

'And Maire a Glan, the decent woman, says that,' Norah whispered to herself and blushed. 'And them laughin' as if there was nothing wrong in it. Then there's no harm in me speakin' to the farmer's son.'

At the table the game was now fast and furious. None of the players heard the women's remarks.

CHAPTER 18

IN THE LANE

I

Sunday afternoon of a week later.

Alec Morrison was walking along a sheltered lane towards the house, his hands deep in his trousers' pockets, a cigarette between his lips, and his mind dwelling on several things which had taken place the week before. On Sundays he liked to walk alone when there was nothing extraneous to distract his mind, and then to ponder over thoughts that thronged his brain from time to time. He was a Progressive, and the term, which might mean anything to the general public, to Morrison meant all that was best in an age that, to him, was extremely reactionary and lacking in earnestness of purpose and clarity of vision. The young man believed that he, himself, realised all the beauty and all the significance of life and the importance of the task allocated in it to man. He also imagined that he possessed unlimited powers and that in the advance of humanity towards perfection he was destined to play an important part. Most young men of sanguine temperament, who read a little, paint a little, and write a little, have at times hallucinations of this kind. The young man's pet idea was that he, by some inscrutable decree of Fate, had been appointed to show the working classes the road towards a better life, towards enlightenment and prosperity.

Up till very recently (he was now twenty-one) he had taken no notice of the great class to which he did not belong. He lived in middle-class society, was cradled in its smug self-conceit and nourished at the breasts of affectation. He spent many years at school and now realised that he had wasted his time there. After leaving school he entered a bank in Paisley and spent a number of hours daily bending over a desk, copying interminable figures with a weary pen.

Seeing the conditions under which labourers wrought on his father's farm caused him to think seriously. Once when he was at home two persons, a man and a woman, Donal and Jean, supposed to be husband and wife, got employment in the steading. These two people were very ragged, very dirty, and very dissolute. The woman's face was hacked in a terrible manner; her nose had been broken, and her figure looked more like a maltreated animal's than a human being's. The man was low-set, stunted, and weedy. Both drew their wages daily and got drunk every night. One night when they had returned from a neighbouring village Morrison saw them in their sleeping quarters. A disused pigsty, no longer tenable for animals, was handed over to these creatures. A pile of dirty straw lay on the floor and on this the man and woman were sleeping, the man snoring loudly, the woman lying face upwards; the blunt nails of her bleeding fingers showed over the filthy bags which covered her body. A guttering candle was dying in the neck of a beer bottle beside them and the smell of beer pervaded the place.

'It must be an awful life, this,' he said to his father, who accompanied him.

'These kind of people think nothin' of it,' his father said. 'They get drunk every night and are very happy. Whisky is the only thing they want.'

'Yes, they want something like that to live in a place like this.'

What struck the young man forcibly at that moment was that the people were like himself; that under certain conditions he might be just as they were, even like the man lying under the dirty bag by the side of the pock-marked harridan; and that man under favourable conditions might be himself, Morrison, and full of glorious dreams for the betterment of the race to which he belonged.

That night Morrison slept little, and when sleep came he dreamt that he lay with the old harridan under the dirty coverlet, his arms round her and his lips pressed against the dry and almost bloodless lips of the woman. In the morning the remembrance of the dream filled him with horror. That such people should exist; that, under certain conditions, he might be the man lying there in the pigsty! He began to think seriously of things. Then he came across a woman in Paisley – a woman who belonged to the club of which he was a member – a woman whom he thought was different to all others. She was progressive and pronounced in her views and explained to Morrison how society from top to bottom, from hall to hovel, from robes to rags, was an expression of injustice, of wrong, of vice, of filth and moral decrepitude, and that in the interest of the future race the social system had to be changed and society to be renovated. Because she was very clever and good looking Morrison fell in love with this woman. She was a typist in a merchant's office.

II

Thinking of many things, he sauntered towards the farm. The cigarette went out; he threw it away and lit another. The evening was calm and quiet; a few late birds were chirruping in the hazel bushes and somewhere in the distance a dog barked loudly. The grey twilight that links day and night was over everything.

Suddenly Morrison perceived Norah Ryan coming towards him. She wore her grey tweed, which showed to perfection the outlines of her slender figure. In one hand she carried a book, the other hand hung idly by her side.

'Are you going for a walk, Norah Ryan?' Morrison asked when he met her.

'I am,' she answered, hardly knowing whether she should stop and talk to him or continue on her way.

'You're reading, I see.' He took the cigarette from his mouth as he spoke, held it between finger and thumb and flicked the ash off with his little finger.

'Yes, I'm readin',' she said, but did not tell him what book she held in her hand; he could see, however, that it was a prayer-book.

'When do the squad go to Ireland?'

'Next Friday, if all goes well,' she answered.

'So soon!' Morrison exclaimed, and in his voice there was a vague hint of regret. 'Are you glad to get home again?' he asked.

'Yes.'

'And the rest of the squad – what are they doing this evening? Are they playing cards?'

'The men are; the women are singin', some of them; and Gourock Ellen and Annie are mendin' their clothes.'

'It is getting dark quickly,' said Morrison. 'Are you coming back now?'

'Is it time?' she asked, then said, 'I suppose it is.'

He was going to the farm and it would be nice to have his company. She had seen him going out and anticipated meeting him coming home. Perhaps that was why she had come; if so she did not dare to confess it, even to herself. She now thought that she should not have come; a tremor shook her for a moment, then she turned and went back along the lane with the young man.

A car drawn by a white pony came up behind them, and they stepped nearer to the line of hazel bushes to let it pass. They were now very close to one another.

'Some of the people on the next farm, coming home from church,' said Morrison as the car was passing. 'Watch that the wheels don't catch you. The lane is very narrow…. There!'

He caught hold of her by the waist, drawing her close to him and pressing her very tightly.

'The car was almost running over you,' he said.

'Don't!' she cried, striving to get free. 'Don't, now; it's not right.'

'The wheel …' he said in a husky voice. 'The lane is so narrow.' He knew that he was telling a lie, but at the same time he felt very pleased with himself. He had dropped the cigarette, which could be seen glowing red on the dark ground. He released the girl, but would have liked to catch her in his arms again. The vehicle went rumbling off into the distance. 'It is so very dark, too,' he muttered under his breath.

They walked along together, both busy with their own thoughts, the girl hot and ashamed, but curiously elated; the young man in some way angry with himself for what he had done, but at the same time desirous of clasping Norah again in his arms.

'If I had someone to tell me what to do,' she said under her breath, but knew instinctively that there was no one but herself to determine what action should be pursued in an event like this. Even if advice were proffered to her she knew that it would be useless. Something was driving her to the brink of an unknown which she feared, and from which there was no retreat and no escape.

'You are stumbling,' said Morrison, and again caught hold of her. She had not stumbled; it was a pretext on his part; he merely wanted an excuse to hold her in his arms. She could see his hand on her sleeve and noticed the gold ring sparkling in the darkness.

In man there are two beings, the corporal and the spiritual; one striving after that happiness which ministers to the passion of the individual to the detriment of the race; the other which seeks for happiness according to divine laws, a happiness that is good for all. Yesterday, today, ten minutes before, this spiritual being presided over Morrison's destiny; now as he walked along the crooked lane, a lone wind sighing in the hazel bushes and a few stars out above him, he felt the animal man come and take possession of him. The rustling of Norah's petticoats as she walked beside him, the slight pressure of her little rough fingers on his large smooth hand filled him with an insatiable animal desire which held him captive.

This was no new experience, and it possessed for him a certain charm which in his saner moments he loathed, but now he could neither conquer nor drive it away.

'I like the bow in your hair,' he said in a hoarse voice that startled the girl. 'It suits you.'

'I must be off and away now,' she said, freeing her hand from his, but not drawing it away quickly enough to prevent him getting possession of it again. 'Let me go,' she said in a low voice. 'Ye must let me go. What would yerself be talkin' to the likes of me for? … There's the farm!'

'Don't hurry away,' said Morrison, bending down and placing both arms round her waist. For some reason which he could not fathom he felt ashamed of himself, but he clasped her more tightly as he spoke. 'Why are you in so great a hurry? You're better here. Is that young fellow – Flynn they call him, I think – waiting for you? Micky's Jim was telling me all.'

'He had no right to,' said the girl angrily, but refrained from drawing herself away. 'Dermod Flynn is nothin' to me.'

'I'm glad of that.'

'Why?'

Morrison did not answer. It would be unwise to commit himself in any way, he thought, and for a moment he mastered the passion which filled his body. The lights of the farm sparkled in front. The open shed was facing them. The fire glowed red inside, and against it dark forms came and went. He stooped down and kissed her three times and she could feel his warm body press passionately against her own.

Someone passed near them and Morrison let her go. She hurried off towards the shed, and he could hear the patter of her boots as she ran. She passed Dermod Flynn on her way; no doubt he had seen Morrison kiss her, she thought. When she entered the shed Gourock Ellen, who was bending over the card table, looked up and saw the flush of colour in Norah's face. Then Ellen noticed Dermod coming in and saw the troubled look in the boy's eyes.

'Dermod's been kissin' ye, lass, I'll warrant,' she whispered to Norah, then turning round to Micky's Jim, she opened his shirt front and ran her fingers down his hairy chest. 'Come on now, Jim, for that'll gie ye luck,' she cried.

'Yes, decent woman, it's sure to give me luck,' said Jim, throwing down the cards and putting a match to his pipe.

III

'What have I done, what's Alec Morrison to me?' Norah asked herself as she looked in her little cracked hand mirror ten minutes later. 'He's nothin' to me, nothin', nothin'; no more than Dermod Flynn is. The two of them might so well be strangers to me. Now why did he kiss me? Dermod never kissed me. I'm glad of that.'

Norah looked round the byre, at the bunks in the stalls, the cattle troughs and the candle burning on the iron stanchion. She was alone, the other women were still out with the card-players in the shed.

'I must be very good-lookin',' she whispered to herself as her eyes sought their reflection in the cracked mirror; then she blushed at her girlish vanity and innocent pride. 'And him so grand, too, a gentleman!' But in some indistinct and indefinite way she felt that she would be raised to his level. 'And he kissed me – here.' She put her fingers over her red lips. 'But he's nothin' to me, nothin'. Dermod Flynn is nothin' either.' She knew that the first assertion was not true; the repetition of the second gave her a certain pleasure.

'Do I love two of them? Can one love two people?' she asked herself. 'But I'm not in love and never was. I like Dermod, but all the girls in the squad like him.... Why did Alec Morrison kiss me, and him a gentleman? It wasn't my fault, was it?' She looked round and addressed an imaginary person, a look of bewilderment settling on her face.

'Did I go out to meet him this evenin'? Did I like his kisses? Is Dermod Flynn angry? I couldn't help liking Dermod; he is so good, so kindly. But I'm a bad girl, very bad; all my life was full of sin. Pride and vanity, what the Catechism condemned, are my two sins. I used to be vain at school. I had two shoes and I was proud, because other people wore only mairteens. I used to dress my hair and try and look nicer than any other girsha; because I was vain. And now I'm vain because a well-dressed gentleman talks kindly to me. God forgive me! Ah, this looking-glass, I hate it! I'll just have one look at myself and then never get hold of a glass again.'

She sat down on the bed and her fingers toyed with the potato sacks that served as quilt.

'Yes, he's very nice and talks to us so kindly,' she whispered, and again her eyes sought the mirror. 'Oh, it was a fine evening, one of the nicest ever I had.... . They're not too red, just pale, and when the blush is in them I'm better lookin' than at any time. Has any one in the squad cheeks like mine? ... Why did he want to kiss me? And my boots to one side at the heels and the toe-cap risin' off one of them. I wish I had money, lots of it, gold, a crock of gold like the fairies leave under the holly bush ... I could buy new dresses and maybe rings. Norah, don't let your hair hang down so far over your forehead, it doesn't become ye. A wee bit back there, no, here; that's it. Now ye're very good lookin'.'

'And to think of it as the first time and he has won fifteen shillin's!' said Maire a Glan, who had just entered the byre. 'Fifteen shillin's, Norah!'

'What?'

'He won!'

'Who?'

'Who but Dermod Flynn?' said the old woman. 'And him playin' for the first time!'

CHAPTER 19

THE END OF THE SEASON

I

In a week's time the squad was to break up: Gourock Ellen, Annie and the two men who joined at Greenock, were leaving for Glasgow; Dermod Flynn who, despite the initial success, had lost all his money at the card table, was going to remain in Scotland and earn his living at the first job that came to hand. Such a little boy! Norah felt sorry for him, but now he hardly deigned to look at her. When at work the far-away look was always in his eyes and at night he played for hours on end at the gaming table. Most of the players said that he was awfully plucky and that he would stake his last penny on a card and lose the coin without turning a hair.

For the whole week prior to departure Norah, who was now very restless, laughed nervously when a joke was passed, but seemingly took no heed of the joke. She was not unhappy, but in a dim, subconscious way felt that she had done something very wrong. Before knowing Dermod intimately he frightened her; it was only after knowing Morrison so well that she became frightened of him. Dermod had never kissed her; she and the boy were only friends, she said to herself time and again. Dermod was only a friend of hers, nothing more. Sometimes when alone she said so aloud, as if trying to drown the inner voice that told her it was not true. If Dermod only ceased playing cards things might right themselves, she thought, but deep down in her heart she wished everything to go on just as at present.

Morrison went to town on the day following the episode in the lane, but, before leaving, told Norah that he would come back to see her prior to her departure for Ireland.

'Don't tell anybody that I am coming back,' he said, and, while wondering at his words, she promised not to tell.

The squad was going on Friday; on Thursday night Morrison returned, a rose in his buttonhole and a silver-handled stick in his hand. She saw him enter the farmhouse as she returned from the field, her knees sore, her clothes wet, and straggling locks of hair falling over her brow. At supper she ate little but took great care over her toilet; scrubbed her hands, which were very sore, until they bled, and spent nearly half an hour before the little looking-glass which she had brought from Ireland. She sorted her tresses, and put in its place an erring lock that persisted in falling over her little pink ear.

She put on her grey dress, tied a glossy leather belt around her waist, laced her shoes, and when she had finished left the byre, which was lit up by a long white candle stuck in the neck of a whisky bottle, and went out to the cartshed where the squad assembled.

Morrison was there before her, sitting beside Micky's Jim on the end of an upturned cart, and speaking to Maire a Glan about the hardships of the field. Willie the Duck played his fiddle, now sadly out of tune; a game of cards was in progress, and Dermod Flynn, who held the bank, was losing rapidly. It was said that he had no money in hand except the wages which he had lifted that day, and now it was nearly gone. What would he do when all was spent? Nobody enquired, but it was evident that he would not return to Ireland that winter.

Norah entered, her head bent down a little, her hands clasped together and a look of hesitation on her face.

'Ha! there's another one that's for Ireland in the morning,' said Micky's Jim, taking the pipe from his mouth and spitting down between his legs to the floor. It was to Norah that he spoke, and Dermod Flynn ceased playing for a moment to glance over the rim of his cards at the girl. But his mind was busy with something else and his eyes turned back almost instantly to the gaming table. He cared nothing for her, Norah thought, and the idea gave her a strange comfort.

'You're going tomorrow as well as the rest?' said Morrison when the girl drew up to the fire. He knew that she was going and felt that he should have said something else. Presently, however, he asked: 'Are you glad?'

'Yes,' she answered, but the look in her eyes might have meant 'No'. Morrison understood it thus, and the sensation which surged through him on Sunday evening surged through him again.

'Not goin' to play any more; skinned out,' someone said at the table. Norah glanced at the players and saw that Dermod Flynn had risen. He approached the fire, one hand deep in his pocket, the other holding a splinter of wood which he threw into the flames. He had lost all his money; he hadn't a penny in the world now. Gourock Ellen offered him a piece of silver to retrieve his fallen fortunes.

'If I don't win I cannot pay you back,' he said, and sat down beside Morrison and facing Norah. Fixing his eyes on the fire he was presently buried in a reverie and the dreamy look of the schoolboy was again on his face. One of his hands was bleeding; it had been torn on a jagged stave which got loose on the rim of Norah's basket earlier in the day; his knees peeped out through his trousers and the uppers of both his boots had risen from the soles.

Norah gazed at him covertly, saw the wound on his hand, the bare knees showing through the trousers, and the toes peeping through the torn uppers. Then something glistened brightly and caught her eyes. It was the ring on Morrison's finger. The young man was speaking.

'… and it will be ten months before you are back in the squad again. Such a long time!'

'It's not much comfort we have in this country anyway,' said Maire a Glan, who was turning the heel of a stocking, stopping for a moment to run one of the needles through her hair.

'I have got to go into the house now,' said Morrison, rising to his feet and holding out a hand to the fire. 'I hope you'll all have a good voyage across tomorrow night.'

'The Lord will be with us,' said Biddy Wor, who had just come in from the byre carrying a small frying-pan in one hand and a pot of porridge in the other.

'How long does it take to cross from Greenock to Londonderry?' Morrison asked Biddy Wor, meanwhile fixing his eyes on Norah Ryan.

'Derry, ye mean,' said the old woman. 'We always say "Derry", but it's the foreigner, bad luck be with him! that put London on to it. From Greenock it takes ten hours, more or less.'

Morrison drew a cigarette from a leather case which he took from his pocket. As he was lighting the cigarette he dropped the case and it fell beside Norah's feet. He bent down hurriedly.

'Come out into the open, for I have something to say to you,' he whispered in a low voice to Norah as he stooped; then he went out, taking leave of the party in one 'Goodnight', and five minutes later Norah rose from her seat and followed him.

'Where are ye goin', girsha?' asked Maire a Glan.

'Down to the byre,' said the girl without turning round.

Morrison was standing in the shadow which fringed the fan-like stretch of light thrown from the shade.

'Is that you, Norah?' he asked, knowing well that it was she, and as he spoke he took her into his arms and kissed her. To Norah there was something dreadful in this kiss, and while not knowing that it gave expression to the pent-up passion of the man, she felt nervous and afraid. She looked back to the shed, saw the faces round the gaming table, old Maire knitting in the corner, her needles showing brightly as the firelight played on them. A disused cart-wheel hung from the wall; she had never noticed it before... . Here in the dark beyond the circle of light something terrible threatened her, something that she could not comprehend but which her beating heart told her was wrong, and should be avoided. Why should she be afraid? Norah had all the boldness of innocence: her virtue was not armed with that knowledge which makes it weigh its every action carefully. Morrison was speaking, asking her to come further out into the darkness, but she still kept her eyes fixed on the shed. Safety lay there; freedom from what she could not comprehend. The man had hold of her hands, pressing them tightly, entreating her to do something. She freed herself from his grasp and ran back to the shed, half glad that the whole incident had taken place, and more than a little desirous to go out again. Her love for the well-dressed youth imparted a recklessness to her timid nature. When she went to her sleeping quarters two hours later old Maire a Glan accompanied her. The gamblers were still playing, the fire blazed merrily, and Ginger Dubbin held the bank and was winning heavily.

'What's that, that's shinin' in front of us?' asked Maire a Glan as she came out. 'Maybe it's only seein' things that I am, for me old eyes play tricks in the darkness.'

'It looks like a live spark lyin' on the ground,' said Norah.

'That's not on the cold ground,' answered the woman. 'See, it's movin'! It'll be the farmer's son with the gold ring on his finger. Now what will he be after waitin' for there?'

'How am I to know?' said Norah, but in such a low voice that the old woman had to draw near to catch the words. 'I'm sleepy,' she said after a pause; 'it's time we were in bed.'

II

On the morning of the day following, the squad prepared for their departure, and gathered up all their spare clothes, their pans and porringers, and packed them in woollen handkerchiefs and tin boxes. The blankets, eighteen in all, were tied up in a parcel, ready to be sent off to the merchant in town.

'God knows who'll sleep in them next year!' said Willie the Duck in a pathetic voice, and everybody laughed, some because they enjoyed the remark and others because it was the correct thing to laugh at every word uttered by Willie the Duck.

Dermod Flynn watched the preparations with impassive face. He was not going home; in fact, he had not as much money in his possession as would pay the railway fare to the nearest town. All his wages had been lost on the gaming table; he had nothing now to rely on but the labour of his own hands and the chance of getting a job.

'What will ye do, Dermod?' Maire a Glan asked.

'I'll try and … But what does it matter to you what I do? One would think to hear you talk that I was a child.'

'I suppose there'll be a lot of drunk people on the boat this night,' said Micky's Jim as he tied a tin porringer in a rag and placed it in his box. 'There'll be some fightin' too, I'll go bail.'

'The Derry boat is the place for fightin', as the man said.'

'Aye, sure, and the Irish are very fond of fightin' when they're drunk.'

'It's more in the blood than in the bottle, all the same,' said Eamon Doherty.

'I mind one fight on the Derrier,' said Micky's Jim, biting a mouthful from the end of his plug. 'I was in the fight meself. (If the cork comes out of that bottle of milk, Owen Kelly, it'll make a hell of a mess on yer clothes.) It started below. "There's no man here," said I, "that could –" (Them trousers are not worth taking with ye, Eamon Doherty. No man would wear clothes like that; a person would better be painted and go out bare naked) "– that could put up his fives to me." (If ye dress yer hair like that, Brigit Doherty, I'll not be seen goin' into Greenanore with ye.) Then a man drove full but for my face and I took the dunt like an ox. (Willie the Duck, are ye goin' to take that famine fiddle home again? Change it for a Jew's harp or a pair of laces!) "That's how a Glenmornan man takes it," says I, and came in with a clowt to the jowl –'

'Stop yer palaver about fightin', Micky's Jim, and let us get away to the station,' said Maire a Glan. 'We'll not auction time while we're waitin', as the man said.'

'If we go off now we'll only have three hours to wait for the train,' remarked Jim sarcastically.

'And poor Dermod Flynn,' said Maire a Glan, tying her bundle over her shoulders with a string. 'Not a penny at all left him. Where's Norah Ryan? She's the girl to save her money.'

At that moment Norah was outside with Morrison and the young man was asking a question. The wish to find an answer to it had kept him awake for nearly half the previous night.

'Why did you run away from me yesterday evening, Norah?'

'I was frightened.'

'Of what?'

'I don't know.'

'Well, I certainly don't know what caused you to run away.'

Morrison knew that, innocent though Norah was, some subtle instinct warned her the night before to hurry off to the safety of the shed.

'I would like to know why you did it, why you ran away, I mean?' he asked, knowing in his own heart that, if she understood, she had good reason to be afraid. 'Does the girl understand?' he pondered. He had heard them talk of most things in Micky's Jim's squad, but perhaps the girl paid no heed to the talk.

'Are you coming back next year?' he enquired.

'It's more nor likely.'

'Do you care for the life in the squad?'

'It could be worse.'

'That's no recommendation,' said Morrison with a laugh, but seeing that Norah failed to understand him, he went on: 'I don't think you could have a life much harder than this.'

'I did not even kiss you last night,' he said after a short silence, 'and now you are going away and maybe never coming back again. I would kiss you now, only some of the squad might see us, and you wouldn't like that.'

But for the squad Morrison cared nothing. He was just on the point of kissing Norah when he noticed his father looking at him through a window of the farmhouse. Although not respecting his father overmuch, for old Morrison was a hard-drinking and short-tempered man; the son did not want the little love affair to be spoken of in the house.

'If you stay tonight in Greenock, Norah, I'll go down with you,' said the young fellow. 'Will you stay?'

'Why should I stay?' asked Norah, who did not understand what Morrison's words meant.

'Because – well, you see –' stammered the youth. 'Oh! I think you'd better go with the rest. I'll see you next year.'

He held out his hand, clasped hers almost fiercely and without another word turned and went towards the house. On the way he lit a cigarette, rubbed a speck of dirt from the knee of his well-creased trousers, and wondered why he wanted to take possession of the innocent girl. Despite his high-flown views on the equality of man, Morrison never thought of marrying Norah. Besides, there was Ellen Keenans, the advanced woman and author of *Songs of the Day*, and it was Ellen who taught him what man's conception of duty towards the race should be. At the present moment Morrison did not see how he could fit in with Ellen's teachings.

That night most of the squad sailed for Ireland; Gourock Ellen and Annie took their way to Glasgow, and Dermod Flynn set out on the open road, ragged, penniless, and alone.

CHAPTER 20

ORIGINAL SIN

I

A year had passed; the potato season was over, but old Morrison, who was making considerable improvements in his steading, had kept the squad to work for him two months longer than usual, and all the party of the previous year, with the exception of Dermod Flynn, Ellen, and Annie, was there. Nobody in the squad knew where Dermod had gone, but rumour had it that he worked during the previous winter as a farm hand on a farm near Paisley. It was also said that he had done very well and had sent ten pounds home to his people in Glenmornan.

Norah Ryan had spent the winter and spring at home; her mother was still alive, but seldom ventured outside the door of the cabin. 'The coldness of the dead is creeping over me,' she told Norah when the girl was leaving for Scotland. 'My feet are like lumps of ice, and when the cold reaches my heart it will be the end, thanks be to God!'

Norah felt deeply for her mother; the old woman had none now but her daughter in all the world. Fergus had not been heard of for the last three years; some said that the boy was dead, others that he was alive and making a big fortune.

Norah always prayed for him nightly when she went down on her knees, asking the Virgin to send him safe home, and 'if he is dead to intercede with her Son for the repose of his soul'.

At the end of each fortnight the girl, who earned twelve shillings weekly, sent sixteen home to her mother. In four months Norah sent six pounds eight shillings to Frosses, and a pound of this went towards the expense of the priest's mansion. The same amount had been paid the year before and Norah was well-pleased, because now her father would rest easily in his grave. 'He'll rest in peace now that all his lawful debts are paid,' the old parish priest said.

Micky's Jim had fallen in love with Oiney Dinchy's daughter and it was said that he was going to get married to her when he went back to Ireland. Owen Kelly was as niggardly as ever. Once during the year he had bought a pennyworth of milk and at night he left it in a beer-bottle beside his bed. In the morning the milk was gone and Owen wept! So Micky's Jim said; and Jim also circulated a story about a rat that drank the milk from the bottle.

'But that couldn't be, as the man said.'

'But it could be. I saw it while all the rest of ye were snorin'.'

'There's no standin' your lies, Micky's Jim.'

'True as death 'twas a rat that drunk the milk,' Jim explained. 'I saw it meself. Stuck its tail down the neck of the bottle and licked its tail when it took it out. Took two hours to drink the whole lot. I once had a great fight and all about a bottle of milk –'

It was Christmas Eve. Norah sat beside the coal fire which burned in the large stove in Morrison's cart shed, seeing pictures in the flames. Outside there was no moon, but a million stars shone in a heaven that was coldly clear. Tomorrow the squad was going home.

'I haven't seen that fellow, young Morrison, for a whole year,' said Maire a Glan, who was sewing patches on her dress. 'I don't like the look of yon fellow; it makes me sick to see him sittin' here, askin' us about how we do this and how we do that, what we do at home and how many acres of land have we got in Ireland, and hundreds of other things that the very priest himself wouldn't ask ye.'

'He's a good youngster, for all ye say,' remarked Owen Kelly, who once got a shilling as a tip from the young fellow. 'That's no reason for ye takin' such an ill will against him, Maire a Glan.'

'I don't like him atall, atall,' said the old woman doggedly. 'There's something about him that I care little for.'

'We all have our faults, Maire,' said old Biddy Wor. 'And it goes against the grain with me to speak ill of anybody, no matter who they are. Ye've noticed that yerself.'

'I couldn't fail to, seein' you've told me so often,' said Maire a Glan.

'There are faults and faults,' remarked Eamon Doherty. 'And some faults are worse at one time than another. D'ye mind the beansho?' he asked, turning to Biddy Wor. 'Of course ye mind her. Well, the man that was the cause of – ye know yerself – he got drounded at the fishin' before he could get married to Sheila. Her fault was not a great one atall, atall.'

'She was a brazen heifer, anyway,' said Biddy Wor.

'Where is she now?' Eamon Doherty enquired.

'No one knows atall, atall,' said Judy Carrol. 'Maybe she's a – a one like Gourock Ellen, God be good to us all!'

'I hear that she's in Glasgow,' said Murtagh Gallagher.

'Glasgow is the town to be in,' remarked Micky's Jim, scraping the wet tobacco from the bottom of his pipe. 'By the hokey! It was a great place for fightin'. One night I had seven fights hand running. A fellow named Droughty Tom was shootin' out his neck on the Docks. "What are ye chewin' the rag for, old slobber chops?" I ups to him and says, shovin' my fist under his nose: "There's a smell of dead men off that fist," I said –'

'We're sick to the bottom of the grave of hearin' about yer fightin', Micky's Jim,' said Dora Doherty, who entered the shed at that moment. 'D'ye know who's out there?' she asked.

'No.'

'It's that youngster, Morrison,' said the woman. 'I saw somethin' black in the darkness, and I thought it would be the farmer's son.'

Norah Ryan started forward in her seat, turned round, looked at Maire a Glan, rose, and went outside.

II

She had not seen Morrison for close on fourteen months, and he had never written to her; but time and again she intended to post one of the letters which she spent part of her time in writing to him. But they were never posted, and often she wondered why she had written them. Why, he wouldn't care for her, she told herself many times. He was far above her, a gentleman; she was only a poor worker, a little potato gatherer. He had never written and perhaps he did not love her one little bit. She felt angry and resentful with him, as she went out from the stuffy shed and looked up at the starlit sky.

Alec Morrison was waiting. Norah could see his dark form showing against the white gable of the byre, and could hear the crunch of his boots on the gravel as he changed his position. He had just come from Glasgow; he was working there now and he had come down to see Norah before she went back to Ireland. He had often intended to write to her but never did. Other more pressing problems, relating to a new sweetheart, a pretty little damsel in wonderful dresses and with no more morals than a bird, took up his attention. He held out his hand to Norah when she approached.

'I'm glad you've come out,' he said in a low voice. 'I've been waiting here for quite a long while.'

He had been waiting for her! Norah's heart gave a bound of gladness.

'But you never wrote to me,' she said reproachfully.

'You didn't write to me and I didn't know your address.'

That was really why he hadn't written! How strange she had never thought of that.

'And ye would write?'

'Certainly, Norah,' he said. He had not let her hand go, now he imprisoned the other. How coarse they were and hard from her season's work! The hands of the Glasgow girl.... But he felt that he was doing something wrong in comparing the two women at that moment.

'Do you mind the last night you were here?'

'I have often been thinkin' of that night,' said Norah.

'Are you going to run away from me tonight?'

'No.'

'Why did you run away the last time?'

'I don't know. Maybe it was that I was afraid.'

She looked back at the shed as she spoke, saw old Maire a Glan bending over the fire, Willie the Duck playing his fiddle; could hear the loud laughter of Micky's Jim. Norah looked up at the face of the man beside her and was not in the least afraid.

'We'll go along the lane a bit,' he said.

They went together hand in hand along the hazel-lined gravel pathway. Overhead the stars sparkled, the trees, showing thin against the sky, waved their bare arms in the slight breeze and moaned plaintively. Willie the Duck was playing 'Way down upon the Swanee River', and it seemed as if the melody drifted in from a great distance.

'That's a wonderful melody,' said the young man. 'In it is the heart and soul of a persecuted people.'

He had heard somebody make that remark in the club and it appealed to him. The girl made no answer to his words. They stopped as if by mutual consent opposite the large shed in the stack yard.

'It's very cold,' said Morrison.

'Is it? No.'

'We'll go in here,' said the young man. He pulled the gate of the stack yard apart and went in, Norah following. A vague sense of danger, of some impending menace, suddenly took possession of the girl. The sight of the fire shining would be comforting, but she could not see the shed now. Between her and it the farmhouse stood up white and lonesome. A light glimmered for a moment in one of the rooms, then went out. Somewhere near a dog barked loudly, another joined in the outcry; an uneasy bird rose from the copse and fluttered off into the night.

They entered the shed. Inside it was warm and quiet and the scent of old hay pervaded the place. A strange fear, blending in some measure with joy, came over Norah. Morrison's arms were round her and she felt as if she wanted to tell him some great secret. No thought of danger was now in her mind. The problems of existence had never given her a moment's thought. All things were to her a matter of course, the world, the trees, the flowers and stars, and men and women. Love in some vague way she knew was related to marriage just as faith had some relation to heaven. But the faith in God which was hers was something which she never strove to analyse, and the love for the young man filled her being so much at present that she could not draw herself apart from it and consider the rights and wrongs of her position.

Everything was so peaceful and quiet that it seemed as if all the world were asleep and dreaming. Some words, hazy as the remembrance of almost forgotten dreams, drifted into her mind. They were words once spoken by Sheila Carrol at the hour of midnight on Dooey Strand.

'When the earth is asleep, child, that will be a dangerous hour, for you may then commit the mortal sin of love.'

What did Sheila mean when she spoke like that? Why was she thinking of those words now? Norah did not know. Before her was a great mystery, something unexplainable, terrible. The great fundamental truths of life were unknown to Norah; no one had ever explained to her why she was and how she had come into being. She walked blindly in a world of pitfalls and perils; unhelped by anyone she groped futilely in the dark for one sure resting place, looked for one illuminating ray of certainty to light up her path. At that moment the soul within the fair body of hers warned her in some vague way of the danger which lay before her. 'You may commit the mortal sin of love.'

What did those words mean? She wanted to run away, but instead she clung closer to the man; she could feel his lips hot on hers and his breath warm on her cheek.

III

Something terrible had happened. The maiden's purity, never sullied by a careless thought, was sullied for ever. To the girl it appeared as if something priceless which she loved and treasured had suddenly been broken to pieces. Morrison stood beside her, his hands resting on her shoulders, his breath short and husky; and his whole appearance became suddenly repulsive to the girl. And the man wanted to be gone from her side. He had desired much, obtained what he desired, but was now far from satisfied. He felt in some vague, inexplicable way that she had suddenly become distasteful to him. With other women he had often before experienced the same feeling. He bent over the girl, who quivered like a reed under his hands.

'Are you going into the house?' he asked. He almost said 'byre'.

'I'll go in myself,' she answered in a low voice. 'Go away and leave me.... Go away!'

'Are you angry with me?' he asked. He was now ashamed of all that had taken place, ashamed of himself and ashamed of the girl. In some subconscious way it was borne to him that the girl was to blame. He thrust the thought away for a moment but when it returned again he hugged it eagerly. He wanted to believe it; he chose to believe it.

'Goodnight, Norah. I'll see you again tomorrow before you go away.' He released her arms and went out through the gateway. She could hear his footsteps for a long while but never looked after him. A great fear settled on her heart; she was suddenly conscious of having done something terribly wrong, and it seemed as if the very fabric of her life had been torn to shreds. Weeping, she stole back to the shed like a frightened child.

The party was in a great state of excitement. A rat chased by some prowling dog had just run into the shed and passed between the legs of Maire a Glan, who was warming her hands at the fire.

'Mercy be on us! a dirty, big grey rat,' Maire was saying. 'It was that long, as the man said.' She stretched a long lean arm out in front of her as she spoke.

'If we caught it we'd put paraffin oil over it and set fire to its hair,' said Micky's Jim. 'That's what scares the rats!'

'Ye wouldn't set fire to a dumb animal, would ye?' asked Bridget Doherty.

'Wouldn't I? What would yerself do with it?'

'One might kill it in an easier way.'

'Any way at all, for it's all the same,' said Micky's Jim. 'Last year me and Dermod Flynn killed a lot on yon farm in Rothesay. The farmer gave us a penny a tail and we made lots of tin. How much did we make, Norah Ryan?' he asked. 'It's yerself that has the memory and ye were always concerned about Dermod.'

'I don't remember,' said Norah, who was standing at the door of the shed.

'The old mad farmer was goin' to cheat us out of a tanner, anyway,' said Micky's Jim. 'But I soon put up my fives to him. "Smell them fists," I says to him –'

'Ye never stop talkin' about fights,' said Biddy Wor.

'That's the kind of him,' said Maire a Glan. 'His people had the contrary drop in their veins always. D'ye mind, Norah Ryan, the way that –'

But when the old woman looked round Norah had disappeared. She had stolen out through the starlight to her bed, her mind groping blindly with a terrible mystery which she could not fathom.

CHAPTER 21

REGRETS

I

In the June of the following year Norah Ryan received a
letter from Scotland. It ran:

> 47 Ann Street,
> Cowcaddens,
> Glasgow.

My Dear Norah,

It is a long while now since you heard a word from
me. I often intended to write to you, but my hand
was not used to the pen; it comes foreign to my
fingers. I am not like you, a scholart that was so long
at the Glenmornan schoolhouse with Master Diver.

I am working away here in Scotland, the black
country with the cold heart. I have only met one of
the Glenmornan people for a long while. That was
Oiney Dinchy's son, Thady, and he's a dock labourer
on the quay. He told me all about the people at home.
He said that poor Marie a Crick, God rest her soul! is
dead. Do you mind the night on Dooey Head long
ago? Them was the bad and bitter times. He said that

Father Devaney has furnished his new house and the cost of it was thousands of pounds, a big lot for a poor parish to pay. He also told me that you were over with the potato squad in Scotland and that you were looked on with no unkindly eyes by a rich farmer's son. But whoever he is or whatever he is, you are too good for him, for it is yourself that was always the comely girl with the pleasant ways. Whatever you do, child, watch yourself anyway, for the men that are in black foreign parts are not to have the great trust put in them.

Mac Oiney Dinchy was saying that no word has come from Dermod Flynn for a long time. He didn't send much money home to his own people and they think that he has gone to the bad. Well, for all they say, Dermod was a taking lad when I knew him.

And old Farley McKeown – the Lord be between us and harm! – got married! What will we see next? I wonder what an old dry stick like him wants to get married for; and Mac Oiney Dinchy says that he gave his wife sixty thousand pounds as a wedding present. Well, well!

I do be lonely here often, and I am wishful that you would take up the pen and write me a long letter when you get this one, and if ever you come to Scotland again come to Glasgow and spend a couple of days with me.

Hoping that yourself and your mother is in good health,

SHEILA CARROL.

'Who would that letter be from?' asked Mary Ryan from her seat in the chimney corner. A pile of dead ashes lay on the hearth; the previous summer had been wet and the turf was not lifted from the bog.

'It's from Sheila Carrol, mother.'

'From that woman, child! And what would she be writing to you for, Norah?'

'She's dying to hear from the Frosses people,' answered the girl. 'And it is very lonely away in the big city.'

'Lonely!' exclaimed the mother. 'If she is lonely it's her own fault. It's the hand of God that's heavy on her because of her sin.'

'That's no reason why the tongue of her country people should be bitter against her.'

'Saying that, child!' cried the woman. 'What's comin' over you at all, girsha? Never let me hear of you writing to that woman!'

Norah went to the door and looked at the calm sea stretching out far below. The waves were bright under the glance of the sun; a dark boat, a little speck in the distance, was moving out towards the bar.

'Where are you going, Norah?' asked the woman at the fire.

'Down to the sea, mother,' answered the girl as she made her way towards the beach.

II

Between the ragged rocks the grass was soft to the feet and refreshing to the eyes. Two lone sycamore trees showed green against the sky; a few stray leaves, shrivelled and filed through by caterpillars, were fluttering to the earth. A long fairy-thimble stalk, partly despoiled by some heedless child but still bearing three beautiful bells at the extreme top, whipped backwards and forwards in the wind, and Norah, reaching forward, pulled off one of the flowers and pinned it to her breast.

The tide was on the turn. The girl sat on a rock by the shore and put her small brown feet in the water. Down under the moving waves they looked as if they didn't belong to her at all. Here it was very quiet; the universal silence magnified the tranquillity of things. Under the girl's feet it was very deep, very dark, and very peaceful; there, where a reflected swallow swept through a wide expanse of mirrored blue, in the sea under her, were no regrets, no heart-sickness, and no sorrow. When the tide went out a fair young body, a white face with closed eyes would lie on the strand. Then the Frosses people would know why the terrible phantom, Death, was courted by a girl.

'It was all a great mistake,' she said to herself, and in the excitement caused by the stress of thought she sank her nails into her palms. The memory of a night passed seven months before came vividly to her mind. How many tearful nights had gone by since then! How many times had she written to Alec Morrison telling him of her plight! No answer had come; the man was indifferent.

'I wasn't the girl for the likes of him, anyway,' said Norah, looking at her feet in the water. 'But why has all this happened to me?'

As in all great crises of a person's life, there came a moment of vivid consciousness to Norah and every surrounding object stamped itself indelibly on her mind. The tide was sweeping slowly out; the seaweed in the pool beneath swayed like the hair of a dead body floating in the water. Two little fish with wide-open eyes looked up and seemed to be staring at her. Beneath in the water the fleecy clouds looked like little white spots against the blue of the mirrored sky, and the bar moaned loudly on the frontier of the deep sea.

'No matter what I do now, no one will think me worse than I am,' said the poor girl. 'I'll have no joy no more in my life, for there's no happiness that I can look forward to.'

She pulled the fairy thimbles from her breast and crushed them in her hand. Out near the bar she could see the little black boat heaving on the waves. Norah rose to her feet.

How dark the water looked under her. The sand sloped sharply from her feet to the bottom of the pool, which was bedded with sharp rocks covered with trailing, slimy seaweed. She peered in, catching her breath sharply as she did so. Then one little brown foot went further into the water, afterwards the other. She bent down, cut the water apart with her hands; a slight ripple spread out on both sides and was lost almost as soon as it was formed.

'Jesus, Mary, and Joseph, pray for me a sinner now and at the hour of my death, Amen,' she said, repeating a prayer which had flowed countless times since childhood from her lips.

A sudden thought struck her and a look of perplexity overspread her face. 'This is pilin' one sin on top of the other,' she said in a low voice and looked round, fearing that somebody had overheard her. Everything about was silent as if in fear; in that moment she thought that the sea had ceased to move, the swallow to circle, herself even to live; the world seemed to be waiting for something – an event of great and terrible purport, hidden and unknown.

Suddenly the child that was in her leapt under her heart and a keen but not unpleasant pain swept through her body. She drew back from the pool, horror-stricken at the thing which she intended to do.

'I'll go home,' she said meekly, as if obeying some command. 'Maybe he'll have pity on me when I go over again beyond the water. This day week Micky's Jim, he goes again. And I can go to Sheila Carrol. She knows and she has the good heart. God in His heaven have pity on me and all that's like me! for it's the ignorant girl that I was…. If anyone had told me…. But I knew nothin', nothin', and I'm black now in the eyes of God as I'll soon be black in the eyes of the world, of Dermod Flynn, of me mother and everybody that knows me. Nobody will speak to me than atall, atall!'

CHAPTER 22

ON THE ROAD

I

A dead weight lay on Norah's heart; the child beneath her heart was a burden. But even yet (it was now the month of August) those in Micky's Jim's squad did not suspect her condition. She knew, however, that she could not conceal her plight much longer, and she wanted to run away and hide. How could she endure the glance of her country people, of Micky's Jim and Maire a Glan, when the truth became known?

The squad would soon set off to Morrison's. Things would go well if once she got there, she assured herself. At present she wished that she had someone to confide in, somebody to whom she could tell her story. But in the squad there was none whom she could take into her confidence. The old women from Glenmornan and Frosses, brimful of a narrow, virtuous simplicity, were not the ones to sympathise with her; they would only condemn. If Gourock Ellen was here, Norah felt that she could sigh her misfortune into that woman's heart; but neither Gourock Ellen nor Annie had turned up for the last two years, and nobody knew what had become of them.

One day Norah felt that her secret was discovered. No one spoke of it; no one hinted at her condition, but all at once a curious feeling of restraint, of suspicion, charged the atmosphere of the barn and potato field. Whenever she asked a question those to whom she spoke fixed on her a stare of thinly veiled pity, not pity in essence but in design, before replying. Once or twice when ploughing through the fields, her head bent upon her work, she glanced round covertly to see the eyes of everybody in the squad fixed on her. No one spoke and all silently resumed their work when she looked at them. The silence terrified and crushed the girl. 'How much do they know?' she asked herself. That afternoon as she ploughed her way through the wet fields Micky's Jim came up and stood behind her. Instinctively she knew that he was going to speak and she waited his words in fear and trembling.

'Norah Ryan,' he said, and his words came out very slowly, 'who is to blame? Is it –'

Jim bent down, lifted a potato which she had passed over, threw it into the barrel and left the sentence unfinished.

It was Friday, the day on which the weekly wages of the party were paid. That night, when Norah received her money, she stole away from the squad intending to call on Alec Morrison.

II

It was the last day of August. The swallows and swifts circled above Norah's head and from time to time swept down over the sodden pastures where the farm cattle were grazing. The birds snapped greedily at the awkward crane-flies that were now rising on their great September flights.

Morrison's farm was twenty miles distant, and not wanting to spend the money which she had earned at her work, Norah travelled all night long. In the morning she found that she had lost her way and had to retrace her steps for full seven miles in order to regain her former course. At a wayside post office she sent half the money in her possession home to her mother. Late in the evening, feeling footsore and very weary, she came to the farm. Although she had not eaten food since leaving the squad she did not feel in the least hungry. Now and again dizziness seized her, however, and a sharp pain kept tapping as if with a hammer in her head.

'Everything will be all right now,' she said as she saw the lights of the farm glowing through the haze of the evening, but for all that she said the grave doubts which weighed upon her could not be shaken away. She entered the farmyard. A few stars were out in the sky, a low wind swept round the newly built hayrick and the scent of hay filled her nostrils. Alec would surely be at home. She uttered the word 'Alec' aloud; she had never given it utterance in his presence, she recollected, and wondered why she thought of that now.

The windows of the house were lighted up, and a long stream of light quivered out into the darkness. Norah approached the door, stood for a moment looking at the shiny brass knocker but refrained from lifting it. She was very frightened; the heart within her fluttered like a little bird that struggles violently against the bars of the cage in which it is imprisoned. One frail white hand was slowly lifted to the knocker; between the girl's fingers it felt very cold and she let it go without moving it. A great weariness had gripped her limbs, and her hand, heavy and dead, seemed as if it did not belong to her.

She came away from the door and approached the window. She could hear loud laughter from inside and somebody was playing on the piano. A dark blind hid the interior of the room from her view, but the light streaming out showed where the blind had been displaced at one corner, and pressing her brow against the pane Norah looked in.

The piano suddenly ceased; a frail shadow came between the light and the window; then a young and beautiful girl passed like a vision across the stretch of room open to the watcher's eyes. Norah's glance took in the girl for a moment; she noticed a fair head firmly poised, a small hand raised to brush back the tresses that fell down over a white brow. Even as the small hand was raised, a hand, larger, but almost as white, reached out and the fingers of the girl were gripped in a firm embrace.

Norah started violently, hitting her head sharply against the window-pane, and with difficulty restraining the cry that rose to her lips. The hand, white as a woman's almost, with the glittering ring on the middle finger, how well she knew it! And who was the fair girl, the fleeting and beautiful vision on whom she looked in from the cold and darkness of the night? Norah did not know, but instinctively she felt rising in her heart a great resentment against the woman in the room. Hatred filled her soul; her breath came sharply through her nostrils and a mist gathered before her eyes.

'I'm not goin' to cry!' she said defiantly, and began to weep silently even as she spoke.

A withered husk of moon crept up the sky; a dying wind moaned feebly on the roof overhead and on the ground beneath the girls' feet; a blundering moth struck sharply against her face, fell to the ground, rose slowly and as slowly disappeared. All around was the vast breathing silence of the infinite, the mystery of the world.

Norah looked into the room again and old Farmer Morrison was facing her, a long white pipe in his mouth and a starched collar under his chin. A broad grin overspread his face, and he looked like a fat, serious frog that had suddenly begun to smile. The upturned end of the blind slowly fluttered down and the whole interior of the room was hidden from the girl's eyes.

'Here am I out in the cold, and everyone is happy inside,' said the poor girl, pressing her hand tightly against her breast as she spoke. 'What was I doin' atall, atall, when I was here before? How I call to mind that night of all nights, a dear night to me! And it is forever written red in my soul … There he's in there and in there is another girl – not me. I'm out here in the cold … Mother of God! What am I to do?'

Norah went back from the window, caring nothing for the noise she made; caring little for what might now happen to her. Her face twitched, her breath stressed through her nostrils, her shoulders rose slowly and fell rapidly. The breeze gathered strength; it swept as if in a light passion around the farmyard and caused the girl's skirts to cling closely about her legs. She leant for support against the shed in which Micky's Jim and his squad had taken up their quarters so often. How bare and lonely the place looked now! Somewhere in the far corner a rat was gnawing at the woodwork with its sharp teeth; presently it ran out into the open, moving along rapidly, but as softly as a piece of velvet trailed on polished wood.

At that moment an intense and sudden revulsion of feeling took place within Norah. She was filled with a strange dislike for everything and everybody. A great change began to operate in her soul. In one vivid flash the whole world lay as if naked before her. Man lived for pleasure only; he had no thought for others; he cared only for himself, his passions and desires. What had she been doing all her life? Working for others, slaving that others might be happy. She worked to bring money to the landlord (ah! the dresses that the landlord's daughters wore!), to Farley McKeown (ah! the lady that got sixty thousand pounds to become his wife!), and to the priest (ah! the big mansion and the many rooms!). At this awful moment she dared not go to one of her people for help. Even her mother would give her the cold glance if she went home; she might shut the very door in her daughter's face. There was nobody to care for her – but even at that moment she recollected Gourock Ellen and Sheila Carrol, and felt that in these two women great wells of sympathy were open and at these she might refresh her weary soul.

Before her for an instant the world lay exposed to its very core; then as if by a falling curtain the sight was hidden again from her eyes and she found herself, a lonely little girl, leaning against the cold wall, her head sunk on her breast and her numb fingers, that almost lacked feeling, pressing against the rough masonry of the shed. A great wave of self-pity surged through the girl and she burst into tears.

She took no heed of the voice near her, did not see the dark forms which stood beside her, and only started violently and looked round when a hand was laid upon her shoulder. Two persons, a man and a woman, were looking at her. But even then in the terrible isolation of her own thoughts she took little heed of the strangers. She gazed at them vacantly for a moment, then turned towards the wall again as if nothing interested her but the bleak shed and the rats squeaking in the corner. When, after a moment, the strange woman ventured to speak, Norah looked round in surprise. She had forgotten all about the two people. Recollection of having seen them before came to her; they were the man and woman that had made such an impression on Morrison when he viewed them sleeping in the pigsty.

'What's wrong with ye?' asked the woman in a not unkindly voice. Norah could detect the odour of whisky in her breath and concluded that both the man and woman were drunk.

'Poor girl!' said the man when Norah did not answer. He looked closely at her and seemed to understand her plight. 'Poor lassie!' he repeated … 'Where's yer folk? Ah, I know who ye are, for I saw ye before. Ye were here with the tattie diggers last year, weren't ye?'

'Come doon to the shed with us,' said the woman. 'It's warmer there than here.'

The woman took the girl gently but firmly by the hand and led her into the sty in which herself and the man lived. Norah made no protest and followed the woman without a word. In the dwelling-place of the man and woman it was very dark and rats were scampering all over the place.

'Jean,' said the man on hearing the scurrying in the corner, 'rats!'

'Last night they ate all our food,' said the woman.

'Last night, Jean?' interrogated the man.

'The night before,' the woman corrected.

The man drew a match from his pocket, rubbed it on his trousers and lit a candle stuck in the neck of a black bottle which stood on the floor. Near it a small pile of wood, hemmed with a few lumps of coal, was ready for lighting. To this the man applied the match and in a few minutes the fire was burning brightly. A dark smoke rose to the roof, which was broken in several places; something small like a bird fluttered out from the rafters and whirred in the air above.

'Jean,' said the man, 'a blind bat!'

'Sit doon here, lass,' said the woman, drawing forward a splintered chest and placing it beside Norah. 'We'll gie ye somethin' to eat in a meenit. Are ye hungry?'

'Not hungry,' said Norah, sitting down on the box, 'but dry.'

'This is what ye need,' said the man, drawing a bottle from his pocket and handing it to the girl.

'I don't drink,' said Norah. 'I've the pledge.'

'Jean,' said the man, looking at his wife and pointing to a tin porringer which lay on the ground beside him, 'water.'

The woman went out and returned in a few minutes with a porringer of water which she handed to Norah, who drank deeply.

'Jean,' said the man, uncorking the bottle which he held in his hand, 'drink!' The woman returned the bottle when she had drunk a mouthful.

'Jean, tea!'

The woman emptied the porringer from which Norah had drunk and went out again.

'She's a rare body that!' said the man to Norah when the woman clattered away through the darkness. 'I like her, I like her like – like –' he paused for a moment and bit the nail of his thumb; 'like blazes!' he concluded.

Norah looked round and took a sudden interest in the place. An instinctive liking for this man and woman crept into her soul. True they were both half-tipsy, and the man now and again without any apparent reason uttered words which were not nice to hear.

'Yer wife is a kindly woman,' said Norah, breaking through the barriers of her silence.

'Wife!' said the man and laughed a trifle awkwardly. 'Wife! Well, I suppose it is all the same.'

The man was a stunted little fellow, unshaven and ragged, but his shoulders were very broad. The little finger of his left hand was missing and his toes peeped out through his boots. HIs teeth were stained a dirty yellow with tobacco juice.

'It's not much of a place, this,' he said. 'We never have much company here 'cept the bat that lives in the rafters and the wind that comes in by the door and the stars that look down through the roof.'

He laughed loudly, but seeing that Norah did not join in his laughter, he suddenly became silent. Norah's eyes again roved round the place. It was dirty and squalid, well in keeping with the occupants. A potato barrel stood in one corner; beside it was a pile of straw covered with a few dirty bags. This was the bed. The guttering candle gleamed feebly in the corner and the grease ran down the bottle. Overhead the bat was still fluttering madly, hitting against the joists every moment.

The woman re-entered the shed and placed the porringer of water on the fire; the man went to the barrel, lifted the bag which served as a cover, and brought out little packets of food.

'Can I be of any help to you?' asked Norah, rising to her feet.

'Ye're tired and worn,' said the woman.

'Jean,' said the man, 'don't let the lass work.'

Norah sat down again. A box came from the dark recess of the room; the woman wiped it with her apron and laid it on the floor by the fire. The man placed a loaf, some sugar, a piece of butter, and a tin mug on the table.

'Donal,' said the woman suddenly, 'milk.'

The man went out and returned in about ten minutes with some warm milk at the bottom of a large wooden pail.

'We just get a wee drop from the farmer's cows when there's nobody about,' he explained.

When tea was ready the girl was handed the tin porringer filled to the brim; the pannikin in which the tea was made served the other two, both drinking from the vessel in turn. Norah ate the bread greedily; she felt very hungry. The man and woman had recourse to the bottle once more when the meal was finished.

'Where is the tattie squad now?' asked Donal.

'Down at G— farm, near S—,' answered Norah.

'Donal, dinna speir,' said the woman in a sharp voice.

'Jean, haud yer tongue,' answered the man, but he did not press the question when he noticed a startled look steal into Norah's eyes.

'Things maun be some way,' said the woman in a voice of consolation, though she seemed to be addressing nobody in particular, 'and things will happen.'

'There's great goings-on in there,' said Donal, pointing his thumb over his shoulder in the direction of the farmhouse. 'Morrison's son has been and engaged to a young lady. Happen that ye may have seen the young man when ye were here afore.'

Norah looked at Donal straight in the eyes and he felt that she was seeing through him into a world far beyond. The man looked at Jean; their glances met and a message flashed between them.

'Him!' said the woman.

'The feckless rascal!' exclaimed the man.

He threw another lump of coal into the fire, kicked the others into a riotous blaze, shook up the straw in the corner and spread out the blankets and bags.

'Bed, lassie,' he said to Norah, pointing at the straw.

'But where'll yerselves sleep?' asked the girl.

'Jean, where'll we doss?'

'By the fire,' answered the woman.

'But it'll be wrong of me,' said Norah; then stopped and left the words that rose to her tongue unuttered. Sleep was stealing over her; she shut her eyes. A gentle arm was laid on her shoulders; she rose, because a voice suggested that she should rise, and afterwards found herself lying on the bed of straw.

A vision of a lighted window came to her; she was looking in at the man she loved and his lips were pressing those of another woman. Then scenes and objects vague and indistinct passed before her eyes, big dark shadows mustered together in the centre of the roof above her, then other shadows from all sides rushed in and joined together, trembled and became blended in complete obscurity. Norah fell asleep.

'Poor lassie!' said Donal, throwing himself down on the floor by the fire, 'poor lassie!'

'God have pity on her,' said the woman; 'and her sic a comely lass!'

CHAPTER 23

COMPLICATIONS

I

On the night of Norah's arrival at the steading Alec Morrison slept well, but wakened with the dawn and sat up betimes. He was very pleased with himself and his position at the bank; things had gone well, his father had doubled his allowance, and on the strength of that the young man had become engaged.

He had broken with the little girl in Glasgow; for while admiring her good looks he deplored her lack of intelligence. She spent a great deal of her time in dressing herself, and Morrison knew that there would come a day when dresses would not please, when a husband would require something more worthy of respect, something more enduring than pretty looks and gaudy garments. Besides this drawback there was another. The girl, who took her good looks from her mother, long dead, had a grasping, greedy father whom nobody could love or admire. Morrison had met him twice and disliked him immensely. He was a dirty little man and generally had three days' growth of hair on his chin. When shaking hands his thumb described a curious backward turn, forming into a loop like one of those on the letter S. The daughter had the same peculiarity. Before meeting the father this movement of the girl's thumb amused Morrison; afterwards it disgusted him. Finally he took his departure and again got into tow with Ellen Keenans, the live woman with advanced views ten years ahead of her age. Morrison fell in love easily, indifferently almost. He was an attractive young man, well built and muscular, who cultivated the art of dress with considerable care. All good-looking women fascinated him, but none held him captive for very long. He had become engaged to the girl with the advanced ideas and took her to his people's home. The old farmer liked her but did not understand many of the things of which she spoke. That was not to be wondered at, seeing that he was a plain, blunt man, although a gentleman farmer, and the girl was ten years ahead of her time.

II

Alec Morrison, the sleep gone entirely from his eyes, his face a little red after shaving, came downstairs to the breakfast-room. Ellen Keenans was sitting on the sofa, a book in her hand.

'Up already, dear?' asked Morrison, and bent to kiss the girl. She laid down the book which she had been reading and met the kiss with her lips.

'The country life is so quiet, so refreshing; one cannot have too much of it,' she said, drumming idly with her fingers on the edge of the sofa.

'What are you reading, dear?' the young man asked.

'Kautsky's *Ethics of Materialist Conception of History*.'

'Rather a big thing to tackle before breakfast.'

She cast a look of reproof at the young man, lifted the book from the table, then, as if something occurred to her, laid it down again.

'You haven't read it, I bet,' she said; then before he could answer: 'You promised last night to let me see some queer people –'

'Wrecks of the social system.'

'– who live on this farm.'

'An old man and woman,' said Morrison. 'A quaint pair they are, stunted and seedy. They seem to have no souls, but I suppose deep down within them there is some eternal goodness, some fundamental virtue.'

'Who are you quoting?' asked the girl, getting to her feet. 'Where are these two people?'

'In an outhouse near by,' he told her. 'It's terrible the abyss to which some people sink,' he went on. 'How many of these derelicts might be saved if some restraining hand was reached out to help them, if some charitable soul would take pity on them.'

'When did you begin to look upon charity as a means of remedying social evils?' asked the girl almost fiercely. 'Charity is a bribe paid to the maltreated so that they may hold their tongues.'

Morrison, as was his custom when the girl spoke in that manner, became silent.

'In here,' he said when they arrived at the dilapidated door of the pigsty.

'In there?' questioned the girl and looked at Morrison.

Morrison entered with rather an important air; he was showing a new world to his fair companion. The girl hesitated for a moment on the threshold, then followed the young man into the dark interior.

Donal and Jean were seated at the fire drinking tea from the same can. On a small and dirty board which lay on the ground between them a chunk of dry bread and a little lump of butter could be seen. The two occupants of the sty took very little notice of the visitors; the man said 'Good morning' gruffly, the woman looked critically at the girl's dress then went on with her meal.

'It must be cold here,' said the young girl, looking curiously round and noticing a streak of grey daylight stealing through the roof.

'Jean, is it cold here?' asked the man by the fire, biting the end of his crust.

'As cold as the grave,' answered the woman.

Ellen Keenans looked closely at the speaker. The broken nose, almost on a level with her face, the pock-marked flesh of the cheeks and chin, the red eyelids, the watery, expressionless eyes filled the young lady with nauseous horror. In the renovated society of which Ellen Keenans drcamt, this woman would be entirely out of place, just as much as her sweetheart and herself with their well-made clothing, their soft leather shoes and gold rings, were out of place here. And these two people, the man who wolfed up his bread like a dog and the woman with the disfigured face, might have something great and good in their natures. Alec had given such sentiments voice often. How noble-minded he was, she thought.

The door of the building faced east. The early sun, rising over a bank of grey clouds, suddenly beamed forth with splendid ray and lit up the dark interior of the sty. This beautiful beam disclosed what the darkness had hidden, the dirt and squalor of the place.

The floor, on which crawled numberless wood lice and beetles, was indented with holes filled with filthy smelling water, and the blank walls were literally covered with reddish cockroaches. The sunlight beamed on a spider's web hanging from the roof; the thin silky threads were covered with dead insects. Rats had burrowed into the base

of the walls and the whole building was permeated with
an overpowering and unhealthy odour. Ellen Keenans
glanced up at the joists where the sun-rays struck them,
then down the stretch of dark slimy wall, down, down to
the floor, and there, in bold relief against the darkness, she
saw in all its youthful beauty the face of a sleeping girl.
Ellen turned an enquiring glance to the woman by the fire;
then to Morrison, whose face wore a troubled expression.

'Who have you here, Donal?' asked the young man.

'A lass that we found greetin' outside your door last
night,' said the man, this time not appealing to Jean for an
answer. 'Happen that ye know her?'

The two by the fire looked at the young couple. The
woman's watery eyes took on a new expression; they
seemed suddenly to have become charged with
condemnation and contempt.

'Is she one of Jim Scanlon's squad?' asked Morrison.
Although putting the question he had recognised
Norah instantly, and now he wished to be away. Donal
and Jean looked suddenly terrible in his eyes; the pity
he felt for them a moment ago now gave place to a fear
for himself. Odd little waves of expression were passing
over the woman's face and in her eyes he read a terrible
accusation.

'It was all her fault, not mine,' he muttered under his
breath. 'That night and the dog howling and the stars out
above us ... But it was all her own fault. Why did she
keep following me about? She might have known that I
could never have ... We'll go back to the house now,' he
said aloud to Ellen Keenans. 'We've seen all that is to be
seen.'

The girl glanced at him interrogatively, curious. 'Who
is she?' came the question.

'Ye'll soon know,' said the woman by the fire, rising and going to the shake-down by the wall. 'Wake up, lass!' she cried to the sleeper.

Norah rose in bed, her mind groping darkly with her surroundings. She had been dreaming of home and wakened with a vivid remembrance of her mother's cabin still in her mind. The light of the sun shone full in her face and she lifted her hand up to shield her eyes. Then in a flash it was borne to her where she had spent the night. Several dark objects stood between her and the door; these developed into a grouping of persons, in the midst of which Alec Morrison stood out definitely. Norah, fully dressed, just as she had gone to sleep, moved towards him.

'Alex Morrison, I've come back,' she said, paused and looked at the girl beside him, then began to talk hurriedly. 'I left the squad the day before yesterday; I travelled all the dark night and lost me way, for me mind would be busy with the thoughts that were coming to me… . Last night I came to yer door… . Alex Morrison, why are ye so scared lookin'? Sure ye're not afraid of me!'

Morrison was in a very awkward fix, and this he confessed to himself. He never intended to marry the girl and never for a moment thought that the adventure of Christmas Eve would lead him into such a predicament. 'And you are as well rid of her,' some evil voice whispered in his ear. 'Look at her as she is now. Is she a suitable companion for you?' Morrison gazed covertly at the girl. Her hair, which had not been combed for two days, hung over her eyes and ears in tangled tufts; even the face, which still retained all its splendid beauty, was blackened by the dust which had fallen from the roof during the night.

'Are ye goin' to do the right thing to the girl?' asked Donal. 'It's the only way out of it if ye have the spirit of a man in ye.'

Morrison gazed blankly at the man, then at Norah. A fierce and almost animal look came into her eyes as she faced him.

'I'll do the right thing,' he said in a hoarse voice and turned and went out of the building, Ellen Keenans following at his heels. Norah watched them go, making no effort to detain them. When they went out she tottered towards the wall, reaching upwards with her hands as if wanting to touch resignation.

'It's all over!' she exclaimed. 'It's him that has the black heart and will be goin' to do the right thing with little bits of money. The right thing!' She leant against the cockroach-covered wall, her little voice raised in loud protest against the monstrous futility of existence.

III

An hour later Morrison returned to the sty, carrying gold in his pocket but feeling very awkward. He and Ellen had quarrelled. When they went out into the open from the sty she turned on him fiercely.

'How many of these souls might be saved if some restraining hand was reached out to help them!' she quoted sneeringly.

'But Ellen, it was more the girl's fault than mine. And when one is young one may do many things that he's sorry for afterwards. And I'll do the right thing for the girl.'

'The right thing?' queried Ellen Keenans, and a troubled expression settled on her face. 'But you cannot. It's impossible. To two –'

'I'm wealthy now, you know. My allowance –'

'Oh, I see,' said the girl and, strangely enough, a suggestion of relief blended with her voice.

'I suppose you'll think me a prig, Ellen,' said the young man. 'But it wasn't altogether my fault, neither was it the girl's, I suppose. I suppose it was fate.... The girl won't be highly sensitive. I've seen ones working here on the farm, young women, and they made a slip. But it did not seem to affect them. And we all make mistakes, Ellen ...'

His speech came to an end and he left her and went towards the house; an hour later he re-entered the sty.

The woman with the pock-marked face looked at him angrily. Norah sat beside her on the upturned box, one arm hanging loosely by her side, the other resting on her knees, the hand pressed against her chin and a tapering finger stretching along her cheek. The old woman had given Norah a broken comb to dress her hair and now it hung to her waist in long, wavy tresses. But in the middle of the work she had dropped the comb and fallen into a deep reverie.

'I've come to see you,' Morrison began with an abruptness which showed that he wanted to hurry over a distasteful job. He was going to make atonement for his sin, and atonement represented a few pieces of gold, a few months' denial of the luxuries which this gold could procure. He looked straight at Norah's bowed head, taking no notice of the other occupants of the hovel.

'I've come to see you,' he repeated, but the girl paid no heed to him. He drew an envelope from his pocket, shook it so that the money within made a loud rattle, and placed it on her lap. The girl roused herself abruptly as if stung, lifted the envelope and looked at the man. Fearing that she was going to fling the terrible packet in his face, he put up his hand to shield himself. Norah smiled coldly and then

handed him back the packet, which he had not the courage
to refuse nor the audacity to return. The girl seemed to be
performing some task that had no interest for her,
something out and beyond the scope of her life. For a
moment Morrison felt it in him to pity her, but deep down
in his heart he pitied himself more.

'I thought ... I would like ... You know that ...' he
stammered. 'I'll go away just now,' he said in a low voice.

'You'd better,' said Donal, crouching by the fire like a
cat ready to spring.

Alex Morrison left the sty. At the hour of noon Norah
bade goodbye to Donal and Jean and set off for Glasgow,
where she intended to call on Sheila Carrol, the beansho.

CHAPTER 24

THE RAT-PIT

I

The address on the letter which Norah received from Sheila Carrol was '47 Ann Street, Cowcaddens', but shortly after the letter had been written the Glasgow Corporation decided that 47 was unfit for human habitation, and those who lived there were turned out to the streets.

It was late in the evening of the day on which she left Jean and Donal that Norah came to No. 47, to find the place in total darkness. She groped her way up a narrow alley to the foot of a stair and there suddenly stepped on a warm human body lying on the ground.

'What the devil! – Ah, ye're choking me, an old person that never done no one no harm,' croaked a wheezy voice, apparently a woman's, under Norah's feet. 'I only came in oot of the cauld, lookin' for a night's shelter. Hadn't a bawbee for the Rat-pit. Beg pardon! I'm sorry; I'll go away at once; I'll go now. For the love of heaven don't gie me up to the cops. I'm only a old body and I hadn't a bawbee of my own. I couldn't keep walkin' on all night. Beg pardon,

I'm only a old body and I hadn't a kirk siller piece[1] for the Rat-pit!'

'I'm sorry, but I didn't know that there was anyone here,' said Norah, peering through the darkness. 'I'm a stranger, good woman.'

'Ye're goin' to doss here too,' croaked the voice from the ground.

'I'm lookin' for a friend,' said Norah. 'Maybe ye'll know her – Sheila Carrol. She lives here.'

'Nobody lives here,' said the woman, shuffling to her feet. 'Nobody but the likes of me and ones like me. No human being is supposed to live here. I had at one time a room on the top of the landin', the cheapest room in Glasgow it was. Can't get another one like it now and must sleep out in the snow. Out under the scabby sky and the wind and the rain. It wasn't healthy for people to sleep here, so someone said, and we were put out. Think of that, and me havin' the cheapest room in the Cowcaddens. If the cops find me here, it's quod. Wha be ye lookin' for?'

'A friend, Sheila Carrol.'

'Never heard of her.' The voice, almost toneless, seemed to be forcing its way through some thick fluid in the speaker's throat. The darkness of the alley was intense and the women were hidden from one another.

'Everybody that stayed here has gone, and I don't know where they are,' the old woman continued. 'Don't know at all. Ye dinna belong to Glesga?' she croaked.

'No, decent woman.'

'By yer tongue ye'll be a young girl.'

'I am.'

[1]Threepenny piece.

'Mind ye, I'm a cute one and I ken everything. It's not everyone that could tell what ye are by yer tongue. Are ye a stranger?'

'I am,' answered Norah. 'I was never in Glasgow before.'

'I knew that too,' said the old woman. 'And ye want lodgin's for the night? Then the Rat-pit's the place; a good decent place it is – threepence a night for a bunk. Beg pardon, but maybe ye'll have a kid's eye (threepence) extra to spare for an old body. Come along with me and I'll show the way. I'm a cute one and I know everything. Ye couldn't ha'e got into better hands than mine if ye're a stranger in Glasgow.'

They went out into a dimly lighted lane and Norah took stock of her new friend. The woman was almost bent double with age; a few rags covered her body, she wore no shoes, and a dusty, grimy clout was tied round one of her feet. As if conscious of Norah's scrutiny she turned to the girl.

'Ah! Ye wouldn't think, would ye, that I had once the finest room in the Cowcaddens, the finest – at its price?'

'The Rat-pit's a lodgin' place for women,' the old creature croaked after an interval. 'There are good beds there; threepence a night ye pay for them. Beg pardon, but maybe ye'll pay for my bunk for the night. That's just how I live; it's only one night after another in my life. Beg pardon, but that's how it is.' She seemed to be apologising for the crime of existing. 'But ye'll maybe have a kid's eye to spare for my bunk?' she asked.

'All right, decent woman,' said Norah.

'What do they cry ye?'

'Norah Ryan.'

'A pretty name; and my name's Maudie Stiddart,' said the old woman.

II

Ten minutes later the two women were seated in the kitchen of the Rat-pit, frying a chop which Norah had bought on their way to the lodging house.

The place was crowded with women of all ages, some young, children almost, their hair hanging down their backs, and the blouses that their pinched breasts could not fill sagging loose at the bosom. There were six or seven of these girls, queer weedy things that smoked cigarettes and used foul words whenever they spoke. The face of one was pitted with small-pox; another had both eyes blackened, the result of a fight; a third, clean of face and limb, was telling how she had just served two months in prison for importuning men on the streets. Several of the elder females were drunk; two fought in the kitchen, pulling handfuls of hair from one another's heads. Nobody interfered; when the struggle came to an end the combatants sat down together and warmed their hands at the stove. At this juncture a barefooted woman, with clay caked brown behind her ankles and a hairy wart on her chin, came up to Norah.

'Ye're a stranger here,' she said.

'I am, decent woman.'

'Ye're Irish, too, for I ken by yer talk,' said the female. 'And ye've got into trouble.'

She pointed at the girl with a long, crooked finger, and Norah blushed.

'Dinna be ashamed of it,' said the woman; then turning to Maudie Stiddart she enquired: 'And ye're here too, are ye? I thought ye were dead long ago. Jesus! but some people can stick it out. There's no killin' of 'em!'

'Oh, ye're a blether, Mary Martin,' said Maudie, turning the chop over on the stove. 'Where are ye workin' now?'

'On the free coup outside Glesga.'

'The free coup?' asked the young girl who had just left prison, lighting a cigarette. 'What's that atall?'

'The place to where the dung and dust and dirt of a town is carried away and throwed down,' Mary Martin explained. 'Sometimes lumps of coal and pieces of metal are flung down there. These I pick up and sell to people and that's how I make my living'.'

'Is that how you do?' asked the girl with a shrug of her shoulders.

'Everyone isn't young like you,' said Mary, sitting down on a bench near the stove. The girl laughed vacantly, tried to make a ring of the cigarette smoke, was unable to do so, and walked away. Mary Martin turned to Maudie and whispered something to her.

'Ah, puir lass!' exclaimed Maudie.

'And the one to blame was a toff, too!' said Mary. 'They're all alike, and the good dress often hides a dirty hide.'

'Beg pardon, but have ye got anything to ate?' asked Maudie.

'Nothin' the night,' answered Mary. 'Only made the price of my bed for my whole day's work.'

'Will ye ate something with us?' asked Norah.

'Thank ye,' said Mary Martin, and the three women drew closer to the chop that was roasting on the stove.

III

The beds in the Rat-pit, forty in all, were in a large chamber upstairs, and each woman had a bed to herself. The lodgers undressed openly, shoved their clothes under the mattresses and slid into bed. One sat down to unlace her boots and fell asleep where she sat; another, a young girl of seventeen or eighteen, fell against the leg of the bed and sank into slumber, her face turned to the roof and her mouth wide open. The girl who had been in prison became suddenly unwell and burst into tears; nobody knew what she was weeping about and nobody enquired.

Maudie, Mary, and Norah slept in three adjoining beds, the Irish girl in the centre. The two older women dropped off to sleep the moment their heads touched the pillows; Norah lay awake gazing at the flickering shadows cast by the solitary gas-jet on the roof of the room. The heat was oppressive, suffocating almost, and not a window in the place was open. Women were still coming in, and only half the bunks in the room were yet occupied. Most of the newcomers were drunk; some sat down or fell on the floor and slept where they had fallen, others threw themselves in on top of the bed and lay there with their clothes on. An old woman whose eye had been blackened in a fight downstairs started to sing 'Annie Laurie', but forgetting what followed the first verse, relapsed into silence.

Norah began to pray under her breath to the Virgin, but had only got half through with her prayer when a shriek from the bed on her left startled her. Maudie was sitting upright, yelling at the top of her voice. 'Cannot ye let an old body be?' she cried. 'I'm only wantin' a night's doss at the foot of the stairs. That's not much for an old un to ask, is it? Holy Jesus! I cannot be let alone for a minute. Beg pardon; I'm goin' away, but ye might let me stay here, and me only an old woman!'

Maudie opened her watery eyes and stared round. Beads of sweat stood out on her forehead, and her face – red as a crab – looked terrifying in the half-light of the room.

'Beg pardon,' she croaked, and her voice had a sound like the breaking of bones. 'Beg pardon. I'm only an old woman and I never did nobody no harm!'

She sank down again, pulled the blankets over her shoulders and fell asleep.

Fresh arrivals came in every minute, staggered wearily to their bunks and threw themselves down without undressing. About midnight a female attendant, a young, neat girl with a pleasing face, entered, surveyed the room, helped those who lay on the floor into bed, turned down the gas and went away.

Slumber would not come to Norah. All night she lay awake, listening to the noise of the dust-carts on the pavement outside, the chiming of church clocks, the deep breathing of the sleepers all around her, and the sudden yells from Maudie's bunk as the woman started in her sleep protesting against some grievance or voicing some ancient wrong.

The daylight was stealing through the grimy window when Norah got up and proceeded to dress. A deep quietness, broken only by the heavy breathing of the women, lay over the whole place. The feeble light of daybreak shone on the ashen faces of the sleepers, on the naked body of a well-made girl who had flung off all her clothing in a troubled slumber, on Mary Martin's clay-caked legs that stuck out from beneath the blankets, on Maudie Stiddart's wrinkled, narrow brow beaded with sweat; on the faces of all the sleepers, the wiry and weakly, the fit and feeble, the light of new-born day rested. Suddenly old Mary turned in her sleep, then sat up.

'Where are ye goin' now?' she called to Norah.

'To look for a friend,' came the answer.

'A man?'

'A woman called Sheila Carrol is the one I'm lookin' for,' said Norah. 'I went to 47 Ann Street last night, for I had a letter from her there. But the place was closed up.'

'Sheila Carrol, they cry her, ye say?' said the old woman, getting out of bed. 'Maybe it's her that I ken. She came from Ireland with a little boy and she used to work with me at one time. A comely strong-boned wench she was. Came from Frosses, she once told me.'

'That's Sheila!'

'And she's left 47?'

'So I hear.'

'Then take my advice and try No. 46 and No. 48,' said Mary Martin; 'and also every close in the street. The people that lived in 47 will not gang far awa' from it. They'll be in the next close or thereabouts. What do they cry you, lass?' asked the old woman, slipping into her rags.

'Norah Ryan.'

'A pretty name it is, indeed. And have ye threepence to spare for my breakfast, Norah Ryan? I haven't a penny piece in all the wide world.'

Norah gave threepence of her hard-earned money to Mary, sorted her dress and stole out into the streets to search for Sheila Carrol.

CHAPTER 25

SHEILA CARROL

I

Norah travelled through the streets all day, looking for her friend and fearing that every eye was fixed on her, that everybody knew the secret which she tried to conceal. Her feet were sore, her breath came in short, sudden gasps as she took her way into dark closes and climbed creaking stairs; and never were her efforts rewarded by success. Here in the poorer parts of the city, in the crooked lanes and straggling alleys, were dirt, darkness, and drunkenness. A thousand smells greeted the nostrils, a thousand noises grated on the ears; lights flared brightly in the beershops; fights started at the corners; ballad singers croaked out their songs; intoxicated men fell in the gutters; policemen stood at every turning, their helmets glistening, their faces calm, their eyes watchful. The evening had come and all was noise, hurry, and excitement.

'Isaac Levison, Pawnbroker; 2 Up,' Norah read on a plate outside the entrance of a close and went in.

'I wonder if Sheila will be here?' she asked herself, and smiled sadly as she called to mind the number of closes she had crawled into during the whole long trying day.

Dragging her feet after her, she made her way up the crooked stairs and rapped with her knuckles at a door on which the words 'Caretaker's office' were painted in black letters. A woman, with a string for a neck and wisps of red hair hanging over her face, poked out her head.

'Up yet,' was the answer when Norah asked if anybody named Sheila Carrol dwelt on the stairs.

'After all my searchin' she's here at last,' said the young woman. 'It's Sheila Carrol herself that's in the place.'

The beansho opened the door when she heard a rapping outside. She knew her visitor at once.

'Come in, Norah Ryan,' she said, catching the girl's hands and squeezing them tightly. 'It's good of ye to come. No one from Frosses, only Oiney Dinchy's gasair, have I seen here for a long while. But ye'll be tired, child?'

'It's in an ill way that I come to see ye, Sheila Carrol,' said Norah. 'It's an ill way, indeed it is,' and then, sitting down, she told her story quietly as if that which she spoke of did not interest her in any way.

'Poor child!' said Sheila, when the pitiful tale came to an end. 'Why has God put that burden on yer little shoulders? But there's no use in pining, Norah. Mind that, child!'

'I would like to die, Sheila Carrol,' said Norah, looking round the bare room, but not feeling in the least interested in what she saw. One chair, a bed, a holy water stoup, a little black crucifix from which the arms of the Christ had fallen away, an orange box on which lay a pair of scissors and a pile of cloth: that was all the room contained. A feeble fire burned in the grate and a battered oil-lamp threw a dim light over the compartment.

'I once had thoughts that were like that, meself,' said Sheila. She placed a little tin pannikin on the fire and fanned the flame with her apron. 'People face a terrible lot in body and in soul before they face death. That's the way God made us, child. We do be like grains of corn under a millstone, and everything but the breath of our bodies squeezed out of us. Sometimes I do be thinkin' that the word "hope" is blotted from me soul; but then after a wee while I do be happy in my own way again.'

'But did ye not find yer own burden hard to bear, Sheila?'

'Hard indeed, child, but it's trouble that makes us wise,' said the beansho, pouring tea into the pannikin that was now bubbling merrily. 'The father of me boy died on the sea and me goin' to be married to him when the season of Lent was by. The cold grey morning when the boat came in keel up on Dooey Strand was a hard and black one for me. Ah! the cold break of day; sorrow take it! The child came and I was not sorry at all, as the people thought I should be. He was like the man I loved, and if the bitin' tongues of the Frosses people was quiet I would be very happy, I would indeed, Norah! But over here in this country it was sore and bitter to me. I mind the first night that I stopped in Glasgow with the little boy. He was between my arms and I was lookin' out through the window of 47 at the big clock with the light inside of it. It was a lazy clock that night and I thought that the light of day would never put a colour on the sky. But the mornin' did come and many mornin's since then, and stone-cold they were too!'

Then Sheila told the story of her life in Scotland, and Norah, hardly realising what was spoken, listened almost dumbly, feeling at intervals the child within her moving restlessly, stretching out as if with a hand and pressing against her side, causing a quivering motion to run through her body.

Sheila's story was a pitiful one. When first she came to Glasgow she took an attic room at the top of a four-storeyed building and for this she paid a weekly rent of three shillings and sixpence.

''Twas the dirty place to live in, Norah, for all the smells and stinks of the houses down under came up to me,' said the woman. 'And three white shillin's and sixpence a week for that place that one wouldn't put pigs into! The houses away at home may be bad, but there's always the fresh air and no drunk men or bad women lyin' across yer door every time ye go outside. 47 was a rotten place; worse even than this, and this is bad. Look at the sheets and blankets on the bed behind ye, Norah, look at the colour of them and the writin' on them.'

Norah gazed at the bed and saw on every article of clothing, stamped in large blue letters, the words: 'STOLEN FROM JAMES MOFFAT'.

'That's because someone may steal the rags,' said Sheila. 'This room is furnished by the landlord, God forgive him for the furnishin' of it! And he's afraid that his tenants will run away and try to pawn the bedclothes. Lyin' under the blankets all night with STOLEN FROM JAMES MOFFAT writ on them is a quare way of sleepin'. But what can a woman like me do? And 47 was worse nor this; and the work! 'Twas beyond speakin' about!

'The first job I got was the finishin' of dongaree jackets, sewin' buttons on them, and things like that. I was up in the mornin' at six and went to bed the next mornin' at one, and hard at it all the time I wasn't sleepin'. Sunday was the same as any other day; always work, always the needle. I used to make seven shillin's a week; half of that went in rent and the other half kept meself and my boy. Talk about teeth growin' long with hunger at times when the work was none too plentiful! Sometimes, Norah –'

Sheila paused. Norah was listening intently, her lips a little apart, like a child's.

'Sometimes, Norah, I went out beggin' on the streets – me, a Frosses woman too,' Sheila resumed with a sigh. 'Then one night when I asked a gentleman for a few pence to buy bread he handed me over to the police. Said I was accostin' him. I didn't even know what it meant at the time; now – But I hope ye never know what it means … Anyway I was sent to jail for three weeks.'

'To jail, Sheila!' Norah exclaimed.

'True as God, child, and my boy left alone in that dirty attic. There was I not knowin' what was happenin' to him, and when I came out of prison I heard that the police had caught him wanderin' out in the streets and put him in a home. But I didn't see him; I was slapped into jail again.'

'What for, Sheila?'

'Child neglect, girsha,' said the woman, lifting her scissors and cutting fiercely at a strip of cloth as she spoke. 'I don't know how they made it out again' me, but the law is far beyond simple people like us. I was put in for three months that time and when I came out –'

A tear dropped from Sheila's eyes and fell on the cloth which lay on her lap.

'The little fellow, God rest his soul! was dead,' said the woman. 'Then I hadn't much to live for and I was like to die. But people can stand a lot one way and another, a terrible lot entirely. After that I thought of making shirts and I got a sewin' machine from a big firm on the instalment system. A shillin' a week I had to pay for the machine. I could have done well at the shirt-makin', but things seemed somehow to be again' me. On the sixth week I couldn't pay the shillin'. It was due on a Friday and Saturday was my own pay day. I prayed to the traveller to wait for the morrow, but he wouldn't, and took the machine away. 'Twas the big firm of – too, that did that. Think of it! them with their mills and their riches and me only a poor woman. Nor it wasn't as if I wasn't wantin' to pay neither. But that's the way of the world, girsha; the bad, black world, cold as the rocks on Dooey Strand it is, aye, and colder.

'Sometimes after the sewin' machine went I used to go out on the streets and sing songs, and at that sort of work, not at all becomin' for a Frosses woman, I could always make the price of a bunk in the Rat-pit, the place where ye were last night, Norah. Ah! how often have I had my night's sleep there! Then again I would come back to 47 and start some decent work that wasn't half as easy or half as well paid as the singin' of songs. So I went from one thing to another and here I am at this very minute.'

Sheila paused in her talk but not in the work which she had just started.

'Not much of a room, this one, neither,' she remarked, casting her eye on the bed, but not missing a stitch in her sewing as she spoke. 'Four shillin's I pay for it a week and it's supposed to hold two people. Outside the door you can see that ticketed up, "To hold two adults", like the price marked on a pair of secondhand trousers. I'm all alone here; only the woman, old Meg, that stops in the room behind this one, passes through here on her way to work. But ye'll stay here with me now, two Frosses people in the one room, so to speak.'

'What kind of work are ye doin' here?' asked Norah, pointing to the cloth which Sheila was sewing.

'Shirt-finishin',' Sheila replied. 'For every shirt there's two rows of feather-stitchin', eight buttonholes and seven buttons sewed on, four seams and eight fasteners. It takes me over an hour to do each shirt and the pay is a penny farthing. I can make about fifteen pence a day, but out of that I have to buy my own thread. But ye'll be tired, child, listenin' to me clatterin' here all night.'

'I'm not tired listenin' to ye at all, but it's sorrow that's with me because life was so hard on ye,' said Norah. 'Everything was black again' ye.'

'One gets used to it all,' said Sheila with the air of resignation which sits on the shoulders of those to whom the keys of that delicious mystery known as happiness are forever lost. 'One gets used to things, no matter how hard they be, and one doesn't like to die.'

But now Norah listened almost heedlessly. Thoughts dropped into her mind and vanished with the frightful rapidity of things falling into empty space; and memories of still more remote things, faint, far away and almost undefined, were wafted against her soul.

The girl fell into a heavy slumber.

II

In the morning she awoke to find herself lying in bed, the blankets on which the blue letters STOLEN FROM JAMES MOFFAT were stamped wrapped tightly around her, and Sheila Carrol lying by her side. For a moment she wondered vaguely how she had got into the bunk, then raising herself on her elbow, she looked round the room.

The apartment was a very small one, with one four-paned window and two doors, one of which led, as Norah knew, out to the landing, and one, as she guessed, into the room belonging to old Meg, the woman whom Sheila had spoken of the night before. The window was cracked and crooked, the floor and doors creaked at every move, a musty odour of decay and death filled the whole place. A heap of white shirts was piled on the orange box that stood in the middle of the floor, one shirt, the 'finishing' of which had not been completed, lay on an old newspaper beside the fireplace. It looked as if Sheila had become suddenly tired in the midst of her feather-stitching and had slipped into bed. She was now awake and almost as soon as she had opened her eyes was out of the blankets, had wrapped a few rags round her bony frame and was busy at work with her needle. Sleep for the woman was only a slight interruption of her eternal routine.

'Have a wee wink more,' she cried to Norah, 'and I'll just make a good warm cup of tay for ye when I get this row finished. Little rogue of all the world! ye're tired out and worn!'

Norah smiled sadly, got up, dressed herself, and going down on her knees by the bedside, said her prayers.

'It's like Frosses again,' said Sheila, when the girl's prayers came to an end. 'Even seein' ye there on yer knees takes back old times. But often I do be thinkin' that prayin' isn't much good. There was old Doalty Farrel; ye mind him talkin' about politics the night yer father, God rest him! was underboard. Well, Doalty was a very holy man, as ye know yerself, and he used to go down on his knees when out in the very fields and pray and pray. Well and good; he went down one day on his knees in the snow and when he got home he had a pain in one of his legs. That night it was in his side, in the mornin' Doalty was dead. Gasair Oiney Dinchy was tellin' me all about it.'

'But they say in Frosses that God was so pleased with Doalty that He took him up to heaven before his time,' said Norah.

'But it's not many that like to go to heaven before their time,' Sheila remarked as she rose from her seat and set about to kindle the fire. At the same moment the door leading in from the compartment opened, and an old woman, very ugly, her teeth worn to the gums, the stumps unhealthily yellow, her eyes squinting and a hairy wart growing on her right cheek, entered the room.

'Good morra, Meg,' said Sheila, who was fanning the fire into flame with her apron. 'Are ye goin' to yer work?'

'Goin' to my work,' replied Meg and turned her eyes to Norah. 'A friend, I see,' she remarked.

'A countrywoman of my own,' said Sheila.

'Are ye new to Glesga?' Meg asked Norah, who was gazing absently out of the window.

'I have only just come here,' said the girl.

'Admirin' the view!' remarked Meg with a wheezy laugh as she took her place beside the girl at the window. 'A fine sight to look at, that. Dirty washin' hung out to dry; dirty houses; everything dirty. Look down at the yard!'

A four-square block of buildings with outhouses, slaty grey and ugly, scabbed on to the walls, enclosed a paved courtyard, at one corner of which stood a pump, at another a stable with a heap of manure piled high outside the door. Two grey long-bodied rats could be seen running across from the pump to the stable, a ragged tramp who had slept all night on the warm dunghill shuffled up to his feet, rubbed the sleep and dirt from his eyes, then slunk away from the place as if conscious of having done something very wrong.

'That man has slept here for many a night,' said Meg; then pointing her finger upwards over the roofs of many houses to a spire that pierced high through the smoke-laden air, she said: 'That's the Municipal Buildin's; that's where the rich people meet and talk about the best thing to be done with houses like these. It's easy to talk over yonder; that house cost five hunner and fifty thousand pounds to build. A gey guid hoose, surely, isn't it, Sheila Carrol?'

'It's comin' half-past five, Meg, and it's time ye were settin' out for yer work,' was Sheila's answer. 'Ye'd spend half yer life bletherin'.'

'A good, kindly and decent woman she is,' Sheila told Norah when Meg took her departure. 'Works very hard and, God forgive her! drinks very hard too. Nearly every penny that doesn't go in rent does in the crathur, and she's happy enough in her own way although a black Prodesan … Ah! there's some quare people here on this stair when ye come to know them all!'

Over a tin of tea and a crust Sheila made plans for the future. 'I can earn about one and three a day at the finishin',' she said. 'I have to buy my own thread out of that, three bobbins a week at twopence ha'penny a bobbin.

'Ye used to be a fine knitter, Norah,' Sheila continued. 'D'ye mind the night long ago on Dooey Strand? God knows it was hardships enough for the strong women like us to sleep out in the snow, not to mention a young girsha like yerself. But ye were the great knitter then and ye'll be nimble with yer fingers yet, I'll go bail. Sewing ye might be able to take a turn at.'

'I used to be good with needle, Sheila,' said the girl.

'Then that'll be what we'll do. We'll work together, me and yerself, and we'll get on together well and cheaper. It'll be only the one fire and the one light; and now, if ye don't mind, we'll begin work and I'll show ye what's to be done.'

CHAPTER 26

THE PASSING DAYS

I

They came and went, days monotonously slow, each bearing with it its burden of sorrows and regrets, of fear and unhappiness. The life of the two women was ever the same: out of bed at five in the morning, a salutation exchanged with old Meg as she went to her work; breakfast – a crust of bread and a cup of tea; the light, weak and sickly, peeping through the narrow, murky window, the eternal scissors and needles, the white heaps of shirts, the feather-stitching and finishing. In the morning the cripple next door clattered downstairs on crutches, the card with the rude inscription, PARALYSED FOR LIFE, shaking to and fro as he moved. All day long he lay on the cold flagged pavement begging his daily bread. Tommy Macara, the lad with the rickets, came out singing to the landing on his way to the industrial school. He stuck his head through the door and shouted: 'Ye twa women, warkin' hard.' Both loved little Tommy, his cheery laugh, his childish carelessness, his poor body twisted out of shape by the humours of early disease. His legs would twitch as he stood at the door, making an effort to control the tremors;

sometimes he would laugh awkwardly at this and hurry away. Thus the morning.

Noon – A quarrel at No. 8. The two loose women who lived there argued about the spoils taken from a drunken sailor the night before, and came to blows. One was dressed, the other, just out of bed, had only time to wrap the blanket round her body. Both came out on the landing tearing at each other's hair and swearing. All the doors in the place opened; women ragged to the point of nudity, men dirty and unshaven, hurried out to watch the fight, which was long and severe. The women bit and scratched, and the younger – Bessie was her name – a plump girl wearing the blanket on which the words STOLEN FROM JAMES MOFFAT could be read at a distance – was deprived of her only article of apparel, and she scurried rapidly indoors. The onlookers laughed loudly and clapped their hands; the elder, a light-limbed lassie with very white teeth, returned to her room closing the door behind her. Now and again a shriek could be heard from the apartment, then a hoarse gurgle, as if somebody was getting strangled, afterwards silence. The watchers retired indoors, and peace settled on the stairhead. Only the two women, Sheila and Norah, never ceased work; the needles and scissors still sparkled over and through the white shirts.

Evening – Meg returned half-tipsy and singing a chorus, half the words of which she had forgotten. The day's work had been a very trying one, the dust rising from the rags did not agree with her asthma. On entering she looked fixedly at Sheila, shook her head sadly, ran her fingers over Norah's hair and began the chorus again, but stopped in the middle of it and started to weep. After a while she reeled into her own room, closed the door behind her, and sank to sleep on the floor beside the dead fire.

Little Tom Macara came up the stair, looked in, the eternal smile on his pinched face, and cried out in a thin voice: 'Ah! the women are warkin' awa' yet. They never have a meenit to spare!'

'Never a minute, Tom,' Sheila answered, and the boy went off, whistling a music-hall tune. Tom's mother was consumptive, his father epileptic; he had two brothers and three sisters all older than himself. After Tom, the man with the crutches came upstairs. From the street to the top of the landing was a weary climb, but often he got helped on the journey; sometimes the two whores escorted him up, sometimes Sheila gave him an arm, and everybody on the stairs liked the man. He was always in good humour and could sing a capital song.

Later in the evening, those who indulged in intoxicants became drunk; an ex-soldier, with one sleeve of his coat hanging loosely from his shoulder, who lived with two women, kicked one unmercifully and got dragged off to prison; the two harlots netted two men, one of them a well-dressed fellow with a gold tie-pin and a ring on his finger, and took them to their room; the paralytic could be heard singing and his voice seemed to be ever so far away. Sheila and Norah were still busy with the shirts, sewing their lives into every stitch of their work.

'And them two women at No. 8, there's not the least bit of harm in them at bottom,' Sheila would exclaim. 'They help the old cripple up every time they meet him on the stairs. And to think of it! There's seventeen thousand women like them in Glasgow!'

'God be good to us!'

Midnight came and quiet, and still the two women worked on. Outside on the landing into the common sink the water kept dripping from the tap. Sheila made a remark about the people away home in Frosses and wondered if they were all asleep at that moment. Outside, the city sank to its repose;

only the unfortunate and the unwell were now awake. The epileptic's wife coughed continually; Bessie, the plump girl, stole the pin from the tie of her lover; downstairs the caretaker, the woman with the red wisps of hair, counted the number of men who went to No. 8; half the profits went to her.

One o'clock came and, as if by mutual consent, the Irish women left their work aside and looked out of the window for a moment. High up they could see the spire of the town hall prodding into the heavens; nearer and almost as high the tower of a church with the black hands passing on the lighted face of a clock; closer still the dark windows of the houses opposite. Glasgow with all its churches, its halls, with its shipping and commerce, its wharves and factories, its richness and splendour, its poor and unhappy, its oppressed and miserable, Glasgow, with its seventeen thousand prostitutes, was asleep.

II

Norah and Sheila went to bed, wrapped the blue-lettered blankets round their bodies and placed their heads down on the condemnatory sentences: STOLEN FROM JAMES MOFFAT. Almost immediately Sheila was asleep, her knees drawn up under her (for the bed was too short for her body) and her arms around Norah. The young girl could not sleep well now; short feverish snatches of slumber were followed by sudden awakenings, and fears and fancies, too subtle to define, constantly preyed on her mind. Sometimes, when under the influence of a religious melancholy that often took possession of her, she repeated the *Hail Mary* over and over again, but at intervals she stopped in the midst of a prayer, started as if stung by an asp and exclaimed: 'What does the Virgin think of me, me that has committed one of the worst mortal sins in the world!'

In the midst of a prayer she dropped to sleep, maybe for the third time in an hour, but immediately was awakened by a sharp rapping at the door. Sheila heard nothing, she lay almost inset, and perspiring a little.

'Who's there?' Norah called out.

'The sanitary,' a hoarse voice answered from the landing.

The girl slipped out of bed, hardly daring to breathe lest her companion was disturbed, fumbled round for the matches, lit the oil-lamp and opened the door. Two strangers in uniform stood outside; one, a tall man with a heavy beard, held a lamp, the other, a sallow-faced, shrunken individual, hummed a tune in a thin, monotonous voice and picked his nose with a claw-like finger. The two entered, brushing against the girl who took up her stand behind the door, making a slight rapping noise with her heels on the bare floor.

'How many here?' asked the tall man with the beard.

'Two,' Norah answered, 'the woman in the bed and me.'

'No one else under the bed?'

'No one,' Norah replied, but the man knelt on the floor, lifted the bedclothes and peeped under.

'Only one in the next room?' asked the sallow-faced fellow, pointing at Meg's door.

'Only one and nobody else.'

They chose not to believe the girl's statement, rapped on the door, which was opened after a long delay by old Meg, who had risen naked from bed and was now hiding her withered body behind a blanket stamped with the blue lettering. The sentence STOLEN FROM JAMES MOFFAT ran from the left knee to the right shoulder; the left shoulder was bare, as was also the left leg from ankle to hip.

'Only one here,' she croaked, glowering evilly at the men who had disturbed her slumber. 'Christ! An auld body has no peace at all here, for there are always some folk crawlin' round when decent folk are in bed. Bed! Callin' it a bed and so particular about it. One would almost be as well off if they were thrown out a handful of fleas and allowed to sleep on the doorstep. God's curse on ye both, comin' at this hour of the night to pull an old woman like me from my scratcher.'

The bearded man entered the room, his companion took out a notebook and wrote something down, shut the book and placed it in his pocket. The tall man came out again; both bade Norah 'Goodnight' in apologetic tones and took their leave. Sheila had slept unmoved through it all.

The young girl closed the door, extinguished the light and re-entered the bed. She was very tired, but sleep would not come to her eyes. An hour passed. Sheila was snoring loudly, but Norah awake could hear the water dropping into the sink on the landing, and the vacant laugh of Bessie escorting a man upstairs. At night this woman never slept; her business was then in full swing.

Someone knocked at the door again, and Norah cried, 'Who's there?'

'Is this No. 8?' enquired a man's voice.

Norah answered 'No', and steps shuffled along the passage outside. Next instant the crash of someone falling heavily was heard, then a muttered imprecation, and afterwards silence.

Norah fell asleep again.

CHAPTER 27

THE NEWCOMER

I

Three weeks, laggard and leaden in movement, passed away. It was late evening; nine o'clock was just striking, and Sheila, true to her usual habit, counted the strokes aloud.

'The clock goes faster now than it did the first night I was here,' she said. 'I suppose they'll all be goin' to bed in Frosses now, or maybe sayin' the rosary. Are ye tired, Norah?' she suddenly asked her companion.

'No, not tired, only ...'

'Maybe ye would like to go to bed,' said Sheila, anticipating Norah's desires and looking very wise.

'I think that ... Oh! it's all right,' answered Norah, an expression of pain passing across her face.

'I know,' said Sheila, laying down her scissors and stirring up the fire, which was brighter than usual. 'Ye must go to bed now and keep yerself warm, child. Ye'll be all right come the mornin'.'

'I'm very unwell, Sheila. I feel.... No, I'm better again,' said Norah, making a feeble attempt to smile and only succeeding in blushing.

She undressed to her white cotton chemise, lay down, and Sheila gathered the blankets round the young woman with tender hands. Norah appeared calm, her fingers for a moment toyed with the tresses over her brow, then she drew her hand under the blankets. Her face had taken on a new light; the cold look of despair had suddenly given place to a new and nervous interest in life and in herself. It seemed as if things had assumed a new character for her; as if she understood in a vague sort of way that a woman's life is always woven of dreams, sorrow, love, and self-sacrifice. She was now waiting almost gladly, impatient for the most solemn moment in a woman's life.

'I'm not one bit afraid,' she said to the serious Sheila who was bending over her. 'Now don't be frightened. One would think …' Norah did not proceed. It was a moment of words half-spoken and the listener understood.

Suddenly Norah sighed deeply, clutched Sheila's dress in a fierce grip and closed her eyes tightly and tensely. She was suffering, but she endured silently.

'I'm better again,' she said after a moment. 'Don't heed about me, Sheila. I'm fine.'

The older woman went back to her work with the large shiny scissors and the bright little needle. Only the swish-swish of the cutting shears and the noise of a falling cinder could be heard for a long while. On the roof wave-shadows could be seen rushing together, forming into something very dark and breaking free again.

'Will ye have a drop of tea, Norah?'

'No, Sheila,' said the girl in the bed in a low strained voice; then after a moment she asked: 'Sheila, will ye come here for a minute?'

'A cinder fell into the grate with a sharp rattle, the scissors sparkled brightly as they were laid aside. Sheila rose and went towards the bed on tiptoe.

'I'm not needin' ye yet,' said Norah. 'I thought … I'm better again.'

The woman went back to her work, stepping even more softly than before. The night slipped away; the noises on stair and street became less and less, the women of No. 8 had retired to their beds, a drunken man sang homewards, a policeman passed along with slow, solemn tread; even these signs of life suddenly abated, and the noise of the cutting scissors, the clock striking out the hours, and the wind beating against the window were all that could be heard in the room.

About three o'clock the sanitary inspectors called. Sheila whispered to them at the door and they went away muttering something in an apologetic voice.

The grey dawn was lighting up the street; the blind had been drawn aside and the lamp flickered feebly on the floor. Sheila turned it down and approached the bed. On Norah's face there was the calmness of resignation and repose. She had suffered much during the night, but now came a quiet moment. Her brow looked very white and her cheeks delicately red. Her face was still as beautiful as ever; even so much the more was it beautiful.

'There's great noises in the streets, Sheila,' she said to the woman bending over her.

''Tis the workers goin' out to their work, child,' was the answer. 'How are ye feelin' now?'

'Better, Sheila, better.'

But even as she spoke the pain again mastered her and she groaned wearily. And Sheila, wise with a woman's wisdom, knew that the critical moment had come.

II

The child who came to Norah, the little boy with the pink, plump hands, the fresh cheeks and pretty shoulders, filled nearly all the wants of her heart. The fear that she had had of becoming a mother was past and the supreme joy of motherhood now was hers. She knew that she would be jealous of the father if he was with her at present; as matters stood the child was her own, her very own, and nothing else mattered much. Sometimes she would sit for an hour, her discarded scissors hanging from her fingers, gazing hungrily at the saffron-red downy face of the child, anticipating every moment on its part, following every quiver of its body with greedy eyes. In the child lay Norah's hopes of salvation; it was the plank to which she clung in the shipwreck of her eternity. All her hopes, all her fortunes lay in the babe's fragile bed; the sound of the little voice was heavenly music to her cars. In Norah's heart welled up this incomparable love, in which are blended all human affections and all hopes of heaven, the love of a mother. The great power of motherhood held her proof against all evils; dimly and vaguely it occurred to her that if that restraining power was withdrawn for a moment she would succumb to any temptation and any evil which confronted her.

She found now a great joy in working with Sheila: both talked lovingly of home and those whom they had left behind. Sometimes Norah mingled tears with her recollections. Sheila Carrol never wept.

'Years ago I could cry my fill,' she told Norah, 'but for a long while, save on the night yerself came here, the wells of my eyes have been very dry.'

At another time when the mother was giving the breast to the child Sheila said: 'Ye look like the Blessed Virgin with the child, Norah.'

A difficulty arose about the child's name: that of the father was out of the question.

'One of the Frosses names for me,' said Sheila. 'Doalty, Dony, or Dermod, Murtagh, Shan, or Fergus; Oiney, Eamon, or Hudy; ah! sure, there's hundreds of them! All good names they are and all belonging to our own arm of the glen. The trouble is that there's too many to pick from. We'll be like the boy with the apples; they were all so good that he didn't know what one to take and he died of fargortha while lookin' at them. Dermod or Fergus, which will it be?' asked the beansho.

'Dermod,' said Norah simply.

'I thought so,' said the woman. 'And I hope another Dermod will come one of these days to see us. Then maybe ... Dermod Flynn was a nice kindly lad, comely and civil.'

CHAPTER 28

THE RAG-STORE

I

Once a week, on Friday, Sheila took a bundle of finished shirts to the clothes-merchant's office. Seven months after Norah's arrival Sheila went out one day with her bundle and in the evening the woman did not return. Midnight came and went. From the window Norah watched the lazy hands of the clock crawl out the seconds of existence. Steps could be heard coming up and going down the stairs; then these suddenly ceased. Far away the flames flaring from the top of a chimney-stack glowed fiercely red against the dark sky. A policeman came along the dimly lighted street, walking with tired tread and examining the numbers on the closed entrances. He suddenly disappeared below; afterwards a knock came to the door.

'A woman was run down by a tram-car,' said the policeman, speaking through his heavy moustache, when Norah gave him admittance; 'she was killed instantly.... She had a slip of paper ... this address ... maybe you can identify.'

Norah lifted the sleeping babe, wrapped it in her shawl and followed the man. At the police mortuary she recognised Sheila Carrol. The dead woman was in no way disfigured; she lay on a wooden slab, face upwards, and still, so very still!

'Sheila Carrol! … she's only sleepin'!' said Norah.

'Sheila Carrol, you say,' said a uniformed man who had just entered and who overheard Norah's remark. 'Twice convicted, once for being on the streets, once for child neglect,' he muttered, looking not a little proud of his knowledge. 'The back of the head and the spine that's hurt. When one is struck hard in them places it's all over.'

Norah felt like a cripple whose crutches have been taken away. That night when she returned to her room she slept none and wept bitterly, at times believing that the dead woman was with her in the room. Being very lonely she kept the light burning till morning, and as the fire had gone out she shivered violently at intervals and a dry tickling cough settled on her chest.

II

The merchant who supplied cloth to the two women had gone bankrupt. Probably Sheila was so much overwhelmed by this that she forgot to avoid the dangers of the crowded streets on her way home. Perhaps she was planning some scheme for the future, and as is the case when the mind dwells deeply on some particular subject, the outside world was for a while non-existent to her. An eye witness of the tragedy said that Sheila had taken no heed of the oncoming tram; that death was instantaneous.

When morning came Norah Ryan was conscious of a dull, sickly pain behind her left shoulder-blade. The child slept badly during the night and coughed feebly when it awoke. There were no matches to light the fire; a half-loaf, a pennyworth of tea and a quarter hundred-weight of coal was all that remained in the room.

Norah went into Meg's compartment. The door was lying open. The woman sat by a dead fire, having just awakened from a drunken sleep on the floor. She was a kind-hearted soul, generous and sympathetic, but fond of drink. A glass of whisky made her very tipsy, two glasses made her very irritable.

'Ye're up early, lass,' said the old woman, rising to her feet and scratching her head vigorously. 'Is Sheila sleepin' yet?'

'She's dead.'

'Dead!' exclaimed old Meg, sitting down on the only chair in the room and raising both hands, palms outwards, to a level with her face.

'A tram struck her last night when she was comin' home,' said Norah. 'Killed at once, the policeman said that she was.'

Meg wept loudly for a few moments, then: 'What are ye goin' to do now?' she asked, drying her eyes.

'I don't know.'

'There's often a chance goin' in the rag-store where I work and it's not a hard job at all,' said the old woman. 'The job may be a wee bit dirty and clorty, but think it over. Six shillin's a week is the pay to start wi', then it rises to eight.'

'Thanks for the help that ye are to me,' said Norah; 'and when d'ye think that I'll get the job?'

'Maybe at any time now, for there's one of the young ones goin' to get marrit a fortnight come tomorrow,' said the old woman. 'Then there's a woman that lives at No. 27 of this street, Helen McKay is her name; 'Tuppenny Helen', the ones on the stairhead ca' her. She takes care of children for twopence a day.'

'I'm not goin' to leave my child,' cried Norah. She spoke fiercely, angrily. 'D'ye think that I would give up my child to a woman like Tuppenny Helen? God sees that I can keep my own child whatever happens to me!'

'Whatever ye say it's not for me to say the word agen it,' said Meg, surprised at Norah's wrath.

'Could I take the boy with me if I get a job?'

'Nae fear; nae fear of that,' said the old woman. 'It would smother a child in a week in yon place. Dust flyin' all over the place; dirty rags with creepin' things and crawlin' things and maybe diseases on them; it's a foulsome den. But folks maun eat and folks maun earn siller, and that's why some hae to wark in a place like a rag-store. But dinna take the child wi' ye there. For one thing ye winna be allowed and for another the feelthy place would kill the dear little thing in less than a week.'

For a fortnight following Norah looked in vain for a job at which she might work with the child beside her. At the end of that time the old woman spoke again of a vacant post in the store where she laboured. Norah put the child out to Tupenny Helen, a stumpy little woman with very large feet and hacked hands, then applied for and obtained the vacant post in the rag-store.

III

In the chill, damp air of the early morning the two women tramped to their work, wearing their boots to save the tram fare. The old woman always walked with her head down, humming little tunes through her nose and breaking into a run from time to time. Her long red tongue was always out, slipping backwards and forwards over her upper lip, her hair, grey as a dull spring morning, eternally falling into her eyes, and her arms swinging out in front of her like two dead things as she trotted along.

The rag-store opened out on a narrow, smelling lane; the office where a few collared clerks bent over grimy ledgers and endless rows of figures was on a level with the street; the place where the women sorted the rags was a basement under the office. There were in all thirty human machines working in this cellar, which stretched into the darkness on all sides save one, and there it now and again touched sunshine, the weak sunshine that streamed through a dirty cobwebbed window, green with moisture and framed with iron bars.

All day long two gas-jets flared timidly in the basement, spluttering as if in protest at being condemned to burn in such a cavern. The women, bowed over their work, were for the most part silent; all topics of conversation had been exhausted long ago. Sometimes Monday morning was lively; many came fresh to their work full of accounts of a fight in which half the women of the close joined and which for some ended in the lock-up, for others with battered faces and dishevelled hair. These accounts roused a certain interest which lasted a few hours, then came the obstinate dragging silence again.

All day long they worked together in the murky cavern sorting the rags. The smell of the place was awful, suffocating almost; the damp and mouldy rags gave forth an unhealthy odour; dust rose from those that were drier and filled the place and the throats of the workers. Each woman knew every wrinkle of her neighbour's face, on all the yellowish white and almost expressionless faces of the spectres of the cellar. And now and again the spectres sang their ghost-songs, which died away in the lone corners of the basement like wind in a churchyard.

It was amongst these women that Norah started work.

'A new start!' exclaimed one, a little sallow-faced thing who looked as if she had been gradually drying up for several years, on seeing the newcomer. 'Ye'll soon get the blush oot o' yer cheeks here, lass!'

'D'ye know that there are only three people in the worl' when all is said and done?' another woman called to Norah. 'The rag-picker, the scavenger, and the grave-digger are the three folk who count most in the long run.'

Everybody but Norah laughed at this remark, though all, save Norah, had heard it made a thousand times before.

'Ah! lass, ye've the red cheeks,' said a bow-legged girl of seventeen.

'They'll soon be pale enough,' another interrupted.

'And such white teeth!'

'They'll soon be yellow!'

'And such long hair!'

'It'll soon be full o' dust.'

But they said no more, perhaps because Norah was so beautiful, and beauty calls forth respect in even the coarsest people.

The new start had many troubles at first. Being new to the work and unable to do as much as the other women, she was paid only five shillings a week. After a while the natural dexterity of her fingers stood her in good stead, and she became more adept at the rag-picking than anyone in the basement. Therefore her companions who had before laughed at her inexperience became jealous of Norah and accused her of trying to find favour with the boss.

But the girl did not mind much what they said; her one great regret was in being separated from her boy for the whole livelong day. Her breasts were full of the milk of motherhood, and severance from the little child was one of the greatest crosses which she had to bear.

The master seldom came near the place; it didn't agree with his health, he said. He was a stout, well-built man with small, glistening eyes overhung with heavy red brows. The hairs of his nostrils reached half-way down his upper lip and he was very bald. When the women saw the bald head appear at the foot of the basement stairs, shining a little as the gaslight caught it, they whispered:

'There's the full moon; turn yer money!' and one of the workers who was very fond of swearing would invariably answer: 'There's not much money in the pockets o' them that's workin' in this damned hole!'

Whenever he came down into the rag-store he took the bow-legged girl to one side and spoke to her about something. The two seemed to be on very familiar terms and it was stated that the girl got a far higher wage than any of the other workers: ten shillings a week was paid to her, some hinted. Suddenly, however, she left the place and did not come back again: but now the master came down the stairs oftener than ever before. One evening just as work was stopping the moon-head appeared, shone for a moment under the gaslight, then came forward.

'There's some linen rags here that I want sorted up tonight,' he said, licking his lips. 'I want one of ye to stay here and do the work.'

He looked round as he spoke and his eyes rested on Norah, who was wrapping her shawl over her shoulders.

'Will ye stay here?' he asked.

'All right,' said Norah, and took off her shawl again.

The rest of the workers went upstairs, a bit envious perhaps of the girl who was picked out for special work in

the fetid hole. Master and servant were left alone, but
Norah wished that she had gone away with the rest; she
wanted so much to see her child. The cough which the
little boy had contracted on the night of Sheila Carrol's
death, ten months before, had never gone wholly away,
and now it was worse than ever. The mother herself was
not feeling very well; the sharp pain in her chest troubled
her a great deal at night.

'Ye're a good sorter, I hear,' said the master, licking his
lips, and Norah noticed the hairs of his nostrils quivering
as if touched by a breeze. 'Ye'll not live well on seven
shillin's a week, will ye?' he asked.

'One must live somehow,' said Norah, bending down
and picking up a handful of rags from the floor. 'And a
few shillin's goes a long way when one is savin'.'

She started even as she spoke, for a large soft hand had
gripped her wrist and she looked up to find her master's
little glistening eyes looking into hers. She could see the
wrinkles on his forehead, the red weal that the rim of his
hat had left on the temples, the few stray hairs that yet
remained on the top of the pink head.

'What would ye be wantin' with me?' she asked.

'I could raise yer screw, say to ten bob a week,' said the
man, slipping his arms round her waist and trying to kiss
her on the lips. If one of the dirty rags had been thrust into
her mouth she could not have experienced a more nauseous
feeling of horror than that which took possession of her at
that moment. She freed herself violently from the grasp of
the man, seized her shawl and hurried upstairs, leaving him
alone in the cellar. In the office she had a misty impression
of a grinning clerk looking at her and passing some
meaningless remark. When she got back to her room she
told Meg of all that had happened.

'Ye're a lucky lass, a gie lucky lass,' said the old woman enviously. 'Just play yer cards well and ye'll soon hae a pund a week in the store. I heard today about the bowdy girl that left us a month gone. The master had a fancy for her but a mistake happened and she was in straw. But it's now all right and she's gettin' a pund a week. Just ye play yer cards well, Norah Ryan, and ye'll have a gey guid time,' she added.

'Meg Morraws!'

'Ha, ha!' cried the old woman, laughing and showing her yellow stumps of teeth, worn to the gums. 'That's the way to act. Carry on like that with him and he'll do onything ye ask, for ye're a comely lass; a gey comely one! Often I wondered why ye stayed so long workin' in the rag-store. Life could be made muckle easier by a girl wi' a winnin' face like yours, Norah Ryan. God! to think that a girl like ye are warkin' in that dirty hole when ye could make ten times as muckle siller by doin' somethin' else!'

IV

Norah did not go back to the rag-store. She took her child from Tupenny Helen and looked for other work. The boy with his round chubby legs and wonderful pink toes, which she never tired of counting, was a wonder and delight to her. Everything was so fresh about him, the radiant eyes, the red cheeks that made the mother so much long to bite them, the little soft lips and the white sharp teeth that were already piercing through the gums. The child was dressed poorly, but, as befitted a sanctuary before which one human being prostrated herself with all the unselfish devotion of a pure heart, with the best taste of the worshipper.

The cold which the child caught months before had never entirely gone away; whenever the cough that accompanied it seized him he curled up in his mother's lap in agony, while she feared that the little treasure that she loved so much was going to be taken away. The thought of the boy dying occurred to her many times and almost shattered the springs of action within her. If he died! She shuddered in terror; her fear was somewhat akin to the fear which possesses a man who hangs over a precipice and waits for the overstrained rope to break. If the child was gone she would have nothing more to live for.

Her funds were very low; when she left the rag-store she had only the sum of nineteen shillings in her possession. This would pay rent for a few weeks, but meanwhile food, fuel, and clothing were needed. What was she to do?

Then followed weary days searching for work. Norah went from house to house in the better parts of the city, offering herself for employment. She left the child lying on a bed on the floor and locked the place up. She no longer sent it out to Tuppenny Helen; Norah could not now spare twopence a day.

Again she got work, this time finishing dongaree jackets, and made tenpence a day. She had now to work on Sunday as well as Saturday, and she usually spent eighteen hours a day at her task. Winter came and there was no coal. The child, whose cold got no better, was placed in bed while the mother worked. The dry and hacking cough shook the mother's frame at intervals and she sweated at night when asleep. She ate very little; her breasts were sore when she suckled her child, and by and by milk refused to come. Her eyes became sore; she now did part of her work under the lamp on the landing and by the light from the window across the courtyard. Old Meg, when she was drunk, had pence to spare for the child.

'Just for the little thing to play wi',' she would explain in an apologetic voice, as if ashamed of being found guilty of a good action. Afterwards she would add: 'Ye should have taken the twa extra shillin's a week when they were offered ye.'

One evening towards Christmas when the old woman was speaking thus, Norah asked:

'If I went back now, would I get a job?'

'The man has got marrit and the place, as ye know yerself, has been filled up ages and ages ago.'

A strange expression, perhaps one of regret, showed for a moment on the face of Norah Ryan.

CHAPTER 29

DERMOD FLYNN

I

When the old woman left her, Norah sat for a while buried in thought, her scissors lying on one knee, one hand hanging idly by her side. The boy was very ill, the cough hardly left him for a moment and his eyes were bright and feverish.

'If he dies what am I to do?' Norah asked herself several times. 'Then it would be that I'd have nothing to live for.'

She rose and followed Meg into the room. The woman sat beside the fire, humming an old song. A candle, stuck in the neck of a beer-bottle, was alight, and a cricket chirped behind the fireless grate. 'I'm goin' out for a while,' said Norah in a low, strained voice. 'Will ye look after the boy until I come back? I'll take him in here.'

'All right,' said the woman, rising to her feet. 'Take the little thing in.'

When Norah re-entered her own room the boy was coughing weakly but insistently in the darkness. She lit a candle, sat down on the corner of the bed and was immediately deep in thought. Her money had now dwindled away; she had only one and threepence in her possession. She even felt hungry; for a long while this sensation was almost foreign to her. The weekly rent was due on the morrow, and the child needed the doctor, needed food, needed fresh air and, above all, the attention which she was unable to give him.

She lifted him tenderly from the bed and carried him in to Meg, who began to crow with delight when the child was placed in her withered arms. Once back in her own room Norah resumed her seat on the bedside and seemed to be debating some very heavy problem. The candle flared faintly in the sconce on the floor; large shadows chased one another on the grimy ceiling ... the cripple came upstairs, Norah could hear the rattle of his crutches ... the noise of the city was loud outside the windows.

Norah rose, swept the floor, lit the lamp, a thing which she had not done for many nights, candles being much cheaper than oil. She went out, bought some coal and a penny bundle of firewood; these she placed on the grate, ready for lighting. The bed she sorted with nervous care, sighing as she spread out the blankets and arranged the pillows.

She then began to dress herself carefully, brushing back her hair with trembling fingers as she looked into the little broken hand-mirror, one of Sheila Carrol's belongings. Her well-worn dress still retained a certain coquetry of cut and suited her well, her broad-brimmed hat, which she had not worn for a long while, gave an added charm to her white brow and grey eyes.

When dressed she stood for a moment to listen to the child coughing in Meg's room. Stifling with an effort the impulse to go in and have one look at the boy, she crossed herself on forehead and lips and went out on the landing. For a moment something seemed to perplex her; she stood and looked round on all sides. The place was deserted; nothing could be heard but the cripple singing 'Annie Laurie' in a loud, melodious voice. Norah again crossed herself, stepped slowly down the stairs, and went out to the street.

II

At midnight she returned for her child. The boy was still coughing, but more quietly than before, and the old woman was lying flat upon her stomach, asleep by the fireside. Norah lifted the child, took him into her own room and placed the frail bundle, in which was wrapped up all her life and all her hopes, on the bed.

The fire was burning brightly, the oil-lamp gave out a clear, comforting light which showed up the whole room, the bare floor, the black walls enlivened by no redeeming feature save the crude picture of the Virgin and Child and the little black cross hanging from a rusty nail near the window; the pile of dongaree jackets shoved into a corner, the orange-box and the bed with the blankets, which Norah had sorted such a short time before, now in strange disorder.

Old Meg suddenly bustled into the room, a frightened look on her face. 'I thought that some yin had stolen the little dear,' she cried, her breath reeking with alcohol. 'Ah, here he is, the wee laddie,' she cooed on seeing the little pink face in the bed. 'I hae got a fright, I hae indeed, Norah Ryan!'

The woman sat down on the orange box and looked curiously round, first at the lighted lamp, then at the fire, then at Norah, and afterwards back to the fire again.

'Hae ye got siller the noo, lassie?' she exclaimed at last. 'Has yer rich uncle kicked the bucket? Fire and light the noo and everything? Ah! what's this?' she exclaimed, bending down and lifting a half-smoked cigarette from the floor. She looked at it for a moment, then threw it into the flames.

'Has it come to this, Norah Ryan?' she asked, and a faint touch of regret mingled with the woman's tones.

Norah, who was bending over the child, turned round fiercely; for a moment she looked like some beautiful animal cornered in its own lair.

'It has come to this, Meg Morraws!' she shouted. 'Did ye think that I couldn't sell my soul? I would do anything under heaven to save my boy; that's the kind of me, Meg Morraws. I've money now and Dermod won't die. I won't let him die! ... What wouldn't I do for him, child of my own and of my heart? ... It's ill luck that's drawin' me to ruin, Meg, but not the boy. He can't help the sickness and it's myself that has got to make him well again.... . I had whisky this night: that made me brave. I could ... Isn't it time that ye were in bed, Meg Morraws? I'm not feelin' kind towards anyone but the child. I want no one here but Dermod, my little boy.'

Meg went into her room, closing the door softly behind her. Norah took some money – five shillings – from her pocket and put it on the mantelpiece, under the picture of the Virgin and Child. It made a tinkling sound as she put it down and the silver coins sparkled brightly.

Then she turned down the light, threw some more coals on the fire, and taking the child from the bed she sat down and held the little bundle of pink flesh against her bosom. She could hear the water bubbling from the tap out on the landing; the noise of footsteps on the stairs; loud, vacant laughter from No. 8. Why did those women laugh, Norah wondered.... . The fire blazed brightly, and as she raised her eyes she could see the silver coins on the mantelpiece shining like stars.

III

Someone rapped; and receiving no answer, the caretaker, the woman with the red wisps of hair, and a string for a neck, poked her head through the door.

'Not in bed yet, Norah Ryan?' she asked.

'Just goin',' the girl answered.

'They're doin' a big trade at No. 8 the night,' said the woman.

'I'm not wantin' to hear; it's nothing to me.'

The caretaker smiled, showing her teeth, sharp as a dog's and in a good state of preservation.

'I'm only just tellin' ye,' said the woman. 'I suppose ye ken, lassie, that half the rooms up this stair are lyin' idle, wi' no yin to take them. What is the reason for that? I'll tell ye. Some people, decent folk, ye ken, will not come to sic a place because they dinna like women of the kind at No. 8. If these two women were put away, this landing would be fillt ev'ry night. But I let the women stay. Why's that? Because I like fair play. Give everyone a chance to live, is what I say. And they're makin' guid siller, them twa lassies at No. 8. Three pounds a night between them sometimes. And I wouldna turn them oot; wouldna do it for wurl's, because I like fair play. But as ye ken yersel', they must pay me a little more than other lodgers.'

'What do ye want me to pay extra?' asked Norah in a hard voice. 'Tell me at once and leave me to meself.'

'Say half and half,' answered the red-haired woman, glaring covertly at the Irish girl. 'That'll be fair, for ye'll earn the money very easy, so to speak. And then ye can stay here as long as ye like. I wouldna turn ye oot, no for onything, because I like fair play. It's not ev'ry house, ye ken, that would... . But ye know what I mean. I wish ye goodnight, and I'll make a note of all the men that come up. And if the police come along I'll gi'e ye the wink. Goodnight and good luck!'

The woman went out, but presently poked her red wisps in again. 'I'll take it that every man I see comin' in here gies ye five bob. If they gie ye more ye can tell me; but five bob'll be the least, and half and half is fair play. Goodnight; goodnight and good luck!'

'A dirty hag she is!' said old Meg, who had been listening at the door during the conversation and who now came into the room. 'Dirty! and her makin' piles of tin. Full of money she is and so is the woman that owns the buildin'. Mrs Crawford they cry her, and she lives oot in Hillhead, the rich people's place, and goes to church ev'ry Sunday with prayer books under her arm. Strike me dead! if she isn't a swine, a swine unhung, a swine and a half. Has a motor car too, and is always writin' to the papers about sanitary arrangements. "It isn't healthy to have too many people in the one room," she says. But I ken what she's up to, her with her sanitary and her fresh air and everything else, the swine! If few people stay in ev'ry room she can let more of them; God put her in the pit, the swine! And the woman downstairs, the thin-necked serpent! is just as bad. If the likes of her finds women like me and you goin' to hell they try to rob us outright before Old Nick puts his mits on our shoulders.'

IV

In the days which followed, Norah learned much which may not be written down in books, sad things that many dare not read, but which some, under the terrible tyranny of destiny, dare to endure. It now seemed to the girl that all freedom of action, all the events of her life had been irrevocably decided before she was born. Deep down in her heart this thought, lacking expression and almost undefined, was always with her.

She bought new dresses, learned the art of making every curl on her white brow look tempting, and every movement of her face and body to express desires which she did not feel. She followed up her new profession like one sentenced to death, with reason clogged, feeling deadened and intellect benumbed. As an alternative to this there was nothing but starvation and death, and even purity is costly at such a price. Dragged to the tribunal which society erects for the prosecution of the poor and pure, she was asked to renounce all that she cherished, all her hopes, her virginity, her soul. Society, sated with the labour of her hands, asked for her soul, and society, being the stronger, had its demand gratified.

But over it all, over the medley of pain and sorrow, over the blazing crucible of existence in which all fair dreams and hopes of the woman were melted away, greater and more powerful than anything else in Norah's life, intense and enduring, unselfish and pure, shone the wonderful flame, the star of passionate love shining in the holy heaven of motherhood.

The child's illness grew worse. One doctor was called in; then another. Both looked wise for a moment, strove to appear unconcerned, passed different verdicts and went away. One condemned the bedclothes; they were unsanitary. Norah procured new clothes; but the child became worse. Medicines were bought one day; they were condemned the next. A pretty pink dress was obtained for the child; it did not suit. When taken back to the clothes-seller he declared it was ruined and charged afresh for new garments.

So day after day, each full of a killing anxiety and bringing its own particular trouble, passed by. Her house had attained a certain fame as houses of the kind rapidly do.

The hooligans who stood at the street corner soon knew her by repute, for an ill name flies far and sticks fast. Little Tommy Macara looked in at her door no more; the boy's mother had warned him against the woman. Life was now to Norah one vast intolerable burden that crushed her down. If only the child were dead things would be clearer; then she would know what to do. If Dermod died everything would be simplified; one easy plunge into the river where it swirled under Glasgow Bridge would for ever end all heartbreak and sorrow.

V

Norah went out into the city on her usual errand; she had now known the life of the streets for fully two months. It was nearly midnight, the streets were well nigh deserted, save for the occasional prowlers and drunken men who were coming home from their clubs or from the foul haunts of the city.

As she walked along, her head held down against the cutting breeze that had suddenly risen and was now whirling round every corner, she heard steps coming behind her, and in these steps she detected something strangely familiar. For a moment she felt like a wayfarer who goes alone, along a dark road, and waits for some horrible apparition to stretch out from the darkness and put a hand on his shoulder. The steps drew nearer, came closer … somebody was passing her. Norah looked up, started a little and cried: 'Under God, the day and the night! It's Dermod Flynn that's in it!'

She was again looking at Dermod Flynn; he stood in front of her, his hand stretched out in welcome.

'Is this you, Norah?' he asked.

The crushing fatality of her years pressed down upon her; she suddenly realised that she had lost something very precious; that all her accidents and faults were bunched together and now laid before her. He had grown so big too; a man he looked.

'Is it yerself that's in it, Dermod Flynn?' she asked. 'I didn't expect to meet you here. Have ye been away home since I saw ye last?' She thought she detected a wave of pity sweeping over Dermod's face and resting in his eyes.

'I have never been at home yet,' he answered. 'Have you?'

'Me go home!' she replied almost defiantly. 'What would I be going home for now with the black mark of shame over me? D'ye think that I'd darken me mother's door with the sin that's on me, heavy on me soul? Sometimes I'm thinkin' long, but I never let on to anybody, and it's meself that would like to see the old spot again. It's a good lot I'd give to see the grey boats of Dooey goin' out beyond Trienna Bar in the grey duskus of the harvest evenin'. D'ye mind the time ye were at school, Dermod, and the way ye struck the master with the pointer?'

'I mind it well,' said Dermod with a laugh, 'and you said that he was dead when he dropped on the form.'

'And d'ye mind the day that ye went over beyont the mountains with the bundle under yer arm? I met ye on the road and ye said that ye were never comin' back.'

'You did not care whether I returned or not. You did not stop to bid me goodbye.'

'I was frightened of ye,' answered Norah, who noticed that Dermod spoke resentfully, as if she had been guilty of some unworthy action.

'Why were ye frightened?' he asked.

'I don't know.'

'And you did not even turn to look after me!'

'That was because I knew that ye yerself was lookin' round.'

'Do you remember the night on the Derry boat?' Dermod asked wistfully.

'Quite well, Dermod,' she replied. 'I often be thinkin' of them days, I do indeed.'

There was a momentary silence. Norah dreaded the next question which instinctively she knew Dermod would ask. He was better dressed than formerly, she noticed, and he was tall and strong. She felt that he was one in whom great reliance could be placed.

'Where are you going at this hour of the night?' he asked, and Norah read accusation in his tones.

'I'm goin' out for a walk,' she answered.

'Where are you workin'?'

'How much does he know?' Norah asked herself. What could she tell him? That she was a servant in a gentleman's house. But even as the lie was stammering on her tongue she faltered and burst into tears.

'Don't cry,' said the young man awkwardly. 'Is there – what's wrong with ye, Norah?'

She did not answer, but low sobs shook her bosom. How much she wished to be away, and yet – how she liked to be beside him! Surely Dermod would think her a very funny girl to weep like that! A momentary remembrance of a morning long ago when she met him on the Glenmornan road flashed across her mind, and she held out her hand.

'Slan agiv, Dermod,' she said in a choking voice, 'I must
be goin'. It was good of ye to speak to me in that nice way
of yers, Dermod.'

His hand closed on hers but he did not speak. The sound
of far-off footsteps reached her ears… . A window was
lifted somewhere near at hand … a cab rattled on the streets.
Norah withdrew her hand and went on her journey, leaving
Dermod alone on the pavement.

CHAPTER 30

GROWN UP

I

To all souls who are sensitive to moods of any kind, whether joyful or sorrowful, there comes now and again a delicious hour when it is not night and no longer day; the timid twilight gleams softly on every object and favours a dreamy humour that weds itself, as if in a dream, to the dim play of light and shade. In that delightful passage of time the mind wanders through interminable spaces and dwells lovingly on vanished hopes, broken dreams, and shattered illusions. In that moment a soul feels the wordless pleasure of a memory that drifts lightly by; a memory to which only the accents of the heart can give life. Old scenes are brought up again and are seen in the delightful haze of transient remembrance; there are waters running to a sea; waves sobbing on a shore; voices speaking softly and low, and trees waving like phantoms to a wind that is merely the ghost of a wind. In these dreams there is a joyful melancholy, a placid acceptance of sorrow and happiness that might have only been realities of an earlier existence of long past years.

An hour like this came to Norah Ryan one evening as she sat in her room waiting for a fight to come to an end on the landing outside. The one-armed soldier, who had just returned from prison had found another man in company with one of his loves, was now blackening the man's eyes. Norah knew that she would be molested when passing outside; she chose to wait until the storm was over. She was dressed ready to go out; old Meg had taken charge of the child; the fight was still in full swing. A fire burned dimly in the grate at which Norah sat; a frail blue fleeting flame flared nervously for a moment amongst the red tongues of fire, then faded away. The blind was drawn across the window, but the lamp had not been lighted yet. Norah sat on the floor, looking into the glowing embers, her chin, delicately rounded, resting in the palm of her hand, her long, tapering fingers touching a little pink ear that was almost hidden under her soft, wavy tresses. The faintest flush mantled her cheeks, her brow seen in the half-light of the room looked doubly white, and her long lashes sank languidly from time to time over her dream-laden eyes.

Norah's thoughts were far away; they had crossed the bridge of many years and roved without effort of will over the shores of her own country. Again she lived the life of a child, the life she had known in her earlier years. The air was full of the scent of the peat, the sound of the sea, the homesick song of the streams babbling out their plaints as they hurried to the bosom of their restless mother, the ocean.

It was evening. The sun, barely a hand's breadth over the horizon, coloured the waters of the bar and the sea beyond, amber, crimson, and dun. The curraghs of Frosses were putting out from the shore; the barefooted men hurried along the strand, waving their arms and moving their lips, but making no sound. Fergus was there, light-limbed and dark-haired; her father, wrinkled and bearded; the neighbours and the women and children who came down to the beach to see the people off to the fishing.

One dream blended with another. It was morning; the sun tipped the hills and lighted Glenmornan; strips of gold in the clouds of the east were drawn fine as the wrinkles on the brow of a woman; a mist rose from the holms of Frosses, and the water of the streams sparkled merrily. In the pools trout were leaping, breaking the glassy surface and raising a shower of rainbow mist that dissolved in the air. A boy came along the road; there was a smile on his face and his eyes were full of dreams, as the eyes of a youth who goes out to push his fortune well may be. In one hand he carried a stick, in the other a bundle. Dermod Flynn was setting out for the hiring fair of Strabane... .

II

So Norah Ryan dreamt, one vision merging into another and all bringing a long-lost peace to her soul. She did not hear the first rap at the door, nor the second. The third knock, louder and more imperative than the others, roused her to a sense of her surroundings. In the fabric of her existence the black thread of destiny again reappeared and she rose, pushed back the erring lock of hair from her white forehead, placed some more coal on the fire, turned up the lamp and lit it, then went and opened the door. A young man dressed in sailor's garb, his face cut and covered with blood, stood on the threshold; behind him on the ground lay a prostrate figure, the man with the empty sleeve.

'Come in,' said Norah. She did not look at the visitor; all men were the same now to her; all were so much alike.

The sailor rubbed a handkerchief over his face, staggered past the girl and sank into a chair.

'What's that one-armed swine doin'?' he cried. 'Strikin' a man, an A.B. before the mast, without any reason; him and his gabblin' fools of women! But I learned him somethin', I did. One on the jowl and down he went. An A.B. before the mast stands no foolin'. Has he got up?' he called to the woman at the door.

The ex-soldier staggered to his feet on the landing, and swore himself along the passage. Norah closed the door.

'He's up on his feet and away to his own room,' she informed the sailor.

'This No. 8?' he asked.

'No,' answered Norah. 'It's three doors round on the left; I'll show you where it is.'

'But is this house one like No. 8?'

'The same.'

'Then I'll stay,' said the sailor, who was still busy with his face. 'I heard tell of No. 8 out abroad. I'm an A.B., you know. Before the mast on half the seas of the world! I met a sailor who was here; not here, but at No. 8. Ah! he had great stories of the place. So I said that I'd come here too, if ever I came to Glasgow. Damn! that one-armed pig he almost blinded me, did the beggar. But I gave one to him on the jowl that he'll not forget.... Where can I wash my face?'

'On the landing,' Norah told him, and handed the man a towel.

He went out and washed. Presently he reappeared and Norah took stock of him. He was dressed in sailors' garb; his eyes were hazy from intoxication, one of his hard and knotted hands was tattooed on the back, his dark and heavy moustache was draggled at both ends and a red scar on his right cheek-bone showed where the soldier had hit him. He was young, probably not over thirty years of age. He sat down again.

'D'ye know what it is?' he exclaimed, striking his fist heavily against his knee. 'A woman of yer kind may be as good as most and better than many. I always say that, always. Some of them may be bad, but for the others –'

He banged his fist again against his knee and paused as if collecting words for an emphatic finish to his sentence.

'Others are as good as pure gold,' he concluded. He was silent for a moment as if deep in thought, then he fixed his eyes on the girl. 'Come here and sit on my knee,' he said.

She sat down on his knee and laughed, but her laugh was forced and hollow.

'Ye're unhappy,' said the man, looking at her fixedly, and stroking her face with his hand. 'Don't say that ye aren't, for I know that ye are. Ye'll be new at this game, maybe.... . D'ye belong to Glasgow?'

'I do.'

'Ye talk like an Irish girl.'

'My father was Irish.'

'Ah! that explains it,' said the man. 'I'm Irish, ye know.'

'Are ye?' exclaimed Norah with a start.

'I am that,' said the man. 'Why do ye jump like ye do? Maybe ye're frightened of me?'

'No.'

'Maybe it's yer first time at this work?'

The girl made no answer. Her cheeks were scarlet and she felt as if she could burst into tears, but stifled bravely the sob that rose in her throat.

'Don't be frightened of me,' said the man. 'We sailors are a rough lot at times, but we respect beauty, so to speak.

My God, ye're a soncy lookin' wench. New to this kind of life as well!'

He paused.

'And what's this?' he cried, glancing at the Virgin's picture and the little black crucifix. He turned to the girl and saw that a tear which she hastily tried to brush away was rolling down her cheek.

'Ye're a Catholic too,' he said in a milder voice. 'It's damned hard luck. I myself am a Catholic, at least I was born one, but now I'm – well, I'm nothin'… . A Catholic feels it most… . I've always said that one may find women a great lot worse than women – than a woman like yerself. The ladies that can gorge themselves at table when ye have to do the likes of this for a livin' are more guilty of yer sin than ye are yerself… . Ye know I'm a bit drunk; not much wrong with me, though, for I can see things clearly. If I'm a bit groggy 'twas mostly the fault of that one-armed swine. But I forgive him … I'm an advanced thinker…. What is yer name?'

'Jean.'

'I mean yer real name. It's rarely that an Irishman calls his children by names unbeknown in his own country. Sit closer. There! ye're a nice girl. I like yer brow, it's so white, and yer lips, they're so pretty. Now, give me a kiss. It's nice to have a girl like yerself on my knee. I'm three sheets in the wind, but I like ye. I'm an advanced thinker and I've read, oh! ever so much: Darwin, Huxley. Have ye ever heard of these men?'

'Never,' Norah answered. 'Who are they?'

'They are the great minds of the world. They are the men who proved that there was no heaven and no God.'

'But there is a God!'

'If there is, why do ye suffer like this?'

'Because I'm bad.'

'Ha! ha!' laughed the man. 'How funny! How very funny! Ye are a child, and God would feel honoured if ye allowed Him to lace your shoes. If ye kept very good and pure He might let ye to heaven when ye died – but would He give ye a pair of shoes in mid-winter? ... There's no God... . Kiss me again. By heaven! If ye weren't so good lookin' and so temptin' I'd be generous. I'd go down on my knees and salute ye as a representative of sufferin' womankind, and then go away feelin' honoured if ye only allowed me to kiss your hand. But ye are so winsome! I should like ye to be always pure, but why do men like purity in a woman? They like it so that they can take it away, so that they can kill that which they love. But what am I talkin' about anyway? I'm drunk; not so much – just three sheets in the wind or so. I can see things clearly. I'm a learned man and I know things, bein' a great traveller, and a worker on half the docks in the world, and a sailor too. A.B. before the mast I am. I've seen things in my time, many things, most of them unjust, very unjust. It's seven years since I left home, think of that! Yer father came from Ireland, ye say. What part of the country did he come from?'

'I don't know,' said Norah in a low voice. 'I never asked him. What part of Ireland did ye come from?'

'I said that it is an unjust world, a danged unjust world,' said the man, pressing her tightly and kissing her. 'And in Ireland ye see more injustice than can be seen anywhere in half the world. I've seen women and girls in Ireland working for a penny a day. They were knittin' socks and they had to travel miles for the yarn; aye, and to cross an arm of the sea that took them to their breasts. In the height of winter, too, with the snow fallin' and the sleet. Ah! if yerself had suffered such hardships ye wouldn't live to tell the tale. And children too had to go out into the cold black water! My sister, a very little girl – just about that size' – the sailor held out his hand about two feet from the ground – 'used to work fourteen hours a day when she was but twelve, and her pay was sevenpence ha'penny a week! The hanged little thing! and she wasn't that size... . But I've made some money – salvage, ye know – and I'm goin' to make my sister a lady when I go back to Donegal. She was such a nice wee girl. Wouldn't it be fine if girls always kept young! I think of my sister now as I left her, not grown up at all... . Ye too are a nice lass, so different from those I've seen in the far corners of the world.'

'What is yer name?' asked Norah in a tremulous whisper. But she knew his name, recognised her brother Fergus, saw in his face that indescribable individuality which distinguishes each face from all others in the world. With tense, strained look she waited for the answer to her question.

III

'Fergus Ryan of Frosses in the county Donegal,' replied the sailor, banging his fist against the corner of the chair. 'Fergus Ryan, able-bodied seaman before the mast. I've sailed ever such a lot. Singapore, Calcutta, New York, and Melbourne; I've seen all those places, aye, and nearly all the countries of the world! ... Ah! and I've come across a lot of trouble, fighting and all the rest of it. Two times a knife was left stickin' in me; more than once I was washed into the sea. Ah! I could tell ye things about other places if I liked... . What's wrong with ye? Ye seem scared. But ye're not afraid of sailors, are ye? They're all decent fellows, honest, though a little careless at times. My God! what's comin' over ye? Ye're goin' to faint!'

Norah had suddenly become heavy in the man's arms; the hand which he held contracted tightly and a sickly pallor overspread her countenance.

'Jean!' cried the sailor, staring at the girl with a puzzled expression. 'Jean! That's not yer name, but it doesn't matter. Ye aren't afraid of sailors, are ye? They're rough fellows, most of them, but good at heart. Has a man never told ye before that he got stuck in the ribs with a knife? Women here know nothin', but in Calcutta.... . What am I talkin' about anyhow? Jean, waken up!'

The man rose unsteadily, and bearing the senseless girl in his arms he approached the bed and laid her down carefully, sorting with clumsy fingers the stray tresses on her brow as he did so. Then seizing a glass that stood on the mantelpiece, he rushed out and filled it with water from the tap on the landing. He came in, held Norah up in his arms, and pressed the glass to her lips. She opened her eyes.

'Drink this,' said the sailor. 'What else can I do to help ye?'

'Leave me to myself,' said the girl. 'Go away and leave me. At once, now!' She sat upright in bed and freed herself from his arms; the glass fell to the floor and broke with a musical tinkle; the water splashed brightly and formed into little wells on the planking. The sailor put his hands between his belt and trousers and gazed placidly at the girl.

'Now, that is too bad,' he said, speaking slowly; 'too dashed bad! All sailors are decent fellows at heart, only now and then they tell stories about their wild life. All that I said about the knifing was just a tale.'

'I haven't mind of what ye said,' Norah replied in a whisper, then in a louder voice: 'Go away! Do go away and leave me to myself.'

'I'm not goin' now,' he said in a voice of reproof. 'I cannot go; it's impossible! I've plenty of money. Look!' He pulled a handful of gold from his pocket. 'My God! I cannot leave ye now, I cannot. Why do ye want me to go away?'

Norah looked at the picture of the Virgin and shuddered as if something had stung her. Suddenly it came to her that Fate had done its worst; that evil and unhappiness had reached their supreme climax. She looked hard at her brother, a fixed and almost defiant look in her eyes, her lips set in a firmly-drawn line.

'Why do ye want me to go away?' he repeated.

'Because I'm yer sister Norah, the one that wouldn't be grown up when ye went back.' She felt a grim, unnatural satisfaction in repeating the man's words, and strangely enough her voice was wonderfully calm. 'I made a mistake and it was all my own fault. This is how I'm livin' now – a common woman of the streets. Now go away and leave me to myself. Fergus, I'm grown up!'

'Ye're my sister, ye're Norah?' said the man as the girl freed herself, almost reluctantly, from his arms. He stepped backwards, paused as if he wanted to say something, approached the door, fumbled for a moment with the knob, and went out. On the stairway he stood as if trying to collect his thoughts?

'Where am I?' he muttered. 'It used to be red creepin' things before, and besides, I'm not very drunk at present, not more than three sheets … But the picture of the Blessed Virgin – that was funny! Fergus Ryan, A.B., are ye drunk or are ye mad? Look around ye! This is a flight of stairs, wooden steps; this is an iron railin', that's a window. Now, ye aren't very drunk when ye can notice these things. That's where the one-armed swine struck me. Now I'll look at my watch. A quarter past nine. If I was in the D.T.'s I couldn't tell the time. Besides, I know where I am at present. On the stairway leadin' to a Glasgow kip-shop, and I've been dreamin'. No, I haven't been dreamin', I'm mad! Talkin' to my sister, to Norah! One does dream funny things. She isn't a person like that... . Seven years is a long time and a lot might happen. I'll walk along the street to the quay and maybe the air off the river will clear me up a bit. I'll come back here and free her from the place, for I've money, plenty of it... . I'm afraid of nothin', nothin' in the world. Why should I, me with the track of two knives in my body? But what is the use of talkin' when I'm awfully sick with fear at this moment! God! I've never ran up against a thing like this in all my life before... . Have I not, though? Are they not all somebody's sisters, some mother's children! I've never thought of it in that way before. I'll go up again.'

He reached the top and tried to push the door open. It did not budge. He put his ear to the keyhole and heard sobs, smothered as if by a hand, very near him. On the other side of the door Norah was weeping.

'That's my sister,' he whispered hoarsely. Looking down he saw the light shining through the splintered door. A cavity through which he might pass his fist lay open before him. He put his hand in his pocket, took out several pieces of gold and shoved them into the room; then turned down the stairs and hurried out into the crowded streets.

IV

At the end of an hour he found himself sitting on a capstan by the river, his elbows on his knees and his head buried in his hands. He could not tell how he had gotten there; his brain was throbbing dizzily and myriad little red and blue spots danced before his eyes.

The place was very dark, the sickly light of the few lamps along the river did not light more than a dozen yards around them. On the deck of a near boat a sailor walked up and down, stamping his feet noisily and whistling a popular music-hall tune. Overhead a few stars glimmered soberly; a smell of pitch was in the air; a boat loosened from her moorings was heading downstream. About fifty paces back from the wharf a public house opened out on the river. Dark forms stood at the bar, arms were waving in discussion, and hoarse voices could be heard distinctly. Against the garish light the smallest perpendicular object was outlined in black. Now and again a fist banged on a table and the glasses raised a silvery tinkle of protest against the striker. A woman came out of the place and went on her way along the street, reeling from side to side and giving utterance to some incoherent song. The water lapped against the wharf, a little wind wailed past Fergus' ears; he rose, stretched his arms, took a cigarette from his pocket but threw it away when it was lighted.

'It's lonely here, but in the pub a man may forget things,' he said. 'I wish to heaven I could think of anything but it! I'll try and forget it, but it's hard, danged hard…. . If I had a fight I'd forget, for a moment at least, what I have just seen. My sister Norah? And once I struck a sailor because he said that no girl was as good as I made out my sister to be…. . A whore! My God, a whore! I'll go'ver to the pub and get drunk, mad drunk! What matters now? I'll not go home, I'll never go home!'

Thrusting his hands under his belt, he crossed the street, entered the public house and called for a glass of whisky at the bar. His face was haggard and the palms of both his hands were bleeding.

'I've driven my nails into them,' he said aloud, and looked round angrily. Those who were staring at him turned away their eyes, renewed their conversation and raised their glasses to their lips with evident unconcern. Fergus lifted his liquor and swallowed all at one gulp.

'The same again!' he shouted to the bartender, and lit another cigarette. 'No, not the same; gi me a schooner and a stick[1] in it. God damn ye! what are ye starin' at?'

The bartender who was examining Fergus attentively made no reply, but emptied out the liquor hastily. For a moment Fergus was deep in thought. Suddenly rousing himself he struck the counter a resounding blow with his fist, ripping his knuckles on the woodwork and causing everybody in the room to look round. Then he swallowed his drink and went towards the door. With his hand on the handle, he looked back. 'I'm sorry for kickin' up a noise,' he said. 'Goodnight.'

He passed out. The ray of light from the door showed him staggering across the street towards the quay. Once there he sat down on the capstan, put his hand in his pocket and brought out a fistful of money. He raised it over his head and for a moment it seemed as if he was going to throw it into the water. However, he kept hold of it and returned to the pub, where he purchased a half-pint of whisky. He placed a sovereign on the counter and went out without his change.

Ten o'clock passed; then eleven. Fergus Ryan paced up and down the quay, his hands deep down under his belt and the half-empty bottle in his pocket. The air was now moist and cold; a smell of rotting wood pervaded the place, and the water under the wharf was wailing fitfully. The mooring

[1]A pint of beer and a glass of whisky mixed.

ropes of the nearest vessel strained tensely on the capstan and the giant vessel seemed eager as a stabled colt to get out, away and free.

'I would like to know where the boat is goin' when she sails,' Fergus said, but instantly his thoughts turned to something else. He pulled out his watch and looked at it.

'Would anyone know a new day if the clocks did not chime?' he asked himself in a puzzled way. 'I suppose not. It'll soon be here, the new day... . There, the clocks are beginnin'. Damn them! Damn them! ... If it had been anyone but my sister! Why did she come to Scotland? Landlord, priest, and that arch-scoundrel, McKeown, livin' on her earnin's. I suppose she'll send home money even now, and some of it'll go to the priest to buy crucifixes and pictures of the Virgin, and some of it to the landlord to buy flounces for his wife, and some will go to Farley McKeown. I was goin' to pay a surprise visit and I was livin' on that goin' home for a long while. Ah! but the world is out at elbow. And I'm drunk!'

He stuck both his hands under his belt again and approached the edge of the wharf. Three dark forms slunk out of the shadows and drew in on the sailor. Only when they were beside him did anything warn him of danger. He looked round into the face of the one-armed soldier, whose loose sleeve was fluttering in the wind.

'Ah! ye swine!' Fergus exclaimed and struggled with the belt which prisoned his hands. But the three men were on top of him and the effort was futile. In an instant he was flung outwards and dropped with a splash into the water that seemed to rise and meet him as he fell. It was as cold as ice and the belt held taut despite his efforts to break free. He had a moment to wonder, 'Why did he want to drown me?' he asked himself. His mouth filled and he swallowed. He was now going down head first, but slowly. He made another effort to free his hands, but was unsuccessful. Then he resigned himself to his fate, and consciousness began to ebb from him. He felt that he had forgotten something that was very important, not to himself but to somebody else. Then came complete darkness, and the book of life, as man knows it, was closed forever to Fergus Ryan.

CHAPTER 31

DESPAIR

I

The light on the mantelpiece grew faint, flickered and was going out; the wick, short and draggled, no longer reached the oil. The fire died down and only one red spark could be seen glowing in the white ashes. Twelve of the clock struck out slowly and wearily, as if the chimes were tired of their endless toil. On the floor beside the door a pile of sovereigns, scattered broadcast, glowed bright even under the dying light; the figure on the black crucifix showed very white, save where the daub of red paint told of the Saviour's wounded side.

Norah sat on the bare floor, one leg stretching out, her hands clasped tightly round the knee of the other, which was almost drawn up to her chin. Action was clogged within her, terrible black monotony was piled around and above her; a silence, not even broken by sighs, had taken possession of the girl.

Old Meg rapped at the door many times before Norah heard her; then she rose, poured some oil into the lamp and turned up the light. Afterwards, not because she wanted to, but because she was desirous of hiding from everybody that which had taken place within the room during the last few hours, she lifted the gold pieces and stuffed them into the pocket of her dress.

'Norah Ryan! Norah Ryan!' the old woman was crying outside the door. A dim, hazy thought of all the good things which the gold would buy for her child crossed Norah's mind as she opened the door.

'The little fellow has taken a turn,' the old woman said as she stepped inside and looked curiously round. Of late Norah's compartment had had a curious interest for her: how many times each night between the hours of six and twelve did she come to the door and listen to all that was going on inside. 'I thought that ye'd never hear,' she said. 'I was knockin' and knockin'.'

'He'll soon be better now,' Norah said in a voice so tensely strained that it caused the listener to look at her with surprise. 'I can now pay for doctors, dresses, everything. D'ye hear that, Meg Morraws?' The last sentence sounded like a threat.

The child was doubled up on Meg's bed, and perspiring freely. The old woman had put on a fire that was now blazing merrily.

'I had twa stanes of coal, and I put them all on because of the kid,' said the woman. 'Have ye a penny and I'll get some oil. There's not a drop in the house and I'm clean broke.'

Norah handed the woman a sovereign and told her to keep it. Meg ejaculated a grunt of surprise, made a remark about the shops being closed, promptly discovered that she really had some oil, and put the coin in her pocket.

The night wore on; the child, breathing heavily and coughing, lay in Meg's bed, one little hand showing over the blue lettered sentence on the blanket. The light burned fretfully, the old woman remarked that the oil was mixed with water and that she had got poor value for her money. Norah talked of removing the child into the other room; Meg said it would be madness, and scraping up more coal, heaped it on the fire. In the morning the old woman intended to get very drunk in the pub outside.

A clatter was heard on the stairs; then the sound of a falling body throbbed through the building. Meg went out and found a man – the one-armed soldier – asleep on the landing. She bent down, fumbled with the man's coat, discovered a bottle of whisky, drank and returned the bottle to the sleeper's pocket. She entered the room again, smacking her lips, threw herself down by the fire and started to weep. In a little while she fell asleep.

She woke instinctively at eight o'clock, the hour when the taverns were opening, and rising to her feet, she rubbed her eyes vigorously with her fingers. She found Norah sitting on the edge of the bed, one hand pressed tightly against her knee, one resting lightly on the head of the child.

'Are the pubs open yet?' asked Meg, then in a lower voice: 'I mean, is the child better, the dear little thing?'

'He's dead,' said Norah quietly. 'He died over an hour ago.'

'An hour ago!' exclaimed the woman. 'And why didn't ye waken me? ... I'm a bad yin, Norah Ryan, a gey bad yin!' Saying these words the woman approached the bed and for a moment stared fixedly at the child. Then she paced backwards across the room, sobbing loudly and muttering meaningless words under her breath. Through the dirty window she could see the beer-shop opposite; the doors were open and a young man in shirt-sleeves was taking off the shutters.

'My heart is wae for ye, Norah,' said the old woman. 'Death is a hard thing to bear. But I suppose it'll come to all of us yin day. Oh! oh! and all of us maun gang some day... . I'm goin' oot the noo,' she suddenly exclaimed, stopping in her walk and looking very serious, as if she had remembered something very important. 'I'll be back again in a meenit or twa.'

Meg tied her shawl over her head, and without washing her face went out and became speedily drunk. The young man with the white shirt, who took down the shutters, made some sarcastic remarks about Meg's dirty face, and Meg, being short-tempered, lifted an empty bottle and flung it in the man's face, wounding him terribly. A policeman was called in and the woman was hurried off to the police station.

Noon saw Norah Ryan still sitting on the bedside, her brother's gold jingling in her pocket whenever she moved, and her dead child lying cold and silent beside her.

II

A month of black sorrow passed by. There was a great void in Norah's heart, a void which could never be filled up. Every morning she rose from bed, knowing that the day would have no joy, no consolation for her. Life was almost unendurable; never was despair so over-powering, so terrible. Nothing but the all-encompassing loneliness of the future existed for her now – that terrible future from which she recoiled as a timid animal recoils from the brink of a precipice.

She had suffered so much, was healed a little; now the healing salve of motherhood was wrenched from her by the hand of death. Nothing now remained to the girl but regrets, terrible, torturing, lingering regrets that tore at her mind like birds of prey.

'No matter what I do now, nobody will think me no worse than I am,' she cried, but the thought left her unmoved; even life did not interest her enough to have any desire to end it. Shame had once covered her, enveloped her as in a garment, but now shame was gone; she had thrust it away and even the blind trust in some unshapen chance which had once been hers was now hers no longer.

She worked no more; only once was she roused to action, and that was when she looked at the gold coins in her pocket. This was Fergus' money, and she had often wondered where he had gone to on that night of nights. She went to a neighbouring post office and sent ten pounds home to her mother. Not a line, not a word went with the money order.

'I'm dead, dead to everyone,' she said. 'To me own mother, to Fergus, to all the good people in the wide world.'

III

She was coming back from the post office and the loneliness weighed heavily upon her. She thought of the letter on its way to her own country. Soon the little slip of paper would be in the old home, would be pressed by her mother's fingers; and she, poor little suffering Norah, would still be hemmed up in her narrow room, for all the world just like a bird prisoned in its cage; hearing nothing but the vacant laughter and sound of scurry and scuffle on the stairs and streets, and seeing nothing but the filthy lanes, the smoky sky, and the misery and squalor of the fetid Cowcaddens.

She went into a public house and purchased a bottle of whisky. That night she got drunk and even happy; but the happiness was one of forgetfulness. She awoke from a heavy sleep in the middle of the night and lit her lamp. Then her eyes fell on the picture of the Virgin, the holy water stoup, the little black crucifix and the white Christ with extended arms and bleeding breast nailed upon it.

'I've prayed to ye for years,' she cried, clutching the picture of the Virgin in her hand. 'And look at me tonight! It's little good me prayers has done me; me a drunkard and everything that's worse nor another!' So speaking, she flung the picture into the dead fire. A spiral of ashes rose slowly, fluttered round and settled on the floor. She brought down the holy water stoup, and resisting with a shudder the desire, bred of long custom, to cross herself, emptied the contents into the fireplace. Then she looked at the confidante of her innumerable vague longings – the crucifix.

'Sorrow!' she laughed. 'Did ye ever know what a mother's sorrow for her dead child was? That's the sorrow, the sorrow that would make me commit the sins, the most awful in the whole world. But what am I saying? It's me that doesn't know all the meanin' of many things. If the people at home, the master at school, the priest, any one at all had learned me all the things that every girl should know I wouldn't be here now like something lost on a moor on a black night.'

She went back to her bed, leaving the light burning and the crucifix standing on the little shelf. She wondered why she had not thrown it into the fire as she intended to do, and wondering thus she fell into a deep and drunken slumber.

IV

She awoke early, dressed, and went down the stairs into the street. It was Sunday, solitary and silent, with a slight shower of snow falling. Glasgow looked drearier than usual with its grimy houses and the wet roofs, its dirty, miry streets where the snow dissolved as soon as it fell. Norah's spirits were in sympathy with the sombre surroundings, and she felt glad that the oppressive noise of the weekdays had abated.

Heedless of direction, she walked along and was passing a Catholic chapel when the worshippers who had been to early Mass showered upon her. It was too late to turn back; she walked hurriedly through the crowd, feeling that every eye was turned in her direction.

'Potato-diggers,' someone said. 'They're goin' back to Ireland tomorrow.'

Norah looked at the speaker, then to the crowd at which he pointed. It was a party of Irish workers, now numbering about thirty in all, and a few stragglers were still coming out to swell the ranks. A young girl with very clear skin and beautiful eyes was putting her rosary, one with a shiny cross at the end of it, into her pocket. An old woman with a black shawl over her head was brushing the snow from her hair. Her face was brown and very wrinkled; the few hairs that fell over her brow were almost as white as the snow that covered her shawl.

A young priest in cassock and gown came out, smiling broadly. 'It's early in the year for snow,' he said, looking at the potato-diggers.

'One may expect anything at this season of the year, yer reverence,' said the old woman with the white hair. The young girl looked closely at the priest, hanging on every word that he uttered.

'Are you all goin' across home, this winter?' asked the priest.

' 'All of us,' said a man.

'You like the old country?' enquired the priest.

'Well may we,' answered the old woman. 'It's our own country.'

Norah was moving away; the last words came to her like an echo.

'Our own country!' Norah repeated half aloud, every word coming slowly through her lips. 'But I have no country at all, no country! He's a nice, kind priest, indeed he is. Speakin' to them just as if they were his own people! I would like to go and confess me sins to that priest!'

The snow fell faster, and presently Norah felt cold. A fit of coughing seized her and the sharp pain which seldom went away from her left shoulder-blade began to trouble her acutely. She turned and went back to her room.

All that evening two pictures kept rising in her mind. One was of the priest with the smiling face talking to the potato-diggers; the other was the picture of the young girl with the clear skin and the beautiful eyes putting the rosary, with the shiny cross at the end of it, into her pocket.

CHAPTER 32

CONFESSION

I

A week passed; the hour was twelve o'clock on a Saturday night. The clocks were striking midnight but the streets were still crowded with people. A boat could be heard hooting on the Broomielaw; a train whistling at Enoch Street station. A woman came along a narrow lane on the Cowcaddens, shouldering her way amongst the people, and abusing in no polite terms those who obstructed her way. She wore a shawl almost torn to shreds and she staggered a little as she walked. Her features were far from prepossessing; dry hacks dented her cheeks and brow; her lips were rough and almost bloodless and wisps of draggled hair hung over her face. As she walked along she broke into snatches of song from time to time.

Under the gaslight staring eyes set in sickly or swarthy faces glared at her; rude remarks and meaningless jokes were made; sounds of laughter rose, echoed and died away. Suddenly a noise, loud as a rising gale, swept through the lane; a man hurried past and rushed along the streets, a young girl followed. The crowd, as if actuated by one common impulse, scurried past the woman, yelling and shrieking. A drunken man stared stupidly after the mob, then fell like a wet sack to the pavement; a labourer struck against the prostrate body; fell, and rose cursing. A whistle was blown. 'The slops! The slops!' a ragged youth shouted, and a hundred voices took up the cry. 'Run! Run!' others roared.... . A little toddling child stood on the pavement crying, one finger in its mouth and its big curious eyes fixed on the rabble.

'What are ye greetin' for?' asked the woman in the ragged shawl. 'Have ye lost yerself?'

'I want me mither!' wailed the child.

'Ye're here, are ye?' cried a stout, brazen-faced woman, ambling up and seizing the infant, who was trying to chew a penny which the stranger had just given it. 'It's a lass that's fainted on the pavement,' explained the mother, pointing to the crowd. 'I think the corner boys, rascals that they are, were playin' tricks on her.'

'That's always the way with people,' said the strange woman. 'See and don't let the child swallow the bawbee.'

With these words she hurried into the press of people, the corners of her shawl fluttering round her. A group of ragged men and women stood on the pavement, chattering noisily. Against the wall a frail form was propped up between two young girls, one of whom had a frightened look on her face; the other was smiling and chewing an orange. A man, lighting a pipe and sheltering the match under the palm of his hand, made some suggestion as to what should be done, but nobody paid any heed.

The woman with the torn shawl elbowed her way through the crowd, and came to a standstill when she caught sight of the girl propped up on the pavement.

'It's Norah Ryan!' she exclaimed.

'That's the name,' a female in the crowd said. 'She lives up 42. She's a woman of the kind that .... But ye ken what I mean.'

'And ye'd let her die here, wi'out givin' a hand to help her!' cried the newcomer, turning fiercely on the speaker. 'Help me to take the lass to her house.'

The two girls assisted by two men helped the woman to carry Norah upstairs. The crowd followed, pressing in and shoving against those in front. Someone made a rude remark and the laughter which greeted it floated far up even to the topmost landing, where the paralysed beggar, somewhat the worse for liquor, was singing one of his cheery songs.

II

The accident to Norah happened in this way.

After seeing the Irish diggers come out of the chapel, she felt a sudden desire to go and confess her sins to the young priest. This desire she did not strive to explain or analyse; she only knew that she would be happy in some measure if she went to the chapel again.

The memory of her sins began to trouble her. How many they had been! she thought. From that night when a ring sparkled in the darkness outside Morrison's farmhouse up till now, when she was a common woman of the streets, what a life she had led! With her mind aspiring towards heaven she became conscious of the mire in which her feet were set; the religion of childhood was now making itself heard in the heart of the woman. Nature had given Norah a power peculiarly her own that enabled her to endure suffering and in turn counselled resignation; but that power was now gone. She required something to lean against, and

her heart turned to the faith of which the little black crucifix
on the mantlepiece was the emblem. On the Saturday
evening following her meeting with the potato-diggers she
went to confession.

She entered the chapel, her shawl drawn tightly over
her head and almost concealing her face, which looked fair,
white and childlike, seen through the half-light of the large
building. Although she tried to walk softly her boots made
a loud clatter on the floor and the echo caught the sound
and carried it far down through nave and chancel. A few
candles, little white ghosts with halos of feeble flame
around their heads, threw a dim light on the golden
ornaments of the altar and the figure of the Christ standing
out in bold relief against the darkness over the sacristy door.
The sanctuary lamp, hanging from the roof and swaying
backwards and forwards, showed like a big red eye.

Outside the confessional a number of men and women
were seated on long forms; one or two were kneeling, their
rosaries clicking as the beads ran through their fingers.
Those seated, with eyes sparkling brightly whenever they
turned their heads, looked like white-faced spirits. An old
man was shuffling uneasily, his nailed boots rasping on
the floor from time to time; a woman having been seized
with the hiccough rose and went out, and the row on the
seat gathered closer, each no doubt pleased as the prospect
of getting in advance of at least one other sinner. Norah
sat down at the end of the row, a strange fluttering in her
heart, and her fingers opening and closing nervously. She
felt that the penitents knew her, that they would arise
suddenly and accuse her of her sins. A man opposite looked
fixedly at her and she hung her head. The low mumbling
voice of the priest saying the words of absolution over a
sinner could be heard coming from the confessional. But

had there ever been a sinner as bad as she was? Norah asked herself. For her sins it was so hard to ask forgiveness.

'Never, never will I get absolution,' she said under her breath.

Then she began to wonder if the young, pleasant-faced priest who talked to the potato-diggers was in the confessional. He would not be hard on her; he looked so kind and gentle!

'I'm afeared, very afeared,' she whispered to herself. 'I'll not go in this time; I'll go away and come back again.'

But even as she spoke the woman with the hiccough came back and took up her position on the end of the seat. Norah found that she could not get away now without disturbing the woman. She bowed her head and began to pray.

III

She could not see the priest in the confessional, but could hear him breathing in short, laboured pants like a very fat old woman. It couldn't be the young man, Norah thought, as she went down on her knees and began the 'Confiteor'. The priest hurried over the words in a weary voice; Norah repeated them after him, stopping now and again to draw her breath. A sensation, almost akin to that which precedes drowning, gripped her throat.

'What sins have ye committed?' asked the priest. 'Tell me the greatest first.'

'I am a woman of the streets.' She had now taken the plunge and felt calmer as she waited to be asked a question.

'God's merciful,' said the priest, and his voice was tinged with interest. 'Go on.'

'I am the mother of a child that died but was never christened,' said Norah. 'It was all through my own fault.'

'You haven't been married?'

'No,' said the girl, with a shudder. 'I often thought of takin' my own life.'

'Yes.'

'I took to drink and then threw the picture of the Blessed Virgin and a stoup of holy water into the fire.'

She paused.

'Ye've given up the life of the streets?' enquired the priest in a voice teeming with curiosity.

'I have,' answered Norah.

'Did ye like it?'

'No.' The answer was the echo of a whisper almost.

'God's merciful,' said the priest. His tones seemed hoarse with the passion of a sensuous youth. 'And yer other sins?' he asked.

IV

She prayed for a long time before the altar, mingling tears with her prayers. Footfalls came and went, but nobody paid any heed to the kneeling woman. Of this she was glad. Norah wanted to do good, as other people commit evil actions, secretly. The trembling shadows thrown by the sanctuary lamp played round the Christ who, with outstretched hand, stood over the sacristy door. How great and serious the Saviour looked! The girl imagined that He was thinking of some great secret belonging to humanity but hidden so deeply that it was unknown to man.

At ten o'clock she returned to her room and sat there for a long while. A great peace had stolen into her soul, a peace that was mingled with no regrets. She had forgotten the pain in her shoulder, forgotten everything but the figure of the Christ over the sacristy door, and the hand that was held out above her head as if in blessing.

It was near midnight when she went out to buy provisions for the next day. The hooligans at the street corner were very drunk and very noisy. There was no policemen about; a fight some distance off was engaging their attention.

'Ah! here's one that'll hae some siller, the kip-shop wench!' shouted one of the roughs, a big, round-shouldered rascal, on seeing Norah. 'Fork out, my pretty, and gie us some tin.'

'Fork out!' roared the rest of the gang in chorus.

Norah stood undecided, one foot in the gutter, one on the pavement. The grocer's shop was a dozen paces away.

'The cops will be here in a jiffy,' someone shouted in a tense whisper. 'Search her!'

Then followed a wild rush and Norah was conscious of many things in the next few minutes. The air seemed suddenly charged with the fumes of alcohol; hands seized her, rough fingers fumbled at her blouse, opened it and rested on her breasts; a whistle was blown, she fell to the pavement, got dragged for a few paces on the wet street and was pulled to her feet again. Someone laid hands on her purse and took it out; a scramble ensued, then a fight for the money. Norah was thrown down again and trampled upon. The hooligans tore the purse and several coins fell to the ground. A second whistle was blown, and the crowd disappeared, leaving Norah lying in a dead faint on the pavement.

V

When she recovered consciousness she was in her own room, lying on the bed. The lamp was lit and she could hear the coal crackling in the fire. She raised herself up in bed and looked enquiringly around. A stranger, a woman who was bending over the fire, hurried forward.

'And how are ye, Norah Ryan?' asked the stranger.

'It's Ellen that's in it,' exclaimed Norah, sinking back on the pillow, but more from surprise than from weariness. 'Where have ye come from, Ellen?'

'I was in the street,' explained the woman, who was indeed Ellen – Gourock Ellen. 'I saw ye lyin' on the pavement and I kent ye at once. A woman in the crowd knew where ye lived…. Ye hae nae muckle changed, Norah Ryan. Ye're just the same as ye was when I saw ye last in Jim Scanlon's squad. And d'ye mind how me and ye was in the one bed?'

'Ellen, I'm glad that ye came,' said Norah in a low voice. 'I used to be often thinkin' of ye, Ellen.'

'Thinkin' of me, lass?' exclaimed Ellen, bending over the bed, but keeping her lips as far away as possible from Norah lest the young woman should detect the smell of whisky off her breath. 'Why were ye thinkin' about me? Someone worthier should be in your thoughts… . The rascals in the streets! Ah, the muckle scamps! They should be run into the nick and never let out again. Ill-treatin' a little lassie like you!'

Norah looked up at the woman. Ellen's pock-marked face was still full of the same unfailing good nature which belonged to her years before when she worked in Micky's Jim's squad.

'Where is Annie?'

'I dinna ken. She went off with a man and I haven't seen her never since.' Ellen smiled, but so slightly that the smile did not change the expression of her eyes.

'Ye don't tell me! And ye've never been back at the squad again?'

'Never back. I was times workin' at the rag-pickin' and times gatherin' coal from the free coup.'

'That's what Mary Martin done,' Norah exclaimed. 'She was a woman known to me.'

'And ye kent old Mary!' said Ellen. 'Me and her have worked together for many's a day, makin' a shillin' a day each at the job.'

The woman paused.

'Are ye feelin' a wee better, Norah?' she asked presently.

'I'm fine, Ellen,' was the answer. 'I could get up and run about and I'm not in the least sleepy. What were the corner boys wantin' to do?'

'They wanted siller –'

'My purse, Ellen! Have they taken it from me?' Norah searched nervously in the pockets of her dress.

'I'm afeared that they have.'

'Mother of God! I haven't one penny now, Ellen, not one brown penny!' Norah exclaimed. 'It'll be the streets for me again.'

'We'll get along somehow, if we work together,' said Ellen.

'We'll work together; that's the way,' Norah whispered after a moment's consideration.

'Twa is always better than yin,' Ellen replied.

Norah looked closely at the woman as if puzzling out something; then her eyes closed gently and quietly and she fell asleep. She awoke several times during the night, mumbled incoherent words, then sank into a deep slumber again. And all night Gourock Ellen watched over Norah Ryan. Morning found her still sitting beside the bed, weary-eyed but patient, her eyes fixed on the face of the sleeping girl.

CHAPTER 33

ST JOHN VIII, I–II

I

In the morning Norah was in a raging fever. She spoke in her delirium of many things, prattling like a child about the sea and curraghs of Frosses going out beyond Trienna Bar in the grey dusk of the harvest evening. She held conversation with people visible to none but herself: with Fergus, with Dermod Flynn, with her mother, with the dead child. The girl's whole history for the last three years was thus disclosed to Gourock Ellen. Days came and went; the patient became no better. A doctor was called in; he applied his stethoscope to Norah's chest and shook his head gravely.

'Well?' asked Ellen eagerly.

'I'll come again tomorrow,' said the doctor, and his tones implied that this was a very important announcement. 'Meanwhile –' and he gave Ellen instructions as to how she should treat the patient.

Money was scarce; Norah had lost every penny of hers on the night that the hooligans attacked her. The other woman had only twenty-five shillings in her possession, and this went very quickly. Then Ellen called on the Jew, Isaac Levison, who had the pawnbroking business on the stair.

'D'ye ken the lass Norah Ryan?' Ellen enquired of the man, an undersized, genial-looking fellow with sharp eyes and a dark moustache.

'I know her,' said the Jew. He knew Ellen by sight and reputation; the kind way in which she was treating the girl was common talk on the stairs.

'I want the len o' three punds,' said Ellen. 'I can only gie my promise to pay it back when I get work. Is that enough of a security?'

'I'll take your word,' said the Jew, who was to some extent a judge of character, and who was kindly disposed towards the woman, having heard much that was good about her. 'Five per cent,' he added. 'That's extra good terms.'

When the doctor came the next day Ellen spoke to him.

'Cash is gey scarce here,' she said, 'but do yer best for the girl and I'll meet the bill some day. I'll meet it, doctor, so help me God!'

The doctor smiled slightly; such protestations were not new to him. Besides, he was a kindly man.

'I'll do my best for her,' he said. 'And as to payment – well, we'll see.'

'Ye'll get paid,' said Ellen fiercely. 'Ye must wait, but it doesn't matter what happens, ye'll get paid, mind that! Though the lass is no blood relation of mine, I dinna want ye to work for charity. And I'll pay ye yer siller; aye, if I've to work my fingers to the bone to do it.'

The doctor looked at the woman and knew that she was speaking from the depths of her heart.

II

Another fortnight, and the tang of spring was in the air. Ellen had procured work as a charwoman in a large school, and being a good, reliable worker, several smaller jobs came her way. Her wages now amounted to nine shillings a week. Norah had recovered a little; the cough was not as hard as formerly; the pain under her left shoulder-blade had lost its sting, but, though hardly noticeable, it was always there. At first Ellen found it difficult to induce Norah to stop in bed; the girl wanted to get about and do some work. Only when she got to her feet did Norah become fully conscious of the weakness in her legs and spine.

As she lay there in her narrow bed she could discern through the cracked window the sky, always sombre grey and covered with low, sagging clouds. Now and again she could see a homing crow fly past on lazy wings or perhaps a white sea-gull turning sharply far up in the sky with a glint of sunshine resting on its distended wings. And often on a clear night, when the moonbeams filtered through the ragged blind, Norah would dream of Frosses, and the sea, the old home, with the moon rising over the hills of Glenmornan and lighting up the coast of Donegal.

'I have been a great trouble to ye, Ellen,' Norah said one evening, turning round in the bed and looking earnestly at her friend. 'I seem to be only a trouble to everyone that I meet, and now to yerself most of all. Ye have been the great friend to me, Ellen.'

'Haud yer tongue, ye muckle simple hussy,' said Ellen with a smile, sorting the blankets on the bed. 'Now gang to sleep and dinna let me hear ye fash any longer. Are ye happy?'

'I'm very happy, Ellen, waitin' for the minit.'

'What are ye haverin' aboot, silly lassie?'

'I used to build castles on Dooey Strand, that's home in Donegal, when I was wee,' said Norah. 'And then when they were big and high the tide would come in and sweep them away in one little minit. Them castles were like people's lives. Used ye to make castles in the sand when ye were wee, Ellen?'

'Not in the sand, but in the air, Norah,' said Ellen reminiscently. 'I began the bad life gey early. My mither – she wasna what some people might cry vera guid; but she was my mither, Norah. Maybe I wasna wanted when I came, but she had the pain o' bringin' me forth. Well, I kent most things before I was sixteen years auld. Sixteen is an age when a girl dinna weigh her actions, and sixteen likes pretty dresses, and sixteen disna like to starve. Though we were poor and often hungry I kept pure for a long while. But to tell the truth I didna think it worth it in the end, Norah.'

She paused for a moment and sorted a piece of cloth to fit on the dress she was patching.

'At eighteen – that's a gey guid wheen of years ago now – I took it in my heid that I wisna goin' to sin ony mair,' Ellen went on. 'I got very religious and bowed myself in the dust before God. "He'll ne'er forgie me my trespasses," I said, "for I'm a poor miserable sinner." I got a Bible then and read in it mony things that were a consolation and an upliftin' to me. And last night I bought one on the streets, Norah. A man with a barrow was sellin' them, and I got one for a penny. I thought that maybe we would read pieces from it together.'

'The Catholic Church doesn't allow us to read the Bible,' said Norah.

'I'll only read one little bit,' said Ellen, taking a dilapidated volume from her pocket. 'Ye'll listen to it, Norah, won't ye?'

'Anything that pleases yerself, Ellen, will please me.'

III

Ellen laid down her scissors, trimmed the wick of the lamp, resumed her seat, wetted her thumb and began to turn over the pages of the volume.

'Here it is,' she said, and commenced to read in a low voice.

"'And early in the morning He came again into the temple, and all the people came unto Him; and He sat down and taught them. And the Scribes and Pharisees" – they were a kind of people that lived in them days, Norah – "brought unto Him a woman taken in" – who committed a bad sin; "and when they had set her in the midst, they say unto Him: Master, this woman was taken" – when she was sinnin' – "in the very act. Now Moses in the Law commanded us that such should be stoned: but what sayest Thou? This they said, temptin' Him, that they might have to accuse Him. But Jesus stooped down and with His finger wrote on the ground, as though He heard them not. So when they continued asking Him, He lifted up Himself and said unto them: HE THAT IS WITHOUT SIN AMONGST YOU LET HIM FIRST CAST A STONE AT HER. And again He stooped down and wrote on the ground. And they which heard it, being convicted by their own conscience, went out one by one, beginning at the eldest, even unto the last, and Jesus was left alone and the woman standing in the midst. When Jesus had lifted up Himself and saw none but the woman, He said unto her: Woman, where are those thine accusers? Hath no man condemned thee? She said, No man, Lord. And Jesus said unto her: Neither do I condemn thee; go, and sin no more."

Tears showed in Ellen's eyes when she finished reading; then without giving Norah time to speak, she went on with her own story.

'I gave up the life on the streets for twa and twa – for nearly four months, Norah. Then my mither took ill and was like to dee. I nursed her for a long whilie, then the siller gaed awa' and hunger came in its place. I had never learnt ony trade; there was only one thing to be done, Norah. I went oot tae the streets again, oot to sin knowingly, and what was before an ignorant lassie's mistake was then and after a fault, black in the eyes of heaven.'

Ellen paused and looked up at the roof. Perhaps she was again seeing herself as she was on that evening long ago, a wistful and pretty girl, a child almost, going out into the streets to earn the money that would buy food and clothing for her ailing mother.

'I came back the next morn, greetin' a wee, if I remember right, and twa pieces of gold in my pocket. When I came into our room I found my mither lyin' on her chair by the fire, and she was dead!'

'Poor Ellen,' said Norah in a low voice. 'Ye had a hard time of it from the beginnin'.'

'Hard's not the word,' cried Ellen, and a fierce look came into her eyes. 'It was damnable!'

There was silence for a moment, when the two women felt rather than thought. As in a dream, they could hear crowds passing like tides along the narrow lane outside.

'Will God ever forgive us for our sins?' asked Norah.

'Ye have never ceased to be pure in the sight of God, lass,' said Ellen; 'and if baith of us are judged accordin' to our sufferin's we needna hae muckle fear. That's the way I look at things, Norah!'

And Ellen, taking up her scissors, restarted her work, a smile almost angelic in its sadness playing in odd little waves over her face. And in the poor woman's soul, glowing brighter even in misfortune, burned that divine and primary spark which evil and accident could never extinguish.

CHAPTER 34

LONGINGS

I

Time wore on and Norah lived for the most part in a world of fancy, spoke to imaginary individuals and at moments addressed Ellen as Sheila Carrol or as Maire a Glan. Sometimes she was gloomy and reserved, made folds in the sheets, murmured in an almost inaudible voice, and seemed to be calculating distances. The least movement of the left arm pained her and caused her to groan aloud. Now and again her eyes were dull, heavy, and glassy; at other times they were relit and sparkled like stars. She ate next to nothing; wrinkles formed round her eyes, her cheeks were sunken; she became the shadow, the ghost of her former self.

After a while the name of Dermod Flynn entered into her prattle; at first she spoke of him, eventually she spoke to him as if he were in the room. When her mind resumed its normal state all this was forgotten. Once Ellen spoke to her of Dermod Flynn.

'I would like to see him again, just once,' Norah said, then added: 'I'm a heart-break to ye, Ellen; to everybody that I ever met. I'm like a little useless wean, useless, of no use at all.'

Acting on Norah's wishes a priest was called in, heard Norah's confession and administered the sacraments. This made the girl happy for many days. Ellen disliked priests, but never gave hint of her dislike to Norah.

'Ye're sic a funny little thing,' she exclaimed more than once. 'I took a fancy to ye when I saw ye for the first time that mornin' on Greenock Quay along wi' Dermod Flynn. He was a comely laddie, and I would like to see him comin' here.'

'I wonder where'll he be now?' said Norah.

'I wunner.'

II

Spring was over the town. The sun shone almost daily through the window and rested on Norah's bed; the birds twittered on the roof; their songs, even in the city slums, were filling the air.

Starvation was very near the two occupants of the room. They were three weeks behind with the rent, the landlord threatened to evict them; the grocer grumbled, the coalman would not supply coals. Added to this, Ellen had lost her job as charwoman in the school. The headmistress, a dear old pious soul! had made enquiries into Ellen's past life, and the result of the investigations was that the charwoman was told to leave the premises.

Ellen was thinking of these things one morning. Norah was tossing restlessly in the bed, when a knock came to the door.

'Come in!' Ellen cried.

A man entered, one hand deep in his trousers' pocket, a worn cap set awkwardly on his shaggy head. He was a powerfully built individual, broad-shouldered and heavy-limbed. He had not shaved for weeks; his beard stood out in sharp bristles from his jaw.

'Moleskin Joe, what d'ye want?' Ellen asked, her voice charged with resentment.

'Did ye know Dermod Flynn?' asked the man, gazing curiously at the woman tossing in the bed.

'I kent him.'

'I'm lookin' for a wench – for an old sweetheart of his, so to speak,' said the man.

'It's Dermod Flynn that he's speakin' about! D'ye know Dermod?' asked Norah, sitting up in bed and gazing intently at the stranger. Her cheeks flushed; all her young beauty seemed to have returned suddenly and settled in her face.

'It's like this,' said the stranger, shuffling uneasily. 'It's like this: me and Dermod's pals. We did graft together on many's a shift, aye, and fought together too. And he can use his fives! Well, Dermod often told me about an old flame of his, called – her name was –'

'Norah Ryan,' said Ellen.

'That's it,' said the man, looking at the girl in the bed. 'Perhaps you'll be her. If you are, you buckle on to Dermod. He's one that any girl should be proud of; and he can use his fives! But women don't understand these things.'

'*Don't* they?' queried Ellen.

'Some think they do,' said the man. 'Well, Dermod went to London and worked on a newspaper as a somethin'. Graft of that kind is not in my line, and the job wasn't in Dermod's line neither. He came back here to Glasgow, and he's lookin' for his old flame. I'm just helpin' him.'

'Well, that's the lass he's lookin' for,' said Ellen, pointing to the girl in the bed. 'Now run awa', Joe, and bring Dermod.'

'By all that's holy! she's a takin' wench,' said the man, looking first at the girl, then at Ellen, then back to the girl in the bed again. 'Well, I'd better be goin',' he said.

'Ye'd better,' answered Ellen.

'Are ye well off here?' asked the man, who was apparently unperturbed by Ellen's remark.

'Gey poorly,' said the woman; 'we'll soon hae a moonlight flittin'; that's when we have anything to flit with.'

The man dived his hand into his trousers' pocket, rattled some money, then as if a sudden thought struck him he went towards the door.

'Send Dermod at once, will ye?' asked Norah.

'I'll do that,' said the man, then to Ellen: 'I want to speak to you.'

She accompanied Moleskin out on the landing and closed the door behind her.

'Isn't she a comely wench!' said the man.

'I know that. Is that all ye have to say to me?'

'Why is she in bed at this hour of the day?'

'She's waitin' for the meenit,' said Ellen in a low whisper. 'She'll maybe no' last another twenty-four hours.'

'And she looks the picture of health!' said the man.

Ellen told of the assault on Norah, her narrative bristling with short, sharp, declamatory sentences. When she finished the man pulled some money from his pocket and put it into Ellen's palm.

'Dermod's my matey,' he explained apologetically. 'I'll bring the youngster here and we'll be back in a jiffy. He's lodgin' near the wharf. And by heaven! we'll cure the girl. She'll be better in next to no time.'

Ellen shook her head sadly. 'Lungs canna be put back again once they're gone,' she said. 'But hurry and bring Dermod Flynn here.'

The man turned and clattered downstairs.

III

'Moleskin Joe is an old friend of mine,' said Ellen, coming in and counting the money as she made her way towards the bed. 'Thirty bob – two – two fifteen – three, three punds nine and sixpence!' she cried. 'And Dermod will be here in a meenit… . My goodness! what's gang wrang wi' ye, child?'

Norah was lying unconscious on the bed, a stream of blood issuing from her lips. One pale white hand was stretched over the blue lettering of the blanket, the other was doubled up under her body.

'Poor Norah Ryan!' exclaimed Ellen, opening the window and drawing back the clothes from the girl's chest. 'It's the excitement that's done it… . Wake up, Norah! It's me, Ellen, that's speakin' to ye. Ye ken me, don't ye?'

She placed her hand on Norah's breast. Although her hand had lost most of its delicacy of touch she could feel the heart beating faintly, almost like the wing of a butterfly flickering against the net in which it is imprisoned.

'She'll be better in a wee meenit! There, she's comin' to. She'll ken me as soon as she opens her eyes!' said Ellen, and she nearly cried with joy.

In a little while Norah recovered and looked round with large, puzzled eyes; then, as if recollecting something –

'Is he comin'?' she asked eagerly, but so softly that Ellen had to bend down to catch the words. 'He was the kind-hearted boy, Dermod,' she went on. 'I always liked him better than anyone, Ellen… . 'Twas the bad girl that I was … and I'm a burden on ye more than on anyone else.'

'God send that I bear the burden for long and many's a day yet,' said the woman. 'Ye've been a guid frien' to me, Norah, and I feel happy workin' awa here by yer side.

Ye'll get better too, for when Dermod comes ye'll be happy, and the happy live long.'

Norah put out her hand and grasped that of her friend. 'God bless ye, Ellen,' she said. 'Ye've been more'n a mother to me. But I'm not long for this world now. Something tells me that I'm for another place. I'm not afeared to die, Ellen; why should I? But sorrow is on me because I'm leavin' you.'

The darkness fell; the two women were silent, their hands clasped tightly and their eyes full of tears. But with them was a certain strange happiness; one bright thought joined another bright thought in their minds just as the beams of a newly lit fire join together in a darkened room.

Norah fell asleep. The lamp, which had become leaky, had now gone out. Ellen lit a candle, stuck it into the neck of a bottle and placed the bottle on the floor. The place looked desolate and forbidding; dead ashes lay in the fireplace; a pile of rags – Ellen's bed – lay in the corner. There was no picture in the place, nothing to lessen the monotony save the little crucifix on the mantelpiece, and this relieving feature was a symbol of sorrow.

Ellen glanced at the sleeper. How strangely beautiful she looked now! It seemed as if something spiritual and divine had entered the body of Norah, causing her to look more like the creation of some delightful dream than an erring human being bowed with a weight of sorrow.

'I'll go out and get some coals,' said Ellen, speaking under her breath. 'Then we'll have a cheerful fire for Dermod Flynn when he comes. He was sic a comely lad when in Jim Scanlon's squad. And poor Norah! Ah! it's sic a pity the way things work out in this life. There seems to be a bad management of things somewhere.'

CHAPTER 35

THE FAREWELL MEETING

I

For the rest of that evening, between short periods of sleep, one bright vision merged with another in front of Norah's eyes, and in every vision the face of Dermod Flynn stood out distinctly clear. She spoke to him; talked of home, of the people whom both had known, of the master of Glenmornan schoolhouse, of Maire a Glan, of Micky's Jim and the squad, Willie the Duck, and all those whom they had known so well a few short years before. But for all she spoke, Dermod never answered; he looked at her in silence where she lay, the life passing from her as a spent fountain weakens, as an echo dies away.

The candle threw out a fitful flame in the room, shadows rushed together on the ceiling, forming and breaking free, dancing and capering in strange antics. Steps could be heard on the stairs; the tap was running outside and the water fell with a hissing sound. Ellen was still out; the room was deserted; nothing there but the shadows on the ceiling and the sick girl on the bed by the window.

She was asleep when Dermod Flynn came, and wakened to find him standing by her bed, looking down at her with

eyes full of love and pity. There was no surprise written
on her face when she saw him; to Norah for days he had
been as near in dreams as he was now in real flesh and
blood.

'I was dreamin' of ye, Dermod,' she said in a low voice,
sitting up with one elbow buried in the pillow and her
bare shoulders showing white and delicate under her locks
of brown hair.

'Ye took the good time in comin',' she went on, but
there was longing, not protest, in her voice. 'Ellen told me
that ye were lookin' for meself.'

Dermod was down on his knees by the bedside. ''Tis
good to see you again, darling,' he said. 'I have been looking
for you for such a long time.'

'Have ye?' she asked, her voice, tinged with a thousand
regrets, rising a little as if in mute protest, against the
shadows dancing on the roof. Sobbing like a child, she sank
back in the bed. 'It's the kindly way that ye have with ye,
Dermod,' she said in a quieter voice. 'Ye don't know what
I am, and the kind of life I've been leadin' for a good lot of
years, to come and speak to me again. It's not for a decent
man like yerself to speak to the likes of my kind. It's meself
that has suffered a big lot too, Dermod, and I deserve pity
more than hate. Me sufferin's would have broke the heart
of a cold mountainy stone.'

'Poor Norah!' Dermod said, half in whispers; 'well do
I know what ye have suffered. I have been looking for you
for a long while, and now, having found you, I want to
make you very happy.'

'Make me happy!' she exclaimed, withdrawing her
hands from Dermod's grasp as if they had been stung.
'What would ye be doin', wantin' to make me happy? I'm
dead to ev'rybody, to the people at home and to me own

very mother. What would she want with me now, her daughter and the mother of a child that never had the priest's blessin' on its head. A child without a lawful father! Think of it, Dermod! What would the Frosses and Glenmornan people say if they met me now on the streets? It was a dear child to me, it was. And ye are wantin' to make me happy! Every time ye come ye say the same…. D'ye mind seein' me on the streets, Dermod?'

'I remember it, Norah.'

He looked at her closely, puzzled no doubt by her utterances. She was now rambling a little again. Dreams intermingled with reality and her fingers were making folds in the sheets. Dermod remembered how in Glenmornan this was considered a sign of death. She began to talk to herself, her head on the pillow, one erring tress of hair lying across her cheek.

'It was the child, Dermod,' she said, a smile playing over her features; 'it was the little boy and he was dyin', both of a cough that was stickin' in his throat and of starvation. As for meself, I hadn't seen bread or that what buys it for many's a long hour, even for days itself. I couldn't get work to do. I would beg, aye, Dermod, I would, and me a Frosses woman, but I was afeared that the peelis would put me in prison. In the end there was nothin' left to me but to take to the streets…. There were long white boats goin' out and we were watchin' them from the strand of Trienna Bay. The boats of our own people. Ah! my own townland, Dermod! … I called the little child Dermod, but he never got the christenin' words said over him, nor a drop of holy water…. Where is Ellen? … Ellen, ye're a good friend to me, ye are! The people that's sib to myself don't care what happens to me, one of their own kind; but it's ye yerself that has the good heart, Ellen. And ye say that

Dermod Flynn is comin' to see me? I would like to see Dermod
again.'

'I'm here, Norah,' said the young man, endeavouring
by his voice to recall her straying fancy. 'I'm here, Norah.
I'm Dermod Flynn. Do ye know me now?'

There was no answer.

'Norah, do ye remember me?' Dermod repeated. 'I am
Dermod – Dermod Flynn. Say "Dermod" after me.'

She opened her eyes and looked at him with a puzzled
glance. 'Is it ye indeed, Dermod?' she exclaimed. 'I knew
that ye were comin' to see me. I was thinkin' of ye often,
and many's the time I thought that ye were standin' by me
bed quiet like and takin' a look at me. Ye're here now, are
ye? Say "True as death".'

"True as death!'

'But where is Ellen?' she asked, 'and where is the man
that came here this mornin', and left a handful of money
to help us along? He was a good, kindly man; talkin' about
fives too, just the same as Micky's Jim. Joe was his name.'

She paused.

'There were three men on the street and they made fun
of me when I was passin' them,' she went on. 'Then they
made a rush at me, threw me down and tramped over me.
I was left on the cold streets, lyin' like to die and no one to
help me. 'Twas Ellen that picked me up, and she has been
a good friend to me ever since; sittin' up at night by my
side and workin' her fingers to the bone for me through
the livelong day. Ellen, ye're very good to me.'

'Ellen isn't here,' Dermod said, the tears running down
his cheeks. With clumsy but tender fingers he brushed back
the hair from her brow and listened to her talk as one listens
to the sound of a lonely breeze, the mind deep in unfathomable
reflections.

Gourock Ellen entered the room and cast a curious look round. Seeing Dermod kneeling at the bedside the woman felt herself an intruder. She came forward, however, and bent over the girl, her shoulder touching the head of the young man.

Norah's eyes were closed and a pallor overspread her features.

'Are ye asleep, lassie?'

There was no answer to her question; the woman bent closer and pressed Norah's breast with her hand.

'Are ye come back, Ellen?' Norah asked without opening her eyes. 'I was dreamin' in the same old way,' she went on. 'I saw him comin' back again. He was standin' by me bed and he was very kind like he always was.'

'But he's here, little lass,' said Ellen, turning to Dermod Flynn. 'Speak to her, man,' she whispered. 'She's been wearin' her heart away for you, for a long weary while. Speak to her and we'll save her yet. She's just wanderin' in her head.'

Norah opened her eyes; the candle was going out and Dermod could mark the play of light and shade on the girl's face.

'Then it was not dreamin' that I was!' she cried. 'It's Dermod himself that's in it and back again. Just comin' to see me! It's himself that has the kindly Glenmornan heart and always had. Dermod, Dermod! I have a lot to speak to ye about!'

Her voice became strained; to speak cost her an effort, and Dermod, who had risen, bent down to catch her words.

'It was ye that I was thinkin' of all the time, and I was foolish when I was workin' in Micky's Jim's squad. It's all my fault and sorrow is on me because I made you suffer. Maybe ye'll go home some day. If ye do, go to me mother's house and ask her to forgive me. Tell her that I died on the year I left Micky's Jim's squad. I was not me mother's child after that; I was dead to all the world. My fault could not be undone; that's what made the blackness of it. Never let yer own sisters go to the strange country, Dermod, never let them go to the potato squad, for it's the place that is evil for a girl like me that hasn't much sense.... Ye're not angry with me, Dermod, are ye?'

'Norah, I was never angry with you,' said the young man, and he kissed her. 'You don't think that I was angry with you?'

'No, Dermod, for it's yerself that has the kindly way,' said the poor girl. 'Would ye do something for me if ever ye go back to yer own place?'

'Anything you ask,' Dermod answered, 'and anything within my power to do.'

'Will ye hev a mass said for me in the chapel at home; a mass for the repose of me soul?' she asked. 'If ye do I'll be very happy.'

These were Norah Ryan's last words. As she spoke she looked at Gourock Ellen, and by a sign expressed a wish to speak to her. She sat up in bed, but, as she opened her mouth, shivered as if with cold, looked at Ellen with sad, blank eyes and dropped back on the pillow. Dermod and Ellen stooped forward, not knowing what to do, but feeling that they should do something. The girl was still looking upwards at the shadows on the ceiling, but seeing far beyond. Then her eyes closed slowly, like those of a child that falls into a peaceful sleep.

Norah Ryan was dead.

THE END